DARK SERPENT

PAUL DOHERTY

headline

First published in 2016 by
HEADLINE PUBLISHING GROUP

1

Cataloguing in Publication Data is available from the British Library

Hardback ISBN 978 1 4722 3369 1

Typeset in Sabon by Palimpsest Book Production Limited, Falkirk,
Stirlingshire

Printed and bound in Great Britain by
CPI Group (UK) Ltd, Croydon, CR0 4YY

Headline's policy is to use papers that are natural, renewable and recyclable
products and made from wood grown in sustainable forests. The logging
and manufacturing processes are expected to conform to the environmental
regulations of the country of origin.

HEADLINE PUBLISHING GROUP
An Hachette UK Company
Carmelite House
50 Victoria Embankment
London EC4Y 0DZ

www.headline.co.uk
www.hachette.co.uk

To Steven Barge, a most supportive yet critical friend.
Many, many thanks for your encouragement.

CHARACTER LIST

John Naseby	Master of *The Candle-Bright*
Laurence Torpel	Leading mariner
Peterkin	Ship's boy
Gaston Foix	Master of *The Black Hogge*
Ysabeau	Gaston's wife
Blanquit	Leading seaman aboard *The Black Hogge*
Sulpice	Sailor aboard *The Black Hogge*
Matthew Fallowfield	Matthew Aschroft, Templar knight
Henry Sumerscale	Henry Poultney, Templar knight
Sir Hugh Corbett	The Keeper of the Secret Seal
Lady Maeve	Sir Hugh's wife
Edward	Sir Hugh's son
Eleanor	Sir Hugh's daughter
Boudon	Sir Hugh's steward

Ranulf-atte-Newgate	Senior clerk in the Chancery of the Green Wax
Chanson	Sir Hugh's clerk of the stables
Walter Creswell	'The Deacon'; one of Sir Hugh's spies in France
Fitzosbert	Chief muniment clerk at the Tower
Robert Burnel	Bishop of Bath and Wells
Gabriel Rougehead	King's approver
Crispin Slingsby	Owner of the Salamander tavern
Philippa Henman	Owner of the Merry Mercy tavern
Raoul Henman	Vintner and alderman of Queenhithe
Matthias Sokelar	Harbour master
Agnes Sokelar	Matthias's daughter
Geoffrey Layburn	Vicar of Holy Trinity the Little
Waldo Henman	Previous vicar of Holy Trinity; Raoul Henman's uncle
Primus	Leader of assassin band
Edward II	King of England
Peter Gaveston	Earl of Cornwall, the king's favourite
Philip IV	King of France
Isabella	Daughter of Philip IV, wife of Edward II
Guillaume de Nogaret	Philip's chief minister
Thomas, Earl of Lancaster	Leader of the great lords

Aymer de Valence	Earl of Pembroke, opponent of Edward II
Sir John Howard	Knight
Ap Ythel	Leader of Edward's body-guard
Chancellor Baldock	King's councillor
Walter Reynolds	Royal chaplain and king's councillor
Pierre du Bois	Lawyer to Philip IV
Amaury de Craon	French envoy
Guido Tallefert	English agent in France
Lord Scrope	English envoy in France
Rochfort	Former Templar
Pietal	English courier in Boulogne
Brother Jerome	Clerk to Amaury de Craon
Jacques de Molay	Grand master of the Templar order
William Boveney	Templar serjeant
Ralph Grandison	Templar knight
Reginald Ausel	Master of St Giles lazar hospital
Edmund Datchet	Templar knight
Master Crowthorne	Leech at St Giles lazar hospital
Walter Burghesh	Templar captain
Roger Stapleton	Templar knight
Sir Peter Mausley	Leper knight
Richard Puddlicot	Master felon
John of St Albans	Mason
Elijah Woodman	Magister Viae, leader of the Fraternity of the Hanged

Matilda Poultney	Owner of the Sunne in Splendour tavern
John Poultney	Son of Matilda Poultney
Penda	At the Sunne in Splendour
Gunhilda	Penda's sister, at the Sunne in Splendour

HISTORICAL NOTE

'Uneasy lies the head that wears the Crown.' Shakespeare's description of English kingship certainly applied to Edward II of England as he fought to protect the great love of his life, Peter Gaveston, during the summer of 1311. Sinister dark forces ranged against both the King and his royal favourite. Across the Narrow Seas, Philip IV of France wove his own tapestry of treason to trap Edward and Gaveston as well as their principal clerk Sir Hugh Corbett. The French king's secret poisonous design had been well planned and cunningly plotted, and was on the verge of full flowering . . .

PART ONE

'What use is it to oppose the king?'
The Monk of Malmesbury, *Life of Edward II*

'From all the terrors of the deep, Lord, deliver us. From those who prowl the seas, wolves seeking those whom they may devour, Lord, deliver us.' John Naseby, master of the two-hundred-tun cog *The Candle-Bright*, quietly murmured his prayer. The journey out of the Thames to Boulogne-sur-Mer in the English-held enclave of Ponthieu in Normandy was short but highly dangerous.

'You are praying, Master Naseby?'

'I certainly am,' the master replied, glancing out of the corner of his eye at Laurence Torpel, his leading mariner. 'I am praying for swift and smooth passage. You there!' Naseby steadied himself against the pitch and swell of the sea. 'You there!' he repeated, bellowing at the ship's boy high on the falcon perch at the top of *The Candle-Bright*'s soaring mast. 'What do you see, Peterkin?'

'Nothing, sir,' the boy's voice carried back. 'Nothing to the north, south, east or west.'

Naseby heaved a sigh of relief and carefully made his way across to the taffrail, gesturing at Torpel to join him. Both seamen stood grasping the rough-hewn wood, feet apart as they braced themselves against the fast-running swell of the Narrow Seas. Naseby glanced across at the great sail billowing out under a vigorous north-easterly wind. A good wind, indeed the best for the crossing they had to make. His heart skipped a beat as he glimpsed a shadow against the sail like that of a man hanging from the great crossbar of the mast, yet it was only a loose rope. He glanced away, staring out over the swollen grey sea broken by ripples of frothy white, his heart and mind thronging with the names of those he had killed at sea, above all those of Matthew Fallowfield and Henry Sumerscale. He glanced over his shoulder at that dangling rope. He had hanged Fallowfield and Sumerscale from the mast of *The Candle-Bright* three years ago. He murmured another prayer.

'Master, you still think of them?'

'Of course I do. How can I forget?' Naseby leaned against the side of the ship, his eyes watering as his face was whipped by the salt-edged wind. 'Three years ago last January, *The Candle-Bright* was part of the royal fleet mustering to leave London and Dover to accompany our noble King Edward across to Notre-Dame de Boulogne; he was to marry Isabella, the twelve-year-old daughter of Philip IV of France, God curse the Frenchman as a sinner and a reprobate.' Naseby was now talking to himself as he recalled the events of that fateful time. 'Yes, January 1308,' he murmured. 'The old king had been dead for six months, his wounded cadaver opened, embalmed and sent to Westminster for burial; his beloved son Edward of Caernarvon had succeeded to the throne. Now the young king did not want to marry Isabella. Philip threatened all-out war against Gascony, and the seizure of all England's possessions in France. Edward conceded, as he did over the question of the Templars. Do you remember, Torpel?'

'Of course. Philip of France had declared the Templars to be warlocks and magicians, corrupt, degenerate and guilty of the most appalling practices.'

'All lies, Master Torpel. Philip just wanted the Templar treasures, their lands and whatever else he could grab. He bullied Pope Clement V for his blessing and approval and,' Naseby sighed, 'as Clement lives in exile in Avignon, he falls within easy reach of Philip's mailed fist. Templars in France and elsewhere were seized and disappeared into Philip's dungeons, where his torturers soon got the answers their master required. At first, however, Edward II of England refused to believe Philip's allegations against the order.'

Naseby drew a deep breath of fresh sea air. He had told this tale to himself as well as to those whom he trusted, time and again. He had to set the scene for what he knew to be the most tragic mistake of his life.

'Gaveston.' Torpel broke into his thoughts.

'Gaveston,' Naseby agreed. 'He is the cause of everything. King Edward is obsessed with him.'

'Are they lovers?' Torpel asked, lowering his voice.

Naseby glanced down at the sea-washed deck, wondering how much he should say.

'That's why we are now crossing to Boulogne, isn't it?' Torpel insisted. 'Peter Gaveston, the Gascon favourite, the beloved friend of our noble king, who has created him Earl of Cornwall and married him off to a royal princess.' He lowered his voice, as if the very wind could carry his words to where he wished they would not. 'They say the great earls want Gaveston exiled. They will force the king to agree, and my lord of Gaveston will have to shelter in Ponthieu, probably in Boulogne itself.' He pointed down at the deck. 'We are taking treasure and whatever else he will need to live in opulent exile.'

'The king has agreed to this; he has commissioned us even against the advice of Sir Hugh Corbett, Keeper of the Secret Seal.'

'Because of *The Black Hogge*?' Torpel queried.

Naseby ignored the question. He stared out over the grey water, the morning mist thinning fast.

'Are you awake, boy?' he yelled up at the lookout in the falcon's perch.

'Awake and watching!' the boy sang back.

Torpel decided to change the subject. 'Master, you were talking about Fallowfield and Sumerscale. I admit I have heard rumours, gossip. I would like to hear the true story, as I did not serve with you then.'

Naseby nodded. 'According to Gabriel Rougehead, a king's approver, a Judas man, Fallowfield and Sumerscale, both members of my crew, became drunk in a tavern, the Salamander, which stands close to the river in Queenhithe. They mocked the king and Gaveston, mimicking them in the sex act, and,' Naseby sighed, 'made matters worse with lecherous comments about Edward's intended wife and new queen. I was ordered to try both men before a hastily convened ship's tribunal at Queenhithe. I was given the power of oyer and terminer.'

'To hear and to terminate,' Torpel translated.

'And I certainly did,' Naseby agreed. 'At the time, *The Candle-Bright* was a royal ship in the king's service, so they were tried in secret according to the articles of war at sea. Rougehead repeated his allegation, which was supported by three other witnesses. No one from the Salamander came forward to vouch for Sumerscale and Fallowfield's innocence. Both men denied the charge, but they couldn't even explain why they were in that tavern in the first place. Anyway, the Judas men had their day.'

'And were Sumerscale and Fallowfield guilty?'

'I doubt it very much. Perhaps slurred comments when they were deep in their cups, but Rougehead and his fellow approvers could not be contradicted. You see, the king had issued a proclamation against anyone attacking Gaveston in word or deed. This same royal proclamation offered rewards to those who laid indictment against offenders and were proved correct. I . . .'

Naseby paused as he steadied himself against the roll of the ship, followed by a sharp juddering as it swerved sideways. The sail was now slapping loudly like the snap of a whip. He waited whilst Torpel screamed at the crew to tack according to the shift of the vessel. The sound of bare feet on the slop-soaked deck echoed like a drum; above them a marauding gull shrieked and swooped. Naseby stared across the sullen waters. He did not really know why he was telling Torpel all this, but he had confessed the same to Hugh Corbett, Keeper of the Secret Seal in the Jerusalem Chamber at Westminster, a room Corbett used to transact the secret business of the Crown. He recalled the clerk's long oval face with its deep-set, soulful eyes, his shaven olive skin and close-cropped hair. Corbett reminded Naseby of a cleric rather than a royal clerk. An official lacking any ornament except for the signet ring of the Secret Chancery on his left hand and a pure silver cross on a filigree chain around his neck. A wedding gift, so someone had told him, from Corbett's wife the Lady Maeve . . .

Torpel returned to his side, and Naseby continued with his narrative.

'Against my better judgement, I found Fallowfield and Sumerscale guilty. Like so many others, I was eager to please the young king. I was ordered to execute them immediately.' He looked askance at his leading mariner. 'I really had no choice. *The Candle-Bright* was governed by the articles of war; we were on royal business. In the end, the will of the prince has force of law. I mustered the ship's company and hanged both men from the mast. I was also ordered to keep the bodies dangling there until we set sail, as a public warning not to engage in contumacious or treasonable talk against His Grace and the king's good friend and brother Lord Peter Gaveston.'

'You hanged them, master,' Torpel said, 'and yet you now seem convinced they were innocent.'

'Look, my friend,' Naseby shook his head, 'I confessed the same to Sir Hugh, how I am haunted by their ghosts, particularly that of Sumerscale. He was very handsome, only a youth, with a gift for mimicking bird calls. He protested his utter innocence until the garrotte knot choked off his breath. You ask about their innocence.' Naseby tapped his stomach. 'From the very start I had this feeling at the core of my being that both men had been betrayed. I believe they were victims of a plot. I suspected that Rougehead had been suborned, lavishly bribed to lay allegations, but I don't have a shred of evidence for this. At the time, everyone was deeply sensitive about the king and his precious favourite, and I was no different.'

He coughed, turned and spat over the side. 'What really convinced me of their innocence was that before they were hanged, a wandering friar heard their confessions. Of course he couldn't say what they had told him, but afterwards he informed me in no uncertain terms that he'd heard the confessions of two guilt-free men. I still see their ghosts.' Naseby's face had drained of all colour, and he grasped one of the sail ropes lashed to the rail.

'Ghosts?' Torpel exclaimed.

'Corbett said you were a good man.' Naseby leaned

closer as the ship plunged and rose. 'He said I could trust you.' He glanced across at the crew busy coiling cordage. *The Candle-Bright* was now cutting sharply through the waves, the morning mist lifting, the sun about to break through. So why did he feel this deep, cloying fear, as if he was entering a violent storm at the dead of night on seas running fast and furious past a rocky coast? After all, the weather was relatively calm, the sea fairly serene. Soon they would be in Boulogne, and when they had delivered what they had to, they could return to Queenhithe, where Naseby, a bachelor, could eat, drink and enjoy himself at the Merry Mercy, that splendid tavern close to Queenhithe harbour.

'Ghosts?' Torpel repeated.

'Oh, more than that,' Naseby replied. 'I've received warnings.' He steadied himself, opened his belt wallet and took out a number of narrow parchment strips, no more than a few inches long. He handed these to Torpel, who, lips carefully mouthing the words, read the warning.

'"Remember Sumerscale. Where the corpse lies, so the ghosts will gather."' He glanced up at a gull that shrieked and swooped, eager to pluck anything tossed overboard. 'How long have you been getting these warnings?'

'For the last two months. Since May Day, yes, just after the Virgin Mary's feast. They are slipped under a door or left on a tavern table when I am distracted or busy with something else. And, no, I don't know why, or why now. As I informed Sir Hugh Corbett,' Naseby wiped his salt-caked lips on the back of his hand, 'recently I made enquiries along the Thames and in the city, and discovered that Gabriel Rougehead and the other three perjurers are dead.'

'Dead?'

'Oh yes. They were apparently attending some celebration in the Salamander, the very place where they claimed Sumerscale and Fallowfield made their treasonable remarks, when a fire broke out, reducing the tavern to blackened timber. Rougehead and his coven were burnt alive in the inferno. Talk about judgement from heaven!'

'What manner of men were Sumerscale and Fallowfield?'

'I don't know. I truly don't. They were good seamen. Served on board this ship for two months. In November 1307, *The Candle-Bright* was berthed along Queenhithe. Sumerscale and Fallowfield appeared bringing a brief letter of recommendation from Prior Cuthbert, the Dominican guardian of Blackfriars. They signed the book and made an indenture with me agreeing to the articles of war on board ship. Fallowfield was dark-skinned, as if he had served in the Middle Sea: he was the more experienced sailor, Sumerscale the more educated one. They could speak the patois of the ports as well as French. I had few dealings with them; in the main, they kept to themselves, and this made other people suspicious.'

'You mean that they could have been lovers?'

Naseby forced a grin and slapped Torpel on the

shoulder. 'Laurence, my friend, love between two men is more common than the preachers would have us think. You know my views. The intimate life of the individual soul is a matter best left to that person and to God. I was more interested in who Sumerscale and Fallowfield actually were. Believe me, I have searched London and I could discover nothing . . .'

He broke off as Torpel walked away to roar orders at a group of sailors engaged in some tomfoolery further down the ship. As he put the parchment strips back into his belt wallet, his fingers brushed his Ave beads. He closed his eyes and swiftly recited the Jesu Miserere – the 'Jesus have mercy' prayer – before Torpel returned.

'And Sir Hugh Corbett was against this voyage?'

'Very much so.' Naseby opened his eyes and pointed to the horizon. 'You know the danger, Laurence, and so do I. You've referred to it already. *The Black Hogge*, a Breton privateer out of La Rochelle. A formidable warship, over three hundred tuns, with strengthened fighting castles on prow and stern; its main mast is as thick as an oak tree and it boasts a smaller one to the fore to provide extra speed. It carries a cohort of skilled men-at-arms and archers, mercenaries who fear neither God nor man. Ostensibly it sails under letters of marque issued by the Duke of Brittany. Of course its real master is Philip of France. A ship from hell!'

'We are a fighting ship too,' Torpel countered.

'Not like *The Black Hogge*.' Naseby paused as if listening to the wind wail, plucking at the tight ropes and taut cordage. *The Candle-Bright* cracked and groaned, pitched and sank as if in reply. 'That ship sails under its own colours and insignia; its master, the Breton Gaston Foix, is one of the finest and cruellest seamen prowling the waves. What concerns Sir Hugh Corbett, not to mention the king's council, the city corporation and the city guilds, is that *The Black Hogge* knows whenever a ship leaves Queenhithe, and what cargo it carries. Not every English merchantman is attacked. Only those that have valuable cargo or might be carrying secret documents to English agents in France, as we do now.

'Now, Sir Hugh wanted *The Candle-Bright* to be given an escort of war hulks and fighting cogs, but His Grace the king and his . . .' Naseby caught himself just in time, 'the noble Gaveston did not want to attract the attention of their opponents, the great lords, led by Thomas, Earl of Lancaster. So,' he pushed himself away from the rail, 'we are committed. Pray God we make a peaceful landfall.'

The ship's bell was ringing for the noonday Angelus when Naseby received the answer to his prayer. Torpel was just about to intone the antiphon, 'The Angel of the Lord declared unto Mary', when the lookout boy high in the falcon's perch blew three wailing blasts on his hunting horn. Silence immediately descended. No patter of feet, no shouts or cries, just the cracking and groaning of the cog as it surged through the water. Naseby hurried out of his narrow cabin beneath the soaring stern castle. He fought to control his panic as he peered up at the lookout.

'What is it boy?' he shouted.

'Sail, master!' came the reply. 'I see sail bearing down on us!' He was now standing precariously, leaning forward into the buffeting wind. 'Two sails!' he cried. 'Double-masted.'

Naseby's heart skipped a beat. *The Black Hogge*, he was sure of it, though he did not know how that devil ship knew about *The Candle-Bright*. It must have followed them from the mouth of the Thames, which meant that it had been standing off the Essex coast. Yet how could its master know the actual hour and day that *The Candle-Bright* left Queenhithe? Naseby's sense of being haunted deepened. Vengeance was swooping like some sinister hawk across the surface of the deep.

'Master Torpel,' he cried. 'Beat to arms, prepare for battle.'

The ship's crew hastened to obey the strident calls from their officers. The men-at-arms opened the barbican; swords, daggers, maces and crossbows along with quivers of bolts were distributed. Braziers were primed, the ship's cook heating the coals to light fire arrows. Every bucket and pail was filled with water in preparation against flames thrown by the enemy. Small barrels of sand were emptied on to the slippery deck. Naseby armed himself with mail hauberk, fighting gauntlets with sharp pointed studs and a conical helmet with a broad nose guard to protect his face. He thanked the sailor who brought them to him, and strapped on the two-sheathed sword belt as he stared despairingly at the fast-running waves.

The Black Hogge was bearing down on them in hideous battle array, its formidable hulk cutting through the waves as its soot-coloured sails caught the wind. The soaring fighting castles at fore and stern would be thronged with archers and slingers; the deck between would house men-at-arms ready with their ropes and grappling hooks. Smoke billowed from braziers, heralding the fiery fury that would soon be unleashed against the English ship. Naseby steeled himself for what was coming, battle sharp and cruel. Surrender would mean nothing. *The Black Hogge* followed the merciless law of the sea. An enemy ship was to be annihilated. No mercy would be asked and none would be shown.

He recalled the documents Corbett had entrusted to him from the Secret Chancery. He must destroy them. He turned, hastening towards his cabin, but *The Black Hogge* was closing fast, archers at the ready. Two well-aimed crossbow bolts smashed into his face and throat, and he collapsed in a bloody pulp on the deck of his doomed ship. Peterkin, the lookout boy, high in the falcon perch, froze in terror as he watched his captain's body being pulled across the deck by Torpel towards the protection of the cabin. *The Black Hogge*, however, was now turning sideways so that it crashed into the side of *The Candle-Bright*, towering above the English cog. The French archers raked Naseby's crew with a deadly hail of crossbow bolts, fire arrows, slingshots and other missiles. Fire caught hold of the sail. Peterkin's terror deepened as the flames leapt hungrily about him, burning through the cordage so that the entire sail collapsed to the deck.

Time and again the French archers loosed, choosing their targets carefully. Torpel was struck, the force of the arrow so intense that he staggered across the deck and seemed to bounce against the rail. *The Candle-Bright* tilted and he fell over the side. Peterkin watched his corpse disappear from view. Grappling hooks were now being used, *The Candle-Bright* being made secure to the side of *The Black Hogge*. Men-at-arms and archers swiftly boarded. Any resistance was soon crushed. A few of the English crew threw down their weapons and raised their hands in the sign of peace, only to receive a sword or dagger thrust to the heart or throat.

The French turned to plundering both the hold and the ship's cabin. They moved swiftly. Fires were now burning fiercely, while at the same time the tilting of the English cog allowed the sea to pour in and swamp it. Trumpets sounded their warning. The enemy retreated to their own ship. Ropes and nets were quickly hacked away, *The Black Hogge* putting as much distance as possible between itself and its victim.

Up on his perch, Peterkin felt *The Candle-Bright* shake like a dying man struggling for those last few seconds of life. Then it turned and rose. The great mast snapped. Peterkin clung fiercely, eyes closed, as the mast fell sheer, crashing into the sea. He felt salt water clog his mouth and nose. Then the mast floated back up, breaking free of the water, allowing the boy desperate gasps of precious air. Soaked, cold and terrified, he held on for dear life. *The Black Hogge* was now in full sail away from the scene of slaughter. Peterkin's last glimpse of *The Candle-Bright* was its bowsprit, from which Naseby's corpse dangled. He closed his eyes. If he could only be a bird and fly back to the warm safety of Queenhithe . . .

Rohesia the rag woman lay fast asleep in the shelter of the wall separating the great meadow of St Giles lazar hospital from the trackway that wound out from Westminster and through Queenhithe ward. She had discovered a clump of sharp thorn bushes clinging to the curtain wall that concealed a small aperture and tunnel, probably the remains of some abandoned sewer or water course running through the base of the ragstone wall. The hatch at the other end of the tunnel was also concealed by a tangle of bramble, which could be pushed aside, giving access to the hospital's great meadow. Rohesia reckoned she would be safe enough sleeping off the ale fumes there. She was confident that no one would filch her purse or the corpses in her sack. After all, few people if any wanted to do business with the living dead, the lepers of St Giles, those rotting grotesques, their faces, heads and hands hidden beneath thickly swathed binding cloths.

She stirred, moving her head on the thick serge sack that held the corpses of the small dogs and cats she had clubbed to death earlier in the day for their meat and skins.

'Not a penny less,' she slurred drunkenly to herself. 'Tomorrow I'll get that big tom, fat as a suckling pig, with a good hide and thick fur.' She closed her eyes, picturing the alleyway that ran past the Merry Mercy tavern; once daylight broke, she would seize that tom cat and club it to death. 'Oh yes,' she whispered to herself as she sat up, 'I will keep its fur and sell the flesh to the mince grinder. He will offer it as wild rabbit or mix it with herbs to fashion good sausages!'

She broke off as she heard a cry, recognising it as the lonely call of some mortally stricken soul. Rohesia had once been a camp follower, accompanying both her husbands, former soldiers, the length and breadth of the wild marches of Wales and Scotland; bleak, battle-strewn border country where death came swiftly as a whirling arrow or the hiss of a dagger cutting the air. She had heard such a shriek many, many times as she combed the battlefields for the wounded and the dead.

Deeply intrigued, she pushed her sack and purse into a thick briar and crawled forward up a slight incline. As she lay peering across the grass glinting under the bright moonlight, she glimpsed a small bench near the reed-fringed mere. She could see it clearly because the lantern-horn that stood to one side glowed fiercely, illuminating the man who sat slumped, arms out, head down. Rohesia studied him closely. No movement, no sign of life. She turned, narrowing her eyes as she peered across the heathland. She could detect nothing untoward. Here and there, the noises of the night: the crack of a twig, the rustle of a bush as a fox or badger hunted for its midnight feast. She glanced up at the cloudless sky. A feathery-winged owl, silent as a ghost, glided above the meadow before making its plunge. This was the hour of the hunter, yet Rohesia had a growing feeling that a much more dangerous predator was prowling through the dark.

Overcome by curiosity, she edged forward, drawn by that dark shadow on the bench. As she drew nearer, she realised that he was an inmate of the hospital; he was garbed in the grey robe of the lazar house, his head and face almost hidden by encircling cloths, his weapons drawn, resting on the bench beside him. She moaned, fingers fluttering to her lips, as she glimpsed the dagger pushed deep into the man's chest. Then she heard a sound and turned. At such close quarters, the small, squat crossbow bolt shattered her face in an instant.

Edward II of England slapped the simple black Purbeck marble slab that covered his predecessor's remains close to the shrine of St Edward the Confessor in Westminster Abbey. 'My father,' he declared, 'demanded that when he died, his corpse be boiled in a large cauldron until the flesh separated from the bones. He insisted that the flesh be buried and the bones preserved so that when the Scots rebelled against us, those same bones could be taken up against them and he would have victory over our Scottish enemies.' Edward stroked the back of Peter Gaveston's head as he brushed by his favourite to stand over Sir Hugh Corbett, who sat on the steps of the tomb. 'What do you think of that, Hugh?'

Corbett pursed his lips as he recalled the words of Robert Bruce, the Scottish rebel leader: how he feared the dead bones of the old king more than the living body of the new. He blinked as he silently promised to keep such treasonable words to himself.

'Your Grace,' he decided to change the dangerous conversation to something more practical, 'why are we three, the king of England, his leading councillor and his principal clerk, squatting amongst the tombs of your ancestors, admiring the shrine of the blessed Edward the Confessor?'

'You mock us, Hugh.' Gaveston laughed. 'You know full well why we are here. The tombs are surrounded by hand-picked retainers. We are free of any eaves-dropper, spy or scurrier hungry for juicy morsels of gossip, titbits of information for Lancaster and his coterie to chew over like dogs gnawing dry bones. Nor must we forget Monseigneur Amaury de Craon, the fox-faced, fox-souled French envoy, whose mouth is a bowl of lies and whose heart the haunt of treasons. De Craon would pay dearly for such scraps of gossip.' Gaveston leaned over and squeezed Corbett's wrist. 'You know that, Hugh.'

'In which case, my lord, let us turn to the business in hand.' Corbett was quick to seize the initiative. Gaveston had announced that they were gathered here to discuss secret matters, and the clerk was impatient to begin. 'First, *The Candle-Bright*,' he declared, 'which was brought to battle eight days ago by *The Black Hogge* and destroyed along with its crew.'

'As you said it might be,' the king murmured lazily, his heavy-lidded eyes drooping, his full mouth slightly twisted as he ran a bejewelled finger around his neatly clipped moustache and beard.

Corbett stiffened. Edward might look handsome, with hair the colour of liquid gold, olive skin and strange blue eyes, but he could also be highly dangerous. The king inherited his good looks from his father and his exquisitely beautiful mother, the Spanish princess Eleanor of Castile. Nevertheless, despite his physical beauty, he nursed a nasty temper. Indeed, his puckered look, his insistence on meeting here amongst the royal tombs, meant that he was in one of his strange moods when he could abruptly erupt into horrific violence, targeting anyone within reach of his sword arm. Corbett's only consolation was that the young king never displayed such ferocity towards his reappointed Keeper of the Secret Seal. Perhaps he realised that the clerk would immediately resign in response to such violence.

Corbett sighed and tried to relax. More importantly, he reasoned, Gaveston was present. Handsome as a peacock, languid, even effeminate in appearance and gesture, the royal favourite would always pacify Edward and quell any tantrum or outburst. Gaveston was the king's mentor and master in all things. Corbett noticed with quiet amusement how king and favourite had their hair, moustache and beard similarly coiffed and wore the same type of gown, edged with ermine, boasting the Plantagenet royal colours of blue, scarlet and gold.

Edward thrust his head forward aggressively, finger jabbing the air. 'Don't be coy, Sir Hugh. Tell us what happened.'

'*The Candle-Bright*,' Corbett replied, 'was taken mid-voyage. *The Black Hogge* must have been standing off the Essex coast when the cog cleared the Thames estuary and entered the Narrow Seas. It simply followed using the night and morning mist as a disguise. Now Master Naseby and his henchman Torpel were excellent mariners. They knew the dangers, as we all did. *The Black Hogge* has two sails and is more powerfully built, a true cog of war; its size means that when it came alongside *The Candle-Bright*, its archers could pour down a veritable arrow storm, a hail of missiles and fire shafts. The privateer closed swiftly and the battle did not last long. I learnt this from the sole survivor, the young cabin boy who served as lookout on the falcon perch. Those crew who survived the arrows were put to the sword.' Corbett crossed himself. 'God have mercy on their souls. *The Candle-Bright* became a floating funeral pyre. Before he cut loose, Gaston Foix, master of *The Black Hogge*, hanged poor Naseby's corpse from the bowsprit of his own doomed ship.

'*The Candle-Bright*'s mast collapsed and the lookout managed to use the wreckage to stay afloat. He was most fortunate. Later in the day, a herring boat, blown off course, found him and brought him back to Queenhithe. Both Ranulf and I have questioned him closely but there is nothing more to be learnt. *The Candle-Bright* should never have left Queenhithe without a suitable escort, but the damage is done.' Corbett paused. 'Naseby was carrying very important letters to one of our most skilled agents in Paris, the French clerk Tallefert. The letters were written in cipher. If they were taken, if the cipher is broken . . .' he rubbed his face, 'then God help poor Tallefert and anyone associated with him.'

'We can send another ship to Boulogne,' Gaveston interjected, 'this time with an escort.'

'But that doesn't resolve the root of the problem,' Corbett retorted. He tried to hide his anger at the loss of *The Candle-Bright*, the brutal death of good men such as Naseby and Torpel, not to mention the life-threatening danger Tallefert and others now faced.

'The root?' the king asked.

'Your Grace, with all due respect,' Corbett declared, 'it is fairly simple. The root, or at least one of them, is *The Black Hogge*, a ferocious, powerful French warship. Oh, I know it claims to be a privateer, sailing under letters and warrants issued by the Duke of Brittany.' He shook his head. 'We all know that's nonsense. Gaston Foix receives his orders directly from the Secret Chancery in the Louvre. Or, more specifically, Monseigneur Amaury de Craon in London.'

He leaned closer so he almost came between the king and his favourite. 'Now, ostensibly de Craon is here to discuss certain items of business: English-held Gascony, the grievances of French merchants in Bordeaux, the need for a common front in dealing with the Templar order and the arrest of its members.' Corbett waved a hand. 'And so on, and so on.' He paused. 'The reality is different and highly dangerous to the English Crown. To be blunt, the French now control the sea lanes to Bordeaux and consequently our entire wine trade with Gascony. They also control the sailing routes across the Narrow Seas to the English-held county of Ponthieu, our foothold in Normandy. They have virtually imposed a blockade and are managing this most effectively through a formidable ship of war, captained by one of King Philip's best mariners.'

Corbett glanced at the king and Gaveston. They had stopped fidgeting and were now listening intently. The clerk had decided not to mention his own secret talks with Naseby. He would not reveal the ship's master's deep fear that he was being haunted by the ghosts of the two men he had hanged for allegedly speaking and acting contumaciously against the two princes Corbett was now advising. To do so would not be politic or serve any good. Corbett had already decided that when he could, he would thoroughly investigate the executions of Sumerscale and Fallowfield.

'Sir Hugh?'

'*The Black Hogge* is dangerous, sire, to you and yours.' Corbett gestured at Gaveston. 'For many, many reasons, be it commerce or communication with officials abroad. Above all, it brings you into grave disrepute with your court, the commons, the merchants of this city and the people of your kingdom. You are being grossly shamed, you are made to look ineffective and weak . . .'

'Yes, yes.' Edward stamped his feet, beating his fists against his thighs like some frustrated child deprived of a toy.

'Edward, Edward.' Gaveston's voice came as a soothing whisper. 'Corbett is Your Grace's most faithful servant. He speaks the truth. He tells you the way things are rather than how they should be. If he cannot advise us, then we are truly lost.' Edward raised a hand in acknowledgement and Gaveston nodded at Corbett to continue.

'*The Black Hogge* hovers somewhere off the English coast in those turbulent northern seas. Its master, God knows how, seems to be miraculously informed about ships leaving London. *The Candle-Bright* was a case in point. Now it is virtually impossible to keep such a ship's sailing a secret – a child standing on a hill can watch it leave.' Corbett played with the signet ring on his finger. 'The true mystery is how *The Black Hogge*, out in the misty vastness, is informed of that event: the ship's name, its destination and the hour it sailed.

'I have learnt from sailors along Queenhithe that there could be a fast-moving herring boat, a fishing smack, which takes up position in the estuary and knows where to take all the information its crew learns about our ships leaving the Thames.' He pulled a face. 'Others dismiss such an idea as fanciful. Nevertheless, *The Black Hogge* is regularly informed. Even if we sent warships, fighting cogs and galleys, these would surely be noted and the information relayed to the privateer, which would simply disappear into the icy vastness of the northern seas to lurk and wait for fresh opportunities. Of course we could direct cogs from one of the Cinque Ports, or indeed any harbour along our coastline, but that would be costly. Even if we dispatched an entire fleet, would they find the enemy ship? We could spend an eternity floundering about. So let's move to what I consider to be the true underlying cause of our present problems.'

'De Craon?'

'De Craon, sire, that master of mischief and lord of liars. He must be dug out, root and branch. I look forward to crossing swords with him. I understand he lodges at the Merry Mercy in Queenhithe,' Corbett shrugged, 'and I suspect he protests his innocence about what is happening. If accused, he would act gravely insulted and insist that his diplomatic rights and all the attendant niceties be observed. He lodges at that tavern because it is opulent and comfortable, but above all, it is close to the heart of the London merchant community, where information about shipping is easily and readily available.

'The Merry Mercy is a splendid tavern under the ownership of Philippa Henman, the beautiful widow of the late Raoul Henman, vintner and alderman of Queenhithe.' Corbett brushed some dust from the sleeve of his jerkin. 'I have yet to meet Philippa. Many years ago, I knew her late husband. We were comrades. A stalwart man, Raoul. A mailed clerk till he discovered that his true talent was choosing a good wine and providing delicious meals. He became one of the finest taverners in London. I can certainly see why de Craon chose the Merry Mercy.'

'Philippa,' the king replied, choosing his words carefully, 'is a true and loyal subject: I know she keeps Monseigneur de Craon under close observation.'

'That is so, sire,' Corbett agreed. 'As she does Matthias Sokelar, harbour master at Queenhithe and elsewhere. Rather fortuitous, isn't it,' Corbett rubbed his hands together, 'that the French envoy lodges at the very tavern where the likes of Naseby sheltered on occasion, and where the man directly responsible for English shipping also has his chambers. Could there be a link between Master Sokelar, Philippa Henman and de Craon?' He raised his hands. 'But that would be too obvious. The searches my henchman Ranulf of Newgate has made, not to mention my other spies, have revealed nothing amiss.'

'Indeed,' Gaveston replied, 'as the accredited envoy of the French king, de Craon has every right to choose his own lodgings. You, Sir Hugh, will make the most exacting scrutiny of de Craon, Mistress Henman and anyone involved in the departure of shipping, be it royal or otherwise, along the Thames . . .'

Corbett tapped his foot, his spurs ringing eerily. 'It all comes back to the problem of *The Black Hogge* and how it knows so swiftly and accurately about the movements of English cogs. That is the mystery we must resolve.' He paused. 'Now, Your Grace, I understand there are other matters. I have heard rumours about strange deaths in the leper house at St Giles, also in

Queenhithe ward, a short walk from the Merry Mercy.'

'You are correct.' The king rose and stretched, staring across the tombs. Corbett and Gaveston also rose. The clerk glanced around the hallowed precincts. Noises from the abbey community echoed faintly. A lector chanted at the far end of the nave in one of the side chapels. Echoing more ominously were the prayers of the Guild of St Dismas the Good Thief, pious men and women who assembled in the abbey every Thursday to pray for the repose of the souls of those executed outside the main gate of Westminster Abbey, sombre prayers that talked of darkness and divine justice.

The king, muttering to himself, walked away to ensure the royal mausoleum was still ringed by his personal guard. When he returned, he indicated that Corbett and Gaveston should retake their seats on the steps of the various tombs that towered around them. Corbett noticed how Edward sat close to that of his mother, gently caressing the dark marble as if he wished to plunge his hand through the hard stone to grasp the very essence of the only woman he had ever loved.

Edward followed Corbett's gaze. 'Not a day goes by but I remember her.'

'The most gracious of ladies, sire.'

'When she died,' Edward murmured, 'my father also died, at least in spirit. He became cold, cruel and capricious, just like Philip of France.' He forced a smile. 'That's another reason why we meet here. Peter, my beloved, the Templars?'

'The Templars.' Gaveston sighed. 'The fighting monks

who became bankers and landowners from here to the far borders of the Easterlings. The Templars have lost their vision. They are no longer what they should be, and their decline has hastened since the fall of Acre and their expulsion from Outremer in 1291, some twenty years ago. Philip of France has dissolved their order. He has seized their property, land and treasure. Templars have been arrested, flung into the dungeons of the Louvre and elsewhere, tortured until they confessed to the most heinous crimes, including devil worship, black magic, sodomy,' Gaveston smiled wryly, 'and a host of other abominations. The order is finished. Their grand master, Jacques de Molay, will probably end up being burnt alive by the Inquisition. Philip has Pope Clement V in the palm of his hand. No one will dare object, except for those Templars sheltering here in England.'

'Yes, yes, I know of some of them from many years ago.' Corbett nodded. 'Young men who believed they could continue the fight in Outremer only to lose and flee back to England. Such a change,' he mused. 'Once the warriors of Christendom, they returned to become merchants and shopkeepers. From what I know of the French, I suspect King Philip is demanding that all Templars be handed over to him, whilst Your Grace,' he bowed towards the king, 'will insist that they are still your subjects and so within your love and protection.'

'Very well put, Hugh,' the king agreed. 'But my beloved father-in-law disagrees. He argues that all Templars fall within his power on the legal basis that he has been appointed by the papacy to manage the dissolution of this once famous order. Consequently he has issued warrants for the arrest of Templars sheltering here.'

'I remember one such,' Corbett mused. 'He served with me as a mailed clerk both in Wales and in Scotland before leaving for Outremer. So long ago.' He screwed his eyes up as he recalled his turbulent youth drinking and carousing with other wild bloods in the taverns along Cheapside. 'Ah yes, Ralph Grandison.'

'Ralph Grandison is dead,' Gaveston declared flatly. 'Murdered two nights ago. His corpse was found on a bench near the mere in the great meadow of the lazar hospital at St Giles in Queenhithe.'

Corbett closed his eyes and put his face in his hands. 'Ralph, Ralph,' he whispered, 'so full of life.'

'It is not the first such murder.' Gaveston patted him on the shoulder. 'William Boveney, a former serjeant in the order, was also stabbed through the heart about a week ago.'

'Yes, I heard about that, as I did about de Craon's insistence that since all Templars are under the authority of the French crown, they should be handed over to him immediately. Ranulf and I have been watching that fox closely.' Corbett paused.

'What?' demanded Edward.

'Your Grace, I understand the Templar order ceases to exist. The papacy has dissolved it?'

'Yes, Hugh,' Gaveston replied. 'All this happened during your retirement. Many English Templars vanished into thin air or travelled across the Rhine to join the Teutonic knights in their fight against the Easterlings. One group, who served as a cohort in Acre, calling themselves the Brotherhood of the Wolf, moved from their manor deep in the forest of Epping and sought sanctuary in the leper hospital, the lazar house of St Giles here in Queenhithe, under the pretence that they are infected by that dreadful disease.'

'And are they?'

'I doubt it very much. However, it provides a pretext for sheltering there, for us doing nothing about them. Very few people volunteer to enter a lazar house.' Gaveston paused, leaning his head back against the marble tomb, staring at the light pouring through one of the lancet windows. He held up a hand. 'We do not have time for details, Hugh. You must collect them. You have no objection to entering a leper house?'

Corbett shook his head. 'I have been well advised. Leprosy is only contracted by close and constant contact with the infected over a long period of time. In particular sharing their food, the water they bathe in. But why do you want me to—'

'A number of reasons.' Gaveston leaned forward. 'First, two English knights have been murdered there; that in itself warrants investigation. Second, these murders may have been perpetrated here in our kingdom, in our principal city, at the behest of Philip of France. We know he wants these knights extradited to Paris. If that can't be done, their deaths would be equally satisfying. Philip fears that when Pope Clement convenes a general council at Vienne, these same knights might mount a vigorous defence of their order and disprove the allegations against them.'

'But how could de Craon plot and perpetrate such murders?'

'We know he is deeply interested in what happens at St Giles, which is probably one of the reasons he lodges at the Merry Mercy, only a short walk away from the hospital. Of course he cannot enter the place. The master knight, Reginald Ausel, a former Templar,' Gaveston grinned, 'and a distant kinsman of mine, was appointed to his post after the papacy dissolved the order. Ausel would resist with weapons drawn any attempt by de Craon to enter St Giles. Indeed, speaking of that,' he scratched at a bead of sweat beneath the high collar of his cambric shirt, 'as you will discover, what is so puzzling about the two murders at St Giles is that both knights had their weapons drawn, yet they were killed silently, with virtually no evidence that they resisted.'

'You say de Craon shows great interest in the leper hospital. How do you know that?'

'From Mistress Philippa Henman, minehost of the Merry Mercy. Mistress Philippa, as a member of the vintners' guild, supplies St Giles with meat and drink at a reasonable price. She is also lady abbess of the Guild of St Martha, a group of merchant ladies, widows and wives who do good work at the hospital. After all, St Giles still houses a considerable number of leper knights.'

'So you think de Craon definitely had a hand in these murders?'

'Oh yes, we do,' Gaveston replied. 'Hugh, the Templars are finished, their members divided. Some now actively work for Philip in his attacks, both public and secret, on the order. The French may well have an assassin, a spy amongst the Templars at St Giles, either one of their company or someone else. Just think how Philip would relish these knights being slaughtered one by one at the very heart of our kingdom.'

'And there is more?'

It was the king who replied. 'Oh yes, my Keeper of the Secret Seal, as you suspect, there is always more. I want you to discover what is truly happening at St Giles.' He bent down and opened the leather chancery satchel close to his feet, drawing out a dark blue velvet cloth. He unfolded this to reveal a long ivory-handled dagger, its curling blade of the finest Damascene steel, the remnants of a scarlet cord still clinging to its hilt.

Corbett took the dagger from the king and carried it over to the candle spigot, a blaze of light before a statue of the martyred King Edmund. Moving the dagger between his fingers, he scrutinised the fine handle. The ivory was slightly chipped and stained, whilst the blade, he was sure, had been recently bloodied.

'Sire,' he called over his shoulder, 'this is Moorish.'

'A blade belonging to one of the assassins who serve the Old Man of the Mountain in his secret fortress high in the hills above Aleppo in Syria,' replied the king. 'They feed on hashish and are dispatched to slay anyone their master has marked down for death. Over forty years ago, my father served in Outremer. His wife, my beloved mother Eleanor, went with him. Father proved to be what he always claimed to be, a true warrior of God, so the Old Man of the Mountain ordered his assassins to slay him. They invaded his tent, but Father, God's own swordsman, killed all three of them, though not before one of them managed to cut him with that blade.'

The king came across and took the dagger from Corbett's hand. 'A flesh wound, but still highly dangerous as the blade had been coated with a deadly poison. My mother, with no thought to herself, sucked out the poison and cleaned the wound with her tongue. My father suffered no lasting effects, and on his return to England, he came here to Edward the Confessor's shrine and dedicated the knife as an offering to the memory of that holy king, placing it with his treasure, the Crown Jewels and other precious items, in what he considered to be one of the safest places in England . . .'

'The crypt of Westminster Abbey,' Corbett declared, 'a great underground chamber with walls twenty feet thick, deep beneath the abbey chapterhouse, entered through a set of iron-bound doors and down a steep spiral staircase with a broad gap that can only be spanned by a set of specially constructed wooden steps.'

'You know it well, Sir Hugh?' Gaveston demanded.

'Tell him,' the king urged.

'Eight years ago last April,' Corbett played with the silver cross on the chain round his neck, 'a master felon, a certain Richard Puddlicot, organised a gang that broke into the crypt. They hired a special mason, John of St

Albans, to work at opening one of the crypt windows overlooking the abbey cemetery. The gang was very successful and stole a great deal of treasure, the Crown Jewels and other precious artefacts. The old king commissioned me to hunt down Puddlicot, that prince of thieves. When I finally apprehended him and some of his henchmen, they were tried, found guilty and hanged. The king ordered Puddlicot's corpse to be peeled and his skin nailed to the door leading to the abbey chapterhouse.'

Corbett pointed at the dagger. 'I recovered a great deal of the treasure, but a goodly portion remained missing and still does. I distinctly recall not recovering that dagger. Your father was desperate for its return.'

'This dagger,' the king replied, balancing it in his hands, 'was used to murder Ralph Grandison, thrust deep into his heart: a killing blow. Whoever committed that murder must have been involved in the great robbery eight years ago. So you see, Hugh,' Edward moved so close that Corbett could smell the rich rose water the king rubbed into his skin, 'my father-in-law, Philip of France, is making a public mockery of me. *The Black Hogge* is his doing. I am sure the murders amongst the Templars can be laid at his door. And now this dagger. Whoever is working for Philip must have some of the treasure looted from the crypt.'

Edward abruptly clasped his hands around Corbett's face. The clerk's fingers fell to the hilt of the dagger on his belt even as he heard Gaveston's sharp intake of breath. 'Hugh, you have been away from royal service for years, locked up with your family, your precious bees, your love of plainchant, whilst I have been drawn deeper and deeper into my father-in-law's snares. In Scotland, Bruce threatens me. A few miles to the north of London, Lancaster and the other earls gather ready for war. I am a king on the verge of becoming a public mockery, and the cause and origin of my great discomfiture sits in the Merry Mercy weaving his web on behalf of His Satanic Majesty in Paris.'

'Edward, Edward,' Gaveston hissed. 'Your Grace.'

The king took his hands away and stepped back. 'Hugh,' he pleaded, 'I need you. Untangle the web. Trap the spider and send him scuttling back into the dark. Will you do that for me?' Corbett stared into the king's eerie light-blue eyes. 'For the sake of the Crown, for the memory of my father and my beloved mother, and for me, Hugh, just for me?' He extended a hand, and Corbett grasped it.

A short while later, the king and Gaveston left the royal enclosure, the household bodyguard closing around them in a clatter of steel, Edward, mercurial as ever, shouting how Corbett should accompany them to the palace at Sheen and study the royal beehives. The clerk listened to the king and his favourite clatter down the abbey nave, rubbing his face where Edward had so roughly grasped him. He walked across to a small altar dedicated to the Virgin and lit a taper. He whispered a requiem for Ralph Grandison's soul, then returned to the royal tombs, staring down at the plain black marble slab that enclosed the remains of his former master, Edward I.

He closed his eyes as he recalled that sunny day so many years ago at Windsor when he had taken the oath of fealty, swearing to be the Crown's servant body and soul, in peace and war, against all enemies both within and without. Edward had leaned down and whispered in his ear, 'Hugh, remember this day. When the time comes and my son needs you, really needs you, answer him. Promise me that.' The old king had taken his face gently between his hands. 'God be my witness, Hugh, keep fealty or I shall come for you from beyond the grave.'

'I have given my oath,' Corbett whispered into the dark, 'and I shall keep it.'

He left the tombs and moved up through the incense-sprinkled air of the abbey nave. He entered the lady chapel and sat down on a plinth, staring at a host of candles blazing before the statues and wondering how his wife, the Lady Maeve, and their two children, Edward and Eleanor, were faring at Leighton Manor. And his bees? Would Boudon, his steward and assistant, take care of everything? He smiled to himself. Boudon knew more about bees than Corbett ever would. The clerk just wished he could go home for a day or two to rest. He would love to discuss with Boudon what he'd recently read in Pliny's *Natural History*: how bees in flight, if overtaken by darkness, would stop, cluster and lie on their backs to protect their wings against the morning air. Was that true?

Corbett pulled his war belt closer as he reflected on what the king and Gaveston had told him. In truth, the real problem was *The Black Hogge*'s ability to attack any English ship. He must remember that and move to the tip of the arrow point. Once that was resolved, the problem could be confronted and cleared. The same was true of the murder of the Templars at St Giles. What was the reason for those deaths? Undoubtedly Philip of France and de Craon had a hand in it all, but the appearance of the assassin's dagger also indicated that the French might have had some involvement in the robbery of the crypt eight years ago.

The English Crown faced a veritable storm of problems. Corbett had heard rumours about them as he worked in the Secret Chancery chambers at both Westminster and the Tower. He had been dealing with reports and news from his spies along the Scottish March when he had begun to be drawn into the mystery of the Templars' deaths and the depredations of *The Black Hogge*. Now he was fully committed. De Craon was ensconced at the Merry Mercy. Corbett had responded. He had already dispatched his clerks to the tavern to make searches as well as to hire chambers for themselves and Corbett. 'It will be best to set up house as close to the fox's den as possible,' he had advised them. 'I am sure de Craon will be delighted to see us.'

He watched the dagger-like flame of a taper fall and rise. He heard a sound, a footfall behind him. He swiftly drew his dagger and turned, but there was nothing. He returned to watching the candle flame, its constant burning soothing him. He missed the Lady Maeve, his children and Leighton Manor. Nevertheless, he was pleased to be back in the Secret Chancery. After an absence of almost six years, he felt as if his wits and brains had become slightly rusted. Now he had to be sharp and sure. The Secret Chancery was like the Great Conduit in Cheapside. All kinds of information flowed through it: chatter, gossip, scurrilous stories, the judgements of the itinerant commissioners, the decisions of manor courts and the constant backbiting and petty infighting amongst the clergy. All this had to be collected, the wheat sifted from the chaff as it was closely scrutinised.

In the end, Corbett was convinced that de Craon was very much the spider, spinning a tangled, treacherous web under the pretence of being here at Westminster to discuss certain items of business with leading royal officials. Ranulf was already on the hunt. By now, the senior clerk in the Chancery of the Green Wax should have moved into the the Merry Mercy tavern: it was time they closed in on the spider.

'Ah well,' Corbett murmured. He made to bless himself, but froze at a sound behind him. This time he was certain. He had half drawn his dagger when something hit the tiled floor beside him and rolled to rest against a pillar decorated with scenes from hell in which demons, giant apes with human faces, plucked the souls of the damned impaled on ugly thorn bushes. Corbett turned slowly, but nothing disturbed the dark hush of this hallowed place. He could detect no threat, no moving shape or flitting shadow. He resheathed his weapon, then walked over and picked up the cylinder-shaped object, the slender remains of a pure beeswax candle with a piece of parchment twined round it. He undid this and stared at the warning inscribed upon it.

Sir Hugh Corbett, Keeper of the King's Secret Seal, put not your trust in those in power. Go back, sir, to your manor, your wife, your children, your estate and your beloved bees. Do not enter the tournament field.

He read the dark-inked message once more, then placed both parchment and candle in the wallet on his belt. 'So the dance begins!' he murmured to the darkness. 'Dance I shall, and in time so shall ye.'

Corbett patted his wallet and stared at the demonic scene painted on the pillar. Warnings did not frighten him. He was intrigued, curious. Who would know he was here at Westminster? He had moved out of the Secret Chancery offices a few days earlier. He had suspected he was being followed, and if so, it must be some henchman of de Craon; who else? De Craon was no friend of his; he would love to take Corbett's head. So why the warning?

'We shall see,' Corbett whispered. 'We shall wait to discover what form this deadly dance takes.'

PART TWO

'By this the whole kingdom had been greatly injured.'
    The Monk of Malmesbury, *Life of Edward II*

Gallows Day at Queenhithe Steps was regarded as a holiday by many. The grisly execution of felons always attracted grotesques, ribalds and rifflers: these swarmed out of their dingy, dank dungeons, eyes bright, wits sharp for any easy mischief. Clothed in filthy rags, they were still well armed with battered daggers, blades and dirks pushed into the rope belts around their waists. Garbed in fluttering cloths, coarse leather sandals on their feet, cowhide cloaks flapping in the breeze, the denizens of London's underworld surged down the broad thoroughfare along Dunghill Lane to the glittering Thames, where the soaring gallows jutted out over the edge of Queenhithe quayside. Here the corpses of eight river pirates would hang, twist and rot for three turnings of the morning tide.

The execution carts would leave Newgate once the Angelus bell had tolled and the daily rota of masses had been completed. The city mob would be joined by the whores from Cock Lane and elsewhere. These ladies of the night would have their heads covered with the most garish wigs fashioned out of horsehair and dyed every colour of the rainbow. Close by, their pimps would shepherd them as cats would captured mice. These squires of the sewer, as they proudly called themselves, would be sharp-eyed for any customer desperate enough to pay the price and lead his chosen whore up some dark, needle-thin runnel to obtain whatever squalid satisfaction he needed. Musicians, troubadours, story-tellers and fire-eaters also set up shop, standing on carts, boxes or barrels. One enterprising itinerant ballad-monger had dressed himself in black and then painted a white skeleton over it, his face covered by a corpse mask. This minstrel of the midden heap stood on a wheelbarrow with a small boy beside him to collect the coins as he bawled out a story about ghosts being seen tramping the coffin paths on the far side of Queenhithe.

Naturally people stopped to listen, and the crowd attracted the food sellers, who, now free of the watchful eyes of the market bailiffs, pushed their movable stoves and grills on filthy hand carts to some suitable enclave. Once there, they would fire the coals to cook chunks of horse, cat and dog meat soaked in the spiciest sauces to disguise both the age and origin of their produce. The taverns, cook shops, ale houses and bakeries also prepared for the surging crowd, the shopkeepers ever vigilant for the nips, foists and legion of false beggars who would come crawling out, eager-eyed for easy pickings. After all, the weather was good for a hanging.

The shit-strewn streets and alleyways had dried and

hardened underfoot, although the lack of any breeze along the narrow thoroughfares meant the foul odours from the public jakes, midden heaps and lay stalls hung like a pall in the air as the sun warmed the fetid streets. The only relief from the stench was the saltpetre being strewn from the gong carts. These same carts caused obstructions and accidents in the tightly packed streets, where the air was riven by the agonising shrieks of dogs and cats caught under their wheels. Prayer groups also gathered to provide spiritual comfort to the condemned: the Guild of the Hanged and the Fraternity of the Good Thief, who perfumed the stinking air with their smoking thuribles and squat beeswax candles.

Ranulf-atte-Newgate, senior clerk in the Chancery of the Green Wax, watched all this as he leaned against the gatepost of the Merry Mercy tavern. The great double doors of this splendid hostelry had been thrown open. Behind Ranulf, others gathered to watch the approaching procession. Mistress Philippa Henman, tavern mistress and prominent member of the vintners' guild, was taking no nonsense. Ranulf watched her admiringly. Philippa, he reckoned, had not yet reached her fortieth summer, though she dressed like an older woman in a gold-edged Lincoln-green dress that covered her from neck to just above her elegant yet workaday boots with their squat heels and silver buckles. She wore fawn doeskin gloves, whilst her thick auburn hair was primly collected beneath an old-fashioned veil secured by a dark brown headband. She glanced up, caught Ranulf's eye, smiled and walked briskly forward.

'Master Ranulf, would you agree,' she indicated with her hand towards the gateway, 'that in view of what is happening outside, perhaps I should arm my household? Though the alderman and sheriffs have promised a formidable cohort of bailiffs. Ah, and I see them here.'

Ranulf followed her direction. Groups of burly individuals, in either the livery of the city or the colours of Queenhithe ward, were now shoving their way through the throng, heavy cudgels at the ready. The crowd greeted their arrival with cheers and boos. Ranulf, however, was more interested in Mistress Philippa's beautiful face: the high, prominent cheekbones, the ivory sheen of her unpainted skin, the full, generous lips and the slightly slanted eyes that seemed to dance with merry mockery. She seemed aware of his scrutiny, turning swiftly and glancing coyly at him.

'You study me, sir,' she teased, 'yet there are many wondering why you are here. A senior royal clerk adorned with his medal of office,' she leaned over and gently tugged at the chain around Ranulf's neck, 'not to mention that you wear the signet ring of the chancery. And yet,' she stood back, swaying enticingly as she looked Ranulf up and down, 'you dress like a man-at-arms in your dark brown leggings and jerkin, though your boots and war belt are of the finest Cordovan, your sword and dagger well hilted, your wallet thick and heavy.'

'You are most observant, mistress. You study sharply.'

'But not as much as you, Ranulf-atte-Newgate!' She now leaned so close that Ranulf could smell her rich perfume, a distillation of crushed fresh lilies. 'You must wonder how a widow woman like myself came to be a vintner, tavern mistress and merchant.' She raised her eyebrows in mock question.

'Your husband?'

'The good Raoul.' Philippa's face softened. 'Dead this last year.'

'Of what?'

'A wasting sickness.' Philippa glanced away as if to hide the expression on her face, before turning back with a smile. 'I am well skilled in this trade, from an ancient merchant family from Queenhithe.' Her voice took on the pompous tone of a guild master. 'A purveyor of fine wines and other similar products from the vine-yards of France.' Her smile faded. 'I am glad that you and Sir Hugh Corbett will be here, a powerful coun-terweight to Monseigneur de Craon. I have heard a great deal about Sir Hugh. My husband was older than me, a self-made man, but in his early days he was a mailed clerk. I understand he and Sir Hugh were comrades. Time eventually separated them, but Raoul always talked highly of Sir Hugh. He had the deepest respect for him, and consequently so do I, which is more than I can say for Monseigneur de Craon.'

'You dislike him?'

'The French have waged war on English ships for decades,' she hissed. 'De Craon is part of all that. I recognise the rules. He hides behind the mask of an accredited envoy and can demand whatever lodgings he wants.' She laughed softly. 'He chooses to set up camp at the heart of London's busiest ward, because he is a spy. He collects information and intelligence. He also flirts with me. However, it is not just my cooking skills and my pretty face that attracted him to this place. The Merry Mercy is a crossroads, the hub of a wide circle of activities, be it the city, the river, the port or Westminster. I am right, am I not?'

'Very much so,' Ranulf agreed. 'De Craon is a hunter who casts his net far and wide. How long has he been here?'

Philippa screwed up her eyes and chewed the corner of her lip. 'At least three months.'

'And it's no coincidence that it was about three months ago that *The Black Hogge* made its presence felt.' Ranulf sighed. 'And yet we cannot object. In Paris, our own envoy, Lord Scrope, insists on hiring chambers that overlook the main entrance to the Louvre. Mistress, apart from playing cat's cradle with our Frenchman, do you have much to do with him?'

'As little as possible.'

'And Master Sokelar, our grim-faced harbour master, and his equally grim daughter?'

Philippa laughed like a girl, gloved fingers fluttering prettily to her lips. She drew a deep breath. 'Master Sokelar is his own man. You know how it is, Ranulf. The city council and the Guildhall hire chambers in this tavern or that for port reeves, harbour masters, collectors of customs and other officials. It's cheaper than buying properties along the river edge or hiring chambers from a landlord. Master Sokelar works from here, though he has his own house, and his records are dispatched to the exchequer at Westminster.'

'And does he have much to do with de Craon?'

'Now, now, Master Ranulf,' she teased, 'I am not your spy. Suffice to say that Sokelar dislikes de Craon intensely.' She paused. The noise from further down the street was growing. The mob was swirling about. The Fraternity of the Hanged, in their earth-coloured robes and white rope belts, were clustered around their leader, the Magister Viae – the Master of the Way – under his billowing standard, a linen cloth emblazoned with a stark black gibbet. The execution carts would be here soon.

Mistress Philippa put a hand on Ranulf's arm as she heard her name called. She glanced back across the tavern yard.

'And here he comes,' she murmured, 'our noble harbour master.'

Matthias Sokelar was one of the most glum-visaged officials Ranulf had ever met. He had a long, horse-like face under a mop of scrawny hair, deep-set, troubled eyes, angry red spots either side of a fleshy nose, and a mouth constantly drooping in disapproval. He was dressed in the blue and white livery of the city, a badge bearing the royal arms emblazoned on his right shoulder. He carried a white wand of office, which he swung threateningly as he strode towards the gate; behind him, almost running, came his daughter Agnes, a slender, mousy-faced young woman, pretty in a severe-looking way but clearly eaten up with anxiety over her father.

She wore a brown smock a little too long that threatened to trip her, whilst her cream-coloured veil hung slightly askew.

Sokelar paused in the gateway and glared at Ranulf. 'I know why you and your master are here. I have my answers. I am totally innocent of any wrongdoing, both now and in the past. Now, I want to be at the quayside before the rabble arrives.' He swept into the street, snapping his fingers at his daughter to hasten along with him.

'Now there goes an agitated man.'

'Ranulf,' Philippa grasped his arm and squeezed it tightly before letting go, 'every official along the quayside is under threat. The ravages of *The Black Hogge* are notorious. They are staple fare, the chatter and gossip of the riverside taverns and ale houses.' She pulled a face. 'Even the brothels. Everybody realises that some malefactor here in London is informing that death-bearing ship of what cogs leave port and when.'

'But we know it is Master de Craon.'

'Yes, Ranulf, but how?' Philippa abruptly started as a flock of birds burst out of a clump of trees near the curtain wall of the tavern. She stared up at them, mouth slightly open, before glancing swiftly at Ranulf. 'Have you broken your fast? You could . . .'

She paused at a roar further down the street. The crowd was now surging backwards and forwards. The two execution carts had arrived, pulled by great dray horses caparisoned in black ox hide, their manes all hogged with scarlet ribbons, their reins and leads a full blood red. Executioners, faces hidden behind devil masks, managed the high-sided carts. The four prisoners in each were made to stand so the accompanying mob could hurl both abuse and refuse at them. Shouts and curses dinned the air, followed by a hail of filth and slops. Bagpipes wailed. Drum beats echoed. Trumpets and hunting horns brayed their shrill, discordant blasts. Relatives of the condemned clung to the sides of the carts, shouting to their menfolk. Warlocks and wizards in dirty robes and funnel-shaped hats pushed rags through the slats of the carts to catch some of the prisoners' bloodied sweat, which they could later use in their midnight ceremonies. Quacks, conjurors and cunning men also tried to keep close; the leavings of men condemned to hang were said to contain certain healing properties.

The carts stopped in a rumble of wheels and a clatter of hooves outside the Merry Mercy, and Ranulf soon realised why the tavern boasted such a name, as Mistress Philippa ordered her steward and master of the hall to serve tankards of frothing ale to the executioners, the condemned men and the city bailiffs guarding the carts. Ranulf, who had retreated further into the yard, could only marvel at the macabre pageant: the prisoners gulping down their drinks and pleading for more; the hangmen, already much the worse for wear, screaming at people to get out of the way whilst beating off in a whirl of clubs those who tried to climb into the carts. The air shrilled with screams, cries and curses. The stench was offensive as the sweaty mass of unwashed bodies pushed and shoved, kicking up the dirt in the filthy lane.

At last, more sober voices were heard and a cohort of mounted Tower archers forced their way through, their captain shouting for the carts to move on. The archers ringed the execution party whilst a group of Franciscans in their reddish-brown robes followed, chanting psalms and hymns of mourning. Ranulf glanced around. Mistress Philippa had disappeared back into the tavern. The clerk tightened his war belt and followed the Franciscans as the execution carts wound their way along twisting lanes under crumbling, tumble-down houses that leaned over to block out both light and air. At last the stench of the streets lifted under the wafting of the stiff river breezes, and the procession debouched out of the warren of rat runs on to the cobbled quayside of Queenhithe.

Ranulf seized a vantage point, a crumbling plinth, the only relic of a former warehouse, from which he watched the condemned being fastened with tightened nooses before being tossed over the edge of the quayside, the mob roaring its approval as each victim was dispatched. Once the executions were over, the crowd began to break up. Tinkers and traders appeared selling tipples of water, fruit filched from elsewhere, the skins of cats and dogs for fabric as well as a choice of day-old fish.

Ranulf pushed these street merchants aside. He watched the Fraternity of the Hanged break away from the mob and process from the quayside under their garish banner. He jumped down from the plinth and followed them up Stinking Lane and into the Hanging Tree, a large, ancient three-storey tavern, its gables held secure by sturdy crutches. The taproom was huge, lit by spluttering oil wicks. At one end stood the counter, a board placed over a row of barrels. At the other, an enclave. Here the corpses of those hanged at Tyburn and Fleet were brought to be dressed and prepared for burial. Kith and kin could claim the remains of relatives at a price. Any unclaimed cadavers were dispatched in a cart to St Mary le Bow for swift burial in the poor man's plot of that church's sprawling cemetery.

A sign proclaimed the enclave to be 'The Purgatory Chamber'. Five corpses lay under linen sheets heavily soaked in pine juice, while smoking pots of herbs and incense, as well as the rancid odour of tallow candles, did something to conceal the pervasive stench of corruption. The entrance to the chamber was guarded by two of the self-proclaimed brothers, sturdy and armed with nail-bearing clubs and cudgels. The Magister Viae sat enthroned in the taproom's one and only window embrasure. Scullions were busy serving him platters of steaming meat and vegetables, as well as deep-bowled goblets of red and white wine.

Ranulf stood waiting in the doorway. The Magister continued to eat, shouting between mouthfuls at mine-host, a veritable tub of a man with a greasy leather apron hanging from neck to toe so he glistened like a lump of lard in the candlelight. Ranulf slowly drew his sword, the scraping steel quietening all sound. The

Magister looked up, smiled and beckoned the clerk across, indicating the stool facing him. Ranulf resheathed his sword and sat down.

'Good morrow, master.'

'Good morrow, Ranulf! How is my learned friend and colleague?'

'Rest assured,' Ranulf murmured, 'my heart leapt like a stag at the sight of your face.'

The Magister's round, weather-beaten features cracked into a smile, though his watery blue eyes remained watchful. He lifted a hand, soft and white as a lily, and rubbed his thinning hair, which stood up all spiked.

'Greetings, Elijah Woodman,' Ranulf declared. 'Sir Hugh told me that you are one of the finest mariners this side of heaven.'

The Magister bowed mockingly. He popped a piece of venison into his gummy mouth before yelling at one of the oafs guarding the Purgatory Chamber to ensure the open eyes of one of the corpses be closed with special weights. 'I thank you for the compliment, but it would seem that there is a better mariner at sea: Gaston Foix, captain of *The Black Hogge*. However, Master Ranulf, you can tell Sir Hugh that I, along with everybody else who lives along the Thames, am truly mystified at how Foix knows what he does!'

'I agree, it is a rare mystery,' Ranulf replied. 'But the other matters Sir Hugh asked you to search?'

'You mean Master Long Face?' the Magister retorted, chortling at Ranulf's discomfort. 'That is your nickname for Sir Hugh, but that too is a secret. So let's grasp the business in hand.' He cleared the table in front of him, pushing cups and platters away, leaning so close that Ranulf could smell his spiced breath. 'I deal with cadavers, Master Clerk, the corpses of the hanged; that's the only trade I could take up. You know my story. I was a pirate caught for the foulest treachery: I attacked a royal ship by mistake. I should have been hanged, but there were those on the king's council, the likes of the Earl of Surrey, who recalled my service in the royal fleet. I was pardoned on the sole condition that I never set foot on a ship, domestic or foreign, under pain of arrest for treason, which,' the Magister shrugged, 'means hanging, drawing, quartering and disembowelling, something that concentrates the mind wonderfully. I merely mention this as I would be grateful if Sir Hugh would kindly consider appealing on my behalf to the king or, even better, my Lord Gaveston. Tell Sir Hugh I have worked very hard on his behalf.' The Magister picked up his goblet. 'Do that and I will give you a good tun of the best Bordeaux.' He grinned. 'I will even throw in a couple of corpses.'

'I would be happy with a goblet of wine now.'

The Magister shouted for Ranulf to be served. Once the clerk had toasted him and sipped at the rich red wine, the Magister leaned forward. 'Henry Sumerscale and Matthew Fallowfield don't exist,' he whispered. 'No, listen. In January 1308, three and a half years ago, our noble king sailed to meet his bride, the lovely Isabella, in Boulogne. The king's cogs gathered at

London and Dover. *The Candle-Bright*, under John Naseby, was one of these ships. It berthed at Queenhithe for two weeks, preparing itself. Remember, it was the depths of winter, and a journey across the Narrow Seas has to be carefully plotted. Sumerscale and Fallowfield were part of the crew. I understand they had been so for a number of weeks.

'Now, just before *The Candle-Bright* sailed, indictments were levelled against the two men by Gabriel Rougehead. They were accused of treasonable talk about the king and my Lord Gaveston in the taproom of a nearby riverside tavern, a rather seedy place, the Salamander. Rougehead became a king's approver: in other words, he was pardoned for past offences in return for testimony that would convict. He was supported by three other rogues, professional Judas men. Both Sumerscale and Fallowfield protested their innocence, but the evidence against them stood.

'Naseby, a good man, a skilled mariner, had no choice but to accept the inevitable decision. Execution was immediate. The pair were taken up on to the deck of their own cog and hanged from the mast, their corpses left to dangle for three days as a warning to others. The bodies were taken down just before *The Candle-Bright* sailed and were handed over to me. I brought them here and was preparing them for burial in the poor man's plot when a priest arrived to claim both corpses.'

'What priest?'

'Parson Geoffrey Layburn, vicar of Holy Trinity the

Little, which stands near the junction of Old Fish Lane and Cordwainer Street. He said he was acting on behalf of someone; he didn't say who.' The Magister waved a hand. 'At the time I didn't care.'

'But you said Sumerscale and Fallowfield didn't exist?'

'When Sir Hugh entrusted me with the task, I began my searches, but there is very little, if any, information about them amongst the river folk. You know how names and news pass from lip to lip, but these two were unheard of except for their service aboard *The Candle-Bright*.'

'I agree,' Ranulf murmured. 'I will report the same to Sir Hugh. I found nothing in the records from the Crown, city or Guildhall. It seems Sumerscale and Fallowfield appeared from nowhere, served on that cog, were arrested and executed.' He paused. 'You went back to that priest, surely?'

'Yes, I did. I was told in no uncertain terms to mind my own business and promptly shown the door. Parson Geoffrey would respond better to a royal clerk rather than a humble soul, a public sinner such as my good self. I live in the twilight world. I sit and eat with the midnight folk. As I have said, a truly humble soul.'

'But this humble soul has further information,' Ranulf tapped the table, 'and you are impatient to share it?'

'Yes, though the prospect of payment would encourage my humble soul even more.'

Ranulf opened his purse and placed three silver coins on the table, which were immediately swept up by the

Magister. 'Master Ranulf, many thanks. Now listen. I confess I was intrigued at finding no reference to Sumerscale and Fallowfield, so I turned on their accuser, Gabriel Rougehead, and for the first time I discovered some involvement by the Templars.'

'The Templars?'

'Gabriel Rougehead was a former Templar. He was expelled from the order at least twelve years ago for filthy sexual practices, violence and perjury. Rougehead came from London, so he drifted back here. He was an outlaw, a wolfshead eager to obtain both a pardon and a reward. An educated man with a knowledge of languages and, when he wanted, most personable. He was a veritable shadow-master: skilled in deceit and disguise, a true mummer who could act many a part and persuade others to work for him. Rougehead's father was English, his mother from Nanterre. He may have been involved in the robbery of the royal treasure in the abbey crypt, as he had his crooked fingers in many a pie. Anyway, he claimed to be in the Salamander when Sumerscale and Fallowfield played out their treasonable pageant.'

'You believe he was lying?'

'I know he was. Look around you, clerk. These are my henchmen who, when darkness falls, go out across the city and visit the taverns to collect gossip, whispers and chatter like gleaners who follow the harvesters. Two of them were in the Salamander that night. They reported that Sumerscale and Fallowfield were deep in conversation and made no such treasonable comments.

Of course, there was no opportunity for any real defence of those two unfortunates whilst the information I learnt came after both men were hanged. Now,' he continued briskly, 'Rougehead was joined by Judas men, professional perjurers. They perpetrated their evil and were rewarded. Afterwards, gossip had it that they not only claimed rewards from the Crown but were actively encouraged in their villainy by others.'

'Who?'

'No one knows.'

'Could it have been the Templars?'

'Master Ranulf, God only knows. But I tell you this. I have also heard about the murders amongst those same Templars at the lazar house of St Giles, and I know that the French envoy de Craon sits ensconced in the Merry Mercy. Gossip has it that the murders are de Craon's doing, and that the French have a secret ally amongst the Templars. More than that, I cannot say.'

The Magister paused, swilling the dregs of his wine around his goblet. 'But to return to Sumerscale and Fallowfield, perhaps the Templars did have a hand in their destruction. After all, Rougehead was a former Templar. For all we know, Sumerscale and Fallowfield may also have been members of that order.' He glanced at the hour candle on its spigot, peering to see how close the flame was to the next red hour ring. 'I had both their corpses for two days. As usual, we inspected them. One of my henchmen is a leech of some repute. Anyway, Fallowfield was a much older man, with the grizzled body of a warrior who had fought in Outremer.

His skin was deeply burnt, whilst his back was scarred as if he had been the victim of a cruel lashing, although the wounds were old and well healed.'

'So he could have been captured and tortured by the Saracens?'

'Or the recipient of severe military punishment such as the Templars inflict on their members. Moreover, he had that order's cross here,' the Magister patted his right shoulder, 'etched with a dagger, self-inflicted, which might indicate he had been admitted as a full Templar.'

'And Sumerscale?'

'A very handsome young man, no more than sixteen or seventeen summers old. He had the body of a woman, soft, white, unmarked. Except,' the Magister drew a deep breath, 'on the buttocks were small wounds almost healed. In a word, given that he was a beautiful young man, I suspect somebody had tried to brutally sodomise him, though that is just conjecture.'

The Magister sipped from his goblet, indicating that Ranulf also drink from his. 'I know nothing else about those two unfortunates. As for their nemesis Rougehead and his companions? Well, Sumerscale and Fallowfield were hanged in January 1308, the first year of the king's reign. Three months later, just before Ash Wednesday, Rougehead and his three accomplices were invited by some mysterious individual to a sumptuous meal in a private chamber at the Salamander. Delicious food and the best wine were served, or so I have learnt. Hours after the banquet began, the alarm was raised. The chamber hired for the occasion had become a raging inferno, which swiftly spread through the tavern, reducing it to a blackened ruin. Everyone escaped except for Rougehead and his confederates; their charred remains were found amongst the wreckage.

'Justice eh? The four accusers were savagely burnt – isn't that the ancient punishment for perjury? – whilst the very place Sumerscale and Fallowfield were alleged to have committed their crime was reduced to smouldering ash.' The Magister lifted his goblet. 'Proof enough that the mills of God do grind exceedingly small. Now, Master Ranulf, give my good wishes to Sir Hugh.'

Edmund Datchet, former Knight Templar, sat in his cell deep in the enclosure of St Giles hospital, the great lazar house in Queenhithe. The day was drawing on, the sun beginning to set. Both its glare and its cloying warmth had made Datchet's last day alive as refreshing as anything he could have wished. Of course he did not realise that death was about to tighten its noose and spring its trap, that the demand had been made for his soul, and he was too involved in the past to consider whether he was in a state of grace. He stared around his cell, the place that had become his refuge, his protection against Philip of France and the heinous allegations levelled against his broken, shattered order. Datchet had become a poor knight of Christ to fight under the piebald standard in Outremer, defending Christ's holy places against the infidel, but that dream had now died. Jerusalem would never be retaken and the coastal towns of Palestine, the castles and great fortified places of Outremer, had fallen one by one to the enemy.

'Acre!' he muttered to himself. 'Acre was the Vespers of us poor knights. Our last great cry against the infidel.'

Datchet, who styled himself a chronicler of his order, picked up his quill pen, licking its feathery tip as he collected his thoughts about the present situation. In truth, everything lay in ruins. Edward of England like many other princes of this world, had declared himself to be against the order, slavishly following the example of Philip of France, who now demanded that every Templar in England be handed over to him.

'Edmund, are you sleepy?' a voice hissed behind him.

Datchet, garbed in his thick, sweat-soaked leper robe, looked over his shoulder, pulling down the cloth that covered the bottom half of his face.

'I feel weak.' He smiled with his eyes at Reginald Ausel, also a former Templar, now master of the lazar hospital. Ausel, a tall, stringy man, lank grey hair falling either side of a deeply furrowed face, smiled back and sat down on the edge of the cot bed. Datchet, as he always did with this particular comrade, hid his unease and turned to face him squarely. 'Poor Grandison and Boveney,' he declared, 'slaughtered, murdered. Brother Reginald, is this the work of that demon incarnate Philip of France? His familiar de Craon lurks only a short walk away.'

Ausel lifted a hand. 'It's all possible, Brother Edmund. The stories coming out of France are hideous . . .'

'We are reaping what we sowed,' Datchet interrupted.

'Minds closed by hostility and suspicion now support the most heinous and vile accusations. Suspicions amongst thoughts are like bats amongst birds. They come out at twilight as darkness descends. Our order is now cloaked in a thick mist of poisonous gossip. We have good reason to believe that the rumour is true.'

'Which rumour?'

'That years ago Philip of France recruited at least a dozen spies to enter our order. Now these have become professional informers against us.'

'He doesn't need such spies now.'

Both Datchet and Ausel startled at the voice and then relaxed as the door, just slightly off the latch, was pushed open and the Templar captain Walter Burghesh, his sun-brown face completely unmasked, his blue eyes hard and cold, strolled into the room, scratching his rough-shaven face, its thick, hard bristles sharp as briars. Burghesh joked that his face had the skin of a dogfish and it suited his temperament. He made no attempt to hide his robust rude health. He simply declared he sheltered at St Giles to be with his brothers, safe from the clutches of those who wished to harm him and his order.

'Philip the dog king, with his thick yellow hair and glassy eyes, doesn't need traitors and spies.' Burghesh shook his head. 'The French king gets his evidence from torture. Our brothers in Paris face the thumb-screw, the boot, the rack and the press, stretched out on cobbled yards or the filthy floors of dungeons to be crushed under heavy weights. They have had their feet burned, thick metal spikes pushed beneath finger-nails, teeth wrenched out and the bleeding gums prodded with red-hot pins. Some of our brothers are of the willow rather than the oak; they bend lest they break. They sing any tune piped to them. We are supposed to have worshipped a demonic bearded head called Baphomet, summoned devil women from hell and venerated idols smeared with the blood of dead children. One of our brothers said that if he faced such tortures, he would confess to murdering God himself.' Burghesh paused, labouring for breath as he spoke so vehemently and passionately. 'Philip, that lord of hell, has pursued us. He will continue to pursue us. He is determined that no Templar attends the planned council at Vienne to speak in defence of our stricken order.'

'But is it just the French?' Datchet protested. 'Brother Walter, others have good cause to hate our order.' He lowered his voice. 'The accusations of the French king's lawyers may be ridiculous, but in some of our houses, as in other enclosed communities . . .' His voice trailed off.

'What are you implying, my friend?' Burghesh demanded.

'You know full well,' Datchet muttered. 'The love David had for Jonathan, which surpasses any love a man has for a woman.'

'We all love the brothers.'

'Even to the extent of sodomy?' Datchet pulled at the folds of cloth beneath his chin. He wore these more as protection against contagion rather than to cover the sores that pitted his face.

His companions did not bother to answer his question, but glanced sheepishly away. Datchet knew that the French king's accusations, in the main, were heinous and false. However, that secret love between individual members was something his order could not deny. Ausel got to his feet, followed by Burghesh, and, clapping Datchet on the shoulder, the pair made their excuses and left.

Datchet closed the door behind them and returned to his chancery desk. He made sure his sword and dagger were close by. After all, poor Grandison and Boveney's corpses were now laid out in the Chapel of the Dead awaiting burial. An assassin was on the prowl and it would be best if he remained vigilant. He turned swiftly as the door opened, but it was only a servitor, masked and hooded, who brought in a tray with a goblet of wine and a platter of small honey cakes. He put these down and left. Datchet nibbled at the sweetmeats and sipped at the goblet as he returned to reflect on what had happened to his order. He recalled a story from Lithuania, where the Teutonic knights attacked an Easterling fortress on the River Niemen. Rather than be captured, the Easterlings built a great funeral pyre of all their goods, cut the throats of their women and children and then allowed an old priestess to decapitate the remaining warriors, a hundred in all, before splitting her own head with a cleaver just as the Teutonic knights forced the stockade.

'Those barbarians could teach us a lesson,' Datchet breathed, sipping at the wine. 'We should have gone into the dark like warriors, sword in one hand, shield in the other.' He grasped his own weapons, turning away from the desk to face the crudely carved crucifix nailed to the wall. He himself had owned a similar cross in the great fortress of Acre, that bastion of the Templar order overlooking the Middle Sea, the last Frankish foothold in Outremer.

'Twenty years ago, to our eternal shame,' Datchet grated to himself, 'Acre fell.' He recalled the arrival of the Mameluke horde, their sultan eager to avenge the slaughter of Saracens massacred in the city. Almost a quarter of a million men with a hundred mangonels, the most fearsome being 'the Victorious' and 'the Furies', along with powerful catapults nicknamed 'the Black Bulls'. Acre had fallen under the incessant, deadly barrage of fiery missiles from these engines of war; those who tried to flee were caught on the quayside and butchered, men, women and children. The city had been consumed by terror. Some Frankish ladies even mutilated themselves, cutting off nose and ear lobe, hoping that such disfigurement would be a defence against rape and violation. Datchet could not credit such stories. He and his companions, the Brotherhood of the Wolf, had escaped by sea. Others now accused them of cowardice, of desertion, of treachery deserving of death. Master Crowthorne, leech at St Giles, had lost kith and kin at Acre and constantly reminded the Templars about that. 'We should have fought on and gone to God as warriors,' Datchet whispered.

He started at a knock on the door and called out, but there was no answer. He rose, opened the door and smiled at the servitor, whose face was almost hidden by his deep hood.

'Oh,' he exclaimed, 'you have returned.' He turned away. The cowled, masked figure followed him into the chamber, closing the door with one hand as the other drove the long stiletto blade deep into the side of Datchet's neck.

Sir Hugh Corbett, Keeper of the Secret Seal, stared down at the corpses laid out on the mortuary tables in the death chapel of St Giles. All three were to be buried on the morrow after a requiem mass. He had instructed Ausel, master of the hospital, to have the cadavers naked, exposed; now he wished he hadn't. All three victims – Grandison, Datchet and Boveney – were free of the dreadful leprosy, though all of them had suffered from some skin infection, whilst old wounds scarred their bony white cadavers from neck to toe.

Corbett closely scrutinised the death wounds. Boveney and Grandison had been struck to the heart, whilst Datchet had received a killing blow to the side of his neck, which had completely severed the blood pulses in his scrawny throat. All three wounds must have been delivered by someone very close to their quarry, yet Corbett could detect no other mark indicating that any of the victims had tried to defend themselves. He was mystified; after all, the dead men had been warriors, with their weapons close by when they were attacked. He shook his head, crossed himself and turned to the narrow, slightly tilting table behind him. He peeled back the stained, tarred sheet and stared at the old woman dressed in a grey smock, her face a hideous mess of congealed blood and bone, caused by the crossbow bolt, which must have been loosed very close.

'Rohesia,' Ausel whispered, coming alongside Corbett. 'An old beggar woman. She skinned cats, dogs and God knows what else for their hides and meat. She was killed near the mere that lies at the bottom of the great meadow, not far from where Grandison's corpse was discovered. We found her sack and wallet close to a disused sewer opening; she probably crawled through this to sleep beneath a bush.'

Corbett nodded and pulled the sheet back over the body. 'I would be grateful if you could show me where they all died.'

Accompanied by Ranulf, Corbett left the death chapel, following Ausel across the cobbled, dirt-strewn bailey and into the tangle of stone passageways that cut through the buildings of the hospital. He considered it a journey across a truly blighted landscape. The hospital lay quiet as the day ended. Bells rang, then fell silent. The patter of feet echoed into nothingness. Ranulf was already highly nervous at entering what he called 'the contagious precincts of St Giles'. The oppressive silence, the first curling of an evening river mist and the glaring stone faces of statues, gargoyles and babe-wyns did little to soothe his humours.

They turned a corner. Ranulf quietly cursed as a figure sitting on a turfed bench abruptly rose. He moved like an apparition through the drifting mist, swathed in cloths from head to toe. The leper stopped, stared at Ausel, then turned and scuttled off, clacking his wooden rattle. They passed other such ghoulish sights as they went deeper into the hospital. Figures emerged from doorways only to swiftly retreat to the ominous clatter of their rattles. The small group skirted the hospital gardens with its various plots – herb, flower, vegetable and fruits – then passed through a majestic lychgate and into the great meadow that stretched down to the high grey ragstone curtain wall in the far distance. A lonely, rather bleak place, a boundary between the hospital buildings and the bustling city beyond its walls. A place where the living dead could walk through the grass with sun, rain and wind on their corrupted faces. The meadow fell away, and at the bottom of the slight hill stretched a mere, a small lake fringed with willow trees, bushes and a tangle of gorse. Like the rest of St Giles, a silent, eerie place, the stillness broken only by the caw of nesting crows and the fluttering of wings as a bird burst out of the trees.

Ausel led Corbett to a wooden bench on the far side of the mere. 'Grandison was found here, facing the wall,' he explained, 'a spent lantern by his side. He was slouched, crouched forward, that strange Arabic dagger thrust deep into his chest.'

'Show us,' Corbett ordered. Ausel shrugged and sat down on the bench, hands dangling.

'Rohesia lay over there.' The master of the hospital pointed to a patch of flattened grass still stained with dry blood. 'Flat on her back, hands out, her face all crushed and bloody.'

Corbett sat down on the bench next to Ausel and stared across at the wall.

'Behind that screen of bushes and foliage,' Ausel observed, 'you will find the entrance Rohesia used. Some ancient watercourse. I suspect she came here often. A safe place. People tend to keep clear of a leper hospital.'

'But not two nights ago,' Corbett retorted. 'Rohesia crawled in; she saw or heard something untoward, edged closer and the assassin struck. He could not allow her to escape. She may have seen something. However, that is not the real mystery.' He stretched out his legs. 'Grandison was an old comrade of mine. A skilled warrior, moderate and calm, or he was when I knew him. So what was he doing here in this lonely, bleak place at the dead of night? He had his weapons?'

'Sword and dagger were out on the bench either side of him.'

'Why?' Corbett rose to his feet. 'Why does a Templar knight come and sit here? Why bring his weapons? Was he expecting to meet someone? Tell me, was Grandison infected?'

'No.'

'Did he fear anything or anyone?'

'Only what we all have to confront, Sir Hugh, the

destruction of our order. You will meet with the rest?'

'Yes, yes, I will. But let me see where the others were murdered.'

Ausel led Corbett and Ranulf back to the main hospital buildings, explaining how Boveney had been found murdered in a small enclave built into the side of the hospital church. Apparently a favourite place for the old Templar to watch the sun set.

'We found him here just before Vespers.' Ausel pointed to an ancient enclave, once part of a now derelict anchorite cell. The wall of the church was spotted with lichen and ivy. There was a ledge that served as a seat. Above this a leper squint, which provided the recluse with a clear view of the high altar to watch the consecration and elevation of the host during mass. 'He was sitting here like this.' Ausel sat down on the ledge and slouched forward, sword and dagger either side of him.

Corbett stared round. The lazar house was a lonely dwelling, but this place was particularly desolate. The clerk suppressed a shiver, winked at Ranulf and said he'd seen enough.

They both followed Ausel across into the main hospital buildings and the master's parlour. A bleak room; a stark black cross nailed to the wall, on either side of this paintings of the Beau-Seant and Piebald banners as well as other standards of the fighting order of monks. Five people sat grouped around the scrubbed table. Two were Templar knights, swathed in robes, their hoods pushed back. Corbett was aware of sharp, lined faces, mouths set grimly, eyes hostile and watchful.

Ausel introduced Roger Stapleton and Walter Burghesh. Both men sketched a bow and welcomed Corbett in harsh, guttural tones, but they offered no hand to clasp so Corbett responded in kind. A third person was the hospital leech and physician, Master Crowthorne, a lanky individual with straggling hair either side of his pockmarked face, made even uglier by the ever-dripping nose above prim lips and receding chin. The two women were in stark contrast. Philippa Henman looked radiant even though she was garbed from head to toe in a grey lazar robe, her lovely auburn hair almost covered by a hood that she kept pushing back with a doeskin-gloved hand; her companion, the young, fresh-faced Agnes Sokelar, was dressed similarly. Both clasped hands and exchanged the kiss of peace with Corbett. Mistress Philippa explained how she and Agnes were leading members of the Guild of St Martha, which took its name from the sister of Lazarus in the Gospels.

'I invited them here,' Ausel explained, indicating the two women, 'at Sister Philippa's behest, because I understand from your henchman that these ladies will attest to the truth of what we say and be witnesses to our responses.'

'I certainly do want to question you,' Corbett declared, 'but there is one further place to visit. I need to see where Edmund Datchet was murdered earlier this afternoon.'

Ausel agreed and escorted him back into the passageway and along a stone-paved gallery into the great cloisters. Datchet's chamber overlooked the ill-kempt garth: its grass had not been cropped, whilst the rose bush in the centre was nothing better than a mass of bramble and briar. Datchet's door was off the latch. Corbett followed Ausel into the austere chamber and stared down at the great bloodstain on the rough carpet. He swiftly measured the distance.

'Datchet,' he observed, 'was killed with a blow to the right of his neck. A deep cut that severed the blood lines in his throat.' Ausel agreed. 'I suspect,' Corbett continued, 'that he opened the door to his murderer, then turned to lead him in. The assassin closed the door behind him, then struck that killing blow. Datchet collapsed and the assassin fled.'

Ausel pointed to the sword and dagger lying to one side. 'Edmund had these at hand,' he declared, 'yet apart from the pool of blood, there was no sign of any disturbance, of Edmund defending himself. Nor did anyone see or hear anything untoward. He died in the same silent way as Boveney and Grandison.'

Corbett pronounced himself satisfied and returned to the parlour, where the others were talking amongst themselves. He took his seat and tapped the table.

'Master Ausel, tell us again why you invited these two ladies to this meeting. I mean in greater detail.'

'Sir Hugh,' Ausel replied, 'you arc going to question us about the murders of three Templars. Others in this hospital do not like us. They resent our presence at St Giles for many reasons. We have no friends or allies here; no one will vouch for us except Mistress Philippa and her good sisters. They know the truth of the situation.'

'And why should others resent you?' Ranulf asked.

'You know full well,' Burghesh retorted. 'The Templar order is now broken and utterly disgraced, due to the malice of Philip of France and his council of demons, led by his chief minister, *Guillaume de Nogaret*. Even before they struck, the Templars faced allegations that we lost Outremer. How we have grown fat and lazy on the backs of others.'

'And of course,' Mistress Philippa intervened, 'our comrades here, including Master Ausel, do not suffer from leprosy. According to Master Crowthorne, other inmates of the hospital – indeed, I know this myself – fiercely resent the Templars being here. They argue that St Giles is not a sanctuary, and they blame them for the violence that has occurred. It is interesting that all three murdered Templars had their weapons close by.'

'They did, mistress!' Corbett smiled. 'I follow your logic: they had their weapons ready in the lonely places where they were murdered because they feared attack by some of the inmates here.'

'It's certainly possible, Sir Hugh, but why they didn't actually defend themselves . . .'

Philippa fell silent as Crowthorne rapped the table.

'I am responsible for this hospital,' he rasped, glaring furiously around. 'I know the humour and condition of all its inmates and I,' he glared at Ausel, sallow cheeks all a-quiver, 'should have been appointed master here.'

'Instead of me, a Templar?' Ausel countered.

'A friend of Gaveston.'

'You mean my lord of Cornwall?'

'Gentlemen, gentlemen.' Corbett too banged the table. 'Let us keep to the business in hand. In brief, the Templar order was dissolved in the winter of 1307 to 1308. Its property was seized. Many of the order fled. You,' he pointed at Ausel, 'were appointed master of this hospital. Yes?' He did not wait for an answer, but pressed on. 'You opened its doors to other Templars seeking refuge. I believe the Templars here once served in Outremer, members of a cohort known as the Brotherhood of the Wolf. You were involved in the defence of Acre. You returned to England and garrisoned the lucrative but very lonely fortified manor of Temple Combe, deep in the forest of Epping. When your order was dissolved, you fled here for sanctuary. Yes?'

Ausel murmured agreement.

'Now,' Corbett continued, 'you may suffer from various ailments but you are not lepers. You dress as if you are, though I suspect this is a disguise as well as a defence against the risk of contagion. However, as long as you do not share the food and drink of an infected person or bathe in their water or have close bodily contact over a long period of time, the risk of contagion is very rare, or that's what the royal physicians advise me. Master Crowthorne, I am correct?' The leech, now more aware of Corbett's status and power, smiled weakly in agreement.

Corbett rubbed his mouth; he felt thirsty, but he and Ranulf had secretly vowed not to drink or eat in this place. 'These hideous murders apart, has anything else occurred out of the ordinary?'

His question was greeted with shrugs and shakes of the head. Corbett stared around, feeling a cold, crippling dread. Something was very wrong here; though he could not place it, he nursed a strong suspicion that what he had been told was a tangle of lies. He felt deeply uneasy in Ausel's company: something in the shift of the master's eyes revealed a cunning soul, a Templar who seemed to have very little feeling, if any, for his comrades, living or dead, not to mention those poor inmates they had passed in their walk through the hospital.

'These murders,' Ranulf demanded, 'who do you think could be responsible?'

'Philip of France,' Stapleton spat back. 'He wants us either imprisoned or dead. He cannot tolerate the possibility of men like ourselves attending the Council of Vienne to defend our order.'

'And will you attend?' Ranulf asked.

'We will be organised,' Stapleton blustered. 'Myself and other Templars, as well as those protected by the Bruce in Scotland.'

'I wouldn't proclaim that too loudly,' Corbett declared drily. 'Bruce is also very friendly with Philip of France.'

Stapleton turned away in embarrassment.

'Datchet and Boveney were murdered in places they were accustomed to be,' Corbett continued, 'but I have asked Master Ausel this, and I repeat the question: what was Grandison doing in the great meadow at the dead of night?'

'Truly, Sir Hugh, we don't know,' Burghesh confessed.

'And you, good sisters?'

'Sir Hugh,' Philippa grasped the hand of Agnes sitting next to her, 'I have been visiting St Giles long before the Templars arrived here.'

'Is that so?'

'Oh yes. Since my marriage to Raoul, my late husband, well over eight years ago.'

'And your husband died . . .'

'About twelve months since.' She blinked quickly and forced a smile. 'The anniversary of his death will be soon.'

'Mistress, my condolences. What is your work here?'

'I bring food, drink and other comforts: oils, jars and essences, salves, fresh linen for bandages. Our guild enjoys the support of all the great and the good in Queenhithe.'

'The sisters do good work,' Crowthorne declared to a murmur of approval from the rest.

'And have you, mistress,' Corbett asked, 'noticed anything untoward?'

'Sir Hugh, when Agnes and I come to St Giles, we each have our own tasks. We do our work, we talk and pray with those who lodge here, then we go. I assure you, we have seen nothing suspicious. Have we, Agnes?'

The young woman gazed adoringly back at her older companion.

'We do good work here,' Philippa repeated. 'The politics of princes do not concern us.' She glanced mischievously out of the corner of her eye. 'I understand, Sir Hugh, that you too will be lodged at the Merry

Mercy, along with your good friend Monseigneur de Craon?'

Corbett grinned back. 'I am sure,' he murmured, 'that de Craon has the same high opinion of me as I do of him.'

'You will be on the floor gallery: our best and most spacious accommodation, the Pendragon room. Monseigneur de Craon, you will be pleased to know, is on the second gallery, a most comfortable chamber in a different part of the tavern.'

'I am sure all will be well, mistress.' Corbett's smile faded. 'But back to the matter in hand: no one here knows why these Templar knights have been slaughtered, or who might be responsible?'

'Philip of France and his minion de Craon,' Stapleton declared, pulling the bandage down from his chapped lips. 'Albeit we have no proof of that or how he carries out his murderous designs.'

No one disagreed.

'Very well. We now have established,' Corbett gestured around, 'that this is all a mystery to you knights and your witnesses, our fair ladies here.'

'We can only say what we see.' Philippa leaned forward. 'The sisters of our guild have different tasks with the various groups at St Giles. Agnes and I deal with the Templars. They are men who have taken sanctuary here with few possessions except for their weapons. I understand their manuscripts and books have been seized.' Her words were greeted with murmurs of agreement.

'Very well,' Corbett said. 'To another matter. Do the

names Sumerscale and Fallowfield mean anything to you?'

'In God's name,' Crowthorne exclaimed, 'who are they?'

'Two mariners hanged by Master Naseby from the mast of his war cog *The Candle-Bright* in January 1308, just before His Grace the king married Princess Isabella. Both sailors were accused of speaking contumaciously against the king and Lord Gaveston and making public ridicule of them, implying that my lord Gaveston was the king's catamite . . .'

Silence greeted Corbett's words. He kept his face impassive and stared around.

'So Naseby, *The Candle-Bright*, Sumerscale and Fallowfield mean nothing to you?'

'We did not say that!' Ausel snapped.

Corbett stared at this former Templar, now master of St Giles. He sensed the man's deepening nervousness and wondered about its cause. He could understand Crowthorne's hostility towards Ausel; the others, however, by the way they sat and rarely looked at the master, also betrayed a dislike, a wariness of their colleague.

'And?' Ranulf demanded.

Ausel snapped his fingers at Agnes.

'I'll answer,' Philippa declared. 'Of course I've heard of *The Candle-Bright*: Master Naseby frequented the Merry Mercy, as do other mariners, but I hardly know much about him or his ship. However, St Giles is in Queenhithe, and its founding charter clearly stipulates that the inmates here must pray for the welfare of the local mercantile community, its guilds, its ships and their crews. Accordingly, Agnes or I, or another member of our guild, would ask Master Ausel to post a notice in the hospital church giving the names of ships leaving Queenhithe, and the date, with a plea for prayer. I'm sure that happened on the day *The Candle-Bright* sailed – yes, Agnes?' The girl nodded. 'Of course,' Philippa added, 'we now know that those particular prayers were not answered.'

'And Gabriel Rougehead, former Templar, king's approver and Judas man, the person responsible for accusing Sumerscale and Fallowfield and so bringing about their deaths?' Corbett paused. 'Gentlemen,' he looked at Ausel and the others, 'I can see that name means something to you.'

'Gabriel Rougehead,' Burghesh replied slowly choosing his words carefully, 'was a rogue born out of hell. He was a Templar serjeant, though one guilty of every sin under heaven and a few more to boot. A man of steady wit and sharp mind, he eschewed wine, ale or any strong drink. He had a number of clever, subtle disguises and hid behind a veritable litany of names beside his own: Nicholas Wray, William Parson, Foulkes Fitzwarren and John Priknash.'

'What!' Corbett exclaimed. 'The last one?'

'John Priknash,' Burghesh repeated. 'Allegedly a defrocked priest out of Lincolnshire.'

'And a . . .' Corbett caught himself just in time: it was best if he kept what he knew to himself. 'I've heard of him before,' he explained. 'You had dealings with Rougehead?'

'Not really. Why should we?' Stapleton demanded. 'He would occasionally visit this Templar house or that, but then he'd disappear again like the dark serpent he was.'

'We heard nothing of him for years.' Ausel spoke up. 'Till news began to seep through about what had happened on board *The Candle-Bright*.' He screwed his eyes up. 'In the spring of 1308, we also heard about that mysterious fire at the Salamander. Minehost Slingsby and all his minions had to flee for their lives. Apparently Rougehead and his three confederates were not so fortunate . . .'

'And so I ask you again,' Corbett demanded, 'none of you here had dealings with this miscreant?' The question was greeted with shakes of the head and murmured denials. 'In which case . . .'

Corbett rose, made his farewells and left. Once they were out in the street, Ranulf plucked at his sleeve.

'You recognised one of Rougehead's aliases?'

'John Priknash,' Corbett murmured. 'Allegedly a leading member of the gang that broke into the crypt and stole the Crown Jewels. Priknash was suspected, but there was no real evidence or proof. As with some other members of the gang, he disappeared like steam from a bubbling pot, vanishing into thin air. Well, well, well.' Corbett stared up at the streak of sky that cut between the grim overhanging houses either side of the street. 'Ranulf, the day is dying, and what a day!

Closeted with His Grace and my lord Gaveston, and you with the Magister Viae. What he told you was interesting enough. I will carefully reflect on it.'

Corbett adjusted his war belt and stared down the street. Dirt glistened on the cobbles; shapes and shadows moved in and out of the mouths of alleyways and other enclaves. A lunatic came dancing out of a runnel garbed in a white sheet, a cresset torch in one hand, a frying pan in the other. He did a wild dance, then disappeared into the murk. Two beggars, one sprawled in a wheelbarrow, the other pushing it, left a courtyard whining for alms, only to hastily retreat at the appearance of a wand-bearing beadle. Shops and stalls were closing for the night. Itinerant cooks doused the flames of their crude stoves and grills. A group of carollers wailed their last hymn, whilst pedlars and tinkers loosened the straps around their necks and disappeared into the alehouses along the thoroughfare. Bells tolled. The evening breeze wafted up the stench of the street and the saltpetre strewn to disguise it.

'What is it, master?'

'The day is done, Ranulf. Soon we will be for the dark.'

'As the poet says, however the day is long, at last the bell will ring for evensong.'

'You have turned to poetry during my absence?'

'I have turned to a lot of things, master. There is a young lady in Southampton, a maiden chaste and pure.' Ranulf drew a deep breath. 'A merchant's daughter, Sir Hugh.' He gestured with his head down the murky street. 'I wonder what she would think if she knew that I was once part of this nightmare world. When I have the time, I am searching for my mother, though God knows whether she's alive or dead. Do I have brothers or sisters? Who was my father?'

Corbett turned to face Ranulf squarely. 'You are a strange one, Ranulf-atte-Newgate.'

'And one who is getting older. I know where I am going, but I also have a hunger gnawing at me to know where I came from.' He punched Corbett gently on the arm. 'I am glad you have returned, Sir Hugh. The present business is a tangled mess.'

Corbett pulled his cloak about him. He suppressed a chill of feverish fear, a sure sign that he faced dire danger, yet he could not articulate either its cause or content. Ranulf was correct. They were moving from their usual worlds, the chatter of the chancery or affairs of the heart, drawn into a dense web of deceit and deadly intrigue. He fingered the hilt of his sword, aware of the other man's gnawing restlessness.

'We'd best visit Holy Trinity the Little and Parson Layburn,' he declared. 'Let's see if he can cast any light on the gathering dark.'

PART THREE

'Wheat is sown and weeds are brought forth.'
The Monk of Malmesbury, *Life of Edward II*

Corbett and Ranulf strode down the street and into a warren-like maze of runnels and alley-ways. The sight of two royal clerks, buckled and armoured, sent the shadow people scuttling back deeper into the dark. An enterprising relic seller, however, tried to interest them in a reputedly sacred hunting horn.

'Very similar,' he gabbled, 'to that owned by St Hubert, which of course is the type the Angel Gabriel uses to blow his Ave to the Virgin. Now, sirs, if you are not interested in that, I have a phial of the Holy Milk of the Blessed Mary kept at Walsingham. I . . .'

He tried to grab Ranulf's arm, then shrieked as the tip of the clerk's dagger blade nicked him beneath the chin. Corbett used the occasion to look quickly back, and glimpsed a cowled figure abruptly stop and turn the other way. He was sure someone was following them. The relic seller fled, shouting curses.

'What is it, master?' asked Ranulf.

'I am sure we are being followed. However, whoever

it was has now disappeared. Do you know who I glimpsed earlier today, just before I entered the lazar hospital?'

Ranulf shook his head.

'The Wolfman!'

'The Wolfman!' Ranulf exclaimed. 'You mean the Earl of Pembroke's retainer, the one who hunts down outlaws for a reward?'

'The same. I don't think he was interested in us; more the gateway to the lazar hospital, as if he was carefully watching people come and go. I wonder what he wants and who he is hunting. Anyway, Parson Layburn awaits us.'

They reached the crossroads of Old Fish Lane and Cordwainer Street and the looming mass of Holy Trinity the Little. They climbed the steps, pushed open the iron-studded door and entered the musty-smelling nave. Corbett peered through the murk. The church's windows were little better than lancets. Candle spigots attached to the squat pillars either side flared, throwing some light on the macabre funeral ceremony being carried out just before the rood screen. A corpse had been laid out for burial in the parish death cart. The cadaver was swathed completely in white cloths, except for the face. On its chest rested a small platter of salt and dried bread for the sin-eater to chew. On each mouldy corner of the death cart a rushlight flickered feebly, while four old women sat around the corpse wailing a death dirge:

'We pray this night, this night,
Every night and all,
Fire and sleet and candlelight,
And Christ receive her soul.'

The ancient withered faces of the mourners were daubed in white paint with streaks of red and twisted in grief. Corbett stepped around them and peered down at the shattered, bloody face of the old woman he had last glimpsed in the death chapel of St Giles.

'Rohesia,' he murmured. 'They must have brought her here within the hour.'

'Can I help you?' A priest dressed in a white surplice with a black and gold stole around his neck came through the rood screen. An old man with a seamed face and scrawny white hair, though his eyes were sharp and bright. 'You knew old Rohesia?' he asked, stepping around the death cart and sketching a blessing above the mourners, who continued their sombre chant.

Corbett introduced himself and Ranulf. He explained how they had visited the leper hospital earlier in the day and now wished to speak to Parson Geoffrey Layburn. The priest, one hand on his chest, bowed mockingly.

'I am Geoffrey Layburn.' He extended his right hand for Corbett to clasp. 'I am greatly honoured by a visit from the king's most senior clerk. Gentlemen,' he gestured at the mourners, 'I think it would be best if I took you somewhere a little quieter.'

He led them into a heavily screened chantry chapel,

closing the door behind them and pulling across the thick velvet curtain. He indicated that Corbett and Ranulf should sit on the wall bench, whilst he brought out a stool from beneath the small table altar. The chapel had a large roundel window through which light poured to illuminate the strange paintings covering the walls as well as the plaster above the altar.

'In heaven's name!' Corbett murmured. He pointed at the crude but vivid scenes, each painted without any reference to the one next to it: St Edmund's severed head being rescued by a wolf; a two-bodied lion with one neck chasing dragon birds with leafy tails; a spoon-bill swallowing a frog, watched by a devil-headed monkey grasping a man with ass's ears by the throat.

'Grotesques,' Ranulf murmured.

'The legacy of my predecessor,' the parson declared. 'Poor man. Waldo Henman had great talents as an artist, but his mind eventually slipped into madness.'

'Henman? The same name as Mistress Philippa, mine-host at the Merry Mercy.'

'Her late husband's uncle. Both Parson Waldo and Philippa's husband lie buried in God's Acre here. This church has been generously patronised by the Henman family. Now, sirs, how can I help?'

'Henry Sumerscale and Matthew Fallowfield hanged from the mast of *The Candle-Bright* in January 1308. You claimed the corpses from the Magister Viae, who usually takes care of the remains of hanged felons.'

'If they were felons . . .'

'You know of them?'

'Very little except that they were accused by a king's approver. A proper Judas man.'

'Why did you claim their corpses?'

The parson pointed to the chantry door. 'I was here one night in the mercy pew, shriving any sinner who knelt on the prie-dieu beyond the curtain. It was growing late, the candles burning low. I was preparing to leave when I heard someone kneel beyond the shriving veil.'

'Who?'

'Sir Hugh, you know I cannot move the veil, but the man was a wealthy one. I did not recognise his voice. Indeed, I suspect he had something across his mouth to disguise it.' The parson smiled wearily. 'I am a shepherd close to his flock; so close I can smell their stink. My mysterious visitor was different. I caught quite a delicate perfume, as if he bathed in the soap of Castile. Anyway,' Layburn shrugged, 'he did not want to be shriven. A gloved hand parted the curtain. He handed over a gold coin, well minted and fresh, one of the first batch issued by the new king. I was then instructed to collect both corpses, shroud and coffin them, sing a requiem mass for the repose of their souls and bury them honourably in God's Acre, which I did. I was also instructed to place two crosses above the graves. They were to be of the best elmwood, the inscriptions carved on them quite stark. I remember them well: "Matthew, faithful servant and friend", and "Henry most beloved".' The parson shrugged. 'And that was that.'

Corbett stared at one of the grotesque wall paintings, a wyvern with a hanging belly biting its own back, whilst above it, a demon with the face of a fierce bat prepared to strike.

'Did anyone attend the funeral mass?'

The parson pointed to a painting of an old woman, hands clasped, lying on her side. 'You see that? It's a depiction of one of the sisterhood, those four old ladies mourning their companion Rohesia; the Sisterhood of the Street, as they call themselves. They attended that funeral, as they do every requiem mass, but apart from them, no one else. And,' he sighed, 'since then, I have heard nothing.'

'And Rohesia?' Corbett stretched out his legs, loosening his war belt. He felt tired and tense, yet still wary of danger lurking close.

'She was a street scavenger.'

'But she was found murdered in the lazar hospital?'

'Rohesia would drink as she hunted cats and small dogs, either the living or just their corpses.' The parson rubbed his stomach. 'She sold their meat to the butchers and their skins to the furriers. At night she would search out some place lonely, quiet and safe. She always maintained the lazar hospital was her favourite refuge, where she could rest undisturbed.'

'Did she now?' Corbett murmured. 'And she never reported anything suspicious, out of the ordinary?'

'No, no. Far from it. She, like all the street people, knew the Templars had fallen, that some of the knights had been given refuge there. She had also heard about the murder of one of them, but that did not concern her.' The parson paused, fingers going to his lips. 'The one place Rohesia tended to avoid was the tavern where you are staying, the Merry Mercy. Comings and goings at the dead of night. Isn't that also the lodgings of the French envoy, de Craon?'

'Yes,' Corbett smiled thinly, 'I am sure de Craon has a legion of midnight visitors.' He rose to his feet and stared down at the priest. 'But you have nothing more to tell us about Sumerscale and Fallowfield?'

The parson sat head down. 'Rohesia!' He glanced up. 'Yes, Sir Hugh, I knew there was something else. I collected the corpses from the Magister Viae and brought them here. Rohesia was also present when they were being shrouded. She usually rambled – she was fey-witted – but I distinctly remember her claiming to have seen both men before. I asked her where and when. "Oh, by the hour of candlelight," she replied, "sometime around the hour of the bat." That was her description for nightfall. I was intrigued. I pressed her on this but she wouldn't or couldn't say any more. That's all I can tell you.'

Corbett thanked the parson for his help. He and Ranulf left the church, walking swiftly through the gathering dark, cloaks pulled tight against the evening breeze.

'Master, was that useful?'

Corbett strode on, but then paused in the light of an alehouse: its door was flung open, and the lanternhorns fixed either side of the entrance bathed the doorway in a warm glow.

'A tankard of ale, Ranulf?'

He led his companion into a taproom reeking of ale as well as the fragrance of ham, bacon, apples and onions hanging in nets from the blackened ceiling beams. The two men sat at a makeshift table, an overturned barrel placed in an enclave. A servitor brought two blackjacks of frothing ale. Corbett grasped his and toasted his companion before taking a generous gulp of the rich dark brown drink.

'Very good, strong and tangy. Ranulf, there are certain things in London I missed during my retirement, and city ale is one of them.' He grinned. 'As well as your good self, of course.' His smile faded as he stared around. 'Ranulf, your Latin is improving. Yes? You have been taught by a master?'

'You know that, Sir Hugh. I continued my studies in the schools during your retirement.' Ranulf sat back cradling his tankard. 'I even considered training for the Church.' He waved a hand at Corbett's smile. 'I know! I have too deep an interest in the ladies for the supposedly celibate life, though that's not the real reason.' He lowered his head, gazing at Corbett from under his eyebrows; a strained, empty look.

'What is it, Ranulf?'

'Look around you, Sir Hugh. In the corner sits a rat-catcher with dirty hands and a filthy face. In the sack between his shit-strewn boots are the corpses of the vermin he has caught, trapped and killed. Close to him is one of the foulest-looking prostitutes in London. Within hailing distance of her, the pimp who sells her raddled body. So many people, Sir Hugh, so many sinners, and yet the Church teaches that God loves us all. But you know, many a day I go to bed and I don't believe in any of it.' Ranulf lowered his voice. 'No God, no Christ, no Church, no sacraments. And after death? No heaven, no hell, no limbo, no purgatory. Nothing but eternal blackness: the oblivion of everlasting night.'

Corbett hid his surprise by drinking from his tankard.

'Sir Hugh, we are creatures of the dark. We care for our bellies and for ourselves. When I was a child, I starved. I was so hungry I would chew a piece of leather whilst only a walk away some fat merchant in a cookshop close to Newgate filled his belly with the softest chicken flesh. So yes, I have been studying, but where it will take me, I cannot say.' Ranulf put his tankard down. 'Sir Hugh, do you believe in everything that's preached from the pulpit?'

'No, no, I don't, but I pretend as if I do. Like you, Ranulf, I have my doubts. However, I look at this life and I have choices. Do I strengthen the light or deepen the dark? When this business is over, you must come and stay at Leighton Manor and we can discuss it further, but now to the matter in hand.'

Corbett hitched off his cloak and loosened his war belt. 'First,' he began, 'I have been away from royal service for six years. During that time the old king has died and his son Edward of Caernarvon has succeeded to the throne. Edward II is determined on advancing his favourite Peter Gaveston as much as he can, in the teeth of intense opposition from his leading earls, led by his cousin Thomas, Earl of Lancaster. However,

Edward's problems are not confined to this kingdom. Philip of France has virtually forced him to marry Isabella, who is now the fifteen-year-old queen of this kingdom. Philip has also compelled Edward to join him in a vicious attack on the Templar order, which to all intents and purposes has ceased to exist.'

Corbett paused, staring at a tinker who had wandered in from the street with his tray still wrapped around him. In one hand he carried a cudgel, in the other a cage containing a squealing ferret. The rat-catcher whom Ranulf had glimpsed earlier shouted abuse at this rival. The scullion boy told him to shut up as he shooed the tinker into the kitchen, where the ferret was to be released along the rat runs beneath the floorboards.

'Isn't it strange?' Corbett whispered. 'That's what we are, yes, Ranulf? Hunters! We pursue sinners, reprobates, even if they are clothed in perfumed silk and enjoy great power and sport gorgeous titles.'

'Including Philip of France.'

'Most definitely. Philip of France,' Corbett continued, 'sees himself as master of Europe, but he has to develop the sinews of such a dream. So we enter the subtle treachery and highly dangerous politics of the situation. Philip enjoys a mastery over our king. Matters worsen with the emergence of *The Black Hogge*, a powerful war cog under a most skilled captain, who takes his orders direct from Philip in Paris and de Craon in London. How that's done, I do not know. *The Black Hogge*, however, is proving to be a true menace, a real threat to English shipping. It is swifter and more powerful than any English craft, and it also seems to know about every ship that leaves the Thames – the time of its departure as well as its destination.'

Corbett sipped at his tankard. '*The Candle-Bright* itself is very much part of a greater mystery. Three years ago, its master John Naseby hanged two men, Matthew Fallowfield and Henry Sumerscale, for speaking contumaciously against the king and Gaveston. Naseby later nourished grave doubts about the guilt of both men and was haunted by their memory. Now, just before his last voyage, Naseby's guilt was cleverly exploited. He was reminded of Sumerscale and Fallowfield's execution, how unfair it was and how he would pay a blood price for their deaths. This made him deeply uneasy, as he confessed to me. If I'd had my way, *The Candle-Bright* would never have sailed, but it did, only to face total disaster.'

'Which means,' Ranulf said slowly, 'that the person or persons who threatened Naseby before he sailed already knew the *The Candle-Bright* was going to its destruction.' He ran a finger around his tankard. 'I don't believe in ghosts and revenants, master. Naseby's mysterious tormentor is flesh and blood; it has to be de Craon. But why threaten Naseby in the first place?'

'I cannot answer that. An equally vexing question is: who were Sumerscale and Fallowfield? Where did they come from? The only person who claims to have seen them in London, away from *The Candle-Bright*, is a fey-witted old woman who was probably murdered because she was in the wrong place at the wrong time.

Apart from Rohesia's rather vague statement reported to us by a third person, both men remain a mystery. The Magister Viae believes that Fallowfield might have been a Templar who served in Outremer. He also asserts that Sumerscale may have been the victim of a nasty sexual assault. Nevertheless, despite all the mystery surrounding these two men, someone here in Queenhithe, and someone fairly rich and powerful, ensured that they received honourable burial.

'In addition,' Corbett pressed on, 'there definitely seems to be a link between Sumerscale and Fallowfield and the Templar order. They were accused by that cunning rogue Gabriel Rougehead, also known as John Priknash, a felon twice as fit for hell as any of them and, more importantly, a former Templar. Why did Rougehead level such accusations? Was he bribed? Were the other perjured witnesses – and I am sure they did lie – also paid to commit such a heinous act? Nevertheless, Rougehead and his coven did not live long enough to enjoy the fruits of their misdeeds, perishing in that mysterious fire at the Salamander, the very tavern where Sumerscale and Fallowfield allegedly committed their offence. In this case, certainly the wages of sin are death.' He paused. 'Ranulf, I must question Slingsby, minehost at that tavern, before he gets much older.'

He took a sip of ale, lips moving as he sifted the various problems. 'Now to the Templars themselves,' he continued. 'The order has been destroyed. Philip has had his way. Edward of England has also agreed to the dissolution of the order, but despite his father-in-law, he drags his feet. He allows certain Templars to take sanctuary in the lazar house of St Giles: its master is Reginald Ausel, a distant kinsman of Gaveston, the others are poor knights. Philip would like all of them to be handed over to him. He certainly doesn't want any of them travelling to the Council of Vienne later this year. It would appear that even here, Philip has had his wicked way. Three Templars have been mysteriously murdered, all with their weapons close by, but with no trace of resistance. One of them, Grandison, was stabbed in the dead of night with a dagger once wielded by an assassin in Outremer, part of the king's treasure at Westminster that was plundered some eight years ago.

'Finally, Ranulf, there is that warning thrown at me in Westminster Abbey, telling me to withdraw, to go back to my bees. Are all these mysteries linked? I suspect they are, and this in turn means there is a common root.'

'Yes.' The force of Ranulf's reply surprised Sir Hugh. 'Yes,' he repeated, leaning over the table. 'Amaury de Craon, self-proclaimed envoy of the French king, is the root of all our present evils. Oh, he can masquerade as an emissary trotting off to Westminster to discuss this and that with senior officials. Nonetheless, master, I have reflected, and I believe that Philip and de Craon have concocted and plotted a game that they now play both fast and furious to secure control of this kingdom and its king. In order to achieve this, certain obstacles have to be removed. One of the most serious—' he paused 'is you.'

Corbett stared sharply at his companion. 'Ranulf, what proof do you have of this? Apart from the warning, I have not been threatened. Before all this began I did not know about Sumerscale and Fallowfield, whilst I am hardly of the Templar order.' He poked Ranulf playfully. 'Come, Master Clerk, what have I taught you? Where is the evidence, where is the proof?'

'Master, you are probably wondering why I am brooding about the darkness in my own soul, but this springs from a fear more of the stomach than the mind. A belief that murderous mischief is being plotted and you are its intended victim. I have no proof, no evidence, just a nagging feeling of real danger. Come, master, you have experienced it: hunting rebels along the Welsh March, or down those dark runnels near Newgate or Southwark where the nightmare people lurk, or along those moon-washed coffin paths out in the countryside where you glimpse shadows deeper than the rest.'

Corbett stared hard at his companion. Now he understood why Ranulf's mood had darkened. Invariably the Clerk of the Green Wax was right; he had a nose for danger. Corbett lifted his blackjack and silently toasted his friend.

'My comrade, you may be correct. I too nurse a secret dread. We have already sustained a grievous blow . . .'

'*The Candle-Bright*?'

'Oh, more than that. Naseby carried secret instructions to a spy I have nourished deep in the Louvre, a man close to the heart of King Philip's dark designs.' He lowered his voice. 'Guido Tallefert, senior clerk in the inner royal chamber; what King Philip and de Craon call the Holy Chancery.'

'Yes, you have mentioned him before.'

'Tallefert had a close bosom friend, a Templar named Rochfort. Before Philip struck in 1307, Tallefert sent a secret warning to Rochfort, who fled Paris to Boulogne and the safety of the English county of Ponthieu. Of course royal serjeants arrested him, but kept his confinement secret. Now I had done business with Tallefert on a number of issues.' Corbett grinned. 'We also share a passion for beekeeping. Tallefert comes from English-held Gascony: a man of Bordeaux, a bachelor, who has no love for Philip or the likes of de Nogaret and de Craon. He begged me to help Rochfort and I obliged.'

Corbett called across to the scullion, who was squatting with his back to a barrel. The boy immediately leapt to his feet and hurried across. Corbett pressed a coin into his grimy hand and pulled him close, whispering in his ear. The scullion, slipping and slithering on the slops on the stone floor, hastened away. A short while later, the ale master appeared. A tall man, fair-haired, face darkened by the sun, wide-spaced eyes crinkling under bushy brows, wiry and quick in his movements. Ranulf immediately recognised a soldier.

'This is Rochfort,' Corbett whispered in Norman French, 'now Master Simon out of Bordeaux. A vintner and an ale master.' When Corbett had finished the introductions, Ranulf clasped the man's hand and smiled.

'I suppose you will soon be a guildsman?'

'In time.' Rochfort's English was tinged by a slight accent. 'Sir Hugh,' he leaned closer, 'any news from Tallefert?'

'No, though I wish to God there was. I do fear for him.' Corbett tapped the tankard in front of him. 'Rochfort, I suspect you have been watching us since we arrived?' The man nodded. 'Are we being followed?'

'I don't think so. Though a man came in, glanced across, turned and left. He was dressed in brown leggings and a Lincoln-green jerkin and had a war belt strapped around his waist and one across his chest.'

'Ah, the Wolfman!' Corbett declared. 'A hunter,' he explained. 'He works for a great English lord. I just wonder what he wants. Did you see anyone else?'

Rochfort shook his head. 'I don't think so,' he whispered.

'In which case,' Corbett tapped the blackjack, 'one more delicious serving would be most welcome.'

Rochfort collected the tankards and strode off, calling for the boy. Corbett watched him go.

'I cultivated Tallefert,' he murmured, 'even while I was away from royal service. I also helped our good friend here leave Boulogne and settle in Queenhithe.'

'And now?' Ranulf demanded.

'Naseby was carrying secret instructions for Pietal, our courier in Boulogne, a letter written in cipher for Tallefert. Now he may have destroyed it before *The Black Hogge* closed, or it might have been lost in the fighting and the destruction of *The Candle-Bright*.

Finally, it might have been taken and the clerks at the Louvre have been unable to decipher it . . .'

'Or they might have done.'

'In which case,' Corbett breathed, 'God help poor Tallefert . . .'

Guido Tallefert had woken long before dawn. Once dressed, he left his narrow house overlooking the gushing grey Seine. One house among many in the long line of tall, sharply gabled buildings that seemed to spring up from the cobbles to dominate the narrow, winding streets of the quarter. Guido felt he was going through a forest of stone: houses of all shapes and sizes, with painted woodwork and across their gables the sculpted faces of exotic beasts. He turned a corner, hurrying beneath a long line of vividly scrolled painted shop signs. He passed the carved fountains at the crossroads, close to the statue of the patron saint of the quarter, a beacon light glowing before it.

The silence of the streets was now being shattered by the traders and tinkers swarming out of their rotting tenements and tawdry dungeon chambers. The shrill yelping of the fishwives carried as they bustled up from the quayside, sweating under the heavy wicker baskets they carried. The shouts of the water and wine criers mingled with singing from funeral processions, which grew more raucous as the mourners stopped at the crossroads to share a deep-bowled goblet of wine. They staggered and stumbled, the purple-draped coffins bobbing like corks on bubbling water.

The deeper Tallefert went into the city, the more raucous grew the noise. The shouts and curses of soldiers, the bawling of mountebanks, the clatter of hooves, the rattle of heavy-sided carts and the booming and jangling of bells. The stench of the sulphur strewn on the muck and odour underfoot stung his nostrils as he tried not to be distracted by the tumult of the city. He pushed by the fur-gowned burgesses, the wheedling beggars, the quacks and cunning men mouthing their nonsense. Tramping groups of men-at-arms mingled with pilgrims heading for Saint-Denis, preceded by cross bearers and thurifers who incensed the smelly air. Tallefert ignored all these, as he did the wedding parties, the manacled prisoners and the bands of jugglers. He had to reach the great charnel house of the Innocents, Paris's vast cemetery, with its yawning gateway and soaring walls and the long, very busy shopping arcade that had sprung up against these.

At the main entrance, he displayed his chancery seal and slipped past the city serjeants into the sprawling, noisy marketplace, which also served as a mansion for the dead. He reached the northern arcade, with its vivid stone-carved frieze portraying the macabre figure of Death grinning terrifyingly at emperors and popes; grasping an abbess by the hand as she read a book, a priest by the shoulder as he wrote his homily, a usurer counting his coins, a drunkard with his goblet. All had to turn and face the hideous countenance, the bony finger nudging them, the skeletal hand summoning them. No one escaped.

Tallefert trembled like a leaf as he studied the frescoes, then stared around, trying to glimpse the red-headed Pietal amongst the surging crowd. A teller of tales climbed on to a plinth to announce 'news from the provinces'. He seemed to be addressing Tallefert personally as he recounted how a monster had been born at Amboise, how a gang of felons had been hanged from a steeple in Provins and how an English ship, *The Candle-Bright*, had been taken by *The Black Hogge* in the Narrow Seas and sunk with all hands. Tallefert's legs began to tremble. *The Candle-Bright*! He recalled how Sir Hugh Corbett, in his missive around Pentecost last, had intimated that Pietal should be in Boulogne to receive fresh instructions for Tallefert in Paris, which would be brought by the English cog. And why had the news about the sinking of *The Candle-Bright* been kept secret? According to the teller of tales, it had been sunk at least eight days ago, so why had it not been known throughout the inner royal chancery?

Tallefert felt sick. He closed his eyes and wondered if this would all end at Montfaucon, the great gallows near Porte Saint-Denis. The massive, macabre scaffold dominated the landscape, soaring up on its six-yard-high mound, its thick black branches festooned with ropes, nooses and chains. 'God in heaven,' he whispered to himself. 'It's over, I must flee.'

The clerk left the cemetery, taking the swiftest route back along the riverbank to his house in the Rue Saint-Laurent, close to the Tour de Nesle. He reached it clammy with sweat and flung open the iron-studded door, stumbling down the narrow paved passageway leading to the kitchen and the garden beyond, where he kept his beehives and, beneath a heavy paving slab, his precious strongbox. He threw open the kitchen door, staggered out into the garden and froze. Guillaume de Nogaret, Philip's first minister and secretary to the royal council, lounged in the garden seat, which had been turned to face the door. Around and behind him were his personal bodyguard, dressed in black and gold, their jerkins emblazoned with the royal silver fleur-de-lis on a dark-blue background, mailed gloved hands resting on the hilt of sword or dagger. The only sound came from Pietal, red-haired and waxen-faced, who had been tightly bound around chest and arms and hoisted to swing from the gnarled pear tree Tallefert had so carefully cultivated over the years. The messenger twisted and turned, groaning at the tight cords.

'Good morning, Tallefert. I see you must have heard our storyteller at the Holy Innocents.' De Nogaret rose and walked slowly over, snapping his fingers. One of his retinue hastened forward: the man wore Tallefert's broad-brimmed hat, heavy gauze veil, stiffened leather gauntlets and quilted jerkin, all intended to protect the wearer against bee stings. In his right hand he carried a leather mask. Tallefert's heart sank. Such a mask was often used in the torture and interrogation of prisoners; with slits only for the eyes – no aperture for mouth or nose – it would be clasped over the face and the leather straps at the back tightened as the interrogator wished.

'Vallon here,' Nogaret's blunt fingers gently stroked

the side of Tallefert's sweaty face, 'is also a student of the beehive. Now,' he took the mask from Vallon's hand, 'we have smeared the inside of this mask with the most delicious flower juice. The bees from your hives will investigate. Once a small swarm of them have filled the mask, Vallon will place it over Pietal's face and tighten the straps. We of course will not wait here but inside your house.'

De Nogaret shoved Tallefert viciously in the chest, sending him staggering back. Orders were shouted. Tallefert was kicked and pummelled into the kitchen scullery. The door was closed, the window firmly shuttered. De Nogaret just stood there listening intently, ignoring Tallefert's cries and sobs. At the first piercing scream from outside, he sighed, smiled and raised a hand.

Corbett could only agree with his hostess that the Merry Mercy was, in all aspects, a magnificent tavern. It possessed a huge taproom where the polished floorboards gleamed beneath spotlessly clean coarse matting. Window boxes crammed with sweet-scented flowers adorned the sills. Pots of fresh herbs, stirred and replenished daily, ranged along ledges or in wall niches next to small brass lanternhorns where stubby candles glowed beneath stretched linen coverings. Hams, bacon, legs of pork and shoulders of lamb basted in tasty sauces and covered in white cloths hung from the rafters in their cream-coloured nets, exuding the most mouth-watering smells. Proper tables and leather-cushioned stools were plentiful, whilst the long common table was scrubbed clean, as were the sturdy benches either side.

Two great kitchens served both the tavern and the houses around. In each of the kitchens a fierce fire roared, whatever the weather, in the mantled hearth adorned with the carved faces of wodewoses, giants and satyrs. All the impedimenta of the kitchen ranged along the hearths: spits, prongs, forks, ladles, basting bowls and jugs of spicy herb sauces. The turnspits were busy from Prime to Vespers. Delicious smells wafted along the galleries and passageways. The Merry Mercy enjoyed a reputation second to none with its three stories of comfortable rooms and chambers. The roof was tiled with gleaming red slate, the chimney stacks firmly embedded to draw off the smoke, strong enough not to bend beneath the gales that swept the Thames

Philippa Henman had proudly led Corbett on what she called 'a grand chevauchee' along polished galleries into cellars, stable yard, washroom, bath houses and slaughter pens. Eventually he had been ushered into the Pendragon chamber, where his clerk of the stables, Chanson, had already stacked his saddle bags. Philippa parted the curtains dramatically around the great four-poster bed to reveal white linen sheets, strawberry-coloured drapes, coverlets and bolsters, the latter filled with the softest down feather. The chamber also boasted stools and a chancery desk beneath the large unshuttered glass-filled window overlooking the most delightful rose garden. Corbett openly admired the painted cloths hanging on the walls, which told the story of Merlin's deep sleep and his protection of the Holy Grail. While Philippa talked, he also made sure that his small manuscript coffers and caskets were secure under their intricately fashioned locks. Finally she escorted him to the tavern council chamber, the Cana room, its walls decorated with exquisitely depicted scenes celebrating Christ changing water into wine.

Corbett now sat at the head of the council table listening to Philippa chatter on about the quality of the turkey rugs and the polish used to bring the oaken and elmwood panelling to a shine. He quietly admired this beautiful widow woman dressed so simply in a quilted brown robe with a dark red cincture. A snow-white veil covered her hair, with bands of the same colour at wrist and neck. A most elegant lady, with delicate manners, very precise in all she did.

Philippa paused as she caught Corbett's eye. 'Sir Hugh, I am sorry. I chatter like a bird in spring. You intend to hold a commission of justice here in this room? Even though de Craon lurks here?'

'And Master Sokelar, the harbour master, also does business here,' Corbett declared. 'It suits me.

'But one of the king's courts?'

Corbett, not wishing to give offence by appearing peremptory, just smiled and shrugged as if it was a matter of little concern.

'Sir Hugh, you knew my late husband, Raoul Henman?'

'I certainly did.' He smiled. 'In the days of our tender

youth, he was a mailed clerk like myself, and a scholar, one with a nose for good wine and a passion for tasty cooking.' Corbett licked his lips. 'When I was a hungry young clerk, Raoul could make the most splendid banquet out of scraps. I recall his gelatine pie was truly delicious, the pastry light, all puffed up and soft, the meat tasty and spiced though not smothered. He shared these dishes with me; he was most kind.'

'He said the same of you, Sir Hugh: a good man, that's what he called you, a truly decent human being.' Philippa smoothed down the folds of her gown. Corbett noticed how spotlessly clean it was, and that included the stiff pure-white cuffs. He gestured around.

'Raoul was poor; he must have worked very hard.'

'He certainly did, Sir Hugh, though I also brought him a most generous dowry. Anyway,' she sighed, 'you must hold your court. A commission of oyer and terminer?'

'Yes, mistress, it will be. I apologise but I must also summon you.'

'At what hour?'

Corbett was about to reply when there was a knock at the door and Ranulf and Chanson entered carrying items for the makeshift court: Corbett's war belt and unsheathed sword, a Book of the Gospels borrowed from Parson Layburn and a chancery case of hardened leather containing quills, pumice stones, ink horns and other clerkly necessities. Ranulf sketched a bow in Mistress Philippa's direction. Chanson, however, was humming a tune, badly as always. When it came to music, or handling weapons, Chanson was truly hopeless.

'Mistress, you asked at what hour.' Corbett spread his hands. 'I appreciate how busy you must be. Will you be returning to St Giles? I mean, it's only a very short walk away.'

'Not today.' She shook her head and glanced briskly at him. 'I understand you have summoned Monseigneur de Craon. I tell you, he is swollen up like any toad, full of sound and fury, protesting at what he called "a totally unacceptable and indeed illegal summons for a foreign envoy".'

'Let him choke on his bile,' Ranulf retorted.

'Mistress,' Corbett rose and bowed, 'I cannot give you the hour when you will be summoned, but it is time we began. If you could send some ale and food, I would be most grateful.' Philippa said she would and bustled out.

A short while later, a kitchen maid brought a tray, three tankards and a platter of dried meats and cut fruit. The clerks broke their fast. Afterwards Corbett washed his hands at the lavarium while Ranulf laid out his writing implements and Chanson, as usual, prepared to act as guard and usher at the door. Corbett also set out his seals and warrants, his authority to hold inquiry on any matter affecting the Crown or its rights.

The first to be summoned was Matthias Sokelar, the harbour master, accompanied by his daughter Agnes, still dressed in the grey garb of the Guild of St Martha. A bustling, busy little man who constantly scratched his stubbled face, Sokelar took the pledge, one hand on the Book of Gospels, the other on a small crucifix, gabbling out the words of the oath before glaring pop-eyed at Corbett.

'I am a royal official as well,' he screeched. 'I have signed . . .'

'Sir,' Corbett brusquely interrupted, 'you are harbour master here in London. You knew when *The Candle-Bright* sailed?'

'As did many along Queenhithe,' Sokelar snarled back. 'It left on the morning tide and made good progress down the Thames to the estuary before tacking south-west into the Narrow Seas.'

'Where it was trapped and destroyed by *The Black Hogge*, which must have been waiting for it, as it has done for so many English cogs.'

'Sir Hugh,' Sokelar's voice turned wheedling, 'my daughter Agnes helps me keep good records. We mingle with those who work and live along Queenhithe.' He rubbed his sweaty hand on his stained fustian jerkin. 'Like everyone else,' he gabbled on, 'we have heard about *The Black Hogge*, but we do not know how that ship's captain knows so much about English vessels leaving the Thames . . .' His voice faltered.

Corbett studied the harbour master carefully. Sokelar could be acting, yet the problem he posed was real enough. Far too many people had known when *The Candle-Bright* had sailed, but how did the French captain know so swiftly and so accurately?

'Do the names Sumerscale and Fallowfield mean anything to you?'

'No, but I heard both names from Agnes after you questioned her at St Giles.'

'Do you have anything to do with the Templars there?'

'Not unless I have to.'

'You don't like them?'

'They are Templars, disgraced and despised.'

Corbett leaned back in his chair. 'Master Sokelar, did you serve in Outremer?'

'I was in Acre with the Christian fleet.' The harbour master had grown decisively petulant, head back, lower lip jutting aggressively.

'Did you flee?'

'Like many,' Sokelar spluttered.

'Such as?'

'Master Crowthorne, the leech at St Giles. We were all there with our friends and kin. The Templars betrayed us to the Mamelukes. I can still recall them swarming up for the attack. Kettledrums booming out their threat, the clash of cymbals splitting the air, a mass of men swarming like ants, streaming up the ladders and siege towers pushed against the walls and fortifications. The city was strong. The Templars should have driven them off. They didn't, they fled.'

'Many of them died there,' Ranulf interjected.

'As did my wife, Agnes's mother,' Sokelar rasped. 'The Templars are to blame. They lost the last great Christian fortress in Outremer. They failed us all. They must now face the consequences instead of hiding and fleeing.'

'Fleeing?' Ranulf asked.

Sokelar turned to his daughter, who just shook her head.

'You are on oath,' Corbett warned. 'I need information urgently. I search for the truth in so many things. Now, Templars fleeing?'

'Rumours along the quayside,' Sokelar confessed. 'Tavern tittle-tattle and ale-house gossip about the Templars hiding in St Giles. How they don't feel safe. How the French king has sent secret assassins to kill them. In a word, they are looking to flee.'

'Where?'

'Robert the Bruce in Scotland. It is well known that he rejects the allegations against the Templars and offers sanctuary to that order.'

'And they cannot go by land,' Ranulf offered. 'They would be vulnerable to attack by assassins hired by the French, as well as by those such as yourself who fiercely resent the Templars.'

'True,' Sokelar agreed. 'Their only path of salvation would be by sea, but God help them if the cog they sail on is attacked by *The Black Hogge*. A strong possibility, bearing in mind how swiftly and accurately the master of that ship knows what is happening in Queenhithe and elsewhere.'

'Do you believe they are about to flee?'

'Sir Hugh,' Agnes interposed, her face slightly flushed, one hand gripping her father's arm, symbolising the close bond between them. 'Why ask my father? He is only the harbour master. He administers shipping to and from Queenhithe. He is not responsible for what happens, as so many seem to believe.'

Corbett questioned Sokelar further, but the harbour master and his close-faced daughter could provide no more information, so he thanked and dismissed them. They had just left when Corbett heard Chanson's voice raised in protest, followed by a loud knocking on the door, which was flung open. A man dressed in the cream and brown robes of a Carmelite swept into the room.

'Sir Hugh Corbett!'

'And who are you?' Ranulf swiftly seized the sword from the table and swung it so the razor-sharp blade rested against the side of the intruder's stringy neck.

'I am Brother Jerome, a lay brother in the order of Carmelites. I am also a member of the household . . .'

'Clerk and secretarius,' Corbett interrupted, 'of our noble French envoy, Monseigneur Amaury de Craon. I have heard of you and your doings. I have come across your name in documents and had it whispered to me in the Secret Chancery chamber at Westminster. Be careful, Brother Jerome! Ranulf's sword is sharp. A mere cut could open a deep wound in not the thickest neck I've seen.' Jerome shifted slightly, eyes as hard as black pebbles, and Corbett glimpsed the stiletto blade appear in the Carmelite's right hand. 'I truly wouldn't,' he warned. 'Please.'

The dagger disappeared, and Corbett stared at this true killer, an assassin who hid behind the robes of a Carmelite. Brother Jerome was a sinister soul: head and face completely shaved, pasty white skin glistening with nard, a long, aquiline nose above prim, bloodless lips. He had the look of a ferocious hawk, yet Corbett also acknowledged his reputation. A brilliant clerk, skilled in all sorts of ciphers and secret alphabets, but also a dagger man; a professional assassin, expert with the knife, garrotte strings or pot of poison.

'Ranulf,' Corbett warned, 'lower your sword. Brother Jerome, it is good to meet you at last. Even in retirement, during the last two or three years, I have heard of your name and reputation. Ranulf!'

Corbett's companion reluctantly lowered his sword. Corbett extended his hand for Jerome to clasp. The Carmelite did so, and Corbett pulled him close for the *osculum pacis*, the kiss of peace.

'*Pax tecum, Frater*,' he whispered. 'Peace be with you, Brother, but be very careful.' He stood back and beamed at a man he knew to be his implacable foe, one who would like nothing better than to take his head. 'So, Brother, what does the monseigneur want? Peacefully now.'

'He is an accredited envoy. He has business with your king's chancellor at Westminster. He cannot,' Jerome gestured at the table, 'be summoned before one of your courts. You have no right . . .'

'He is not summoned to a court. The chancellor and his advisers at Westminster are not expecting your master today. I simply wish to meet the envoy of the king of France at the request of my king, who is also the son-in-law of yours. Now,' Corbett clapped his hands and gestured at the door, 'go tell your master I will see him in due course . . .'

Crispin Slingsby, once minehost of the Salamander tavern, was sworn next. Ranulf and Chanson had done diligent work and discovered the unfortunate taverner to be residing at the Hope of Heaven, a cramped, greasy hostel not far from the blackened ruins of the Salamander. A large, pot-bellied man with an aggressive red face and the rolling gait of a former mariner, Slingsby almost sauntered into the Cana chamber. He took his seat and slowly mouthed the words of the oath before leaning back in the leather chair and staring at Corbett from under bushy eyebrows. The clerk gazed back, narrowing his eyes as he racked his memory. He recognised the man but couldn't recall the details.

'Will the Salamander be rebuilt?' he asked abruptly.

'I hope so,' came the muttered response. 'I am casting about amongst the merchants and river traders for finance. The Salamander was popular in its time, and of course the site belongs to me. I have the necessary charters and indentures.' Slingsby stumbled over his words. Corbett suspected that, despite the early hour, the taverner had imbibed considerably before presenting himself. He stared hard at Slingsby and then smiled.

'Puddlicot!' he declared. 'Richard Puddlicot, leader of the coven that, eight years ago, broke into the crypt at Westminster and stole the royal treasure.' Slingsby paled, gawping nervously. 'I recall questioning you, sir,' Corbett pressed on, turning to wink at Ranulf. 'According to reports, when Puddlicot was planning his outrage, he allegedly did so at the Salamander. He and his fellow malignants hired a chamber there.'

'One of the many taverns he used,' Slingsby blurted out. 'Sir Hugh, of course I remember you visiting me, your questions, but I was an innocent bystander.' He ignored Ranulf's burst of sarcastic laughter.

'If I recall correctly,' Corbett insisted, 'you were accused of sheltering Puddlicot and his coven after the robbery.'

'All lies. No witnesses came forward, no proof was offered for such an outrageous accusation.'

'Yes, yes,' Corbett replied impatiently. 'But isn't it strange, Master Slingsby, that Gabriel Rougehead, also known as John Priknash, an alleged henchman of Puddlicot, reappeared in your tavern three years ago last January, probably to drink and wench.' Slingsby stared bleakly back. 'He later accused two of your customers of speaking contumaciously about the king and Lord Gaveston and making public mockery of them by simulating the act of sodomy.'

'Of course I recall that.'

'And the names of the two accused?'

'Sumerscale and Fallowfield.'

'Had you ever met them before?'

'No.'

'Do their names mean anything to you?'

'They didn't then,' Slingsby sniffed, 'and they don't now.'

'And were you a witness to this contumacious talk, you being the owner of the tavern?'

'You must have read the record of the court, Sir Hugh. I understand the master of *The Candle-Bright*

drew up a memorandum about the trial.' Slingsby
paused, licking his lips. 'I did hear shouted mockery
about His Grace the king, laughter, raucous remarks.
Being His Grace's most loyal subject, I objected, threatening to eject the perpetrators if I identified them. I
then went down into the cellar, and was some time
there as one of the casks had split. I did hear shouting
and roars of laughter, raised voices, but when I returned
to the taproom, Sumerscale and Fallowfield, apparently
much the worse for drink, had left. I was summoned
to the tribunal on board *The Candle-Bright*, where I
told Naseby what I have told you.'

'And you never recognised Rougehead from years
earlier when he and Puddlicot frequented the taverns
of Queenhithe?'

'Of course I didn't.'

'Of course I didn't,' Ranulf mimicked, raising his
head. He took a fresh quill and sharpened it.

'What does that mean?' Slingsby screeched.

'It means I think you are lying through that filthy
bowl you call a mouth. Sit down and keep still,' Ranulf
snarled. 'I suspect you did recognise Rougehead.'

'I did not.'

'You knew he was a rogue, a king's approver, someone
who laid testimony against another in the hope of a
pardon and a reward.'

'Never, and nor did Master Naseby. Rougehead's
testimony was supported by others.'

Corbett glanced away. He had read and studied the
brief transcript of the trial, which provided very little.

Sumerscale and Fallowfield had faced a military tribunal. Evidence was laid, in this case the testimony of at least four witnesses, and the two accused could produce nothing to counter it.

'Liars fit for hell.' Corbett pointed at the taverner. 'Do you know, Master Slingsby, I believe Sumerscale and Fallowfield were trapped, indicted and executed as part and parcel of some bizarre plot, the reason for which is as yet unknown. In my view, as the angels be my witness, Rougehead and his coven were guilty of the most heinous perjury, worthy of death – as, when we discover the truth of the matter, you might well be too . . .'

'I know nothing of this,' Slingsby blustered. 'I . . .'

'Never mind that.' Corbett smiled bleakly, fingering the pommel on the sword lying close to his right hand, its blade pointing directly at Slingsby. 'Let's move on in time to the spring of 1308, just before Lent began. Rougehead and the three other perjured witnesses gathered at your tavern for a banquet. A feast of good food and wine in a chamber especially hired for the occasion.'

'God damn his eyes!'

'God damn whose eyes, Master Slingsby?'

'The stranger. You are correct. It was before Ash Wednesday, the time of feasting before the rigours of Lent. I adhere to them, as does Mistress Slingsby . . .'

'I am not interested in your spiritual life, Slingsby.'

'Of course, Sir Hugh.'

'Then tell me?'

'One evening around Vespers. The curfew bell had tolled, beacon lights glowed in the steeples . . .'

'Master Slingsby!'

'Yes, yes, a tap boy came to me. He said a stranger was waiting outside. He needed to speak to me urgently, that it would be to my great profit.'

'You were not suspicious?'

'It was only outside, not far from the main door. I took one of my cellarmen with me. The stranger stood deep in the shadows, cowled and visored. He hid behind the light of a lanternhorn hanging on a post. He tossed me a silver coin and held up another.' Slingsby smirked. 'I told the cellarman to go back. I asked the stranger his business. He told me to organise a splendid repast for Shrove Tuesday on the sole condition that Rougehead and the other three witnesses attended. I was to publicise this and say that the invitation was at the behest of a henchman of my lord Gaveston, a token of thanks for the destruction of two felons who had besmirched his master's honour and that of the king.'

'Would Rougehead believe that?'

'The stranger passed over four silver coins. One for each of them as a further token of favour. He also gave me a heavy purse to cover the costs of the banquet and the hire of a private solar in the first gallery of the Salamander, a truly spacious chamber. The walls were beautifully decorated . . .'

'Yes, yes, what else?'

'I was to serve the courses then leave Rougehead and his coven to their revelry. In addition, the stranger warned that he intended to visit his guests later in the evening. He would enter by a postern door, and was not to be troubled. He assured me,' Slingsby added bitterly, 'that I would, after the meal was over, receive an extra unexpected return for my troubles.' He snorted noisily. 'I certainly did!'

Corbett stared hard at this veritable rogue, a man who lurked in the twilight world of the city. His tavern had been the meeting place for wolfsheads, night slinkers and other dark prowlers. The man who had hired that chamber had known that Slingsby would rise to the offer of good silver as any fish to the bait and it would be easy for the taverner to pass on the invitation to those concerned.

'Sir Hugh, why are you staring at me?'

'Oh, I am just reflecting, Master Slingsby. Now tell me, what actually happened on that evening?'

'Rougehead and his three henchmen blundered into the trap, for that is what it was. They truly believed they were being rewarded. The prospect of a sumptuous meal, as well as good silver, with the possibility of earning even more, sharpened their greed.'

Corbett covered the lower half of his face with his hand to hide his laughter. Slingsby was describing kindred spirits, and he recalled Scripture's words about sinners coming to judgement. He dropped his hand.

'Continue.'

'Rougehead and his company arrived at the appointed hour on the appointed day. The solar was prepared, the table laid with fine linen, pewter cups and platters, and the banquet was served: sorrel soup with figs and dates, lentils and lamb, fresh venison and dilled veal balls . . .'

'Very good,' Ranulf snapped. 'With wine and ale?'

'That flowed like a river,' Slingsby agreed. 'Though Rougehead had a reputation for avoiding strong drink.'

'And then what?'

'A manservant saw the stranger enter, cloaked, cowled and visored. The scullion summoned me. I watched the visitor climb the stairs.'

'No other description?' Corbett interrupted.

'He was tall, well-spoken; his robes exuded a pleasant perfume as he swept by me.'

'Like soap of Castile?' Corbett recalled his conversation with Parson Layburn.

'Yes, yes, it was. I have bought similar for my lady wife as a gift for Twelfth Night . . .'

'Continue.'

'The stranger arrived late. The tavern was emptying, the chimes of midnight could be heard. The Salamander was settling for the night.' Slingsby blew his cheeks out. 'Then the alarm was raised: a fire had erupted on the first gallery. The building was old, the wood very dry. Those who tried to fight the fire maintained it started in the solar.'

'It could have been an accident?'

'I thought that. Rougehead's coven were drunken bastards. One of them could have been clumsy, knocked a candle over. Anyway, the fire raged through the tavern, reducing it to nothing more than blackened timbers.' Slingsby's head went down as he looked from beneath his brows at Corbett. 'That's when we found Rougehead and his coven all murdered.'

'Murdered?'

'Sir Hugh, this was not proclaimed abroad. Oh, their corpses had been reduced to blackened bones, their flesh nothing more than hardened globules of gristle. But before they were burned, their heads had been sheared off like you would snip a rose flower. It was hard to tell one from another, but they had all been decapitated.'

'Four fighting men,' Corbett exclaimed, 'dispatched so quietly and easily. You and yours heard no swordplay, no clash of steel, no disturbance?'

'None.'

'So this stranger, well-dressed and well-spoken, went into a solar where four daggermen were celebrating their sins. Undoubtedly they were merry, mawmsy with drink, yet this stranger took the heads of each of them?'

'He promised me unexpected recompense,' Slingsby muttered bitterly.

'Do you have any suspicion about who it was?'

'None.'

'But the slaughter of those four men must have something to do with the two unfortunates Sumerscale and Fallowfield?'

'Of course, Sir Hugh.'

'The four perjurers were punished,' Corbett remarked, 'and so were you, Master Slingsby. The Salamander, the place where Sumerscale and Fallowfield allegedly committed their treason, was totally destroyed.'

'So it would seem, Sir Hugh.'

'Tell me,' Corbett rubbed the side of his face, 'when

Puddlicot broke into the crypt and I listed his henchmen – I could never obtain a clear description of Rougehead.'

'True, Sir Hugh. When I saw him, he had long hair, a bushy moustache and beard; it was difficult to see who he really was. A master of disguise.' Slingsby pointed to Ranulf. 'What you said earlier about recognising Rougehead – very few did.'

'Aye.' Corbett watched the candle flame fall and rise in the faint breeze through the room.

'Sir Hugh? May I go now?'

'I think you are a liar, Slingsby.' Corbett turned back to the taverner. 'No, don't puff yourself up like a barnyard cock. I find it difficult to believe that everything that happened was mere chance. I believe you knew Rougehead and possibly the other three. They used your tavern to destroy two men. Time passes, these perjurers are trapped and killed and your tavern is burnt to the ground. I believe that beneath all this lies a tangled tale that we have scarcely brushed. But don't worry, Master Slingsby, you know me by reputation. I will hack away until the tangle is clear. Until then, you are dismissed.'

'Do you really believe that?' Ranulf asked as soon as Slingsby closed the door behind him.

'I truly do, my friend.' Corbett pushed himself away from the table, using his fingers to emphasise his points. 'First, Rougehead and Slingsby were both, to a greater or lesser extent, suspected of being involved in the robbery at Westminster eight years ago. Rougehead destroys two apparent strangers, Sumerscale and Fallowfield, who happened to be drinking in Slingsby's tavern, a place where they had no friends or allies to counter Rougehead's allegations against them. Slingsby says he knows nothing about the incident, though he cleverly hints that something may have happened. Yes?'

Ranulf nodded in agreement.

'I know what you are going to ask,' Corbett grinned, 'which is my second point. Why did Sumerscale and Fallowfield go to the Salamander? They gave no reason for that during their trial. Were they invited there? Were they lured into a trap, or was it just sheer coincidence? Third, just who were these two mariners? Where did they come from? They cannot be traced; their names do not appear in any document. At first they can be dismissed as two hapless souls drifting into this city like so many others, and yet somebody, somewhere close by, had deep affection, even love for them. The mysterious stranger who approached Slingsby was intent on a deadly revenge: the execution of Rougehead and his coven followed by the destruction of the Salamander. Not only that, but Naseby, master of *The Candle-Bright*, was grimly reminded about the execution of Sumerscale and Fallowfield and warned of the dire consequences of his involvement. Such dark prophecies came to hideous fruition. *The Candle-Bright* was attacked by *The Black Hogge*, Naseby, Torpel and their crew were slaughtered and the ship that served as the gallows for Sumerscale and Fallowfield was totally destroyed. This in turn begs a further question.' He paused. 'Was *The Candle-Bright* annihilated as part of Philip's secret, dark design against Edward of England, or as an act of vengeance for Sumerscale and Fallowfield?'

'Or both?'

'Yes, Ranulf, or both. And if that is the case, then I ask myself: were Sumerscale and Fallowfield somehow involved in Philip and de Craon's treacherous plotting against this kingdom and its king? You see,' he played with the miniature paperweights on the table, carved in the shapes of grotesques and gargoyles, 'we have these two men here in the middle. We do not know who they truly were. Here to the left are the forces that destroyed them, and to the right, the powerful response to their untimely deaths. Yet how all this merges together remains a mystery.'

'The source of the present evil,' Ranulf remarked, 'is Rougehead and his accusations. Why did he make them? Is it possible that if Rougehead and Slingsby were linked to the great robbery at Westminster, Sumerscale and Fallowfield were also involved? Was that the connection, one the two mariners dared not raise at their brief summary trial?' He paused to collect his thoughts. 'If they had even hinted that the allegations were being made by men who, like themselves, were involved in that robbery, they would be virtually confessing to treason, which would invoke the most horrible punishments: hanging, drawing, disembowelling.' He waved a hand. 'In the end, such an admission had nothing to do with the accusations against them; it would not help them in any way and could make matters much worse.'

'You may be right,' Corbett mused. 'Perhaps there

was some link between Sumerscale and Fallowfield and Rougehead. Yet at the trial, neither man described Rougehead as an enemy or someone they knew. Indeed, Rougehead depicted himself as a law-abiding citizen, a complete stranger to Sumerscale and Fallowfield: this would have convinced Naseby that he had no malignant motive for accusing the men.'

'Yet we heard from the Templars how Rougehead was a renegade steeped in sin. A possible suspect, or so it might appear, in the great robbery at Westminster.'

'Ah yes, though back then he successfully hid behind the name Priknash. He may have enjoyed an unsavoury reputation in his former career, but I suspect there are many such as he. What I cannot discover is any link between Rougehead and his victims.'

'Interesting, too,' Ranulf murmured, 'that both the accused were mariners. From what I have learnt, *The Candle-Bright*'s usual sea routes were across to Boulogne or down the west coast of France to Bordeaux.'

'Good, good,' Corbett agreed. 'Was there a reason for both men serving on that ship? They cannot have been fleeing, as the vessel kept returning to London. And why were they connected with Queenhithe and not some other quayside?' He paused. 'Ranulf, you have brought Peterkin from Greyfriars?'

'Yes. The good brothers have truly cared for him; he is well recovered.'

'I must have words with him.'

A short while later, Peterkin the lookout boy, the only survivor from *The Candle-Bright*, was ushered into the

Cana chamber. He certainly looked better than the last time Corbett had met him. He had been bathed, his hair carefully cropped and washed. Colour had returned to his face, whilst the Franciscans had bought him a new jerkin, hose and boots. He smiled and bowed, all nervous as Corbett brought him down the table to sit opposite Ranulf. A thin, lanky boy, Peterkin looked to be no older than fourteen summers, an orphan whom Naseby had taken on board as an act of compassion.

Corbett offered the sweetmeats Chanson had brought in. 'Go on, lad, cram your belly, and take this too.' He slipped a coin across the table that the boy snatched up swiftly.

'In the twinkling of an eye,' Ranulf laughed.

'You are well, Peterkin?' Corbett asked. The boy nodded vigorously. 'I can secure a post for you here. Mistress Philippa will look after you. You would have comfortable lodgings, warm food, decent clothing and even a coin or two.' Again the vigorous nod. 'Now, Peterkin, you were ship's boy on *The Candle-Bright* when two of the crew, Sumerscale and Fallowfield, were hanged by Master Naseby for contumacious speech and public mockery of the king and Lord Gaveston. Yes?'

'I didn't see them hang,' the boy replied. 'I hid away. The crew said it was a terrible, hideous choking sound. I don't like to see hangings.'

'No one does, boy,' Corbett replied. 'But what did you know of them?'

'They were quiet. Fallowfield especially. Sumerscale could imitate bird calls to amuse us. He was good at that, but they didn't mix with the others. They kept to themselves. Some of the crew thought they were men-lovers, which made them all the more guilty.'

'Were they good sailors?'

'Fallowfield, certainly. Gossip had it that he had served on cogs, hulks and galleys in both the North and Middle Sea.'

'Did you ever hear them converse?'

'You mean overhear?'

'Yes, overhear.' Corbett smiled.

'Oh yes, on our sailings to and from Boulogne. Much good it did me. They spoke in Latin and a strange tongue. One of the crew said it was the ling . . .' Peterkin cleaned his mouth with his tongue.

'Lingua franca?' Ranulf supplied. 'The common language of the Middle Sea?' Again Peterkin nodded.

'Can you tell us anything more about them?' Peterkin shook his head. Corbett glanced away. References to Boulogne evoked memories of the clerk Tallefert. He wondered if his secret colleague was safe. He had not heard from him or Pietal; that could be ominous. Despite the presence of *The Black Hogge*, ships were still safely criss-crossing the Narrow Seas, yet he had learnt nothing. No one had come out of Boulogne with news or intelligence. He feared that the secret letters carried by Naseby on *The Candle-Bright* had been intercepted. If that was the case, and the letters had been deciphered, both Tallefert and Pietal were in dire peril. Corbett had agreed with the French clerk that if the danger proved too much or the situation too threatening, Tallefert would not wait but would flee either to Boulogne or Bordeaux and secure immediate passage to London. Even during his retirement, Corbett had kept up communication from his own private chancery. Tallefert had confidently reported that no one suspected him.

Corbett beat his fingers against the tabletop, staring at one of the exquisitely woven tapestries decorating the far wall. He dared not send anyone to Paris or dispatch a second letter. He could only put his confidence in the Deacon, an English scholar studying in the halls of Paris. A consummate mummer, a young man who liked nothing better than to perform in miracle plays, the Deacon was a master of disguise who made considerable profit in pretending to be a relic seller recently returned from Jerusalem with a wide range of interesting artefacts: nails from the Crucifixion or the wine jug used at the Last Supper. He was one of Corbett's inner circle, a clever spy who along with Pietal often carried messages to and from the English envoy in Paris, Lord Scrope. He was prudent, cunning and sly. He reminded Corbett of a weasel in the way he could slip in or out of any situation or place. One of the Deacon's duties was to visit Tallefert at least once a month to make sure all was well. Corbett reckoned it was about time such a visit took place.

'Master?' Ranulf spoke. 'Do we still need the boy?'

Corbett broke from his reverie. He glanced at Peterkin and winked. 'Is there anything else you can tell us?' The boy shook his head. 'In which case,' Corbett sighed, 'I am finished.' He paused. 'Tell me, Peterkin, one last thing. Sumerscale and Fallowfield had boarded *The Candle-Bright* only a short time beforehand.' This time a nod. 'Who recommended them? Every captain looks for a guarantee about the men he hires: someone who can vouch for them. Did someone speak up for Sumerscale and Fallowfield?'

Corbett felt a twinge of excitement as Peterkin blinked, lips moving.

'Yes, yes,' the lad murmured. 'A Master Prior.'

'Master Prior?'

'You know, the monks who dress in black and white and call themselves the Hounds of God.'

'The Dominicans!' Corbett exclaimed. 'Their mother house, Blackfriars, is not far from here. Of course, of course.' He rubbed his hands together. 'Blackfriars is the main priory of the Dominican order in this country, yet they have houses all over Europe. They depend on ships like *The Candle-Bright* to fetch and carry produce and take messages here and there. I wager they did good business with Master Naseby. Peterkin, thank you. Seek out Mistress Philippa, she will look after you. Chanson,' he called, 'quick as you can to the Hanging Tree. Order the Magister Viae to meet me at the entrance to Blackfriars. Oh, and give my profound apologies to those waiting, and tell them they will have to wait a little longer.'

PART FOUR

'The love of the people has turned to hatred.'
The Monk of Malmesbury, *Life of Edward II*

Corbett and Ranulf left the Merry Mercy and made their made up Vintry and into Thames Street. The weather was fine. The streets were busy, the crowds surging along the narrow lanes beneath the four-storey houses, so tall they tipped to meet each other. Windows, casements and shutters had been flung open. Neighbours shouted greetings as they hung out sheets and coverlets to be aired. Carts and barrows forced their way through, a crashing sound that forced people to talk all the louder. Corbett found the noise disconcerting after the silence and serenity of the tavern.

Two greyhounds appeared, broken free from the young woman bringing them in from coursing hares in a nearby field. Corbett had to push by a wedding party shouting, 'Wassail, drink ale!' as the revellers passed around a maplewood mazer slopping with wine. The wedding guests tried to draw him into their company, but soon retreated when Ranulf shouted,

'King's men!' and unsheathed his sword. The royal clerks passed on, the crowd jostling along: burgesses in their samite gowns, city fops in brightly coloured jerkins and hose, monks shrouded in dark-brown robes, as well as the sober-clad officials of both the ward and market.

Corbett bought pomanders as some protection against the stench. The dung carts were out cleaning the mess from the lay stalls, public jakes and midden heaps. The sun had curdled the filth and turned the air rancid. The foul fog of fumes drenched and drowned all the sweet smells from the surrounding bakeries, cook shops and stalls. The noise and clamour of the traders grew worse as the two men turned right, up past Knightrider Street. A great set of stocks stood at the entrance to this thoroughfare: close by rose a soaring four-branched gallows. Each arm of the gibbet carried the corpse of a felon executed earlier in the day, the naked dirty-white cadavers swaying slightly at the end of oiled hempen rope.

Beneath the scaffold, archers held two forgers, who screamed and thrashed around as the executioner, brazier glowing, irons red-hot, branded a fiery 'F' on the right cheek of each. The gruesome punishment had to be witnessed by those who had broken the king's peace the night before and now sat clamped in the stocks, fastened tight by neck, arm or leg. Further on, a group of brightly garbed moon people swirled by, singing and dancing to the beat of a solitary drum and the clash of cymbals. Beggars, grotesque in their injuries, true or false, followed the music in the hope that they would benefit from spectators.

Corbett, one hand on the hilt of his sword, strode on, his left side protected by the doorways with Ranulf, as usual, trailing slightly to his right. On one occasion he paused abruptly, turning to see if they were being followed. He glimpsed an individual garbed like a royal forester in green and brown. The figure turned away as if interested in a stall, but Corbett was sure he had seen the same man just as they'd left the Merry Mercy.

'Master?' Ranulf queried.

'Nothing,' Corbett whispered. 'Not for the moment.'

They left the tangle of narrow coffin paths and entered the great cobbled expanse that stretched up to the dark stone curtain wall of Blackfriars, with its majestic fortified gatehouse.

Corbett plucked at Ranulf's sleeve. 'Look,' he whispered, 'our friends have arrived.' The Magister and six of his entourage, all garbed in their earth-coloured robes, strode across to meet them. Any similarity to Franciscan friars proved to be an illusion when their spurred boots and war belts bristling with weapons became apparent. The Magister stopped in front of Corbett and bowed mockingly.

'Welcome, sir.' Corbett gestured at the Magister's companions. 'These will have to stay outside, while Prior Cuthbert will demand you surrender your weapons.' He didn't wait for a reply, but pulled at the calling bell under its coping carved in the shape of a smiling angel.

A lay brother opened the postern door and beckoned Corbett, Ranulf and the Magister inside. He then slammed the door shut and gruffly demanded they unstrap their war belts and leave all weaponry in the entrance parlour. Satisfied, he hurried out to inform his superior and returned to lead them across the paved bailey to Prior Cuthbert's reception chamber. The ancient Dominican was sitting enthroned on a chair at the top of a long table. He tapped the floor with his cane, gesturing at all three visitors to sit close by him. Corbett did not stand on ceremony. He showed the prior his seals of office, then put them back in their velvet pouch and nodded at the Magister Viae.

'Father Prior,' he began, 'in January 1308, my learned colleague here collected the corpses of two seamen hanged from the mast of the fighting cog *The Candle-Bright*. Their names were Henry Sumerscale and Matthew Fallowfield. I believe you recommended them to the ship's master, Naseby?'

'Yes, yes.' The prior smiled, opening his red-gummed mouth. 'Yes, I did recommend them.'

'Why, were they known to you?'

'No, they were not. Oh, by the way, Sir Hugh, I know you by sight and reputation, and I must advise you that what I learnt from both men is covered by the seal of confession.'

'You heard their confessions?'

'Yes, I did, and it made dire listening. I felt deeply sorry for them, which is why, after I pronounced absolution, I acceded to their request and provided them with a memorandum of recommendation to Master Naseby, an excellent mariner and a good man. The older of the pair, Fallowfield, had served on galleys in the Middle Sea.'

'Father Prior, you are sure of this?' Corbett turned to the Magister. 'Describe their faces, their hair.'

The Magister shrugged and gave a pithy description of both men. The prior, head turned away, heard him out, then caught Corbett's eye and nodded.

'Yes, yes,' he murmured, 'those are the two unfortunates, God have mercy on them. Sir Hugh, do you wish for some refreshments?'

'No, Father Prior, I must return to the Merry Mercy.'

'Ah, yes. That tavern was mentioned . . .' Prior Cuthbert caught himself just in time. 'Sir Hugh,' he continued, 'what is spoken in the confessional must remain sealed. But I can tell you the following, as it had nothing to do with the sacrament.' He lowered his voice. 'Both men were former Templars. Both men feared their order and wished to speak to the Inquisition, which, as you know, had been appointed by Pope Clement to investigate the allegations against the Templars.'

'Of course,' Corbett breathed, 'and the Inquisition is the Dominican order, which explains why they approached you. Where were they from?'

'They did not tell me and I did not ask. Both were English. The older one was a cynical fighting man. The youth a dreamer, a romancer, but still one badly hurt, alienated.'

'Did they have friends and family in London?'

'Yes, they did, but they did not refer to them; it was something I deduced.'

'Did they produce any documents?'

'No, they spoke *ex corde* – from the heart.' Prior Cuthbert cupped his hands together. 'The two men came here to be shriven, to confess. They wanted to speak to the papal inquisitors either here or in France regarding the Templars. I forwarded their request to the legates in this country. No, no, nothing in writing. A verbal message carried by a courier. The inquisitors were busy, they did not respond.' The Dominican shrugged. 'Of course, we eventually heard about the executions on *The Candle-Bright*. In this vale of tears, death comes swift and brutal.' He rose. 'Sir Hugh, I have other duties, and in conscience I can say no more.'

'Father Prior,' Corbett replied, 'may I stay here and use this chamber to talk to my colleague the Magister?'

'By all means.'

The Dominican had virtually ignored Corbett's companion, but now he sketched a blessing in his direction, tapped his cane on the floor and left. Corbett waited until he had closed the door behind him before turning to the Magister.

'My learned friend,' he teased, 'I know your nature. You have carried out your own investigation into this mystery, haven't you?'

'With nothing to show for it,' the Magister retorted. 'I mean that. I am not playing Hodman's bluff. Sumerscale and Fallowfield are dead, Rougehead and the other three villains have followed them to judgement.'

'Then I have two further tasks for you. First, discover if you can what rumours persist about Puddlicot and his gang, the rogue who broke into Westminster Abbey and stole the king's treasure eight years ago. What legends have flourished? What stories have emerged? Sift the rumour, the tittle-tattle, the gossip. Remember, some of the coven were caught and hanged either by the neck or the purse. Others fled or managed to weasel their way out of any indictment.' Corbett paused. 'And the French,' he added. 'What are the whispers along the alleyways, the tavern chatter?'

'The merchants curse *The Black Hogge*; they blame His Grace the king and, of course, Lord Gaveston.' The Magister squirmed on his stool. 'Sir Hugh, I have heard gossip from Paris and Boulogne. How certain individuals, persons probably known to you, have disappeared, either fled or been taken up.'

Corbett glanced away. He stared at a painting on the far wall, a fresco depicting a battle between two monkey-faced demons garbed in the purple robes of a cardinal of Rome. Each demon was armed with a twisted dagger and jagged mace. War dogs were lashed to their waists, evil-looking beasts with spiked collars and ferocious jaws. In the background, streams of black earth erupted to stain a flame-streaked sky. Corbett conceded to himself that his own life and career were in a tumultuous, turbulent state and he quietly mocked his own self-conceited arrogance. He must confess to that and be shriven. He had thought he would sweep back into royal office and push through changes and make things better when in fact they appeared to be going from bad to worse.

The destruction of *The Candle-Bright* was a major blow. Having listened to the Magister, Corbett was certain that the documents Naseby carried had been found, deciphered and acted upon. He felt in the very core of his being that Tallefert had been seized along with the courier Pietal. The likes of de Nogaret would have no mercy. There would be no public trial and execution. Both men would be gruesomely tortured, racked and burned till they screamed for relief. Death would be most welcome. Corbett had hoped to build a fine net of spies and informers with Tallefert and Pietal at the centre. *The Black Hogge* had brought such a scheme to a sudden and brutal end.

Corbett slouched in the chair, narrowing his eyes. If Tallefert and Pietal were dead, then sooner or later his other spy, the Deacon, that gregarious eternal scholar with his gift for mimicry and disguise, would establish the truth, though by then it might be too late.

'Sir Hugh!'

Corbett stared at the Magister's weather-beaten face under its mop of spiked white hair. Could this villain, he wondered, provide a way out of the tangled mysteries and problems confronting him? A seed of an idea had taken root in Corbett's mind. He entertained no illusion about the source of the murderous mayhem about to engulf him, along with de Craon, and behind him, deeper in the shadows, those two sinister souls Philip of France and Guillaume de Nogaret.

'Sir Hugh?' Ranulf was concerned at his master's deep detachment.

'Ranulf, a parchment script,' Corbett pointed at the hour candle, 'some wax, a quill pen and a little ink. Magister, please wait.' Ranulf hurried to comply. Corbett seized the proffered quill pen, wrote out his message on the script, sealed it with his chancery ring and then pushed it towards the Magister. 'First, sir, you must listen to all the chatter of the alleyways on the matters I've raised with you. Sift such gossip carefully and report back to me. Understood?' The Magister, studying the parchment, murmured that he would. 'Second,' Corbett continued, 'you would deeply love a pardon for all past crimes?' The Magister looked up, astonished. 'You would be even happier if you were offered the post of king's mariner?'

'Of course, Sir Hugh.'

'Very well.' Corbett tapped the parchment script. 'This will gain you entry to the chancery office at Westminster. Now, besides the other duties I have assigned you, you must spend your time studying the king's sea charts, which describe the coastline from the mouth of the Thames north to the Wash. Do you understand?'

'Yes, yes, I do.'

'You enjoy the reputation of being a master mariner. In your previous life you were Elijah Woodhead, a seaman of distinction. Well, I want you to go back to that. I need you to become Gaston Foix, master of *The Black Hogge*. You must set up house in his soul to see the world through his eyes. You must then become his nemesis, his implacable opponent, and plot how you would, if you could, destroy him totally. Remember,' Corbett held up a hand, 'this is no easy task. Gaston Foix knows which ships leave the Thames. Even if a fleet of war cogs went hunting him, he would know it soon enough. He could hide, do what he wished. Even if our ships sought him out for battle . . .'

'The outcome would not be inevitable,' the Magister excitedly intervened. 'Gaston is skilled in war. He is also master of a powerful cog, which, according to all reports, can outsail and outfight anything fielded against it.'

'So,' Corbett insisted, 'think as his implacable enemy. If you were the king's admiral, from the Thames north to Berwick, how would you trap Gaston and *The Black Hogge*?' He clutched the Magister's wrist. 'In this I trust you, and I assure you, if you are successful, I shall move heaven and earth for you. Betray me and the cause I serve, and I swear, not even St Michael and all his angels will be able to save you. Remember what I have said about the other matters. I know you have your spies, your legion of minions, the swallows of the alleyways. Set up watch on both the lazar hospital of St Giles and the Merry Mercy tavern. Discover who comes and who goes. Where they go and what they do. Do you understand?'

'Sir Hugh.' The Magister clasped Corbett's hand, nodded at Ranulf and left the chamber.

'Chanson!' Corbett called over his clerk of the stables, who was crouched on a stool close to the door. He handed him a small waxen copy of the secret seal. 'As swift as a bird, Chanson, go to the muniment room in the Tower. Search out Fitzosbert, the chief muniment clerk.'

'You mean the Ferret?' Chanson burst out.

'Aye.' Corbett grinned. 'Fitzosbert the Ferret among the records.'

'He certainly looks like one,' Ranulf laughed, 'with his pointed face and his little black eyes, constantly sniffing over the dust that clogs his nose – or so he claims.'

'Search him out,' Corbett ordered. 'Fitzosbert is to go through all the documents seized from Templar holdings throughout this kingdom. He is searching for two names, Matthew Fallowfield and Henry Sumerscale. If he can't find these, I would like him to concentrate on their forenames, any Templars called Henry or Matthew. Describe the ages of both men and whatever else we know about them. Fitzosbert must also be given the names of the Templars now sheltering in St Giles. I want to know where they served before their order was dissolved.' He held a hand up at the sound of distant shouting. 'For the moment we shall return to St Giles . . .' He paused as the door was flung open and Peterkin the ship's boy burst in, followed by an irate lay brother who had tried to stop him.

'Sir Hugh,' the boy pleaded, 'you must come back to the Merry Mercy! A most hideous murder! Master Slingsby has been found cruelly stabbed in a jakes house!'

Gaston Foix, master of *The Black Hogge*, sat in his small cabin beneath the stern castle of his formidable fighting ship. He moved restlessly on the armless leather-backed chair bolted to the deck floor and plucked at a loose thread on his stained thick blue hose. He was glad his ship had anchored. They had been at sea for days; now they could reprovision and take on fresh purveyance. Gaston had sunk *The Candle-Bright*, then sailed on to deliver certain letters and packages to officials in Calais before returning to his continual prowling along the Essex coast. He had charts that accurately described the various estuaries, ports and natural harbours of the rugged and desolate coastline. Of course there were the fishing smacks, but Gaston, an experienced sailor, knew what hour the fishing boats sailed and what hour they returned. Occasionally a mistake was made, but no fishing boat ever escaped *The Black Hogge*. If danger really threatened, Gaston could sail further north, tacking into the frozen seas, or due east, well away from the usual trade routes. Raised on the savage, treacherous seas off the Breton coast, he knew how to play the ghost, slipping in and out of the mist. The real danger was the way he and his crew felt now: dirty, dishevelled, tired of stale bread, hard meat and brackish water.

Gaston stared down at his scuffed boots, ran a hand around his unshaven chin and grinned. He was truly dirty. He must reek like a midden heap, whilst his clothes were so salt-soaked, they were beyond any washing. Thankfully Ysabeau, his wife, could not see or smell him now. Immediately he felt a sharp pang of homesickness. It would be so good to be sailing into the harbour of La Rochelle with its soaring tower defences, to be aiming like an arrow towards the quayside, where his wife and family would be waiting.

Gaston murmured a prayer and crossed himself. He drank the brackish ale from the leather blackjack, his stubby fingers gathering the bits of dried meat and coarse bread on the platter before him. Instead of sailing home, he reflected, *The Black Hogge* was hiding off the windswept coast of Essex, where, despite the summer sun, the breeze could turn cold and biting, with sudden squalls rushing in to send the cog pitching and twisting. As the ship shuddered, tugging and pulling against the anchor stone, he steadied himself, listening keenly to the cries of the lookouts that all was well, clear on land and sea. Usually *The Black Hogge* harboured at night and was gone by dawn, away from any spy on shore or sea, but today was different.

A knock on the door made him turn. His leading seaman, Blanquit, pushed his ugly face through to assure him that their precious cargo was fed, comfortable and resting. All was going well, he declared, and the landing party would soon be ready. His master grunted, and Blanquit left.

Gaston sat back as he recalled how he and his ship had come to be here. Philip of France's tapestry of treasons, as Gaston called it, was now being swiftly woven. The mariner recalled that eventful day when he had been ushered into the secret chamber of the Holy Chancery at the Louvre. A strange star-shaped room, its walls covered with polished Spanish leather sheets, and over these a dark-blue arras displaying the royal silver fleur-de-lis. The thickest turkey rugs carpeted the floor. As far as Gaston could see, there were no windows or apertures. The darkness was kept at bay by a host of fluted snow-white beeswax candles; these provided pools of light over the thick oaken table where Philip of France presided.

Gaston closed his eyes as he recalled meeting the French king for the first time. No wonder they called him the Iron King: thick yellow hair tumbling down to his shoulders, those eerie light-blue eyes never flickering or blinking in their stony gaze. His face was ghostly white, yet his lips were so red Gaston wondered if they had been carmined. To the king's right, de Nogaret, Philip's nefarious soul comrade, his sallow, hard face a mask for a mind that teemed like a box of worms. On the king's left, Monseigneur Amaury de Craon, russet-haired, white-faced, all eager to be dispatched as Philip's envoy to Edward of England. Next to him the truly sinister-looking Brother Jerome, a demon soul if there was ever one.

Gaston had been sworn to the utmost secrecy as the tapestry of treason was unfurled. There was a king to be trapped, mocked and weakened, both within and without; a kingdom to be held to ransom; a treasure seized, and the greatest source of protection and comfort for Edward of England to be brutally removed. There were enemies to be destroyed and men in their scores to be killed, either silently in the dark or during the blood heat of battle.

De Nogaret and de Craon drew Gaston in and showed him his role in what Gaston secretly considered to be a murderous, macabre courtly masque. The ship's master was flattered, praised and, as he quietly realised, threatened. He was told what he already knew, that he would be foolish to sail to and from a port on the Narrow Seas. Instead, he would take up position in the misty, mysterious and empty vastness of the northern ocean. He was instructed on the singular way he and de Craon would communicate. He was informed how he had been chosen because of his skill and reputation as a mariner and because of the unique skills he had learnt during his years of service with the Genoese. He would use what had become a most enjoyable pastime in the service of Philip of France, and so confuse and confound the French king's opponents. Summer would pass, autumn would come, and by then, de Nogaret assured him in a whisper, everything would have come to fruition.

Gaston had certainly played his part to the full. He had taken ships like *The Candle-Bright* and seized their secret papers. Already he knew from the messages he'd received how delighted de Nogaret was at capturing and silencing all those agents of the English Crown. Now they were set to remove the principal obstacle.

Another knock on the door, and Blanquit came in again.

'Master,' he declared, 'the shore boats have brought fresh provisions.' He tapped Gaston's cup. 'Good Bordeaux, the finest Rheinish, roast capon and coney, fresh linen, clean water. We will wash, change and feast well tonight.'

Gaston rose, clasped his henchman on the shoulder and went out on deck, which his crew were swilling down with buckets of water. A strong breeze buffeted his face, cooling the sweat on his skin. *The Black Hogge* strained and creaked in a groan of wood, cordage and sail, like some destrier eager to break free and charge into battle.

'Soon enough, my terrible beauty,' Gaston murmured patting the great middle mast.

The Black Hogge was turning on the tide, pulling constantly against the anchor stone rope. The sails were reefed but the crew stood ready to loose them at the first hint of trouble. Gaston, eyes blinking against the salty breeze, stared out across the mist-hung water. The sea was still a sullen grey mass; the sun had yet to rise, but the shoreline was becoming more distinct as the mist shifted and thinned. Others were coming up from beneath deck: de Nogaret's assassins, well-armed and buckled for war beneath their cloaks, hoods hiding their faces. Professional killers, mercenaries from de Nogaret's personal retinue, each of them carried a saddle bag. They moved gingerly towards the side of the ship, where the taffrail had been removed and a rope ladder lowered.

Gaston stared around. The ship was now reprovisioned with all the necessary purveyance. Once the assassins had finished their business, he would return for them and fresh supplies.

'It is time,' he declared.

He followed the mercenaries down the rope ladder to one of the two bobbing shore boats. He sat in the prow and shouted to cast off. The rowers leaned over their oars, straining mightily as both boats clattered against the side of the cog towering above them, then pulled away, heading for the shore. Gaston breathed in the smells of salt, dead fish, and that distinctive tang from the brambles and briars that stretched down to the beach. At last the surge of the sea weakened, the boat's keel scratching the shale. The oarsmen leapt out to pull the boats as far from the waterline as possible.

Gaston leapt over the side and strode across the beach, climbing the sand hills on to the wild heathland of gorse and sturdy trees. He glimpsed the cart and horses that brought the provisions. A man broke free of these and strode up the beaten-earth track. He pulled back his hood to reveal a dark, close face, full lips strangely twisted, narrow-set eyes wary and aggressive as those of a war dog.

'Gaston Foix.' The stranger clasped the mariner's hand. 'It is good to see you again. Your companions?' He gestured at the eight men behind the mariner.

'You have your orders,' Gaston replied. 'You must take these comrades to the meeting place and wait.'

'What is your name?' The leader of the assassins stepped forward.

'You have your papers?' the stranger retorted, ignoring the question.

'Our documents are all in order,' the leader of the assassins replied, 'signed and sealed. Master Foix here did not give us your name; what are you called?'

'My name is Rougehead,' the stranger replied, 'Gabriel Rougehead. Once a Templar serjeant but now the most faithful servant of His Grace the king of France.'

The Deacon was also, at least ostensibly, the most faithful subject of Philip of France. In reality, he was one of Sir Hugh Corbett's most resourceful spies in Paris. Baptised Walter Creswell over the ancient font in the village church of Castle Acre in Norfolk, he was an actor, a mummer, who sheltered deep in the shadows. The eternal student, he had migrated from the halls of Oxford and Cambridge to study in the colleges and schools of the University of Paris. He could often be seen walking the cloisters of the Abbey of St Victor. Despite his sacred title, the Deacon was most skilled in lying. He often admitted the same to himself. He was a liar by nature, by upbringing, by training, by profession and by permission of his own free will. The only person he did not lie to was Sir Hugh Corbett.

For the rest of his time, the Deacon sold lies. Not only his name, his profession, his so-called loyalty, but a wide array of false relics, from which he made a considerable profit. He assured his buyers that they would be saved for eternal life whilst quietly conceding, in those sombre early hours of each day, that he himself would be closeted with the damned. Yet he could not stop or change, because he did not want to. He loved what he did, and Sir Hugh Corbett recognised that. The Deacon lived, thrived and feasted on deception. He could change his appearance and his trade to be a furrier, a barrow man, a baker, a butcher or a candlestick maker. When he tired of selling relics, he traded in lard, selling it in glazed earthenware jars sealed against the rats; or fresh eggs, waxed and embedded in straw and sand. He was always eager that every deception be successful. He would openly discourse on the Sentences of Abelard, at the same time sitting on a stool and pretending to be a cook boy turning a spit, his face protected from the raging fire by a wicker screen. He used his access to kitchens to provide him with the wherewithal to make relics of the highest quality; be it the cord worn by the Saviour, or Goliath's foreskin.

On that bright summer's day, the Deacon was sheltering in one of the student auberges close to the Tour de Nesle and, more importantly, the narrow street that was home to Guido Tallefert, clerk of the Holy Chancery in the Louvre, close friend and secret ally of Sir Hugh Corbett. He sipped at his watered wine and quietly cursed as one of the city provosts, surrounded by men-at-arms, pushed a movable gallows into the auberge's stable yard. The city authorities often did this as a public warning to the riotous, lusty students and scholars who thronged that quarter, feasting and revelling once released from the halls and schools. The sight of a sun-dried blackened corpse with crows poking and pecking at its hollowed eyes was judged to be the most powerful deterrent to riotous behaviour. The Deacon was tempted to rise and leave, but that might attract attention, so he sat as if listening to the sounds of the streets: the songs of the taverns, the cries of the daughters of joy, the clink of goblets, the thud of running feet and the slamming of shutter or door.

At last the provost's men decided to take their grisly memento mori back out on to the street. The Deacon waited for a while, then followed. He needed, as usual, to check that all was well with Tallefert. He crossed the thoroughfare, glancing across to the greenish-grey moss-covered wall that ran along the Seine. The various enclaves in this barrier were used to exhibit criminals in the stocks, gibbets for hanging river pirates, and the corpses of those fished from the river, stripped and stretched out on hand carts in the hope that someone might recognise them. Two corpses, naked as newborn babes, occupied one enclave. The Deacon stopped and stared at them in horror. They were unrecognisable. The faces of both appeared to have been furrowed or ploughed by some malevolent worm that had turned and twisted in the rotting flesh to create buboes and suppurating boils. The damage had been worsened by the nibbling of fish and of the vermin that swarmed along the riverbank. The eyes had sunk deep into their sockets. The noses were swollen lumps of putrid flesh, the thickened lips gaping and corrupt.

Hand over his mouth, the Deacon hastened on. He reached Tallefert's house and slipped along the spindle-thin runnel leading down to a small postern gate in the garden wall. The Deacon, highly skilled with keys and picklocks, quickly forced an entry. Once inside, he leaned against the gate and stared around. He had never approached this house by its narrow main door. He always entered as he had now. If Tallefert was there, he would welcome him. If he had left, there would be a sign. Today the Deacon was deeply uneasy. Both house and garden appeared desolate and deserted. The rooms were shuttered and locked. The flower beds, herb plots and beehives looked sorely neglected.

The Deacon slipped like a shadow across the unattended garden, under the ancient pear tree, pushing aside the garden furniture. Fighting the fear and panic welling within him, he forced the kitchen door and entered, listening keenly as he hurried from one chamber to another. Tallefert was gone, and so were his panniers and satchels. No precious objects could be seen. The chancery desk was swept clean, the larder, pantry and buttery devoid of all drink.

'Where could he be?' the Deacon whispered. He

crouched down, arms across his belly. No Tallefert, no Pietal. He closed his eyes and then abruptly opened them, his throat growing dry as he recalled those two corpses taken from the Seine. Two grotesques from a nightmare, yet on reflection, their hair, the shape of their bodies, the vestiges of what they had looked like in life, all was familiar. The Deacon's fingers went to his lips. Were they Tallefert and Pietal? How was it that two corpses fished separately from the Seine should be exposed together in death? Was that a reflection of some relationship in life? And the hideous, gruesome injuries – surely those were not the effects of a malignant disease or the nibbling of some rodent, but more the work of torture, of human cruelty. Were those cadavers the mortal remains of Tallefert and Pietal? The corpses had been found in the river close to this house. The two men must have been captured swiftly. Corbett had always instructed his spies that if they were in danger, they should send him or each other a quotation about beekeeping. This had not happened.

The Deacon rose to his feet. 'I have fought the good fight. I have run the race. I have kept faith,' he whispered, 'and now I must be gone.'

He hurried out into the garden and opened the gate, stumbling down the alleyway, desperate to reach the sanctuary of the English envoy's chambers at the Golden Hart tavern. It was all over. Tallefert had apparently disappeared, and the Deacon couldn't forget those grotesque cadavers, their rotting, suppurating faces.

Enough was enough. He too needed to disappear, and Sir Hugh had to be warned . . .

Mistress Philippa met Corbett just within the courtyard of the Merry Mercy. She looked calm and collected in her dark-blue gown with its white bands at neck and wrist, though her eyes brimmed with tears and she kept biting her lip as she tried not to weep. She clutched Corbett's arm, then slipped her soft hand into his.

'Sir Hugh,' she whispered, 'why all this in my beautiful tavern?'

'Mistress,' Corbett touched her on the cheek, 'show me this mischief.'

She shook her head and led him across the cobbled stable yard, Ranulf going before them, pushing his way through the throng outside the postern entrance. Just inside this stood a garderobe. Philippa let go of Corbett's hand, pulled open the door and stepped back. Slingsby, fully clothed, sat on the jakes seat, slightly hunched. The dagger, which must have killed him instantly, was thrust blade-deep into his heart. He slouched, head to one side, mouth gaping, eyes popping from the shock of death. Corbett touched his hand; it was still slightly warm and soft.

'Who found him?' He turned and addressed those gathered behind him.

'I did.' Sokelar the harbour master pushed his way through. 'Agnes and I were about to leave. I needed to relieve myself.' He gestured at the garderobe. 'I opened the door; that's what I found.'

Ranulf organised a group of servants to take Slingsby's corpse across to an outhouse, using an ancient hand cart as a bier. Mistress Philippa fetched lanternhorns. Corbett followed her, ordering Chanson to keep the curious still thronging around well away. Ranulf closed the outhouse door and Corbett began his inspection. He could find no other mark of violence, nothing to indicate that Slingsby had tried to protect or defend himself. Once he had finished, he thanked Philippa, adding that he and Ranulf would return to the Cana chamber and continue their investigation, and inviting her to join them for supper. She smilingly agreed, adding that she would send an urgent message to Parson Layburn at Holy Trinity the Little so the corpse collectors could take care of Slingsby's cadaver.

Once by themselves, Corbett and Ranulf removed cloaks and war belts, cleaning themselves at the lavarium, and ate the light collation a servant brought: dried quail meat, small white rolls, some butter and a jug of tangy ale.

'Why murder Slingsby?' Ranulf murmured between mouthfuls.

'Why not?' Corbett joked. 'But,' he sipped from his tankard, 'a truly mysterious murder. First, notice how on Slingsby's person and in the garderobe we could detect no other mark of violence whatsoever, apart from the death wound, either from Slingsby's assassin or the victim defending himself. Yes?' Ranulf agreed. 'Second,' Corbett smiled, 'when I go to the garderobe, I close the door and bring the latch down so that if someone else tries to enter, they know it's occupied. But according to Sokelar, the latrine door was off the latch. Third, I could detect no blood on the floor outside the garderobe, so I suspect Slingsby was killed inside. Fourth, most men when they use the jakes undo their belts and the points on their hosc. Yet there is no sign of Slingsby even beginning to do this. If he had wanted to relieve himself in a public jakes, his need must have been urgent and the shock of such a blow would have caused him to urinate or defecate, but there is no evidence of this. So what was he doing in that garderobe?'

He glanced at Ranulf, who simply shook his head.

'Was he killed somewhere else and taken there? But that would be nigh impossible in a busy tavern. Finally, Ranulf, your question: why? Why was Slingsby murdered here and now? Yes, he was involved in the destruction of Fallowfield and Sumerscale over three years ago, so is his murder connected to that?'

'And there is who?' Ranulf declared. 'Who could kill a man like Slingsby? Let's be honest, master, I am sure that when it came to sword or dagger play, our dead taverner could hold his own. Surely his killer must be a professional assassin? Someone like our good friend Brother Jerome, who floats around this tavern as if he owns it?'

'We could try to find out where he and others were when Slingsby was murdered,' mused Corbett, 'but there are so many fluctuations, not to mention the downright deceit and deception that would confront us . . .'

He paused at a sharp rapping at the door, which was

flung open and de Craon swept into the chamber, followed by Brother Jerome. The French envoy's face was creased into a false smile, a sure sign that he had apparently decided that courtesy, however false, was the best path to follow.

'Hugh, Hugh!' He advanced on Corbett, arms extended. 'I am so pleased to see you. So happy to hear that you have returned to your king's service. Believe me, Philip of France is delighted. He sees us as uniting against any foe. Come!'

Corbett bit his lip to stop the laughter from bubbling out. He winked at a smirking Ranulf as he embraced de Craon, kissing him on both cheeks.

'Amaury,' he murmured, 'my heart sings with joy at seeing you again. I assure you, you are never far from my thoughts.'

'Likewise, Hugh.' De Craon stepped back. 'And how is the Lady Maeve?'

Pleasantries and compliments were exchanged. De Craon threw his cloak over the table and, uninvited, sat down on a chair, drumming his fingers on its carved arm as he greeted Ranulf and beckoned Brother Jerome to sit beside him.

'Well, Hugh,' the envoy spread his hands, 'it is, as I said, good to see you. What can I . . .'

'*The Black Hogge*,' Corbett retorted, sitting down opposite so de Craon had to turn in his chair, 'and its murderous attacks.'

'Hugh, Hugh . . .' De Craon laced his fingers together and shook his head sorrowfully. '*The Black Hogge* is a privateer sailing under the sealed mandate of the Duke of Brittany. Of course we have heard about its depredations, but let's be honest, English privateers, Scottish privateers, not to mention those of Flanders and Hainault, also prowl the Narrow Seas. Of course we deeply regret the hideous losses you have sustained. I've already expressed our profound concerns to your chancellor and treasurer. My master King Philip of France has remonstrated with the Duke of Brittany.' He shrugged. 'But as you know, Hugh, such matters take time . . .'

'So you have no communication with *The Black Hogge* whatsoever?'

'Of course not. Why, do you think I can fly with messages? We deplore your losses! *Quel dommage! Je suis desol*é.' De Craon gave the most Gallic of shrugs.

Corbett glanced at Ranulf and raised his eyes heavenwards. The room fell silent. De Craon sat blinking as if he was on the verge of tears, distraught at the thought of such English losses at sea. His accomplice in crime, Jerome, sat head down, his hands tucked inside the voluminous sleeves of his cream-coloured robe.

'Do the names Sumerscale and Fallowfield mean anything to you, Amaury?'

'No, why should they?'

'And the Templars sheltering at St Giles?'

'Are there Templars sheltering there, Hugh? If there are, surely they should be handed over to my master. The order has been condemned by Pope Clement. The Holy Father has ordered that its members be arrested, and that includes any Templars in England.'

'And the death of Slingsby?'

'Who?'

'The taverner murdered here in a garderobe earlier today.'

'Sir Hugh,' de Craon waved his hands, 'of course we heard the clamour, but the death of an innkeeper in a shit-house has nothing to do with me or mine.'

'So, Amaury, why are you actually here in London, invoking your rights as an envoy to stay in this most comfortable tavern?'

De Craon, eyes all fluttering, shook his head like some master in the schools dealing with a not-so-bright scholar. 'Sir Hugh, it's well known. We are here to discuss with your king's council certain questions regarding Gascony, in particular the building of a bastide at Saint-Sardos. Of course there are other matters. King Philip would dearly love to see his son-in-law and daughter in Paris. We also have the question of Scotland and English intervention there. A whole host of problems . . .' De Craon's smile was so false, Corbett had to glance away.

'In which case, monseigneur,' he murmured, 'I shall not detain you any longer from your pressing business.'

He leaned back in his chair and fluttered his fingers at de Craon. The two Frenchmen rose, bowed and swept out of the chamber, Brother Jerome slamming the door behind them. Corbett listened to their footsteps fade as he stared down at the tabletop.

'Master, we learnt nothing there.'

'Nothing comes of nothing.' Corbett straightened up.

'In fact, Ranulf, I learnt a great deal. De Craon is thoroughly enjoying himself. He is no more here to discuss the bastide of Saint-Sardos in Gascony than he is to fly to the sun with St Michael and all his angels. He is here to manage and facilitate some subtle, devious plot, a dish cooked in Paris and served in London. The problem is to discover all the ingredients and what they hope to achieve.'

Corbett rose to his feet, suppressing a chill of fear. De Craon, he knew, was deep in some truly deceitful and highly dangerous plot.

'The Templars?'

'Do you know, Ranulf, I don't think de Craon gives a mouldy fig about the Templars. After all, why should he concern himself with a gaggle of frightened, perhaps diseased and probably broken old men whose order has been shattered by both prince and pope over the last four years? What real threat do they pose? True, they can mount a defence of their order, but who cares? What good will it do? Oh no, Ranulf, our dear spider de Craon is spinning a web of deceit. Our first problem is that we do not even know what he intends to catch. Now, let's turn to something more pleasant and rewarding, Mistress Philippa Henman . . .'

By evening, the Merry Mercy had grown even busier. The strains of a song trailed from a taproom, whilst out in the courtyard, perched on a barrel, a storyteller delivered his tale. He claimed to have crossed the Rhine and mingled with the Easterlings, blood-drinking hordes massing for attack in their snow-bound forests. Next to him, a boy with a harp would pluck a few notes as the storyteller paused for effect. Despite Slingsby's murder, the tavern lived up to both its title and reputation as the people of Queenhithe flocked into its taprooms and gardens once the Vespers bell had clanged its evening message.

Corbett and Ranulf sat down with Mistress Philippa and her constant companion Agnes to a delicious meal of swan-neck pudding, partridge in nutted wine sauce, and spiced minced chicken, along with platters of fresh bread, bowls of thick butter and specially diced herbs. Two long-neck jugs held the best wine from Bordeaux and the Rhine. Corbett did not feel hungry, but he did not wish to appear rude and was secretly pleased that Chanson and Ranulf had, as usual, ravenous appetites. Mistress Philippa, face glowing and looking fresh and delightful in her dark-blue gown, insisted on serving portions to all whilst keeping up a constant chatter about tavern matters.

'Slingsby,' Corbett intervened as Mistress Philippa took a sip of wine, 'Master Slingsby, formerly of the Salamander. Did you have dealings with him?'

'I knew of him by reputation, a fellow taverner.' She smiled. 'My late dear husband believed Slingsby sheltered in the twilight world. A genial enough host, though one with strong links to the Fraternity of the Dark, the outlaws and wolfsheads of London.' She pulled a face, bringing her hand prettily up to her mouth. 'Of course, such an accusation could be levelled at any taverner.'

'Your late husband?' Ranulf asked. Corbett could see the Clerk of the Green Wax was both deeply intrigued and attracted by this very singular hostess.

'What about him?'

'He died of . . .?'

'As I have told you, about a year ago. Indeed, I must see Parson Layburn to arrange the requiem for the anniversary of his death.'

'Was he a sickly man?'

'No, but he became so, his heart grew weak. Now, as regards Slingsby, Sir Hugh?'

'Did any of your household notice anything suspicious or untoward this morning?'

'No.' Mistress Philippa shook her head. 'I have heard no whispers, no gossip.' She dabbed her mouth prettily with a napkin. 'I was closeted, God help me, with Monseigneur de Craon over certain delicacies for his diet. He has what he calls a most tender stomach. He cannot eat this, he cannot eat that.' She imitated de Craon's flowing hand gestures so accurately that Corbett and Ranulf burst out laughing.

'From the little I have learnt,' she continued, 'I suspect Slingsby made to leave after the Angelus bell sounded and my household had gathered in the taproom to break their fast.'

'So that part of the tavern,' Corbett asked, 'where the garderobe was?'

'Fairly deserted,' Philippa declared. 'I understand Slingsby was seen arriving here this morning. People knew you wished to question him, but I cannot say anything about his murder, who might be responsible or why he was killed.'

'And de Craon?'

'Sir Hugh, de Craon would have nothing to do with Slingsby, surely? All I can say about our French envoy is what I have said before.' She put her napkin down on the table. '*The Black Hogge* dominates Queenhithe. Everyone knows that de Craon plots mischief all along the riverside. The constant chatter is about how *The Black Hogge* learns so quickly and pounces so successfully.'

'My father is obsessed with it.' Agnes, all petulant, spoke up. 'People blame him, as they do for other things, yet what can be done . . .?' Her voice trailed off. Mistress Philippa insisted on refilling their goblets and the conversation turned to more mundane matters.

After they had finished eating, Corbett thanked his hostess and adjourned to his own chamber. He wrote a letter to Maeve, signed and sealed it, then pored over a piece of scrubbed vellum, trying to marshal his thoughts. *Item*, he wrote: Sumerscale and Fallowfield, whatever their true names, were Templars. Why were they disaffected with their order? They had definitely been trying to meet with the papal inquisitors investigating the accusations against the Poor Knights. Yet who exactly were these two men? Where did they come from? *Item*: Gabriel Rougehead. Corbett was convinced somebody had bribed that renegade Templar, wolfshead and outlaw to lay the most serious allegations against the two men known as Sumerscale and Fallowfield.

Who was behind Rougehead and why had those two men been destroyed? *Item*: who had invited Rougehead and his coven to that fatal meal at the Salamander? How had one individual, according to the evidence, managed to kill all four daggermen, severing their heads from their bodies before setting fire to that place of ill repute? Surely an act of revenge following the execution of Sumerscale and Fallowfield, yet there was no evidence of either man having a powerful protector. They had even had to seek the good offices of Prior Cuthbert at Blackfriars to secure employment on board *The Candle-Bright*. And why did this mysterious vindicator wait almost three months after the executions to take his revenge?

Item: what had been Slingsby's role in all of this? Was he part of Rougehead's conspiracy, hence his tavern being burnt to the ground? Who had murdered Slingsby earlier today? Why now, over three years after his tavern had been destroyed? And why here in the garderobe of a Queenhithe tavern? How had the murder been carried out so skilfully with no sound or sign of any resistance? A fairly powerful daggerman himself, Slingsby had been killed quickly and quietly with one deadly thrust to the heart. *Item*: the Templars sheltering at St Giles, a defeated, frightened, cowardly group. Who was killing them, why and how? What danger or threat did they pose to de Craon, the power of France, or indeed anyone else? *Item*: *The Black Hogge*, a fighting ship under a master mariner that inflicted so much damage on English shipping. Who kept it so carefully appraised of cogs leaving the Thames? How was this done? And surely there must be some connection between that privateer's depredations and Sumerscale and Fallowfield. Naseby, master of *The Candle-Bright*, had been specifically reminded just before his last fateful voyage about how he'd executed the two men. Indeed, he had been threatened here in the Merry Mercy, though such messages could have been left by anyone hired for the task.

Corbett paused in his writing. He too had been warned, in Westminster Abbey. Why and by whom? Only de Craon would have known he was there, but would de Craon warn him? The French envoy would love nothing better than to take Corbett's head and silence forever the English clerk who had bested him so many times in the past.

Item: there seemed to be some connection between the present mysteries and the robbery of the royal treasure in the crypt of Westminster Abbey some eight years ago. How did that precious dagger, part of the robbers' plunder, end up being thrust into the heart of a former Templar in the dead of night on a bench in the great meadow of St Giles lazar house? There were other links to that infamous robbery. Rougehead, under a different name, had been suspected as a member of Puddlicot's coven, whilst Slingsby and the Salamander had also fallen under suspicion of being involved.

Corbett sighed noisily. He felt a deep, creeping weariness. He put his quill pen down and rubbed his eyes. 'And finally,' he whispered to himself, 'there is de Craon.

I know you, you fox.' He stared at the dancing candle flame, then wetted his fingers and doused it. 'You truly lie at the root of all this,' he whispered to the dark, 'but that root runs deep and tangled, and will take a great deal of digging out.'

PART FIVE

'This arrogance will cause his ruin and total fall.'
The Monk of Malmesbury, *Life of Edward II*

The assassin, the Vengeance as he called himself, swept furiously across the meadow in the lazar hospital of St Giles. Dusk had fallen. The sky was darkening as nature greeted the gathering night. An owl hooted from a copse of trees, the ghostly sound echoing above the deserted wind-swept meadow. The bracken and gorse rattled as night hunters began their search for prey. The assassin kept to the shadows, moving soundlessly, taking full advantage of the trees and bushes, ready to sheathe his naked sword if approached, when he could assume another guise and put on a different mask.

He reached a line of buildings, paused, waited and watched. The lepers always preferred the dark. After their evening meal in the hospital refectory, they would creep out to take advantage of the evening breeze. They liked to sit and watch the last rays of the sun, the moon wax stronger and the stars blossom full against the summer sky. Once free of their companions, they would unwind the putrid bandages from around their rotting mouths. They liked nothing better than to expose their skull-like faces – lips, eyelids and noses half eaten away – to the balmy coolness of the breezes.

The Vengeance moved on, passing through the lychgate into God's Acre, slipping like a ghost along the coffin path. In the twilight the assassin glimpsed his first victim: Otho, a leper knight, greatly eaten by the disease. The old soldier sat on a table tomb. On his right, a capped candle; on his left, a small parcel of bread and cheese. Otho liked nothing better than to sit there chewing clumsily on his food, basking in the calmness of the night. The assassin approached, his razor-sharp sword gripped tightly in both hands. Otho, who had fought out in the redlands of Outremer, taken part in furious struggles at this oasis or that, sensed that something was wrong. The assassin was moving quickly, booted feet scraping the ground. Otho turned, alarmed, but the killing blow was faster, scything through the leper's neck, a clean, sharp severing so the blood erupted like water gushing through a spout as the head came clean off to bounce like a ball along the pebble-dashed path.

Satisfied, the assassin moved soundlessly as a shifting shadow back along the coffin path to the death house. Another victim was caught unawares. An inmate, crouching to tie the string around his leggings, stretching out neck and head, which made him vulnerable to the cutting blow of the assassin's two-edged sword . . .

*

Corbett had just broken his fast in the taproom of the Merry Mercy when a breathless Ausel burst into the tavern shouting his name, so choked with fear, the former Templar could hardly speak. Corbett managed to calm him and learnt that hideous murder had been committed in the lazar hospital. He summoned Ranulf and Chanson, who were sharing a stoup of ale in the garden, enjoying the freshness of a new day. War belts were collected and strapped on. Once ready, Corbett followed Ausel through the narrow lanes to the hospital.

They found Crowthorne and the two remaining Templar knights, Burghesh and Stapleton, in the master's parlour. Frightened men, they sat with swords drawn behind a locked and bolted door, which they reluctantly opened to admit Ausel, Corbett and his two companions.

'They blame us,' Ausel gasped, mopping his sweaty face with a rag. 'They blame us.'

'For what?' Ranulf demanded. 'In God's name, you are Templar knights, warriors.'

'This morning.' Ausel drew a deep breath. 'As you know, it was mist-strewn. The lazar hospital came to life, if you can describe it like that,' he added bitterly. 'We gather every day in the church for our dawn prayer, just to make sure all is well. Anyway, this morning our way was blocked by leper knights. You explain!'

He gestured at Crowthorne, the leech, who, face all pale and unshaven, sat trembling on a stool, fingers constantly scratching his right cheek. 'They were angry,' he began. 'It was still half-light. The mist had yet to lift.' He waved a hand. 'We were walking to the church and they just came out of the mist, swathed in their robes and bandages. They were not yet buckled for battle, though I saw their war belts nearby. They screamed how the disgraced Templars had no right to be in their lazar house, how they had shattered the peace and harmony of St Giles.' Crowthorne grabbed a goblet of minted water and gulped noisily. 'I asked them what had happened. Their leader – I am sure it was Mausley – talked about abominations being found, leper knights foully slain, their heads severed. How their corpses were now laid out in the charnel house, the crypt beneath the church.' Again he paused to sip from the goblet.

'That's where the leper knights lay out their dead,' Ausel explained.

'Why?' Ranulf asked.

'That's the way it has always been. The death house is usually for those who serve here and die in that service.'

'So what happened next?' Ranulf asked.

'It became more and more violent,' Ausel replied. 'They said we had brought nothing but trouble. Stones and clumps of earth were hurled at us.' He shrugged. 'We retreated. We had no choice.'

He paused at a rapping at the door. No one went to answer. Eventually Crowthorne gave a deep sigh, rose to his feet, drew the bolts and stepped outside. Corbett went to follow and caught the stench of rottenness seeping in, the reek of putrid, unwashed bandages. Crowthorne returned, pale-faced and trembling. He closed then barred the door and leaned against it. He scratched his cheek again and pointed at Corbett.

'Mausley and the leper knights want to meet with you outside the crypt. They insist you come alone.'

'Master!' Ranulf warned. Chanson got to his feet, shaking his head.

'I will go. I doubt if they will hurt me.' Corbett rose, tightened his war belt and glanced around. Once again he wondered if Philip of France or his minion de Craon would really concern themselves about these knights. The Templars looked what they were: cowed, beaten, exhausted men well past their prime: Roger Stapleton, his lined, severe face all petulant like that of a tired old monk; Walter Burghesh, cramped and furtive in his movements; Ausel was different: concerned about himself and lacking any real moral leadership. Now and again Corbett would catch an expression, a twist of the lips, the cast of a glance. Ausel was a man who had a great deal to hide, or so it appeared. Could one of these knights, Corbett wondered, be a spy for de Craon, a renegade paid to kill the others and so cause agitation? And was Crowthorne innocent of any wrongdoing? A leech who made it obvious that he should be in charge here and fiercely resented the Templar presence?

'Master,' Ranulf warned, 'I should come with you.'

'No,' Corbett retorted. 'All of you stay here.' He pulled up the hood of his cloak, left the chamber and made his way across to the church. He felt as if he was walking through a land of ghosts. The hospital fell ominously silent around him. Now and then a shape would glide by; occasionally Corbett heard the chilling rasp of a leper, their mouth, nose and chest rotting to nothingness.

He left the huddle of buildings, moving across to the crypt. The sun remained hidden, the clouded sky reluctant to break, whilst a cloying river mist swirled in to cloak, hide, deceive and disguise. Corbett, one hand on his sword hilt, approached the steps leading up to the main door; to the right of these a second set led down to an iron-barred gate, which provided entrance to the crypt and the charnel chamber it contained. The gate now hung open, two lanternhorns gleaming either side of the entrance.

Corbett went down, stooping to enter the crypt. He straightened up and stared around. A cavernous chamber, the crypt was dark as any dungeon except for the thick tallow candles that had been lit and placed at the head and foot of three makeshift biers laid out on the floor, close to a heavy iron rail. Beyond this rose mounds of gleaming bones: skulls, ribcages, shards of legs and arms, all piled up in tangled heaps. These were the remains of the long-buried and forgotten dead, plucked from their graves and tombs in God's Acre to make room for the more recently deceased. Corbett walked slowly towards the three biers and immediately turned away gasping, trying to control his stomach. On each bier sprawled the mangled remains of a leper: the bandaged, severed heads and decapitated torsos stinking and drenched in congealed blood. A hunchbacked, knobbly-headed rat scampered out of the dark, scurrying across the corpses, snout twitching, eyes bright.

'God have mercy,' Corbett whispered, then froze at the rasp of steel from outside. He drew his own sword, carefully climbed the steps and stared at the four grotesques confronting him. Leper knights, faces and hands swathed in bandages, hoods pulled close, cloaks thrown over their shoulders to reveal the war belts strapped around their waists. One crept forward soundlessly, slinking like some ghost, his two-edged sword held before him. Corbett crouched, holding his own weapon steady in both hands. The leper lunged, sword whirling. Corbett struck back, blocking the blows whilst parrying with the tip and razor edge of his own weapon. He sensed the leper knight was skilled but weak, easy to fend off.

Corbett's opponent retreated. The clerk expected another to take his place, but the leper knight, breathing noisily, abruptly dropped his sword, and the others followed suit before crouching to sit on the ground. Corbett sheathed his own sword and watched as the knights undid the bandages across their faces to reveal the sheer horror of their disease. He fought to hide his revulsion. He could only stare pityingly at the swollen, liverish faces, deformed and corrupted, eyelids thinned, eyeballs popping, noses collapsed, lips wasted away, mouths locked in grotesque, gaping smiles.

'Sir Hugh Corbett,' their leader murmured, 'we, the living dead, greet you. Look at us, our clothes sticking to our rotting flesh. We look like corrupted corpses. We eat snouting like pigs. No woman would approach us.

No friend greet us. My name is Mausley, Sir Peter Mausley; on behalf of my companions, I salute you.'

The leper knight covered his face, indicating that the others should do the same.

'It was good to cross swords with a fellow warrior,' he declared, 'though I could not have sustained that for long.'

'The Templars are fellow warriors.'

'I don't think so, Sir Hugh. They were forced upon us, and because of them, three of our brothers, venerable, weak, sickened unto death, were executed yesterday evening, decapitated like felons, heads severed as if they were some filthy weed. Sir Hugh, you are the king's man. Ausel was appointed here because of his relationship with Gaveston. We want them gone.'

'I beg your pardon?'

'We want the Templars gone. They are not lepers. This cohort once called themselves the Brotherhood of the Wolf, but in truth, they are toothless and clawless. Because of them and their ilk, Acre fell and the cross was expelled from Outremer. Philip of France wants to arrest them. Let the devil have his way, that's what we say.' Mausley's words were greeted with grunts of approval from the others. 'They came here,' he continued, 'pretending to be lepers even though they are not. They lord it over us whilst we have to sit and watch. A murderous mayhem has engulfed our community. The deaths are because of them. Sir Hugh, have pity on us. We came here to die with honour, with peace, yet the harmony of this lazar house has been shattered by horrid slaughter and cruel stabbings. Now three of our brothers have been murdered, though by whom and why is a mystery. We understand that where Templars go vengeance follows, but poor, aged, diseased leper knights? We want the Templars gone now. The usurper Master Ausel should hand over the hospital to the care of Master Crowthorne.'

'Or?' Corbett demanded.

'There is an alternative. We will kill them all in self-defence, and why not?' Mausley spread his hands. 'What do we have to lose? What punishment could be inflicted on us? All we want is to live our lingering lives in peace.'

Corbett stared at these hapless warriors and his heart went out to them. The sea of troubles they faced had been totally ignored in the violent swirl of politics engulfing both the court and the city.

'I agree,' he replied. 'I will see to the Templars' immediate removal. But tell me, you talk of murderous mayhem. Do you know anything about it, the cause, the purpose, the perpetrator?'

Mausley turned and spoke swiftly to his companions, a muffled conversation in what Corbett recognised to be the lingua franca.

'Grandison.' He turned back to Corbett. 'Grandison was most pleasant. A true knight, courteous and gentle, though much troubled.' Mausley paused to clear mucus from his mouth. 'He would meet with us. We would talk about the fall of Acre, the savage attack by the Mamelukes on the Accursed Tower . . .'

'I know,' Corbett intervened, 'the principal defence

of Acre; when it fell, so did the city. Many people blame the Templars for the disaster.'

'Well, we would debate that. Grandison became more relaxed and apologetic. He openly admitted that he and his colleagues should not be sheltering at St Giles. Apparently they all came from the same Templar house, deep in the forest of Epping: Temple Combe Manor, a fairly wealthy establishment due to its brisk trade in timber. It has now been seized by the Crown pending the final stages of the Templars' dissolution.' Mausley paused to sip from a small waterskin kept beneath his cloak. 'Now listen to this, royal clerk. We also discussed the allegations levelled against the Templar order. At first Grandison was defensive, certainly when his companions were present or close by. One night, however, he was alone, sitting out on that bench in the great meadow nursing a jug of the richest Bordeaux. I went out to enjoy the evening breeze and joined him there. We shared the wine.' The leper shrugged. 'I carry my own cup. Grandison then made the startling confession that, in so far as he was concerned, many of the allegations levelled against the Templars were true.'

'What?'

'That's what he claimed. He called Temple Combe a den of robbers, a coven of warlocks, a brothel full of impure desires and acts. Oh, he went around armed, but it was his Templar comrades he feared and avoided.'

Corbett stared speechlessly at these muffled, hooded figures.

'And if those allegations are true,' Mausley continued, 'then why should the French want the Templars dead? Indeed,' he chuckled, 'the French envoy de Craon would pay good silver for such testimony.'

'Why indeed?' Corbett murmured almost to himself. 'Is there anything else?' he asked.

'No, my lord clerk.'

Corbett got to his feet.

'You will keep your word, Sir Hugh?'

'Rest assured the Templars will leave.'

When Corbett arrived back at the master's parlour, he found his words were prophetic. Ausel, Burghesh and Stapleton were already gone.

'Fled,' Crowthorne declared triumphantly. 'Ausel received some message; they have all left.'

'Where to?'

'God knows,' Crowthorne replied.

'Holy Trinity the Little. It's the nearest church that offers sanctuary.'

Corbett turned. Mistress Philippa, garbed in the voluminous gown of the Guild of St Martha, stood in the doorway.

'As I arrived,' she walked into the chamber, 'they were leaving, saddlebags over their shoulders, war belts strapped on. I asked them where they were going. They replied that it was no longer safe here. They felt threatened, truly frightened . . .'

'I would say terrified.' Crowthorne spoke up.

'Who was the message from?' Corbett demanded.

'Heaven knows,' Crowthorne sneered, 'but they have gone. Now we can have our hospital back, peace within our walls.'

Corbett beckoned at Ranulf to follow him out. 'They've fled now,' he declared, 'because it is still early morning: there will be no crowds and little risk of being apprehended.'

'Sir Hugh, Sir Hugh!' Corbett paused on the path leading down to the main gate of the hospital. Mistress Philippa and Agnes Sokelar came hurrying down behind them. 'Sir Hugh, please,' Philippa pleaded, 'can we come? We do have some influence with these men. We could help.' Both women paused, breathless. 'And there is one other matter,' Philippa whispered, 'that I must inform you of.'

'What?'

'Brother Jerome, de Craon's shadow. He is a Carmelite lay brother or supposed to be.'

'So he claims.'

'Well, did you know he slips out of the Merry Mercy? And on occasion he dons a different robe: the brown of the Franciscan, the grey of a Friar of the Sack or sometimes just a military cloak. He has been glimpsed doing this in the lanes and runnels around my tavern.'

Corbett closed his eyes and sighed. He had overlooked this. De Craon and his sinister shadow would play one role in the tavern publicly, even ostentatiously, but would act differently when secrecy or the darkness of the night provided the opportunity.

'I shall remember that.' He opened his eyes. 'And yes, you can accompany us, though what good any of us can do . . .'

They continued on. Corbett secretly conceded to himself that de Craon and Brother Jerome had the better of him. They were masters of the game. He was deeply mired in the morass of lies swirling about him. Sometime and somewhere in the past, a grievous sin, or sins, had been committed, a searing, hellish offence had taken root to grow and flourish; only now was it reaching bloody fruition.

Lost in his own thoughts, Corbett allowed Ranulf to lead him and the two ladies through the streets. The mist still clung tenaciously, reluctant to shift or break free and allow the first of the sunlight to bathe the houses that towered either side. Nevertheless, despite the murk, stall owners and tinkers were preparing their merchandise. Water tipplers and milkmaids were readying themselves. A dung cart had been summoned to clear the squelching, bloody mess of two mongrels and a cat squashed under the wheels of a heavy barrow carting hunks of meat from the fleshers' stalls outside Newgate. The smell was rank, and Corbett was grateful for the small perfumed pomander Mistress Philippa pushed into his hand. Somewhere a boys' choir intoned the Benedictus. On any other occasion Corbett would have paused to listen, but he pressed on.

London was coming to life: bailiffs, their sharp canes at the ready, were leading a long line of drunkards, curfew breakers and roisterers to the stocks and pillories along the waterfront or up to the great cage on the Conduit in Cheapside. Rougher justice was being meted out to a housebreaker caught red-handed by the watch. The felon had been hoisted on to a gibbet cart with its makeshift gallows, a noose placed around his neck, the box he stood on shoved away so he kicked and danced as he choked whilst a clerk read out the reason for this brutal and abrupt execution. 'The children of the dark', as Ranulf called the denizens of London's underworld, were scurrying back to their dungeons and caverns. The moonlit men, the street crawlers, squires of the sewer and other night walkers hastened to hide. The noise along the streets was beginning to rise, the clash of carts, the clatter of hooves and iron-shod wheels; windows and doors were flung open, lamps and lanterns extinguished.

Holy Trinity the Little was also preparing for the day, its main door pulled back as early risers streamed out after attending the dawn mass. Beggars and cripples, both the real and the counterfeit, had taken up position to whine and plead for alms. As he mounted the steps, Corbett sensed excitement amongst these departing churchgoers and realised that the Templars must have already reached the holy place and proclaimed their right to sanctuary. They would do so as publicly as possible to protect themselves against any law officer who then tried to curb, set aside or interfere with such an ancient and sacred right. Corbett paused on the top step as if to admire the tympanum above the main door, a striking carving in stone of Christ the Judge coming at the end of time.

'Master?' Ranulf queried.

Corbett had turned quickly, taking his companions by surprise as he stared back along the route they had taken. 'There!' he exclaimed. 'So there you are!'

'Who?' Ranulf demanded.

'Our learned colleague Brother Jerome. I am sure I glimpsed his Carmelite robe. He is on the hunt; let him run for a while.'

Corbett led his companions into the sweet-smelling nave. Candlelight glowed before various shrines. Shadows moved as pilgrims visited their favourite statues in the small enclaves dedicated to London saints such as Erconwald and Becket. Corbett walked up the nave and waited for the others hurrying behind him. He pulled back the heavy velvet curtain that hung over the doorway to the cleverly crafted rood screen. The door beyond was open, the sanctuary still bathed in candlelight after the Jesus mass. Precious vessels stood on the altar. Young boys who acted as acolytes and servers scurried about, bowing and genuflecting towards the fiery red sanctuary light that glowed beside the bejewelled pyx holding the sacred host.

The Templars were already in the refuge built into the sanctuary wall to the right of the high altar. The enclave housed two cot beds, stools and a small table. Stapleton and Burghesh squatted on the floor just inside the entrance, eating hot oatmeal from pewter bowls, their saddle bags, panniers and war belts piled behind them.

'Good morrow, Sir Hugh!'

Both Templars startled. They put their bowls down, clambering to their feet as Parson Layburn, resplendent in a red and gold chasuble, swept out of the sacristy to stand between Corbett and the two fugitives.

'Parson Layburn.' Corbett unbuckled his sword belt and laid it on the floor. Ranulf did likewise. 'Before you begin your homily, I know, recognise and accept the law of sanctuary.'

'Especially in this rather unique situation.' The parson's pompous red face suited his waspish tone. 'These are Templars, Poor Knights of Christ. They are not felons but sanctuary seekers in mortal fear for their lives. No warrant has been issued for their arrest or crime proclaimed against them.'

'They are suspects in murder,' Ranulf heatedly replied. 'Indeed, in more than one unlawful slaying.'

'We are innocent of any crime.' Burghesh walked forward to stand beside the parson. 'As our priest has said, we are in mortal fear of our lives. We have been attacked by lepers and harassed by some stealthy killer. His Grace the king promised his protection. My lord Gaveston appointed Ausel as master at St Giles to assist us . . .'

'Where is Ausel?' Ranulf demanded.

'Gone,' Burghesh murmured. 'He fled before I could ask him anything, telling us that we would meet again.'

'That is true.' Stapleton came to stand beside his comrade.

Corbett studied the worn, haunted faces of these desperate men. He suspected what they were planning.

St Giles had proven to be a death trap; now they wanted to be free of both the hospital and London.

'You will stay here the forty days and then you will be gone,' he declared. 'You will demand to be taken to a certain ship berthed at Queenhithe. Once aboard, you will flee far beyond the power of King Philip of France. And where is that? The Hanseatic ports and the Teutonic knights? Or to Sancho of Castile, who has founded the Order of Santiago to take in former Templars?' Neither man replied. 'Has Ausel gone ahead to prepare for all this?'

'Sir Hugh, you cannot infringe the Church's rite of sanctuary,' Parson Layburn declared. 'You should not even be here questioning these men. You know the law. You cannot break sanctuary.'

'I am not. Nor do I intend to.' Corbett gestured at Ranulf and then at Mistress Philippa and Agnes, who stood behind him just inside the rood screen. 'We bring you comfort,' he declared. 'I assure you, I will do all I can for you, both within and without. But I do need to question you. After all, I am a royal clerk, a king's man. I carry his seal and I am in pursuit of justice.'

The parson turned to Stapleton and Burghesh, who nodded.

'We will answer your questions, Sir Hugh but then you must be gone.'

Corbett murmured his agreement, and Mistress Philippa offered to prepare refreshments for them all. The parson readily accepted, adding that Philippa already knew where everything was. She left and the priest followed, muttering to himself. Ranulf stayed by the sanctuary steps as Corbett followed Burghesh and Stapleton across into the sanctuary enclave. He took the offered stool and sat down facing them.

'Somebody is hunting you,' he began. 'He hunts, he traps then he kills you. You recognise that?'

'Of course we do,' Stapleton snapped. 'That's why we took refuge here.'

'What do you think is the cause of all this?'

'We don't know, Sir Hugh.'

'You came from the manor of Temple Combe, deep in the forest of Epping. A day's ride away, yes?'

'We were ordered there,' Burghesh replied, 'after the fall of Acre. We left Outremer, journeyed to France then dispersed to different houses in England. Eventually we all gathered at Temple Combe, a fortified manor, comfortable enough and prosperous in its trade. Peasants, cottagers, charcoal burners and foresters also made their living around the manor. Then in December 1307, orders were issued for our arrest.' He paused as Mistress Philippa and Agnes brought across a jug of ale and a tray of blackjacks. Corbett and Ranulf refused the offer of drink, but the two Templars seized their tankards and gulped greedily.

'I've asked you this before, but do the names Sumerscale and Fallowfield mean anything to you?'

'No, Sir Hugh.'

'I think you are lying.'

'Think what you want, clerk,' Stapleton snarled. 'We are here in sanctuary, then we will be gone.'

'The others may have known something,' Burghesh added tactfully.

'And Rougehead?'

'A rogue, a former Templar,' Burghesh replied evasively. 'He floated like a piece of wreckage through our lives.'

'And Ausel? Has he gone somewhere to help you, or has he just fled?'

'We don't know.'

'You said you were in mortal fear of your lives. The sheriff and his bailiffs will demand to see good cause for that.'

'We are Templars, members of a doomed order.'

'You were that a year ago but you didn't seek sanctuary in a London church. You must prove you are now in deadly peril.'

Stapleton rubbed his mouth and glanced quickly at Burghesh, who nodded. Stapleton undid the wallet on his belt and handed over a strip of parchment. The writing was that of a scribe, clerkly and clear. The threat it contained was a variation on a quotation from the prophet Isaiah: *Vengeance is coming. Retribution hovers like a hawk. Put not your trust in princes or their promises.*

'Ausel received that, pushed under his chamber door,' Burghesh declared. 'The threat is clear enough.'

Corbett agreed and handed the strip back.

'And the source?' he asked. 'The origin?'

'It could be de Craon. Either he or some hireling.'

'Who cares,' Stapleton retorted. 'It's the threat that matters.'

Corbett sensed he would learn nothing more from these men, terrified, cowed and desperate to escape. He and Ranulf left the church and made their way back to the Merry Mercy. They passed de Craon and Brother Jerome in the entrance hall; both looked smug, as though sharing some secret joke at Corbett's expense. Corbett ignored them, asking Chanson to take care of certain items and informing Ranulf that he wished to be alone in his chamber. Once there, he kicked off his boots, undid his war belt and lay down on the mattress, gazing up at the tester that stretched between the four bedposts. He felt confused and dispirited, with little to show for his investigation. He quietly prayed that the king and Gaveston would not summon him to Sheen to render an account.

Corbett's dark mood did not lift when he later discussed matters with Ranulf, who reported how de Craon appeared very full of himself. The French envoy had apparently inveigled Mistress Philippa to prepare a splendid supper to celebrate some French saint's feast, and she would be his one and only guest.

'Minehostess is furious,' Ranulf observed. 'She cannot abide the man, but I suppose she must oblige.' He grinned. 'She is already threatening to plead her monthly courses and retire early to bed.'

Corbett heard him out and decided to visit the kitchens, where the turnspits, cooks, waferers and bakers were preparing a meal in accordance with de Craon's instructions. Brother Jerome, no less, stood in the great kitchen, lecturing the tavern retainers on what was to be done and how it was to be achieved. Corbett glimpsed their surly faces and quietly smiled. He was sure Mistress Philippa's cooks would delight in getting things wrong.

Around evening time, Corbett had two visitors. The first arrived just as the bells were tolling for Vespers. Fitzosbert the Ferret was a small man with a narrow, pointed face, eyes ever blinking, fingers fluttering, a clerk who thrived on searching the records, a task he deeply relished. Dressed in dark-brown and green fustian, he scurried in to squat on the stool Corbett offered him.

'You are most welcome,' Corbett declared. Fitzosbert squeaked his reply. Corbett had to glare at Ranulf and Chanson, who stood behind their visitor trying to muffle their laughter. Corbett hid his own amusement at Fitzosbert's earnestness, his spidery fingers coated with dried sealing wax and ink stains.

'I am very busy on your business, Sir Hugh,' Fitzosbert gushed. 'Very busy indeed. From Matins to Compline and then some. My lady wife is quite overcome by the hours I am working. Oh, thank you, sir.' He plucked the silver coins from Corbett's open hand, then glanced around. 'Perhaps I could bring my lady wife to a fine hostel such as this. The smells, Sir Hugh, the smells!'

'The names,' Corbett broke in. 'Did you search for those names?'

'I did, and I found them. Henry Poultney could be Henry Sumerscale and Matthew Aschroft could be Matthew Fallowfield. Poultney and Aschroft were both members of the community at Temple Combe. I can trace them on the list of tax returns up to the dissolution of the order in 1307, almost four years ago. After that, they disappear. There is nothing to explain what happened to them; they seem to have vanished from the face of the earth.'

'Did you learn anything about them?'

'Aschroft was a serjeant, a veteran who had served on Templar galleys in the Middle Sea. He was captured by the Saracens but escaped.'

'And Poultney?'

'Apparently a squire on his path to knighthood.'

'So,' Corbett declared, 'Aschroft may have passed his fortieth summer. And Poultney?'

'At the time he disappeared, about sixteen summers old. Apparently he entered Temple Combe as a young page. He was placed there by the good sisters of St Francis, the Minoresses; they have an orphanage close to the Tower, where they take in abandoned children, waifs and unwanted babies.' Fitzosbert smiled in a display of cracked yellow teeth. 'Sir Hugh, I anticipated you. I approached the good sisters, but they could tell me nothing. They are vowed to secrecy. Once a child leaves their care and is placed somewhere else, all records, letters, indentures and memoranda are—'

'Totally destroyed,' Corbett intervened. 'Yes, my friend, I have heard of that, whilst Templar records would only tell us what happened from the time that young man joined them, and those, I suppose, will be scarce enough.'

'Very little, Sir Hugh,' came the mournful reply.

'Ah well.' Corbett waved at the door. 'If you could wait a while . . .'

Chanson ushered the lugubrious clerk out into the taproom, assuring him he could drink the finest London ale. Corbett stared at Ranulf and shook his head.

'Two men,' he sighed, 'who appear to be of little importance when they were alive. However, once dead, judicially murdered, the most hellish vengeance is unleashed.'

'Master, what is the logic of your argument?'

'A paradox, Ranulf, a contradiction. Two vulnerable men with no protection or defence whilst alive, but once they are murdered – and that is what happened to them – those responsible, Rougehead and his coven, are cruelly destroyed.'

'Could it be the work of de Craon?' Ranulf said. 'Were Sumerscale and Fallowfield, or Poultney and Aschroft, agents of the French Crown? Consequently, was the destruction of Rougehead and his coven, as well as the murders amongst Templars, de Craon's revenge? Moreover, if de Craon is behind the murders at St Giles, he is also slaughtering men who might threaten or weaken his master's attack on the Templar order.'

'Possible, Ranulf; that too has a logic all of its own. Were Sumerscale and Fallowfield – and we will call them that for clarity's sake: after all, those were the names they lived under, the names they died with – well, were they killed because they were Philip's henchmen? Is that why we know so little about them? De Craon certainly had the means to unleash a ferocious response against Rougehead's coven, followed by the total destruction of the Salamander.' Corbett paused. 'Speculation, speculation, Ranulf, and once we begin to develop possibilities, we must consider all that is possible.'

'Such as?'

'What if there is another party, a group or individual, hiding deep in the shadows who regarded Sumerscale and Fallowfield as kin, allies or close comrades? Who were not swift enough to save their friends from the gallows but are now committed to vengeance. Yet if that is the case, why wait three years? Rougehead and his coven were slain within three months of Sumerscale and Fallowfield being hanged. So perhaps the murder of these Templars has nothing to do with those deaths. Perhaps the simplest and easiest solution is the most logical. Forget Sumerscale and Fallowfield; they are another mystery. Philip and de Craon are slaughtering the Templars at St Giles because they regard them as a threat. Yet how does Slingsby's murder fit in with all this?'

'Master,' Ranulf broke in, 'Sumerscale and Fallowfield, whatever their true names, were tried by military tribunal on board *The Candle-Bright*. Naseby discussed their deaths with you, and his feelings of guilt.'

'Yes he did, Ranulf. And, to anticipate your next question which I have answered before: according to Naseby there was no reference during the trial to the accused recognising Rougehead. If they had recognised him from a former life, they would surely have used it in their defence and depicted him as a rogue, a malicious liar or their lifetime enemy, yet Rougehead had also been a Templar.'

'Perhaps Sumerscale and Fallowfield did not want to reveal their true identities. Perhaps they thought it would make matters worse? But that takes us round and round in circles. At the end of the day, Sir Hugh, I truly believe the two men did not know or recognise their accuser. Now I admit that's strange, both the accuser and the accused being members of the same order. Perhaps the solution is that Rougehead had nothing to do with the English Templars.' Ranulf smiled and shook his head. 'Yet if that's the case, what was he doing in England roistering in a tavern like the Salamander?'

Ranulf paused as Chanson re-entered the room.

'Master, our noble Ferret is supping ale as if his very life depends on it. You have another visitor, whom I have sat at the same table as the Ferret: the Magister Viae.'

Once summoned, the Magister swept into the chamber as if he was a legate from the Pope, capuchon pulled dramatically over his head, his heavy ermine-lined cloak floating about him, exuding quite a delicious fragrance. He unstrapped his war belt, took off his cloak and flung them both over the table. He clasped Corbett's hand, bowed to Ranulf and sat down on a chair.

'Funny little man.' The Magister gestured towards the door.

'You mean Chanson?' Ranulf replied impishly.

'No, that moving blob of ink Fitzosbert. Interesting character. I would love to secure his services on that task you assigned me, Sir Hugh.'

'You are making progress?'

'Slowly, but bear with me. Fitzosbert would be of great assistance. I need to study the tax returns from the Essex shoreline, as well as any reports from the seneschals of custom.'

Corbett agreed, mystified by what path the Magister might be pursuing.

'You also entrusted me with another task,' the Magister continued. 'A close scrutiny of this tavern, who visits and who leaves. Well, Mistress Philippa goes into the city, but that is of little consequence. I know she is very busy at the behest of our noble French envoy . . .'

'And him?'

'Oh, Sir Hugh, innocence itself. Monseigneur leaves the Merry Mercy. He takes a barge along to Westminster, where he meets with whom he is supposed to and then returns to this tavern to rest, eat and drink.'

'He never goes out for further entertainment and refreshment?'

'Never.'

'He never leaves to meet a lady, to keep an assignation? Monseigneur de Craon has needs like other men?'

'I doubt that, Sir Hugh. I tell you, he doesn't leave. His companion the Carmelite Brother Jerome does, however, and sometimes changes into different robes.'

'So I have heard.'

The Magister looked a little crestfallen. Corbett leaned over and squeezed his hand.

'Where does the Carmelite go to? What does he do?'

'The same place as Master Sokelar the harbour master, a rather comfortable brothel called the Queen of the Night, where all kinds of delicacies, both male and female – and everything else in between – are served up to the discerning customers.'

'Both Sokelar and Brother Jerome are visitors?'

'Oh yes, and from my sources inside that august establishment, they seem friendly enough to each other, though there is no crime in that.'

'I wonder . . .'

'Whether there is a crime, Master Ranulf?'

'No, whether we are supposed to think there is. Wouldn't you agree, Sir Hugh?' Ranulf turned to Corbett. 'De Craon and his sinister dark shadow know they are being watched. They love to create confusion and illusion, dangle Sokelar as a possible suspect to distract us from the truth.'

'A strong possibility,' Corbett replied absent-mindedly, though in fact he was more intrigued by de Craon's almost hermit-like existence. According to Corbett's spy Tallefert, de Craon loved the ladies of the night and patronised them generously in Paris. Corbett glanced down at the ground. He had still not heard from Tallefert or Pietal. Nor had he been visited by Rochfort with any news. He closed his eyes briefly in desperation.

'Anything else?' Ranulf asked.

'No,' replied the Magister.

Corbett raised his head. 'And *The Black Hogge*?'

The Magister sighed and tapped the side of his fleshy nose. 'Sir Hugh, if I can borrow the services of your colleague Fitzosbert and be given the right to work amongst the chancery records, I believe I can make some progress.'

Corbett agreed and the Magister left. Ranulf said he would walk around the tavern, and Corbett decided he would accompany him. They visited the kitchens, both the great and the petty, to find ovens, stoves and spits all busy, the air fragranced with delicious odours. A red-faced Philippa assisted by an equally perspiring Agnes, together with the tavern cooks, boilers, bakers, waferers and spit boys, were all intent on preparing de Craon's feast, which included salmon, currant dumplings, porpoise pudding, venison cooked in pastry, veal custard pie, baked pheasants and other delicacies. Corbett pushed his way through the busy household to greet Mistress Philippa, who beneath her thick white apron had donned a gown of dark-red murrey fringed with gold.

'Mistress? All these people are of your household? You know their names?'

'Of course.'

'Do the names Sumerscale and Fallowfield mean anything to you?'

'Sir Hugh, remember you asked me this before? The answer is no.'

'Or Poultney and Aschroft?'

She smiled, shaking her head. 'Common enough names, my lord clerk, so what are they to me?'

Corbett walked on. He glimpsed Peterkin in the buttery, called the boy over and slipped a coin into his greasy hand.

'Peterkin, when *The Candle-Bright* berthed at Queenhithe and the crew came ashore, those two sailors who were hanged, do you know where they stayed? I gather there are hospices and havens for sailors along the riverside, fairly tawdry places, not too clean, but somewhere to sleep. Did they ever mention where they rested?'

The boy pulled a face and shook his head. 'I can't say, Sir Hugh, but they always returned on board looking fresh, their clothes clean, changed, as if they had stayed with a family, been comfortable, not like me and others, who were lucky if we could rent an alehouse doorway.' He looked longingly into the kitchen. 'That is all I can say, Sir Hugh.'

The lad scampered off. Corbett heard de Craon's voice braying like a donkey, praising the delicious odours permeating the tavern. The bells ringing for Vespers carried faintly. Corbett plucked at Ranulf's sleeve.

'My friend, God willing, I will eat tomorrow. De Craon is about, so it's time I went.'

Ranulf muttered about getting something to eat and left for the taproom. Corbett finished his walk around the tavern, quietly marvelling at the business acumen of his former comrade, Raoul Henman, who had arrived in London as a simple clerk, then left the chancery to build up and develop this splendid inn. The sound of a viol echoed across the small courtyard where Corbett was standing looking up at the stars.

'De Craon certainly loves his festivities,' he murmured to himself. He went inside and glanced at the hour candle on its heavy brass spigot, the flame dancing just over the eighth red circle. 'Time to adjourn.'

Corbett was roused by Ranulf shouting and pounding on the chamber door.

'Sir Hugh, master!'

He opened the door.

'Holy Trinity the Little,' Ranulf gasped, struggling into his leather jerkin. 'Burghesh and Stapleton have been murdered.'

'Sweet God!' Corbett exclaimed. 'What hour is it?'

'About the fifth. Master, you must come.'

They reached Holy Trinity a short while later. Sconce torches spluttered against the darkness, lanternhorns glowed through the murk. The main door to the church was locked. Corbett, watching his step as he crossed the tangled gorse and bracken, followed the coffin path to the side entrance through the sacristy. Parson Layburn, bleary-eyed and unshaven, stood in the doorway, around him gathered members of his parish council. The clerk, a scrawny-haired beanpole of a man who found it difficult to keep still, explained how they had arrived at the church to prepare the nave for the feast of Trinity Sunday at the end of the week. They had wanted to enter the church before the dawn mass began. The clerk stamped his feet and wiped his mouth on the back of his hand. Corbett could smell the tang of fear from these men, as well as the pervasive smell of vomit. The clerk gulped and would have continued in his chatter. Corbett held a hand up.

'I am Sir Hugh Corbett, Keeper of the Secret Seal, the king's own officer. What has happened here?'

'Yes, yes,' the clerk spluttered, 'Parson Layburn told us about you.'

'What has happened?' Ranulf demanded. 'Show us now.' He snapped his fingers and pointed at the entrance.

Preceded by torchbearers, Corbett entered the sacristy. He paused to quickly scrutinise the door, which had been forced, the lock ruptured, and now hung askew. The sacristy itself was undisturbed, but the door to the sanctuary had been similarly rent and swung all awry from its top leather hinge. The sanctuary looked like a battlefield, ominous and macabre. No furniture had been disturbed. Nothing overturned or smashed. The red sanctuary light still glowed as a telling witness to the divine presence, though looking round, Corbett felt the angels of heaven must weep at the sight of such bloodshed.

Burghesh and Stapleton, cloaked and booted, their war belts close by, lay sprawled on the sanctuary floor, pools of blood from the stab wounds to their hearts glistening around them. Corbett leaned down and studied the gashes: deep, savage cuts like those inflicted by a razor-sharp two-handed sword.

'Sweet heaven,' he whispered, 'what is this?'

'Lord have mercy! In God's name . . .'

Corbett turned. Mistress Philippa, Sokelar the harbour master and his daughter Agnes stood in the sacristy doorway. The tavern mistress and her companions walked slowly over.

'We heard the clamour,' she explained, 'the alarm being raised. I cannot believe this. Sir Hugh, what can I do?'

Parson Layburn stood shaking, a man overwhelmed by fear.

'Mistress, if you could . . .' Corbett gestured at the priest. Philippa nodded and took Parson Layburn over to the other side of the sanctuary as Corbett quickly scrutinised the scene. The two corpses sprawled dead-eyed, their saddlebags fully strapped as if ready to leave. Everything else was in order. Corbett and Ranulf picked up the water and wine jugs, sniffed their contents.

'Mistress Philippa?' Corbett called. She came over and Corbett handed her the jugs. 'Take these back to the Merry Mercy. Place them over some bait for rodents; see if there is anything untoward.'

He walked across to the offertory table, but the platter was empty except for a few crumbs of gristled meat. He poked these with his finger, then sat down on a stool in the sanctuary enclave, watching the others move around. They all stayed as far away as possible from the two corpses, which lay as if floating in blood. Corbett beckoned to Ranulf and gestured at the grue-some scene.

'They were dressed as if waiting to leave, so who

were they waiting for? Come, Ranulf, let's study this murderous mystery play.'

Corbett led his companion across to the first door. There were no bolts, but the lock was strong and of good quality, badly ruptured when the door was forced. Corbett pointed to the huge log lying to one side in the shadows.

'This murderous masque is both short and brutal,' he murmured. 'The killer locked the sanctuary door behind him; the parish council used that log as a battering ram. I suppose the outer door is no different.'

They walked down to the door leading from the sacristy into the cemetery beyond. Its wood was of good quality, strongly reinforced with iron bands, the hinges of the thickest and toughest leather, the ruptured lock very similar to that on the sacristy door. Corbett asked Ranulf to bring the parish council into the sacristy. The scrawny clerk led them in even as he tried to brush vomit stains from his gown, mumbling his apologies.

'No need, sir.' Corbett patted him reassuringly on the shoulder.

'I am no soldier, Sir Hugh.'

'And I am, my friend,' Corbett replied. 'I have seen many a corpse on the battlefield, but the horror in that sanctuary would turn the most hardened of stomachs. So tell us, what happened?'

The clerk, now consoled, pithily described how they'd entered the main door of the church but found the door through the rood screen into the sanctuary bolted from the inside.

'We knocked and called,' he explained. 'We knew two Templars had taken sanctuary within. When there was no response, we became truly alarmed. We could not force the rood screen door: it's sacred and very costly to repair . . .'

'So you came round to the sacristy?'

'Yes, we knocked, shouted and yelled so loudly that Parson Layburn came out of the priest's house to discover what was happening.' The clerk glanced sheepishly at his colleagues. A few coughed, others shuffled their feet and looked away. 'Parson Layburn was very tired: he had been busy on parish business. Still,' the clerk continued briskly, 'he instructed us to force both doors, and so we did, to expose the abomination within.'

'And they were locked from inside?'

'Aye, and all the bolts on the rood screen had been tightly clasped.'

'And the keys to the doors that were forced?'

The clerk pulled a face and shook his head.

Corbett turned to Ranulf. 'Search the corpses.'

Ranulf did so whilst Corbett thanked the parish clerk and his companions, adding that they needed to visit the Bishop of London's archdeacon as a matter of urgency. 'Blood has been shed in the most sacred part of your church,' he explained. 'It is now polluted. Mass cannot be celebrated until it is reconsecrated. You understand?'

'Of course.'

'Master,' Ranulf came back shaking his head, 'no sign of the keys on either corpse or elsewhere in the sanctuary.'

'Very well,' Corbett replied. 'It's time we questioned the priest.'

Parson Layburn had, under the tender solicitations of Mistress Philippa and Agnes, as well as the strength from a deep goblet of Bordeaux, regained his composure if not his pomposity. He sat on a sanctuary stool clutching the wine cup. Corbett crouched down to question him.

'Parson Layburn, who had the keys to the sacristy door and that leading into the sanctuary?'

'Oh, they had.' The priest pointed across at the two corpses before taking another gulp of wine. 'They locked themselves in and would only open to me or someone they knew and trusted.' He shrugged. 'That's what sanctuary men do. They won't be the first, nor the last.'

'Did you hear anything untoward, Parson Layburn? After all, the priest's house is not far from the entrance to the sacristy.'

'I was absent,' the priest mumbled, head down, refusing to meet Corbett's eye. 'I was visiting parishioners.'

Corbett glanced up at Mistress Philippa, who smiled and raised her eyes heavenwards. 'So you never heard or saw anything amiss?'

'Nothing.'

'Mistress Philippa,' Corbett glanced up again, 'I suggest you have the parish council remove both corpses to the church's death house, or even back to St Giles . . .'

'Sir Hugh, Sir Hugh!' Corbett turned as the parish clerk came hurrying up the sanctuary steps. 'The Sisters of the Street are here. They want to speak to the king's man.' He pointed at the open rood screen door. 'They are waiting near the baptismal font.'

'Ranulf,' Corbett ordered, 'go through Stapleton's and Burghesh's possessions to see if there is anything of interest. As for you, sir,' Corbett gestured at the parish clerk, 'it might be best if you looked after your priest and saw to the removal of those corpses.'

Corbett went down the sanctuary steps and out into the cold, murky nave. Thankfully someone had lit the candle spigots fixed to the drum-like pillars, and these afforded some meagre light. Corbett found the four sisters huddled beneath a wall painting of St Christopher, in which the holy man was fighting a horde of hellish imps, nightmare creatures with monkey faces and bat-like wings. The juddering lights of the candles against this macabre fresco made the four women clustering so close even more sinister. Garbed in a collection of foul-smelling rags, white hair falling down either side of bony faces, the four ancients looked like sisters from the same womb. They were certainly sharp enough, and confident in themselves.

'You're the king's man.' Their leader poked a bony finger at Corbett. 'You're snooping all over the ward. Everyone knows you are here, isn't that right, sisters? King's men! But what are you doing about *The Black Hogge* or that Frenchman, full of mischief he is! You didn't save poor old Rohesia, did you? You can't bring her back or even catch the malignant sinner who murdered her. We watch the streets, we do. We see them come and go.'

Corbett squatted down and opened his belt purse. He plucked out a silver coin, which he spun, caught and placed on the paving stone beside him. 'That's for you and your good sisters when we are done. Now tell me, do you remember the funeral of the two sailors from *The Candle-Bright*?'

'Yes,' they replied together, heads moving in unison.

'You see everything,' Corbett flattered. 'Particularly Rohesia. She had a glimpse of those two corpses. She told Parson Layburn that she had seen both men before. Did she ever remark on that to you?'

'No,' they chorused.

'Rohesia,' their leader leaned forward, red-rimmed eyes all bright, 'did see things, yes.' She turned to get the approval of her companions. 'She did tell us how she saw both men leaving a house in Cheapside.'

'Which house, which street?'

'King's man, I don't know.' She began to hum beneath her breath, the refrain taken up by her sisters, swaying backwards and forwards in macabre harmony.

'And tonight,' Corbett asserted himself, 'what did you see?'

'We gathered at Glistening Corner: it's called that because of the dirty lard thrown on to a lay stall there, taken from a nearby flesher's yard.' The leader held up a hand to still her companions' eerie liturgy. 'Isn't that right, sisters?'

'Oh yes,' they sang back.

'And what did you see?' Corbett insisted. 'Mother, time is passing. I hunt a murderer.'

'We saw them. They swirled past us,' the old woman gabbled. 'We saw them long after the Vespers bell; the curfew lights were glowing in the steeple.'

'Them?'

'Two men!'

'Are you sure?'

'They were garbed in cordovan boots and woollen cloaks, devils incarnate. They slipped through the lych-gate, hurrying from the sacristy, darker shadows than the rest, then they were gone.'

Realising he would get no further sense out of them, Corbett made his farewells, rose and walked back up to the rood screen, where Ranulf was waiting.

'Nothing, Sir Hugh, nothing in their saddlebags.'

'Then let's return to our chambers.'

PART SIX

'He resisted loyal service and did not keep his fealty with the King of England.'
  The Monk of Malmesbury, *Life of Edward II*

They left the church, crossed the cemetery and went out through the lychgate. The streets were becoming busy: bells tolled, carts rattled, the rumble of wheelbarrows a constant noise. The morning mist was lifting and the citizens of the ward were eager to begin another day's trading. Stalls, booths and display tables were being busily prepared by heavy-eyed apprentices. The owners of ale houses, cook shops and roasting places were firing stoves, ovens and braziers. The air was polluted by the smell of night soil freshly deposited, though the sweet perfume of freshly baked bread also drifted out to tease the nostrils. Debtors from a nearby compter, chained and manacled, had been released with dish, cup and bowl to beg for food, drink and alms.

Corbett turned swiftly at a corner and glimpsed someone he had noticed waiting for them outside the lychgate. He recognised the man's Lincoln-green jerkin, like that of a royal forester, the close-cropped head of a soldier. The Wolfman, that hunter of outlaws and malefactors, was pretending to be busy at a leather stall. He then turned away, disappearing up an alleyway. Corbett smiled. Sooner or later, he concluded, the Wolfman would leave the undergrowth and make himself known. He wondered what business that eerie individual was pursuing.

'Is all well, master?'

'No it isn't.' Corbett smiled. 'But let's pray that it ends so.'

They reached the Merry Mercy. Once closeted in its chamber, Corbett asked Ranulf to prepare parchment and pens as he filled two blackjacks from an ale jug. He thrust one of these into Ranulf's hand and quickly toasted him. Once his companion was ready, Corbett began to pace up and down the chamber.

'Let us gather our thoughts, Ranulf. First the Templars. They are now a disgraced, proscribed and broken order. In France they are being harassed even unto death. Here in this kingdom they have been given some leeway. A number of Templars from their house at Temple Combe in Essex took shelter in that lazar hospital at St Giles. One of them, Reginald Ausel, being a distant kinsman of Lord Gaveston, is appointed as temporary master. Their presence at the hospital was fiercely resented by other inmates. Individuals such as Crowthorne and Sokelar also despise the Templars. They regard them as abject failures responsible for the fall of Acre and the expulsion of all Christian armies from Outremer.

'Murders occur in the lazar hospital. Templars are slaughtered in the most macabre and mysterious circumstances. Boveney is killed in an enclave outside the church. Grandison on a bench in a lonely meadow at the dead of night. Datchet in his chamber. All three had their weapons close by. All three offered no resistance to their slayer. There is not a shred of evidence that they defended themselves. Meanwhile, the other inmates of the lazar hospital become more and more resentful, probably agitated by Crowthorne, who wants the mastership for himself. Such resentment spills into violence after the brutal murder of three leper knights, decapitated like criminals. To all intents and purposes there is neither rhyme nor reason for these deaths. The lepers have had enough. They rise in revolt, terrifying their unwanted guests. Is that what the killer intended? That the Templars would be driven out and become even more vulnerable? In which case he certainly succeeded.

'Ausel, Burghesh and Stapleton flee. They cannot tolerate the rising violence, the mysterious assassin who hunts them, the deep hostility of the lepers and, of course, that warning left about vengeance coming. Ausel disappears. Where has he gone? Temple Combe? Or is he trying to secure safe passage for himself and his companions to Scotland? They have mentioned the protection the Bruce has offered to other members of their order. Ausel is one mystery; the other is Burghesh and Stapleton. Fugitives, sanctuary men sheltering in a London church.' Corbett tapped his boot against the turkey rug. 'Nevertheless, Ranulf, they were still warriors, experienced soldiers, desperate and dangerous with their weapons close by. They lock themselves in sanctuary and think they are safe.'

'Are you sure about that, master, that they had the keys?' Ranulf put the quill pen down and seized another, closely inspecting its sharpened point before dipping it into the ink horn.

'Oh yes, I am sure. Parson Layburn would have to give them the keys. They ate and drank and would need to go out to relieve themselves. Nevertheless, apart from that, they would keep themselves safe. They would bolt the rood screen as well as locking those two doors, one leading to the sacristy and the other going into the sanctuary. I believe that this is what happened. Night falls. Parson Layburn goes out on his business, whatever that is. Our two Templar fugitives prepare to leave. Saddlebags were packed and the men were cloaked and booted. I suspect they were expecting a visitor: someone who might help them, provide money, horses, food and safe passage elsewhere.'

'Ausel?'

'Perhaps. Either he or some other killer was allowed through those doors. In a word, their expected saviour proved to be their executioner.'

'Without any resistance or sign of a struggle?'

'Again, Ranulf, I concede that's a mystery, but the assassin must be someone close to them, trusted by those men. So it must have been Ausel. Somehow he killed them without any sign of struggle, then left locking both doors behind him and taking the keys.'

'Why that?' Ranulf asked. 'After all, the deed is

done; what does it matter whether the keys are taken or left?'

'I agree.' Corbett paused in his pacing. 'Why take the keys? Perhaps the answer is obvious: the assassin wanted to create the longest possible delay before the corpses were discovered. If Parson Layburn returned and decided to check on his uninvited guests, he would find the door locked and, exhausted after his work and perhaps the worse for drink, decide to leave matters be. Then of course there are the four old ladies.'

'Those ancient crones?'

'Yes, the Sisters of the Street. I am sure they scamper around looking for any profit. They would certainly try doors and so discover the crime, or . . .'

'Or what, master?'

'Was the killer someone the two men expected? If not, did the assassin know they were waiting for someone else and so locked both doors to impede that person? Let us say, for sake of argument, they were expecting Ausel but someone else arrived who knew them and was allowed in? The assassin strikes, then flees but locks the doors so Ausel will find it impossible to enter.'

'So who is the killer?' Ranulf asked. 'I cannot imagine Mistress Philippa being a sword carrier or having the strength or skill to kill two knights, and, even if she did, what motive would she have? Of course there is Sokelar the harbour master, Crowthorne at St Giles, and we must not forget Parson Layburn.'

'The parson?'

'Perhaps he is connected to this mystery but as yet we are unaware of it.' Ranulf paused. 'Or perhaps it is someone we have not encountered. The Wolfman we glimpsed earlier?'

'The Wolfman a hired killer?' Corbett shook his head. 'A killer, yes, but one who acts within the law, however barbaric that may be.'

'In which case, Monseigneur de Craon, though he is too much of a fox and a coward to prowl the streets of London.'

'Brother Jerome is another matter though, eh, Ranulf? A true blood-drinker. But how could he win the confidence of the Templars to allow him into a locked sanctuary, unless of course he and de Craon are playing some intricately byzantine game and suborned the likes of Ausel. Jerome is a swift, sure and deadly assassin. Ausel could have allowed him into the hospital at St Giles and the sanctuary of Holy Trinity the Little. Now that could be a possibility: the Sisters of the Street claim they glimpsed two men, cloaked and cowled, leaving the church. I have studied Ausel: he is a weak man, vicious, but not a warrior, man against man. Did he take a killer with him? Brother Jerome? Yet why should Ausel be suborned by Philip's man?'

'Sweet heaven, master,' Ranulf breathed. 'It's like being lost in a maze. We follow tangled paths that twist away, and the more we move, the further we are from the truth.' He paused. 'Sir Hugh, any news out of Paris?'

'Silence, and that worries me deeply. Tallefert always promised that if he was discovered, he would simply flee in the clothes he was wearing and with whatever he was carrying. He would go either to Bordeaux or Boulogne. The same is true of our messenger Pietal. I impressed upon them never to delay, never tarry, never think that they could be overlooked, but to flee and to get word to me as soon as possible. So far nothing. No sound, no word, no voice is heard,' Corbett added despairingly.

'Is there anybody else?' Ranulf asked. 'Anyone we can use in Paris?'

'There's the Deacon. You met him on one occasion, the lifelong scholar with his holier-than-thou expression.'

Ranulf smiled. 'A truly consummate actor, a mummer for any masque.'

'Very true.' Corbett scratched the side of his face, lost in thought. 'You see, the Deacon is different from Tallefert. He's a magpie looking for the odd glinting item, a snapper-up of trifles. He listens to the chatter and the gossip of the halls, the taverns and the eating houses of Paris. He rubs shoulders with clerks from the Louvre, men-at-arms from the Hôtel de Ville. Now the Deacon has a routine. About once a month he will visit Tallefert. He won't knock on the door; he simply gets himself in, his one task to ensure all is well. I am going to wait for his next report; that's all we can do. Meanwhile,' he sighed, 'we still have *The Black Hogge*. So far we have heard nothing about any new attacks. If only . . .'

He paused at a knock on the door, and Chanson came in.

'Sir Hugh, you have a visitor. He came into the

taproom, ordered a wine and sat on his own for a while. When I left, he followed me to the stables. He sends his regards, apologises for both following you and troubling you, but he needs to speak to you about Reginald Ausel.'

A short while later, Chanson and the Wolfman slipped into Corbett's chamber. The clerk of the stables stayed near the door as Corbett and Ranulf clasped hands with their unexpected guest, who then sat down on the proffered stool, placing his heavy war belt on the floor beside him and the goblet he carried on the table.

'Ranulf,' began Corbett, 'we are in the presence of the most skilled and dangerous hunter of men. If a price is placed on your head and the Wolfman decides to collect it, not even the king himself will save you. He has hunted malefactors the length and breadth of this kingdom and beyond.'

'Though he is not very good at following people in the streets,' Ranulf remarked. 'We saw him.'

'No, no,' Corbett retorted, 'we were meant to see him. You do that, do you not, Wolfman? You like to tell your quarry you are pursuing them?'

'All those things done in the dark,' the Wolfman replied lugubriously, 'will one day be seen in the light. What is whispered in chambers will be shouted from the rooftops. I am not a child of the light, Master Ranulf, but I certainly work for their cause. When a wolf hunts, he lets his quarry know. The more they run, the more tired and desperate they become.'

Ranulf stared at the grizzled, swarthy face of the

hunter. He was lean and sinewy, his grey hair cropped very close to his head, light-blue eyes ever watchful. He was smoothly shaven and Ranulf noticed how his fingers were tapered, clean and pared. He was dressed in earth-brown hose and Lincoln-green jerkin, very similar to a royal verderer, with good leather boots on his feet. He wore a woman's ring on the little finger of his right hand and a matching necklace around his throat.

'My late beloved wife's,' the Wolfman explained, following Ranulf's stare. 'Gone to God these last fifteen years. Murdered, Master Ranulf, raped by wolfsheads. I was absent being the king's forester in Sherwood. We had a comfortable lodge, with a stable yard and a garden. Matilda divided that up: herb beds for the kitchen and a spice plot. She also loved to grow wild roses. She was the gentlest of people, my little mouse. Six wolfsheads called by. I found her naked corpse some distance from the lodge. We were expecting our first child. Anyway, I buried her in St Swithin's graveyard, then took her necklace and ring and hunted her killers down.'

'And?'

'I kept them in a cage until all six were caught, deep in the forest where it was dark even during the brightest sunlight. I kept them there, then I set fire to the cage and watched them die. The Lord delivered them into my hands. The Strong One of Jacob heard my plea. I pulled them up root and stalk. I told all six, like I tell all my quarry, to convert, to turn back to the Lord and confess. How they must never put their trust in the swift and the strong. Those who cry out to the Lord may sow in tears but they will sing when they reap.'

'An interesting ballad worthy of any minstrel.'

'I am God's own minstrel, Master Ranulf. I am the Lord's bowman. I have been put on this earth to be God's retribution, the humble servant of he who is the Alpha and Omega of all things.'

'And why do you tell us this?'

'Because,' the Wolfman gestured at both Corbett and Ranulf, 'the good Lord and my angel guardian have ushered me into the presence of other hunters. In this matter you are my brothers. We avenge one of the seven deadly sins, the murder of innocents who shriek to heaven for justice. The Lord has no hands on earth except ours to deliver justice for such crimes.'

'And so,' Ranulf jibed, 'what do you want to say to us, your long-lost kin?'

'Your clerk of the stables must have told you. We pursue the same quarry: Reginald Ausel.'

'Why?' Corbett demanded.

'I suspect – indeed, I believe as the Lord has directed me – that Reginald Ausel, former Templar, is also the abuser and killer of innocent young people.'

'Nonsense,' Ranulf snapped. 'For all his faults, Ausel is a Templar, a warrior, a swordsman . . .'

The clerk's voice faltered as Corbett nudged him with the toe of his boot.

'Believe me,' the Wolfman placed a hand on the necklace around his throat, 'I swear that I speak the truth.'

'You are Pembroke's man – Aymer de Valence, Earl

of Pembroke, one of the great barons who oppose the king and Lord Gaveston. Ausel is a distant kinsman of the king's favourite. When you strike at him, you also strike at Gaveston.'

'Sir Hugh, I truly don't care if Ausel is the king's brother. Yes, I am Pembroke's man, though in this matter I work for Sir John Howard.'

'Ah.' Corbett sat back in his chair.

'Master?'

'Howard,' Corbett replied, 'a very ambitious knight from a very ambitious family who own manors and meadows, ploughlands and cornfields, towns, hamlets and villages throughout Norfolk and Essex. Howard is not yet an earl, but he and his powerful kin nurse dreams of supping and dining with the greatest in the land.'

'Be that as it may,' the Wolfman continued, 'it is the Lord who scrutinises the heart; it is he who guides the will, as he did with me. I have studied Reginald Ausel. He returned to this kingdom eighteen years ago, after the fall of Acre. Like many of his order, he moved around between various preceptories. Most of these, as with many Templar holdings, were out in the wild countryside. Temple Combe in Essex is one such. Now, whilst Ausel was at these different preceptories, horrid murders occurred, young men and women sexually abused before having their throats slit. Of course,' the Wolfman added cynically, 'who cares about some peasant? I suspect Ausel would have acquired a taste for such abominations when he served in Outremer. I have talked to men who fought there. Saracen children and their young womenfolk were regarded by some of our so-called warriors as natural prey. They could ravish, rape and kill and never be brought to justice.'

'How old were these victims?'

'Between seven and seventeen summers.'

'You were asking who cares?'

'Yes, Sir Hugh, and who does? Ausel would have escaped justice if hadn't been for one murder he committed in Essex.' The Wolfman sipped at his goblet. 'Ausel fled to St Giles lazar hospital when the Templar order in this kingdom eventually collapsed. Once the Templars had left Temple Combe, rumours surfaced, tavern tattle . . .'

'Which was?'

'Well, the Templars leave and the sinful slayings cease. Has the good Lord sent us a sign? people asked. Now one of the victims murdered in Essex was a very comely blonde-haired wench, the daughter of a royal forester, a keeper of one of Howard's lodges deep in the forest of Epping. She had caught the eye of Sir John; he regarded her as he would some beautiful rose growing to please him.' The Wolfman sighed deeply. 'Young, tender and very beautiful. Apparently the assault on her and the way she died was particularly horrific. Howard wanted both revenge and justice, so he hired me. Pembroke agreed. I prayed and fasted first, as I always do. You have heard of the Triduum?' The Wolfman slurped from the goblet.

'The three-day fast?' Ranulf replied.

'Yes, I always do that for the Lord before I begin my hunt. I speak the truth. I have travelled the length and breadth of this kingdom. I have visited all the Templar houses where Ausel resided. In virtually every locality where he served, I discovered that young people had been brutally assaulted and killed.'

'You are sure it was Ausel?'

'Sir Hugh, like you, I have studied logic in the schools. Remember, if there is only one probability, then it is most probable that it is also the truth. Ausel was the only probability: he served in all the localities where these blasphemies occurred. I believe him to be a ferocious killer, an assassin, a Herod who slays the innocent for his own filthy pleasures.'

Corbett shook his head, got to his feet and walked to stare out of the window at the rose garden.

'I know what you are thinking, Sir Hugh.'

Corbett turned. 'Do you really?'

'That a man like Ausel, a Templar knight, vowed to poverty and chastity, could not be guilty of such heinous crimes. A man dedicated to good in the eyes of God and man.' The Wolfman sipped from his goblet. 'Sir Hugh, I have hunted his like before. Men who love the sheer violence and brutality of attacking and ravishing the young and the innocent. As I have said, in Outremer such demons could do what they liked amongst the poor, and often did. This type of killer suffers from a truly dangerous leprosy of the soul. To all intents and purposes they appear upright and honourable; they can be a priest, a monk, a friar, a merchant, a knight,' he smiled, 'even a royal clerk. They can be openly virtuous except when the malignancy within them forces them to go on the hunt. I have studied them over the years: the only cure for such a disease is death.'

'So what will you do when you find Ausel?'

'I have been waiting for my opportunity,' the Wolfman replied. 'Ausel took shelter in that lazar hospital for years; he was in sanctuary, protected by the king. I now understand that he and two others have fled that place. The other two, or so I am given to believe, have been murdered, possibly by Ausel himself.'

'Why do you say that?'

'Perhaps they either learnt of or suspected Ausel's deadly secret sin. I don't know.'

'What you say is possible,' Corbett murmured. 'Where do you think Ausel will go next?'

'Temple Combe, that deserted, lonely manor deep in Epping Forest.'

'Why there?'

The Wolfman smiled to himself. 'Sir Hugh, when the royal treasure was stolen from the abbey crypt, how much of it was never recovered?'

'Why?'

'Please, Sir Hugh, how much?'

Corbett narrowed his eyes as he recalled lists and indentures. 'I would say,' he mused, 'a good third at least. Many of the smaller items: coins, miniature gold bars, jewels and other such priceless objects. Again, why?'

'And where do you think the treasure is now?' the Wolfman insisted, ignoring Corbett's question.

'According to rumour, certain merchants, goldsmiths and silversmiths in London and Essex profited greatly.'

'Did you know that Rougehead was part of the gang?'

'At the time he was calling himself John Priknash. He was, as with many of the gang, much suspected, but nothing was proved. We did not even have a clear description of him.' Corbett shrugged. 'We still don't.'

'Oh yes,' the Wolfman agreed, 'that's Rougehead, a subtle trickster, madcap and fey. A former Templar, certainly a friend of Ausel.' He paused at Corbett's exclamation of surprise. 'Oh yes, they were comrades; their paths have certainly crossed. Because of Ausel, I have learnt a little more about his ally Rougehead. The Lord has sent me out like a lamb amongst wolves, but he has also given me the cunning of serpents.'

'A saint among sinners?' Ranulf observed.

'I am innocent of all sin, but I move through a world weighed down and sinking beneath an ocean of it. Now, Sir Hugh, I have learnt that Rougehead was a leading member of Puddlicot's gang. He broke into the crypt and kept what he stole, then disappeared into the wilds of Essex along with his plunder. Rougehead, or Priknash, kept well clear of Temple Combe: he would not be welcomed by the other Templars, but Ausel would protect and sustain him. They were comrades in crime.'

'So,' Corbett agreed, 'Rougehead takes part in the robbery then withdraws into the green fastness of Epping. Ausel gives him shelter and sustenance. Other Templars may suspect all this but there is nothing much they can do; that's what my old comrade Grandison was referring to. He may have had his suspicions about Ausel and would certainly be wary of a renegade like Rougehead. Anyway, what does it matter now that Rougehead is dead?'

'Is he, Sir Hugh? Not what I've heard. Oh yes, three years ago he allegedly attended that fateful supper that ended in a feast of murder. According to common report, Rougehead and his three accomplices were decapitated and that hive of sin, the Salamander, was burnt to the ground. However, those who live in the shadows chant a different hymn. They say that four skeletons and four heads were never actually counted; that somehow Rougehead suspected a trap and escaped. Rougehead is a master conjuror, skilled in disguise. I heard one rumour that for a while he led a troupe of professional mummers made up of whores, defrocked clerics and renegade Templars.' The Wolfman patted his jerkin. 'Rougehead hides his appearance. Allegedly he has a scar here on his right shoulder where the Templar insignia was removed; he also has a healed wound on his thigh, the legacy of a Saracen dagger left during their ferocious onslaught on the Accursed Tower at Acre. The fall of that fortress led to Rougehead reneging on his order. A skilled linguist, a man of many appearances, he slipped back into England then away again in a flutter of shadow.'

'To France?'

'Possibly.'

'A Templar,' Corbett declared, 'a renegade who could

fabricate and lie. Rougehead would certainly do Philip of France's bidding. Could he have returned? Could Rougehead, that master of disguise, be responsible for the murders at St Giles, even that of Slingsby at the Merry Mercy?'

'He is a master of disguise,' the Wolfman agreed. 'He could be here, there or anywhere.'

'He and Ausel could be confederates working together.' Corbett returned to his chair and pointed at the Wolfman. 'I have already asked you this. What will you do if and when you capture Ausel?'

'He is a criminal. I will make him confess, then I shall take him back to Sir John Howard, who, I believe, is also a local justiciar.'

'And execution will follow immediately,' Corbett murmured.

'Ausel is a Templar knight,' Ranulf exclaimed.

'They no longer exist,' the Wolfman retorted. 'And who would care for one who is also a slayer of innocents? I know Sir John Howard. In the end Ausel will confess.'

'I am also the king's commissioner,' Corbett declared, 'I need to interrogate Ausel. When do you leave?'

'I will lodge here tonight. Tomorrow I will travel to Temple Combe and begin my hunt. Ausel is like any wild beast: he can roam, toss his head, display his tusks, but he can also be hunted, trapped and eventually killed.'

'But not before I question him?'

'Then come with me.'

Corbett glanced at Ranulf. 'Perhaps one of us should? But let me think . . .'

Once the Wolfman had left, Corbett asked Ranulf to lay out his writing tray.

'Interesting,' he declared. 'I charged the Magister Viae to discover more about Puddlicot's gang and the robbery of the crypt, but the Wolfman certainly seems to know a great deal.'

'You hunted Puddlicot, Sir Hugh.'

'Precisely, Ranulf. He was my special quarry. Puddlicot, however, presided like an abbot over a widespread gang that comprised every layer of society in London: powerful merchants and wealthy goldsmiths as well as some of the most ruthless rifflers and robbers you could pray not to meet. But let us leave that and put together what we have now learnt. We will match the pieces and see if we can glimpse any picture in all of this puzzle.'

'Will we go to Temple Combe?'

'Let me first think clearly, and you can assist me.'

The Clerk of the Green Wax sat down. Corbett patted him on the shoulder, asked Chanson to keep close watch on the door and then began to pace up and down.

'So what do we know, Ranulf, eh? Henry Sumerscale and Matthew Fallowfield: we suspect their true names were Poultney and Aschroft, but this is not a verifiable truth. More importantly,' he paused, 'what do we know about them?'

'Fallowfield,' Ranulf replied, raising his head, 'was the older man. A Templar who probably served on board ship both in northern waters and the Middle Sea. He had stripes on his back that could be due to military discipline or being captured as a slave by the Saracens. He was definitely the more experienced of the pair, and could converse in both Latin and the lingua franca. I have the distinct impression that he was the younger man's protector. This would accord with the epitaph carved on the funeral cross above his grave in God's Acre at Holy Trinity the Little, "Matthew, faithful servant".'

'Excellent, Ranulf. Write that up later. And Sumerscale?'

'A younger man. Very handsome. No more than a youth. He was a foundling raised by the Minoresses, who placed him as a page within the Templar order. A worthwhile venture. The boy would be schooled in both his horn book and the use of arms. A young man dedicated to being a knight.'

'Good. What else?'

'Sumerscale and Fallowfield were members of the Temple Combe preceptory. There is a deep suspicion that this manor was a haven of sin. Rougehead had ties with it, but I suspect these were highly secret. I also believe that Sumerscale and Fallowfield were known to those Templars, who may well have been aware of their real names. Anyway, Temple Combe certainly wasn't a manor to be proud of. According to your old comrade Grandison, the Templars, individually or those of the Temple Combe community, were corrupt, guilty of the most heinous sins. I suspect he was thinking of Ausel, who was a prime example of such wickedness.

Ausel indulged in the most devilish lusts and may have been involved with Rougehead and others in the robbery of the king's treasure at Westminster.

'Master, Temple Combe is shrouded in mystery, a lonely, deserted manor. We must imagine Ausel, Rougehead and possibly others slipping in and out so that it became more of a robbers' den than a house of prayer and discipline. The Templars there were old men. They had seen their order expelled from Acre. Perhaps they had grown cynical. Maybe they indulged in their own sins and turned a blind eye to those of others. I concede this is only conjecture, especially my belief that Ausel's comrades may have been aware of the secret sins of some of their colleagues.'

'I agree.' Corbett nodded. 'I truly believe Sumerscale was a member of the Temple Combe community. A handsome young man, he may have been foully abused by Ausel and perhaps others. The Magister Viae suggested this. Anyway, in time, a protector, somebody with integrity, emerges to defend the boy: the Templar Fallowfield. I suspect it would be very difficult for a young novice Templar to voice complaints: Sumerscale would have been ignored, ridiculed and possibly threatened. I've seen the same happen in the households of some of the great lords, who regard their pages and squires as fair fodder for their lusts.

'But then something unexpected happens. Philip of France intervenes. The Templar order in Europe, and eventually here, begins to disintegrate as the most heinous accusations are levelled against it. Others can refute these, argue against them, but Sumerscale is living proof that in certain Templar houses such vile sins were committed. Sumerscale and his protector use the disintegration of their order to flee, assume false names and plot their own salvation. They seek an audience with Prior Cuthbert at Blackfriars. Both men have serious grievances against the Templars. They also need employment and the means, if necessary, to flee the kingdom. Prior Cuthbert listens to them under the seal of confession, and what he hears deeply concerns him; that was more than obvious.'

'Probably the abuse young Sumerscale suffered. He may even have referred to other hideous sins committed in or around Temple Combe.'

'True,' Corbett agreed. 'Prior Cuthbert helps them. He gives them a recommendation to Naseby. Fallowfield is a former mariner and *The Candle-Bright* is an answer to a prayer. They can leave this kingdom legally and have a swift route, if necessary, to France and the Inquisition, not to mention Philip and de Nogaret, who were also conducting their own ruthless investigation into the order.' Corbett paused. 'However, Fallowfield is an experienced soldier, probably no fool. He would prefer to speak to the Inquisition rather than the French. Oh yes, after all, dealing with de Nogaret could, in the eyes of the English Crown and its lawyers, be portrayed as possible treason.'

'Then, master, we have what you call a paradox, a contradiction. Two very vulnerable men who, when accused of treasonable talk, have no protector. However, once they are dead, someone exacts terrible vengeance for their executions.'

'And who could that be?' Corbett wondered.

'What about Parson Layburn? Did he concoct the stories he told us? We only have his word for what truly happened. Did he collect Sumerscale and Fallowfield's corpses at the behest of someone else, or for his own private reasons? After all, he did bury them; it was he who placed those crosses over their graves.' Ranulf sipped from his goblet. 'Or could it be the harbour master Sokelar, a man, I believe, who hides deep in the shadows?'

'I can't answer your questions, Ranulf but I am fascinated by that contradiction. Two mariners who seem to have few friends, and yet when their ship berths in Queenhithe they have a place to shelter, and when they are destroyed, the most virulent revenge is extracted. Yet even here there is further mystery. According to the Wolfman, Rougehead may have escaped.'

'And the murders of the Templars?' Ranulf asked. 'It could be Ausel, Rougehead, Brother Jerome, either by themselves or together, and there are others: Sokelar, Parson Layburn, Crowthorne the leech . . .'

'So many loose strands,' Corbett murmured, 'and some of those don't fit at all into the pattern we are trying to create. Slingsby survived the destruction of his tavern three years ago, yet he comes here to be questioned by the king's commissioner and is brutally stabbed. Why now, why here? Then there's the dagger used to kill my old comrade Grandison, an item stolen from the crypt at Westminster eight years ago. Where has it been? Why was it used again? Then there is the warning to me. Why warn me? Who would do that . . .?'

'And,' Ranulf added, 'the execution of those poor lazar knights. It's obvious that they were deliberately killed to foment rebellion against the presence of the Templars at the hospital.'

Corbett sat down, clenching and unclenching his hands. 'If I could only trace everything back to a common root,' he whispered, 'but let me think . . .'

Ranulf took the hint. He decided he had other business to attend to, signalling to Chanson to follow him out of the chamber and leave Master Long Face to his thoughts. Once they were gone, Corbett stretched out on the bed, Ave beads wrapped around one hand, the other tapping the hilt of his dagger. He thought of Maeve and the children, letting his mind drift between memories and prayers, quietly conceding to himself that so far he was making no sense of the tangled mysteries confronting him. He relaxed and drifted into a deep sleep.

Ranulf shook Corbett awake.

'Master,' he hissed, 'the boy from the ale house is here. Rochfort has sent him. He demands to see you.'

Corbett struggled to sit up, dazed with sleep. 'The hour?' he demanded.

'Long after Compline.'

'Where?' Corbett demanded. 'What are we to do?'

'Rochfort wants to see you now. He insists that you come alone, but that's a nonsense. I will accompany you. I have asked the Wolfman to trail behind, to make sure we are not followed. I have left Chanson fast asleep in the stables.'

Corbett readied himself, and he and Ranulf left, hurrying along the darkened streets. The night life of the ward, its prowlers and predators, the squires of the knife and the garrotte, the beggars true and false, hastily withdrew at the sight of two men all buckled for war. The stench of the streets had diminished; their clamour had fallen to discordant bursts of sound, be it the wailing of a child, the yell of a man or the screeched speech of some denizen of the night protesting at the pain he or she felt. When they reached the ale house, the hour was very late, the yard and the taproom completely deserted. The boy took them into the narrow kitchen, where Rochfort, deeply agitated, sat on an overturned barrel. He rose to greet them.

'Sir Hugh, I meant you alone.' He gestured at Ranulf. 'You must be alone. I cannot talk. Oh, Sir Hugh, we need to leave here. Perhaps we can go to your manor at Leighton. I could help you with your bees.' His voice faltered as he stared hard at Corbett, who felt a deep, clammy chill seize his belly. He watched Rochfort intently, waiting for what the Frenchman would say next. 'Remember what Palladius said in his *De re rustica*? How in June the gentle murmur of a full hive can be distinguished from the harsh sound of a hive emptying? June is also the month for the outlawing of the drones.'

Corbett's hand fell to his dagger as he stared into Rochfort's panic-filled face. Ranulf caught his master's mood, throwing back his cloak, half easing his sword from its scabbard. Rochfort was fearful and wary; the boy sheltering in a corner began to whimper.

'As I said,' the former Templar declared, 'I will only speak to you alone. Your companion must leave.'

'Yes, you must, Ranulf.' Corbett turned and surveyed the narrow kitchen, realising that there was only one door out. 'You must leave,' he repeated, forcing himself to remain calm. 'Beekeeping is not for you. Anyway, remember what I told you from Theophrastus, how bees violently attack anyone who reeks of scent . . .'

'Enough, enough, enough!'

Corbett and Ranulf whirled round as the door to the kitchen crashed back and the room filled with armed men, cowled and cloaked, black as night, with arbalests and crossbows primed at the ready. Ranulf went to draw his sword, only to receive a cruel blow to the face. Corbett stood watching as the leader pulled the small turnspit boy towards him, the edge of his serrated Welsh dagger digging into the soft young throat.

'I will slit him,' the leader warned, his voice muffled by the visor covering the lower half of his face. 'I will slit this boy from ear to ear, then anyone else. Sir Hugh, tell your daggerman to obey.'

'Ranulf,' Corbett murmured, 'follow me.' He loosened his war belt, letting it fall to the floor. Ranulf, nursing the bruise to the side of his face, did the same. The leader stepped forward, pulling back his visor to reveal a long, sallow face with soulless eyes and a broken, twisted nose above a rat-trap mouth. 'My name is Rougehead, Gabriel

Rougehead. I welcome you here. I appreciate your references to beekeeping: a sure sign of warning between you and Rochfort and, it would seem, Ranulf too. I am glad you came, Corbett: I told that ale house brat that if he did not bring you without fuss and calm, I'd slit his master's throat. Well, Sir Hugh!' He pushed his face close to Corbett's. 'What do you say to that?'

'You're supposed to be dead.'

'He soon will be,' Ranulf added. Rougehead immediately hit the clerk again with the edge of his arbalest. Ranulf, spitting blood and cursing, lunged forward, but Corbett stepped in between the two men and sent the Clerk of the Green Wax crashing against the table in a clatter of flying pots and platters.

'Ranulf,' he hissed crouching down beside his companion, whose face was now a mass of bruises, 'this is an order. Do what they say, as will I.' Ranulf nodded. Corbett clasped him by the hand and pulled him to his feet.

'Not here,' Rougehead ordered. 'The drinking chamber.'

Corbett, Rochfort, Ranulf and the terrified boy were pushed into the taproom. In the meagre glow of spluttering rush lights, the place lay shuttered, locked and bolted from the outside; no one could look in or out. Corbett and the others were made to sit at a makeshift table pulled into the middle of the room; their captors set four bowmen over them as guards. Corbett watched as the rest of the cohort now relaxed, pulling back hoods, undoing cloaks and loosening war belts. Ranulf was nursing his face. Rochfort tried to comfort the boy, whilst Corbett continued to study their captors.

Rougehead he recognised as a villain, a devil incarnate, hell-spawned and fit only to be sent back. A ruthless killer who enjoyed inflicting pain and death. The rest were mercenaries, hard of face and hard of heart. Corbett had served with their kind during the old king's wars and knew their souls, if they possessed such a thing. Professional killers, they would be totally loyal to whoever paid them; when the silver ran out, so would they. Their heads and faces were shaven, and beneath their cloaks, their chests and backs were protected by Italian steel mesh, whilst their war belts – one across their shoulders, the other around their waists – were equipped with dagger, dirk and sword. Each carried a hand-held arbalest and wore fighting gauntlets reinforced with the sharpest metal bolts. Corbett listened to their conversation. Their native tongue was that of Languedoc, though occasionally they would lapse into a strange patois and sometimes English. Ruthless and pragmatic, they were here to complete a task, and they would do it.

Rougehead squatted down in front of Corbett, tongue clicking as his dead eyes studied the royal clerk.

'You asked me a question, Corbett: aren't I supposed to be dead? Well let me tell you, I am clearly not, because three years ago, I escaped. Slingsby was a fool . . .'

'Was?'

'Oh, I heard about him being stabbed in that shit-house of a tavern you shelter in.'

'Along with Monseigneur de Craon, your paymaster?'

'I don't know a Monseigneur de Craon,' Rougehead mocked.

'You were telling us about your wonderful escape,' Ranulf taunted.

Rougehead shifted slightly to face the clerk; behind him, one of the assassins brought up his crossbow, primed and ready.

'You have had two warnings, Ranulf-atte-Newgate. I know who you are. Corbett's daggerman, his war dog. I sense, as does my comrade behind me, that you may spring again. If you do, Primus, the captain of my escort, will surely kill you. Now, about my wonderful escape, as you call it . . .'

'I will kill you,' Ranulf interrupted. 'Not now, but I will watch you die.'

Corbett glared at his companion. Ranulf's rages were hideous: a berserker mood would descend, a battle fury that would not be brooked or controlled. He held Ranulf's gaze as he fought to control his own fear. He truly believed they were in the most terrible danger. Ranulf visibly relaxed, slouching, hands going down. Corbett stared around. Primus and his companions stood armed and ready.

'Did you have a hand in Slingsby's death?' Corbett was desperate to divert Rougehead, who was looking strangely at Ranulf, fingers twitching as if wondering what to do next. Rougehead tore his gaze away.

'No,' he replied, 'but I wish I had. I would have loved to have severed his balls, thrust them into his mouth then taken his head. Oh, I had not forgotten Slingsby! He was never far from my thoughts, but I am under strict orders.' He grinned as he realised he had conceded that he was not acting on his own. 'Nevertheless, as the Good Book says, or used to when I read it – a complete and utter waste of time – nevertheless, there is one verse out of all that drivel I believe in.'

'And that is?'

'Why, Sir Hugh, "There is a season under heaven for everything, a time for living, a time for dying." Believe me, in the fullness of time, I would have taken Slingsby's head.'

'And your wonderful escape?'

'I sensed a trap. I asked a comrade to join us for the feast, to come later, to slip in unobtrusively. When he arrived, I left and watched. I saw the killer creep into the Salamander, I watched him leave. A short while later, flames erupted out of the window of the chamber where the feast was taking place. Enough was enough, my lord clerk. I left, I changed my appearance,' he added dreamily.

'And the person who nearly killed you, who executed your companions?'

'Companions is a good word, Corbett. They were not really comrades. Looking back, I realised how they laughed behind their hands at my disguises, especially the wigs.' He wagged a finger disapprovingly at Corbett. 'Which reminds me, time to put one on.'

'And the slayer at the Salamander?'

'I like that, Corbett.' Rougehead edged forward, long

fingers fluttering. 'You have a way with words. Yes, the slayer at the Salamander . . .' His smile faded. 'I wish I knew who it was.'

'But what did he look like? You said you saw him.'

'A tall, well-built man. Heavy: I heard him breathing hard. His cloak was expensive, of pure wool, I could see the damp glistening on it. He had the rolling gait of a mariner but he reeked of perfume.' Rougehead began to hum under his breath, moving his head backwards and forwards. Corbett glanced quickly at Ranulf and winked. He prayed that Ranulf realised they were dealing with someone as mad and as bad as a box of malevolent frogs.

'So where did you flee?' he asked. 'Temple Combe?'

Rougehead opened the leather sack on the floor beside him, took out a reddish wig, the type worn by a whore, and put it over his shaven head. The dyed horsehair fell to his shoulders, framing his narrow, evil face, making him appear even more macabre. The renegade Templar rose to his feet and, imitating the gait of a prostitute, walked over to the common board and poured himself a goblet of wine. Corbett glanced at Ranulf. The Clerk of the Green Wax had now calmed, his sharp wit warning him that they were very vulnerable to this highly dangerous man. Rougehead squatted down, gulping greedily, staring at Corbett over the cup. Corbett gazed into his adversary's eyes and glimpsed something predatory, malicious, truly evil, as if Rougehead's soul housed a number of demons all jostling for dominance.

'So you don't know who tried to kill you?' Corbett demanded. 'Executed your companions, then set the Salamander alight?'

'Of course not. I would have sought him out and killed him.'

'Do you know why he did it?' Rougehead just smirked. 'Sumerscale and Fallowfield?' Corbett pressed on. He recognised what a foul fire flared in this madman's soul. Rougehead was wasting time here because he wanted to be admired by someone like Corbett. He wanted to show how clever and cunning he truly was. 'Their real names were Poultney and Aschroft,' Corbett continued. 'But tell me, since I am deeply baffled, truly mystified by it all, Sumerscale and Fallowfield – we shall call them that – were Templars, yes? They had been part of the community at Temple Combe, but fled? They wanted to lay allegations against their former order, but you stopped them. Who hired you?'

'You know full well. My good friend and hunting companion Reginald Ausel.'

'Ah,' Corbett murmured, 'so you and he . . .?'

'We share a common taste. He will be waiting for us at Temple Combe.'

'And what else is there?'

Rougehead clawed at the wig, turning to look at Corbett out of the corner of his eye. 'You remember me,' he lisped, 'of course you do. You hunted me and mine eight years ago after Puddlicot broke into the crypt at Westminster on the eve of the feast of St Matthew. You had my name at the time, John Priknash.

Oh yes.' He got to his feet, sipping at the goblet. 'So little evidence, mind you. At Temple Combe you will find out more. But not now.' He walked away.

Corbett breathed in deeply and glanced at his companions. They were all in mortal danger. He suspected that some of the royal treasure plundered from the royal crypt was hidden away at Temple Combe. Ausel would be waiting for them, two killers and a retinue of assassins. They would never allow Corbett and the others to live. They were going to their certain deaths.

'Chanson?' Corbett whispered to Ranulf.

'Fast asleep in his beloved stables.'

Corbett closed his eyes. 'And the Wolfman?'

'He may have followed us here, master, but he will not realise what's happening within.'

'How will they take us out of London,' Rochfort hissed, 'at the dead of night?'

Corbett opened his eyes. He was about to reply when Rougehead, still wearing the garish wig, returned, a fresh goblet of wine in one hand, a piece of dried meat in the other. He squatted down next to Corbett as if they were old friends.

'I escaped to France,' he declared. 'I now work for His Grace King Philip, who,' he cleaned his mouth with his tongue, 'has instructed all princes to hand over to him every recalcitrant and defiant Templar. He does this at the behest of the Holy Father Pope Clement.'

Corbett nodded understandingly at the abrupt shift in Rougehead's mood and tone. 'And I suppose you have been helping the Holy Father's representatives in their investigation?'

Rougehead grinned wolfishly. 'That and other matters.' He was now imitating the voice of a young woman.

'So you are responsible for the murders at St Giles?'

'Lord forfend! No, no, no! Those deaths, pleasing though they may be, are not to be laid at my door.'

'Then whose?'

'I don't know,' Rougehead scoffed. 'I have my own killings to take care of. Such a busy life!'

'But you are de Craon's creature?' Corbett flinched at the hatred that flitted across Rougehead's face.

'I am no man's creature, Master Clerk. I do not work for de Craon. He is the envoy of the French king.'

Corbett nodded and glanced away. Rougehead was probably following strict instructions. On no account, lest matters go wrong, was de Craon, an accredited envoy, to be implicated.

'And how do you intend to take two royal clerks, not to mention a former Templar and a kitchen boy, out of London in the middle of the night?'

'Oh, that is very easy. You, Corbett, are the key to everything. You carry the king's seals. Doors and gates will open, bars will be lifted and guards will step aside. Don't you worry, we won't even tie your hands and feet. Instead,' Rougehead pointed at Rochfort and the boy, 'any attempt by you or your war dog to escape, raise the alarm or do anything to threaten myself or my retinue, and they will die immediately. Primus and his comrades are skilled in the arbalest; they carry theirs fully loaded.' He leaned forward and snapped his fingers in Corbett's face. 'Like that, Master Clerk, a matter of heartbeats and both will be dead, a bolt to their skulls. A few heartbeats later, you and your war dog will be silenced. We will then fight our way through.' He made a face of mock sorrow. 'Now you don't want that, do you? But it will happen if you anger me. I swear on my mother's soul.'

'So you had one, and she had a soul?' Ranulf jibed even as Rougehead's hand fell to his dagger hilt. Primus and one of his companions stepped closer.

'I apologise,' Corbett intervened quickly. 'I regret that remark.'

'Accepted.' Rougehead rose to his feet, then turned abruptly, smashing his fist into the side of Ranulf's face. The blow toppled the clerk from his stool. He made to get up, but Corbett lashed out with his boot, pinioning him against the filthy wall of the taproom.

'In God's name, Ranulf!' he hissed. 'Do you want our deaths?'

'Obey your master!' Rougehead snarled, bending down only inches from the bruised, bleeding face of his victim. 'Keep to heel, dog.' He tapped Ranulf under the chin and turned to peer at the hour candle on its wooden stand. 'An hour after midnight,' he sang out. 'Guards are sleeping, taverns lie empty, the streets are deserted. Come, it is time we left.'

Corbett and the others were dragged to their feet and hustled out into the cobbled stable yard strewn with straw, the horses waiting there placid after being fed, their nosebags now removed.

'Remember.' Rougehead swung himself up into the saddle and pointed at Corbett. 'Remember,' he repeated, 'any attempt to escape and you will all die. Come, come!'

Corbett put his foot into the stirrup held by one of the assassins and climbed up into the saddle. Ranulf, nursing his bruised face, followed suit. Rochfort also mounted, the tavern boy placed on the saddle before him. Rougehead lifted his hand and the cavalcade went out on to the lane. In the light of a doorpost lantern, Corbett glimpsed one of the ancient Sisters of the Street, her wrinkled face, furrowed brow and squinting eyes looking even more ghoulish in the juddering light. As the riders passed, she pulled her ragged cloak about her and fled up an inky-black alleyway.

Rougehead led his group swiftly through the darkness across the meadows of midnight. London, once the sun had set, became a different city: His Satanic Majesty the Devil, as one preacher proclaimed it, wings spread like those of a giant bat, swept in to hold court over his legion of minions. Corbett, reins in one hand, the other on the high saddle horn, quietly applauded Rougehead's cunning. They were travelling at the most desolate hour, a group of mounted armed men, ostensibly led by a royal clerk with the Crown's authority to go where he wished, untroubled by anyone. They would not be stopped and searched. Corbett feared that his life was now as frail as breath on a frosty morning.

He pleaded with Ranulf, hissing at him quietly not to provoke Rougehead any further. Now and again, he would look around, yet as Rougehead had taunted him, nobody knew where they were going. Chanson was fast asleep in some stable, whilst there was no sign of the Magister Viae's retainers or any trace of the Wolfman.

They were soon free of the city. Corbett had to use his seals and licence to pass through Aldgate, going out close by the Tower on to the moon-washed road into Essex. The riders moved close together as they followed the ancient route north along Mile End to the village of Bow. It was the same route Corbett would take if he was journeying back to Maeve at Leighton Manor. He felt the sweat of fear chilling his skin and glanced around. Ranulf was now sullenly nursing his injuries, Rochfort trying to calm the terrified boy. Corbett wondered wildly about what would happen and what chance they had of escape. Rougehead's retainers were seasoned veterans. Now and again two or three of them would hang back to hide and watch to see whether they were being pursued or shadowed.

The cavalcade moved on, making progress to Bow village, which they reached just before dawn. A deep, heart-wrenching homesickness seized Corbett. He was now within easy reach of Leighton Manor. Instead they turned north-east and soon entered the green fastness of Epping. A long line of horsemen threading their way through the trees, following winding paths, curling around ancient oak, beech and chestnut. The trees grew so close, their branches, rich with summer greenery, embraced and entangled with each other to block out the morning light, an eerie green darkness broken here and there by pools of dappled sunshine. Corbett felt they were processing through some cavernous ancient cathedral dedicated to long-forgotten pagan gods. They passed strange cairns of moss-covered stone and made their way carefully around meres, marshes and morasses, all laced with a light-green covering. Birdsong was muted. The silence was made even more ominous by the rustling of an animal through the gorse or the flurry of feathers as a bird broke free.

Rougehead led the way. He followed markings on certain trees and took his bearings from signs carved on to rocks or posts set up by verderers. Corbett realised they must be following some secret path, as he never glimpsed any of the forest people. He fought against the mounting despair, the realisation that it would be difficult, if not impossible, for anyone following them to remain undiscovered. He recalled that verse from Isaiah: 'I set my face like flint.' He was determined to remain calm, yet he wondered what would happen once they reached Temple Combe. De Craon's plot was coming to heinous fruition. Ranulf had been correct: Corbett's destruction was part of the French envoy's dark design, but what would be the last steps in this macabre, murderous masque? More importantly, how were he and his companions to escape it?

He glanced across at Ranulf, who pulled back his hood to reveal his bruised face, mouth all swollen, one eye almost closed. He tried to smile, though Corbett glimpsed the murderous fury in his companion's good eye, the violence curdling within him. He raised his fingers to his lips as a sign to keep the peace. Ranulf nodded before spitting blood on to the trackway. They paused to water their horses at a brook that bubbled through a cleft of raised rock, then journeyed on.

At times the forest became so dark, the trees crowding in so close, that the young boy on Rochfort's saddle whimpered with fear. Corbett caught his unease, but then the trees began to thin, and after about two hours' riding, they debouched on to a trackway that, according to Rougehead, would lead them down to Temple Combe.

At last they reached their destination. The manor was fortified and protected by a high curtain wall, though its heavy wooden gate hung askew, the courtyard inside was choked with weeds and rubbish and the derelict outbuildings were open to the elements. The manor house, a wooden building on a red stone base, was much decayed, the main door, snapped off its leather hinges, being cracked and splintered whilst the windows were mere gaps in the woodwork. Corbett did not like the place. The atmosphere was oppressive, sombre and not good for the soul: eerie, haunted, rife with memories of former glory, when Temple Combe had supplied much-needed timber to the merchants of London, Colchester and elsewhere. He stared around at the derelict store-rooms, cutting sheds, stables and smithies. Here and there he glimpsed the Templar cross or other insignia of the order. The manor house, like other such properties, had been left derelict until the Pope confirmed his decree of dissolution and condemnation at the forthcoming council at Vienne; until then, this was church property, untouchable.

Corbett tried to distract himself by concentrating on his surroundings. He watched the assassins dismount and unsaddle their horses, unclasp cloaks and loosen war belts as they shouted and called to each other. He eased himself out of the saddle. Ranulf dismounted still nursing his face.

'Master!' he hissed.

'Watch and wait, Ranulf. Let us see what happens and prepare for the unexpected.'

Primus, leader of the assassins, sauntered up. Corbett called to him in Norman French, asking a spate of questions about why they were here. Primus ignored him. Corbett deliberately repeated the questions, trying to discover what would happen next. Primus just pulled a face and shrugged. Rougehead came hurrying up. He had heard Corbett's raised voice but did not understand what was being asked. Primus translated in the patois of the lingua franca. Rougehead told Corbett to mind his own business.

Further conversation was futile as Primus and his retinue herded Corbett and the rest up the crumbling steps into what must have been the manor solar: a long, dank, filthy chamber with smoke-blackened walls and roof. The hall reeked of feral smells, the stench of badger and fox as well as other vermin whose squeaking and scrabbling could be clearly heard. They were forced to sit on greasy benches along a filthy common table. At Rougehead's order, Corbett and Ranulf were bound hand and foot. They could move in a shuffling walk, eat and drink, but escape would be hampered and hindered.

Ausel entered, slipping in like a ghost, grey-haired and grey-faced. Ranulf spat in his direction. Corbett shouted a litany of questions, accusing him of murder and other abominations, but Ausel just ignored him and scurried out again. Corbett watched him go and felt hope surge within him. Of course, the Wolfman knew about Temple Combe and so did the Magister Viae, but would they use their knowledge?

He startled from his reverie as Rochfort clambered to his feet, dragging the boy with him.

'Are you so barbaric?' Rochfort shouted. 'This child needs food and drink.'

'Yes, yes, I had forgotten,' Rougehead hissed. 'My apologies, I overlooked you.' He walked towards the table, Primus the leader of the assassins alongside him. Corbett glimpsed the hand-held arbalests both men carried and struggled to his feet screaming a warning, but it was too late. Rougehead brought up his arbalest and loosed a bolt, which smashed into Rochfort's face, shattering flesh and bone in a messy splatter of blood. He then grabbed the arbalest held by Primus and released a second bolt, which caught the boy full in the forehead, sending him staggering back to collapse against the wall.

'Hell's spawn!' Ranulf screamed. 'Blood-drinker, devil incarnate!'

'Yes, yes.' Rougehead kicked Rochfort's corpse, then glanced up and smiled. 'I have been called worse, and look, here I still am.'

'Not for long,' Ranulf rasped. 'I will kill you.'

'Promises, promises!'

'Now, Primus.' Rougehead kicked Rochfort's corpse again. 'Tell two of your lovely boys to take these out and bury them deep in some forest swamp.' The leader of the assassins seemed disconcerted, but nodded in agreement when Rougehead repeated his order in the patois they often used. He hurried away and returned with two companions, who dragged both corpses out to a waiting cart. The horses were speedily harnessed, and Corbett heard the cart rattle off across the yard and out through the gate.

As he and Ranulf sat helpless at the table, greasy platters of hard bread with globules of fatty meat were pushed in front of them, along with two cracked cups of wine.

'Ranulf, eat, drink,' Corbett urged, pushing a platter towards his companion, 'and for the last time, be warned.' He pushed his face closer to Ranulf's. 'Rougehead has an unquenchable thirst for human blood. He loves to kill as other men love to savour a goblet of fine wine, listen to the chant of a choir or seduce a beautiful woman.' He gestured at the glistening streaks from table to door where the corpses had been dragged out like hunks of meat in a flesher's yard.

Rougehead and Primus came back into the hall carrying four sacks made of blood-red cordovan leather. The royal insignia and fine gold stitching could be clearly seen.

'Exchequer sacks,' Corbett murmured, 'the type used to contain jewels and other precious objects in the royal treasury.'

Rougehead moved into the shadows and dragged out a chest bound in iron and boasting four locks. Placing three of the sacks inside the coffer, he brought the fourth over to the table. He undid the metal clasps and pushed the sack up against Corbett's face, shaking its contents. Corbett peered down and glimpsed jewels: rubies, amethysts, precious rings, collars, bracelets and pectorals.

'You were once hunting for these, clerk, without much success, and now they have found you.' Laughing softly to himself, Rougehead, who had now donned a silver-white wig, minced off across the hall and deposited the last sack in the chest. Then the locks were turned, each with a different key: two of them were held by Rougehead, the other two by Primus.

Corbett listened to the two men's chatter, the patois of mercenaries, and learnt that they were to leave at first light for some tavern or hostelry along the Essex coast. Three guards were ordered into the hall; Rougehead and Primus left. Corbett, shuffling along the bench, watched them cross the cobbled yard into a small lodge built alongside the manor house. Then he sat tensely, watching the day fade, as Ranulf, despite his bruised jaw and mouth, delicately ate and drank what had been placed in front of him.

'We are going to die, master,' Ranulf muttered. 'That moon-touched bastard is intent on killing us.'

'No, Ranulf, do not despair. They are not as cunning or as subtle as they think.'

'Master?'

'As far as I know, the death cart hasn't returned; those two assassins who took Rochfort and the boy have not come back yet. True, these men are strangers here, but even a simpleton would soon find a morass or marsh close to the manor: the forest is peppered with them. Take heart, Ranulf. I don't believe a caval-cade of men could leave London unnoticed. Say your prayers, my friend. I have a strong feeling that the demand has not yet been made for our souls.'

Corbett made himself as comfortable as possible, straining his hearing, waiting for the noise of the death cart's return. Primus and other assassins came and went. Rougehead swaggered in to check their bonds. The sun set and still there was no cart. He sensed the deepening anxiety amongst his captors. Apart from Ausel and Rougehead, they were professional mercenaries, soldiers in a foreign field, possibly one profoundly alien to their training and service. Epping Forest was a dark, deep world in itself, its unbroken green canopy concealing a multitude of hideous surprises, from a well-concealed morass to brutal and sudden ambush.

'Master,' Ranulf whispered, 'you are so watchful.'

'Rougehead is as mad as a moon-struck hare,' Corbett

replied hurriedly. 'He is no soldier; we should not have come here. Temple Combe is well known to the Magister, the Wolfman and Chanson, as well as others.' He paused at the howling of some forest dog protesting against the dark, the blood-tingling sound followed by a second, which trailed the darkness to be greeted by another. He lowered his head: he did not wish to raise Ranulf's hopes, since his companion wore his heart on his sleeve. Nevertheless, that howling reminded the clerk of military service in Wales, places very similar to this, camped out deep in the trees of some mountainous valley with the Welsh sloping through the darkness towards them. He rubbed his face and watched the doorway. Rougehead came out into the yard deep in agitated conversation with some of his escort. 'Good,' Corbett hissed, 'they are becoming highly anxious. Believe me, Ranulf, matters are not proceeding as they would wish. Two of their company have still not returned. Let us wait, pray and hope.'

The two clerks had hours of broken sleep. The night passed, uneventful except for the guards occasionally checking them. In the early hours, Rougehead, much the worse for drink, his wig all askew around his unshaven head, lurched in, dagger in one hand, goblet in the other. Corbett glanced at Ranulf, warning him not to bait this most dangerous of men. Rougehead slurped at his wine.

'Clever Sir Hugh Corbett.' He leaned closer, his breath reeking of wine, spices and the corruption from his yellowing wolf teeth. 'You think you are such a subtle clerk,' he taunted, 'but you never realise what game you are in, neither now or in the past.'

'True, true, Master Rougehead, you dance in rings that are hard to follow. Tell me,' Corbett urged, 'here in this lonely place at this desolate hour: did you know Sumerscale and Fallowfield, the men you laid evidence against?'

'Oh no.' Rougehead clawed his wig. 'After Puddlicot was taken up and hanged, thanks to your good self, Sir Hugh, I fled back to France – my mother was born in Auxerre – leaving my portion of the treasure here. I dared not take it with me lest I be stopped and arrested. At the time, all the documents I carried declared me to be John Priknash.'

'So you sheltered abroad?'

'Yes, Corbett. I won't tell you how I came to the attention of Monseigneur de Nogaret after King Philip's edict on the Templars . . .'

'You volunteered information?'

Rougehead grinned, a macabre parody of some shy girl smirking. 'I proved helpful,' he lisped, 'to the French Crown in establishing the full truth about the Templars.'

'And then you were dispatched back to this kingdom?'

'Well, yes and no.'

'You were more worried about your treasure?'

'Yes, I was. Ausel had also been involved in the robbery. A strange man, Ausel. Honest in his own way; more concerned about young, soft flesh than anything else. Anyway, he sent me urgent messages. When I returned, he confessed that he'd tried to seduce . . .'

'You mean rape?'

'*Seduce* young Poultney. How the callow youth had won the protection of an older serjeant, Aschroft. Both entertained deep suspicions about Ausel. Other members of the order here in Temple Combe also believed something was wrong, but they were old, flatulent men, disgraced and dejected. Anyway,' he sniffed noisily, 'Sumerscale and Fallowfield, whatever their names, were eager to confess to so many things about the Templar Order. Now I admit,' Rougehead was becoming grandiloquent, 'I would have helped them, but you see, they were going to point the finger at my dear colleague Ausel, who, by the way, is as drunk as any fiddler.' He swayed on his feet.

'So you decided to act as king's approver?' Corbett pressed. 'You would receive a general pardon for previous offences under any of your names,' he shook his head in mock wonderment, 'which could include participation in the robbery of the crypt. You earned a reward and at the same time destroyed the threat to your colleague Ausel, who, if taken up and arrested, might confess to all kinds of mischief.'

Rougehead nodded drunkenly. 'I stayed for a while,' he slurred, 'but the fire at the Salamander convinced me it was time to leave.'

'I apologise,' Corbett lifted his bound hands, 'I have asked you this before, but you don't know who tried to kill you? I mean, Gabriel, you are so cunning . . .'

Rougehead staggered to his feet, wagging a finger at Corbett.

'I know you, clerk, so soft and subtle, but I repeat, I don't know who killed my companions. I saw him enter the tavern, a tall man, well clothed and fed, his head and face cowled and visored, a good sword in his war belt. He wreaked hideous damage, as he has at St Giles.'

'You believe it's the same man?'

'It must be. Ausel was terrified of him, hence his flight. Good man, Ausel,' Rougehead slurred, 'but broken.' He narrowed his eyes. 'And I have spoken too much. But Sir Hugh Corbett, Keeper of the Secret Seal, whom can you tell?' Wagging his finger, he staggered off across the hall and out into the courtyard.

'A true fool, a jackanapes,' Ranulf whispered as he pushed a narrow stiletto across to Corbett. 'Kept it in my boot, master. Slash our bonds at wrist and ankle, then we will be gone.'

Corbett seized the knife and felt its razor-sharp edge. It could easily slit the hempen rope, but he shook his head and pushed it back.

'Master, we should go.'

'No,' Corbett replied. 'That is not enough. Let's wait a while. Trust me, Ranulf.'

'Who will come?'

'Wait and see. I expect them at first light, just before dawn fully breaks.'

'But master, who? Why are you so confident?'

'Pray and wait.' Corbett nodded towards the half-sleeping guards resting against the treasure chest at the far end of the hall. 'They will scrutinise us again. Keep the knife concealed until I say.'

Corbett and Ranulf dozed for a while before being roughly shaken by the guards, who pulled and tugged at the ropes around their wrists and ankles. Corbett sat and watched the darkness dissipate. The manor came to life. Horses were led out, the morning air broken by the clink and clatter of armour; the faint smoke from crackling fires carried the sweet odour of oatmeal being stirred in pots. Corbett and Ranulf were given stoups of water, some dry bacon and hard rye bread. They were allowed to relieve themselves then herded back close to the main door to stand and blink at the early-morning light. Rougehead appeared, still mawmsy with drink. He became involved in a heated argument with the leader of the assassins. Listening carefully, Corbett drew comfort. The two men had still not returned with the death cart.

Rougehead turned and shouted an order. Corbett and Ranulf were pushed back out into the yard. Corbett raised his head at the clamour. The gate crashed open and the death cart trundled in: two assassins cloaked and cowled sat on the bench, one rippling the reins. Corbett bit back his disappointment, only to gasp in astonishment as figures leapt out of the cart, which had now stopped, blocking the entrance. More men appeared, archers in brown and green, though even from where he stood, Corbett glimpsed the royal insignia on their right shoulders. Welsh archers from the king's own bodyguard, master bowmen with their long war bows, their quivers crammed with arrows.

'King's men down!' a voice shouted. 'King's men down!'

PART SEVEN

'Cursed be greed and all its doings through which love is driven and loyalty exiled.'
The Monk of Malmesbury, *Life of Edward II*

Corbett lurched across, pulling Ranulf to the ground even as the royal archers loosed, their arrow shafts whistling through the air, plucking men from the saddle, making the horses rear and shy. He glanced up. Two of the assassins who had come hurrying out of the hall now lay thrashing on the ground with arrow shafts to the throat, chest and stomach. Ranulf had already used his hidden dagger to free his own wrists and ankles; hot-eyed, he did the same for Corbett, then pushed his master away as he plunged into the melee of horses, assassins and archers, who, with sword and dagger, had now closed with the enemy. The chill morning air and the stillness of that lonely, haunted manor were shattered by the clash of scraping steel, the clatter of hooves and the battle cries of men locked in a blood-chilling fight to the death.

Corbett swerved to avoid a horse and was picking

up a sword when he heard Ranulf's yell. He glanced about. Ranulf was confronting Rougehead. The clerk had snatched a two-edged axe from a nearby stack of wood and was now using this against the renegade Templar. Rougehead, stumbling from his drink, lunged at Ranulf, who stepped aside and deftly opened Rougehead's stomach with the axe. The Templar stood gasping, dropping his sword as he tried to close the long slit wound to his belly, now opening like lips to spout blood. Corbett shouted that Rougehead should be taken prisoner, but Ranulf was locked in his own wild world. Rougehead collapsed to his knees. Ranulf stepped forward. He raised the axe with two hands and brought it down, a savage, powerful blow that split Rougehead's head as if it was a dry log.

As his enemy's body spurted blood, Ranulf kicked it away, then looked over his shoulder at Corbett only to shout a warning. Corbett abruptly swung round, blade out to parry with Ausel, who had crept up behind him. Ausel hastily retreated, then abruptly went slack, sword falling from his hands, mouth gaping, head back, gurgling on his own blood. He staggered forward, arms flailing, to topple to the ground, where he jerked for a while and lay still, blood oozing from his mouth. The dust-strewn mist shifted. The Wolfman, Ausel's killer, lifted the visor of his fighting helmet and smiled at Corbett.

'Judgement delivered!' he called out. Corbett clasped his hand and moved away.

The fighting was over, ending as abruptly as it had begun. The morning haze was dissipating, the dirt and dust of the courtyard resettling. Corbett glimpsed Chanson and raised his hand in acknowledgement. The Magister Viae came running across in his dun-coloured robe, a chain-mail hauberk over his chest, a sword in one hand, a morning star mace in the other. Corbett greeted him, then, sweat-soaked, peered at the archers milling about.

'Who is your captain?' he shouted. 'I am the king's officer, Keeper of the Secret Seal . . .'

'And I am your old and loyal comrade,' a voice answered from behind. Corbett glanced around as the captain of archers strode forward, easing off his pointed steel war helmet.

'Ap Ythel, my friend!' Corbett grasped the gauntleted hand of this veteran Welsh archer, a personal favourite of the king and leader of the royal bodyguard. The Welshman's face, brown as a nut, his greying hair and goatee beard closely clipped, creased into a smile. 'The fighting is over, Hugh.' He gestured around. 'All dead, no prisoners. Three of them died immediately in our first onslaught.'

'And the two yesterday?'

'We came across them in the forest. They were tossing two corpses into a deep morass. We heard their voices, the splashes.' The captain of archers shrugged. 'Each took an arrow to the throat and joined their victims. Hugh, what is going on? I know something about this, but not all.' He gestured with his head. 'The Magister and the Wolfman, I have had dealings with them before. They came hurrying to Westminster demanding to see Chancellor Baldock: he immediately dispatched a warrant for myself and thirty of my boys to follow you.'

'Look,' Corbett intervened, 'it's lovely to hear your sweet voice, but this is urgent. You must make sure there are no survivors.' He found his mind turning and twisting at all the possibilities. 'Nobody must leave, and ensure that none of the horses break free. Lay out the dead and mount a strong guard on the chest, a four-locked coffer in the hall. Hurry now.'

Ap Ythel nodded in agreement and strode away. The Wolfman and the Magister approached, wiping their weapons on cloths ripped from corpses. Corbett greeted and thanked them but insisted that they must join Ap Ythel to ensure all was well. He glanced around. Chanson was now tending the horses, using his consummate skill to calm them and usher the animals back into the small paddock just within the wall. Ap Ythel's archers were gathering the dead and laying them out in a line. Thankfully the cohort had suffered only minor injuries, as most of the assassins had died in that first deadly rain of over forty shafts. Corbett counted the corpses: eight in all, six assassins and the two gruesome, bloodstained cadavers of Rougehead and Ausel.

Remembering the keys, he searched the clothing of both Rougehead and Primus until he found them, and immediately went back into the hall to ensure they would open the intricate locks. They did. Corbett looked inside the coffer. He unclasped one of the exchequer bags and marvelled at the sheer beauty of the precious stones. In this, at least, Rougehead had been clever, collecting miniature items that could easily be hidden and transported.

Hearing shouts and cries from outside, Corbett hastily relocked the chest. No one else, he decided, should see this: the prospect of such riches would turn many a man's soul. He went back into the stable yard and told Ap Ythel that he did not need the archers to guard the coffer. Instead he summoned Chanson, ordering him to leave the horses and mount a discreet but close watch over that great iron-bound chest. He believed this was a wise decision. Ap Ythel's men were already searching the dead for anything valuable; nothing would escape their eagle eye: coins, rings, bracelets, as well as the dead men's weapons, highly prized as many of them were of Milanese and Toledo steel. Corbett, his mind intent on what to do next, ordered the corpses to be stripped of all clothing, which was to be kept apart. Once he was satisfied, the corpses would be buried in the nearest and deepest morass.

'In the meantime,' he ordered Ap Ythel, 'I want you and some of your archers to scour the forest. No one, and I mean no one, must leave this manor or be allowed in without my permission. The news of what happened here must be kept only to us.'

'Master, what now?'

Ranulf had returned, having found their war belts, purses and his chancery satchel. Corbett gripped his companion's shoulder.

'We should have kept Rougehead alive,' he hissed.

'And Ausel?' Ranulf retorted.

Corbett laughed and withdrew his hand. 'Touché, Ranulf, too true.'

'Master, either of them alive, Rougehead in particular, would have plotted our destruction. He would have twisted and turned, lied and misled. He hated us more than life itself.'

'In which case,' Corbett replied, 'he paid the price. Ranulf, the Magister Viae is jumping from foot to foot, desperate to speak. Swill down the common table in the hall. Do what you can to clean that filthy place, then we, the Magister, the Wolfman and Ap Ythel can meet to swiftly discuss what has to be done next.'

The morning drew on, the air warming as the sun strengthened. The noise from the forest increased as the liquid coo of wood pigeons mingled with the constant cawing of crows. The creatures of the green darkness, deer, boar, fox and badger, blundered and careered through the line of trees, their constant bustling keeping Ap Ythel's men on edge. Weapons were piled. Food and drink shared out. The hall table and its floor swilled and cleaned. A brazier lit so the herbs sprinkled on top of the coals could fend off the rank smell. Corbett watched it all as he sat on a stone plinth built into the manor wall.

At last he marshalled his thoughts and gathered the rest to hold council around the common table. Ap Ythel's lieutenant had found some food, a cask of ale, a few battered platters and ancient pewter cups. They hastily broke their fast and waited for proceedings to begin. Corbett had fashioned a makeshift cross; he passed this round for each of them to clutch, kiss and bless themselves as he put them all on oath, declaring that what was going to be said, planned and executed at their meeting was the Crown's own business, highly secretive and confidential, and must be regarded as such on pain of forfeiture and death.

'Very good,' he declared once they were all sworn. 'Let us thank God,' he crossed himself, as did the others, 'that Rougehead made a fatal mistake. He brought us here first rather than to the mysterious place he was preparing to move on to before your good selves emerged like Robin Hood and his merry band from the fastness of the forest. You guessed that he would come to Temple Combe?'

'I knew Ausel would flee here,' the Magister replied. 'A natural choice to hide in, a manor he once served, deep in the forest. We watched you leave; well, not us,' he grinned, 'but those we pay to watch while we sleep. The Sisters of the Street, the beggars in the shadows, the whores and pimps peeping through the shutters. We had similar eyes and ears along the highway to Mile End and Bow village. We were like the mist, all around you.'

'The Magister,' the Wolfman spoke up, 'came enquiring

at the Merry Mercy asking to see Chanson, your clerk of the stables. I had followed you to the ale house but then returned to the tavern. I learnt what was going on and I joined them.'

'Not openly, surely?' Corbett demanded. 'It is essential that de Craon does not suspect what has happened.'

'No,' Chanson called out as he sat on his stool close to the treasure coffer. 'We immediately went to Rochfort's alehouse, God have mercy on him.' He swiftly crossed himself. 'The place was as empty and deserted as an old tomb. So I told the Magister and the Wolfman what you had instructed me to do, Sir Hugh, should you mysteriously disappear.' Ranulf would have clapped his hands in mock approval, but Corbett glared at him. Chanson pulled a face. 'I knew something was wrong. We immediately went to Westminster and Chancellor Baldock. He met us in the Secret Chancery and we told him what we knew.' Chanson pointed at Ap Ythel. 'We were given a warrant and sent to the Welshman at the Tower.'

'I acted as swiftly as I could.' Ap Ythel took up the story, his voice lilting. 'We threaded the forest, moving silently as shadows. We saw no one until we heard the noise of those two assassins disposing of the corpses, the Frenchman Rochfort and that poor boy. It was too late for them, but we ensured that the killers kept their victims company on that long journey into eternal light. May God judge them kindly and show them pity.' He sighed and sketched a cross on his forehead. 'We reached

Temple Combe just before dusk, but decided to wait until morning.'

'Wolfman,' Corbett turned to that hunter of outlaws, 'how good is your memory?'

'Excellent, Sir Hugh.'

'First,' Corbett drew a deep breath, 'in your brief stay at the Merry Mercy, do you think de Craon sensed any change or that something was wrong?'

'No,' Chanson spoke up, 'I don't think so.'

'I would agree,' the Wolfman confirmed. 'Sir Hugh, my memory?'

'De Craon and Brother Jerome must not learn what has happened here. So, Wolfman,' Corbett continued, 'I want you to return as swiftly as possible to Westminster and seek out the king's close councillors, Chancellor Baldock and Chaplain Reynolds. Tell them that when de Craon and Brother Jerome journey to Westminster tomorrow morning for more of their spurious negotiations, they are to be detained there. Tell Baldock to create some crisis to frighten de Craon. He must point out how the attacks by *The Black Hogge* have created deep resentment along Queenhithe. How violent unrest is imminent and how the king fears for the well-being and safety of the French envoy. Ask for de Craon and his sinister shadow to be kept in comfortable, even luxurious confinement at Westminster. The chancellor can also stir the pot even more by saying how distraught both the king and my lord Gaveston have become by the sudden and mysterious disappearance of Sir Hugh Corbett and his clerk,

Ranulf-atte-Newgate. How they have scoured the city but can find no trace of us. That,' Corbett added meaningfully, 'will keep our crafty-eyed minion of Satan both happy and distracted until our return, which,' he joined his hands as if in prayer, 'please God, will not be long.'

Corbett felt that matters would have moved swifter if Rougehead had not been killed, yet he conceded to himself that Ranulf was probably correct. Rougehead was best dead. God knows what tangle of lies that wicked limb of Satan would have spun. And yet? Corbett recalled everything he had learnt about the villain: there was something very wrong. Memories and events did not match. Rougehead was skilled at disguise, at slipping and slithering away like a snake, yet he'd been trapped and cut down like some common outlaw . . .

'Sir Hugh!' The Wolfman interrupted his reverie.

'You have my message for the chancellor?' Corbett asked. The Wolfman nodded, and Corbett ordered him to repeat it. When he was satisfied, he turned to the magister.

'You wish to speak? You have something to tell me?'

'I do, Sir Hugh. You asked me to collect and sift stories and legends about the robbery of the royal treasure from the crypt at Westminster Abbey.'

'And?'

'Sir Hugh, I learnt very little. True, I did hear whispers about renegade Templars being involved, but that was all shadow and no substance. You see,' the Magister leaned his elbows on the table, 'at that time, I was busy trading with the Hanse. I was in the Baltic. I don't know what truly happened.' He paused. 'However, the evidence indicates that Queenhithe, being one of the London wards closest to Westminster, was deeply implicated in the robbery. Time and again the justices returned to question this person or that, though it is one thing to accuse and another to prove. Nevertheless, more were involved than the old king or any of his officers knew, and that is the problem: gilders, smelters, gold- and silversmiths, jewellers, engravers, taverners and merchants were all interrogated.'

'I know, I know,' Corbett intervened. 'The justices moved from ward to ward. People were put on oath and compelled to confess what they knew. I remember the returns being brought into the royal archive at the chancery, stacks upon stacks of documents. It would take a lifetime to read them. When it was all over, the old king came into that room to view them and lost his temper, indulging in one his murderous rages. He kicked the manuscripts, threw them about and even tore at a few with his teeth. The list of suspects was endless. My task was to pursue Puddlicot, the leader of the gang, while other clerks and justices investigated those who possibly bought, stole and moved the treasure.'

Corbett rapped the table. 'But to move to the matter in hand, Magister, we await your wisdom.' He recognised the Magister Viae as a man who loved the masque, the mystery play, the mummery and the pageant, and who was biding his time for his great revelation.

'Sir Hugh, you may not know where Rougehead was taking you, but I do. No,' the Magister gestured at Ranulf, 'let me speak. My lord clerk, you gave me a commission. You asked me to pretend that I was Gaston Foix and to reflect on how I would manage *The Black Hogge*. You also asked me to become his inveterate enemy, and so I have.' He plucked from his wallet a roll of parchment, which he dramatically opened, using cups and platters to keep it straight.

Corbett glanced at the doorway. The sunlight was midday strong, the smell of the forest lush, its noisy life carrying across the yard.

'The day goes on,' he declared, 'the hours swallow each other up. Remember, magister, Rougehead was preparing to move out swiftly. I suggest we do not have much time.'

'We walk in the darkness,' the Wolfman intoned. 'We seek the light of the Lord.'

'And we have found it!' The Magister Viae now came into his own, straightening up and almost filling out as he prepared to speak. '*The Black Hogge* is a war cog. Fierce and predatory under its cunning master Gaston Foix. The ship ostensibly sails as a privateer under letters sealed by the Duke of Brittany . . .'

'Nonsense,' Ranulf broke in. 'It's the war cog of Philip of France, Guillaume de Nogaret and Amaury de Craon.'

'Of course it is, but how they communicate remains

a mystery.' The Magister shrugged. 'Perhaps we can discuss that in God's own time . . .'

'Which is swiftly passing,' Corbett declared.

'Sir Hugh, I suggest we still have perhaps two to three days to prepare. *The Black Hogge* is a powerful predator, but it does have weaknesses. It has sailed from a French port in the Narrow Seas but it very rarely returns, and the reason for that is simple. The Narrow Seas are crowded. If it remained there, it would be noticed time and time again. Moreover, if it sailed into a port like Calais and we learnt of this, we could set up a blockade. It would then have a choice: to stay and rot or sail out to face cruel and bloody conflict. Now I am sure that *The Black Hogge* does return now and again to harbours in the Narrow Seas, but I suspect this is rare and its stay is very short.'

'So any supplies would have to be put on board hastily?'

'Precisely, Master Ranulf. *The Black Hogge* is a lonely hunter; it depends on surprise. It keeps out of the Narrow Seas, hiding in the misty fastness of the northern ocean, taking up a battle position somewhere to the east of the Essex coast . . .'

'And as we have discussed,' Corbett intervened, 'it could take an eternity to find. Even if we did locate it, any English fleet setting out into the wilderness of the northern seas would break up under the wind, storms and sudden squalls.'

'Yes, they'd become separated,' the Magister agreed,

'and God help any ship if *The Black Hogge* found it alone and vulnerable. Moreover, we now suspect that news of an English war fleet being dispatched from the Thames would be relayed to Gaston Foix.'

'So,' Corbett demanded, 'you said *The Black Hogge* has weaknesses?'

'Water,' the Magister retorted. 'The crew need fresh water.'

'Easy enough,' Ranulf declared. 'Even I know about the streams, brooks and rivulets that flow out of Essex: the coves, inlets and natural harbours along its coastline.'

'Water brings *The Black Hogge* in,' the Magister agreed. 'There is also the need for food. Remember, it is very rarely seen in the Narrow Seas except just before it attacks some hapless English ship, yes? So it must provision elsewhere.'

Corbett, sitting at the end of the table, felt a thrill of excitement. The Magister was stating the obvious, yet, as often in logic, sometimes the obvious was ignored.

'True, true,' he murmured. 'It must be at sea for weeks, even months. Gaston has a full fighting crew, men like those assassins. I am sure they came from *The Black Hogge*, landed somewhere along the Essex coast.'

'I agree,' the Magister replied.

'Let me think.' Corbett listened to the sounds from outside: the archers setting up camp, preparing pots of whatever food they had found; the neigh and whinny of horses. He rose and walked over to the doorway, shielding his eyes against the sunlight. The Magister was correct. There was more time and he had to prepare well. He stared across the stable yard. The assassins' naked cadavers sprawled in a gruesome line, faces masked with dust, torsos smeared with congealed blood where their wounds had opened. Corbett crossed himself and whispered a hasty requiem. How many more, he wondered, would die before this deadly game was played to its final throw?

'Sir Hugh?'

'Magister,' Corbett turned back, 'I accept the logic of your argument. Gaston Foix not only needs to feed and water his crew of many souls but nourish them well, to sustain their strength.'

'But where would he get such food?' Ranulf demanded. 'If *The Black Hogge* landed foraging parties to raid farms and villages, the alarm would soon be raised. It would become common knowledge that a French privateer was plundering the coast.' He winced and gently touched his jaw. 'A hunting party,' he continued, 'would be equally hazardous and not necessarily successful.' He forced a smile. 'They would have to kill or plunder a great deal. The crew of *The Black Hogge* must be at least a hundred and twenty men: mariners, soldiers.'

'I agree.' The Magister was enjoying himself. Like a master in the schools, he was leading his audience to the inevitable conclusion. Corbett secretly prayed for patience, steeled his face into expectancy and gestured at the Magister to continue.

'A farmer could provide food, but that amount would

be beyond his capabilities. It would certainly attract attention and provoke suspicion.'

'A tavern?' Ranulf intervened.

'A tavern it must be and a tavern it is,' the Magister trumpeted. 'Sir Hugh, as you know, a taverner has every right to buy all kinds of purveyance from farms and markets, be it salted pork, chicken, beef, vegetables, ale, wine, medicines, herbs and ointments, even clothing and weaponry. The list is endless. A tavern master could do this without attracting attention or creating suspicion.'

'It must be!' Corbett exclaimed. 'The assassins whose corpses are now stiffening outside were undoubtedly brought here by *The Black Hogge*. They carried their own war belts and saddles, but the horses they rode would have been bought or hired at some market or horse fair. Yes, yes,' he curbed his mounting excitement, 'it must be a tavern out on the wild wastes of the Essex coastline; that's where Rougehead and his coven were taking us. They were going back to meet *The Black Hogge* with their prisoners and the treasure hidden here. Accordingly, *The Black Hogge* will return in the very near future, either today on the evening tide or certainly soon after. But . . .'

'This tavern,' Ranulf asked, 'where is it?'

'With my learned colleague Fitzosbert, I went back through the tax returns for all establishments along the coast of Essex. Now, between the mouths of the Blackwater and the Colne stretches a marshy tract. Rivulets run like veins through this treacherous morass, sudden surge tides are common, sweeping swiftly in so the land seems to float as if it were an island in a great lake.' The Magister glanced up. 'Fitzosbert knows the terrain well. Apparently his wife's kin hail from those parts.'

'Very interesting,' Ranulf declared drily, 'please continue.'

'The sea has encroached most grievously on the land. Villages, hamlets and farmsteads have disappeared. Saltcot is such a place. Once it was a small but thriving village; now it lies deserted. However, there is a tavern on Saltcot Hill, the Sunne in Splendour.' The Magister lowered his head as he consulted his memorandum. 'I admit it is rather ill-named and curious. In its prime, the tavern was quite majestic. Its last owner was Matilda Poultney, widow. Matilda apparently died in the autumn of 1281. Because of the decay and desertion, her son and heir, John, abandoned the tavern, stripping it of all movables, and decided to become a vintner in Queenhithe in London.' The Magister sat back, looking pleased with himself.

'The Templar called Sumerscale,' Corbett declared, 'his real name was Poultney. So what happened to John Poultney? Magister, time is passing.'

'Oh, he worked at the Salamander for a while, but he died of the sweating sickness in 1293 and lies buried in Holy Trinity the Little. He was only an apprentice, not a full guild member, and he died leaving no heir. The Sunne in Splendour at Saltcot was considered to be derelict, deserted and part of the wasteland, so it became forfeit to the Crown. Two years ago, Reginald Ausel, former Templar, applied to the barons of the exchequer to purchase the tavern, which he did for quite a meagre price.'

'Angels in heaven!' Corbett exclaimed, staring around the table. 'And are you sure there is no connection, no link, no relationship between Henry Poultney, also known as Sumerscale, hanged on *The Candle-Bright*, and this John Poultney, vintner?'

'Not that I can see, Sir Hugh. Poultney is a common enough name, and from all our searches we found that Matilda had only the one son, this John, who died without issue.'

'So we have it.' Corbett rubbed his hands together. 'Two years ago, Reginald Ausel applies to purchase the Sunne in Splendour. Ausel depicts himself as a former Templar looking to build a new future for himself. In truth, he hands the ownership to Rougehead, who, under another name, acts the jovial tavern master hungry for trade. He purchases food and all the tavern needs, but he has no guests, no customers except for Gaston Foix and the crew of *The Black Hogge*. All this quietly supported by French gold. In the spring of this year, the murderous masque begins.' Corbett sipped at his cup of ale. 'So how do we trap this monster and kill it? We know *The Black Hogge* will sail close to some inlet near the Sunne in Splendour, perhaps tonight, certainly within the next few days. We could send couriers to Harwich or elsewhere. The admiral of the eastern seas has his master cog, *The Holy Ghost*, in one of the eastern ports. He could assemble a small fleet.'

'But that could take days, even weeks,' the Magister protested. 'Even if they did assemble, how would such a fleet find *The Black Hogge*? And once gathered, would they be successful, or would *The Black Hogge* escape and be warned off ever returning to Saltcot?'

'We cannot allow what we know to become public knowledge,' Corbett agreed. 'So, how do we close with this formidable ship?' He smiled. 'I did ask you to become Gaston Foix . . .'

'Indeed you did, and I have a plan.' The Magister drew a deep breath. '*The Black Hogge* will sail in on the evening tide, drop its anchor stone and ride at anchor, its sails rolled and reefed. Its shore boat will be lowered to collect purveyance. If English war cogs appeared and attempted a blockade, *The Black Hogge* would fight its way through. What we must do, Sir Hugh, is inflict on that ship every master's nightmare . . .'

'Fire!'

'Precisely. We must board *The Black Hogge* through stealth and trickery and create a fire. Anywhere would be good, but if the main mast was destroyed, *The Black Hogge* could become a floating coffin.'

Corbett put his face in his hands, closed his eyes and murmured a prayer. He took his hands away and looked around.

'Let us begin.' He gestured towards the doorway. 'Those corpses must be buried quickly by a small guard of archers whom we will leave here. Understood?' Ap Ythel nodded in agreement. 'The same guard will ensure that no one else is allowed into the manor. Anyone who approaches Temple Combe must be detained. Until we strike at *The Black Hogge*, no one must discover what has happened here. Nor must we in any way proclaim it. No messages from Temple Combe or Saltcot are to reach London.' He pointed down the table. 'Wolfman, you will ensure my orders are carried out.'

'I will, Sir Hugh.'

'Remember,' Corbett insisted, 'nothing must be proclaimed or even whispered until, God be pleased, I return safely to London.'

'And us?' the Magister demanded.

'Tell me more about the lie of the land. You know how we can reach Saltcot?'

'Oh yes,' the Magister replied, 'but it will take us about three hours in all. We will strike north-east, threading our way through the forest; this eventually peters out into wasteland, which rises to a steep hill. The Sunne in Splendour stands on that hill, along with a huddle of other dwellings. The hill then falls away to more wasteland, which stretches down to sand hills overlooking the pebbled beach of a narrow but fairly deep inlet.'

Corbett straightened up, tapping the table. 'We will leave first. Myself, the Magister and Ranulf. If we are approached,' he indicated the Magister's brown robe, 'you are a wandering Franciscan who came upon us by chance. Two clerks journeying to Chelmsford who became lost and were attacked by wolfsheads; this would explain why we were in the forest.'

'Sir Hugh.' Ranulf gently touched his own face, where the blows inflicted by Rougehead had blossomed into nasty-looking bruises. 'This is proof enough of any attack.'

'Ap Ythel,' Corbett continued, 'you will leave six of your archers here under an officer to bury the dead and keep strict watch over this manor. As for the treasure chest, it might be best if we took it with us.'

'I agree,' said the captain of archers. 'Rumours are already rife about what that chest contains.'

'Chanson,' Corbett declared, 'you will organise the chest on to the cart. We will use two horses for that. Where that chest goes, you follow. I also want the clothing of the dead assassins piled on to the cart; we may well need it.'

The meeting ended. Corbett and Ranulf finished what was left in their cups and platters, then they scrutinised their war belts, ensured everything was in order and prepared to leave. Chanson readied the horses as well as the cart, on to which, assisted by Ap Ythel and two of his archers, he loaded the heavy treasure chest. Beside this, under a canvas awning, the captain of archers also stored the clothes of the dead assassins. Corbett demanded that the manor be searched for oil. Some was found, a few barrels and half a dozen skins. The magister said it might suffice but they really needed more. Corbett quietly prayed that they might find what they needed at the Sunne in Splendour.

The clerk had one last meeting with the Wolfman, repeating his instructions, then that cunning hunter loped off down the trackway and into the trees. He also conferred with Ap Ythel. The captain and the remainder of his archers were to wait an hour before following Corbett. He was to look for a column of smoke from the derelict tavern as a sign that all was well.

A short while later, Corbett and Ranulf left the manor, the Magister riding before them. They re-entered the forest, the Magister assuring them that he knew the way like the palm of his hand and that he had left strict instructions with Ap Ythel about what route to take. Ranulf was about to question Corbett when the Magister reined in to ride alongside them.

'Sir Hugh, you asked me to keep . . .' He paused as a great raven, black feathery wings fluttering furiously, burst out from a clump of greenery, wheeling up against the light. The Magister, shading his eyes, watched it go. 'Just like all our troubles, eh, Sir Hugh? We are surrounded by greenery, the warmth of a summer sun, and then the raven appears. According to the ancient ones, the bird is a harbinger of impending doom.'

'I hope not.' Corbett turned in the saddle. 'Magister, you have done well. Let us pray it all ends happily. You have more?'

'As I have said, Sir Hugh, I made my own enquiries about the robbery of the royal treasury in the crypt at

Westminster. I discovered that Master Sokelar was suspected of moving the treasure, which is why he has received no advancement but remains simple harbour master in Queenhithe.'

Corbett wafted away a fly and pulled a face.

'Is it surprising, Magister, that a harbour master dabbled in theft?'

'Ah, but he may have dabbled in a great number of things.'

'Such as?'

'You know that his wife, Agnes's mother, was with him when Acre fell. He and the girl escaped but his wife was one of those who was raped and slaughtered when the Mamelukes stormed the Accursed Tower. Master Sokelar has no love for the Templars.'

Corbett, slouched in the saddle, reined in. They had entered a forest glade dappled with sunlight. Insects danced in the golden shafts, bees buzzed greedily above a cluster of wild flowers. A shadow moved and a roe deer in all its horned majesty loped like a dancer from one pool of dark greenery into another. Corbett sat, one hand raised, listening to the sounds of the forest. He glanced back over his shoulder. Ap Ythel would be preparing to leave; soon they would all meet at the Sunne in Splendour.

'Sir Hugh,' the Magister insisted, 'there is more.'

'There always is!' Corbett urged his horse forward.

'De Craon seems very sweet on Agnes Sokelar.'

'What?'

'Oh yes, she visits him secretly in his chamber when

Mistress Philippa is engaged elsewhere. Most fond of her he seems!'

'Well I shall reflect on that,' Corbett replied, spurring his horse forward, indicating that Ranulf join him.

'You heard that, Clerk of the Green Wax?'

'I certainly did.' Ranulf winced, touching his bruised face tenderly. 'But so what, Master? What is more relevant,' he continued, 'is the capture and destruction of *The Black Hogge*. All other business must wait on that. If we succeed, all to the good. If we fail, what is the use of speculating on other matters?'

'Too true, Ranulf. However, let us, as we ride, review what we know.'

Corbett relaxed, letting the reins slip through his hands. Ahead of them the Magister was following a winding trackway. The forest clustered close, though occasionally the treeline would break. Corbett was sure they had turned fully east; now and again on the summer's breeze he caught the salty tang of the sea.

'Master?'

'Ranulf, I am reflecting. Do we have the truth of it or not? First Philip of France and the tangling web His Satanic Majesty is trying to spin around this kingdom and its king. To a certain extent he has had his way. Edward of England has been compelled to honour the papal arbitration of 1298 and marry Philip's daughter Isabella. The French king now has a member of his family at the very heart of the English politic. Not satisfied with this, Philip keeps spinning. In Scotland, Robert Bruce receives French gold and weapons, as do the great lords of Edward's court to encourage them in their opposition to Gaveston and the power of the king. Next we have *The Black Hogge* hiding in the fog-bound vastness of the northern seas, then slipping like a hawk through the clouds to pounce on some English cog fresh out of the Thames. In doing so, not only is English shipping and merchandise being grievously hurt, but our king's authority is much maligned. Finally we have our own capture and abduction. I am sure, indeed I would swear over the Sacrament, that Rougehead fully intended to kill us after we had been tortured to discover what we know.'

'About what?'

'About everything, Ranulf. I do not intend to flatter myself, but I state what was plotted, namely our deaths. The removal of two clerks who, in the eyes of Philip, de Nogaret and de Craon, could counter their many malignant schemes.'

'Sir Hugh, I agree. As you know, I have always believed that your death was something de Craon deeply prized.'

'Chess,' Corbett retorted. 'Ranulf, think of Philip as a chess master, moving all these pieces across the board.'

'And the endgame, surely, control of the English king?'

'Or his removal. I have read the writings of Philip's lawyers, creatures such as Pierre du Bois, author of a treatise titled *On the recovery of the Holy Land*, though it is really nothing of the sort. Du Bois declares that Philip is a new Charlemagne, a pope-emperor of Europe. He argues that he should control all of Europe's kingdoms through the marriage of his children, Isabella being a case in point.'

'And he has succeeded.'

'Though perhaps Philip's endgame is something much more deadly. Listen, Ranulf. A hundred years ago, during the minority of our king's grandfather Henry III, a French fleet actually sailed up the Thames. A Capetian prince named Louis occupied the Tower and set up government. What if Philip wishes to repeat this, but more successfully? He weakens Edward both at home and abroad. He removes people such as ourselves, so that when the corn is ripe he may move in with his sickle and collect a rich harvest: the occupation of England, ruling it in the name of his daughter, the widow queen Isabella. I wonder . . .'

Corbett fell silent. Ranulf was about to question him further when the Magister shouted, lifting a hand. They were now leaving the forest, riding out on to moorland swept by sharp sea breezes. The forest gave way to a mix of bramble, gorse, sturdy bushes, ancient thorn trees and small pools fed by rivulets that glistened in the sun. Wild flowers such as maiden's blush, lily white in colour, thrived and blossomed along with sea lavender grass. The land rose to a fairly steep hill crowned with buildings. Even from where they sat on their horses at the forest edge, Corbett could see that these buildings, now decayed, had once been impressive.

'The hill falls away on the other side,' the Magister reminded them, 'to more wasteland, which runs down through a fringe of trees and bushes to sand hills over-looking a pebble beach.'

Corbett quietened his horse, staring carefully around, wary of riding into an ambush. The place looked deserted, but he was sure they were now approaching the inlet where *The Black Hogge* would sail in to reprovision.

'Shouldn't we hurry?' Ranulf asked.

'No, no,' Corbett replied, 'we take our time. *The Black Hogge* comes and *The Black Hogge* goes, but it must return to make landfall to take us prisoner.'

'An ideal place,' the Magister declared, patting his horse's neck, smoothing the sweat from its hair. 'Nothing but wasteland. The winds bring in sand and gravel. Sometimes the sea floods the land, feeding both the marshes and the salty pools. There is no soil to plant, no crop to be gathered here. On a summer's day like this it's bleak enough, but can you imagine it when the weather turns? Moreover, the place is reputedly haunted, or so I read in a chronicle. A place of blood. According to local lore, that hill is supposed to be an ancient funeral barrow.'

'And?' Corbett asked, intrigued. 'Tell me; I want to know as much as possible about the place.'

'Before the Conqueror,' the Magister replied, 'the Vikings used to winter on Mersea Island. When spring came, they would cruise along the coast, burning and plundering. They were led by twin brothers born in the same hour who loved one another dearly. One spring, they sailed up to what we now know as St

Osyth. They killed Osyth but carried off her beautiful sister. When they returned to Mersea, each of the twins wanted her for himself and their love turned to jealousy. Drawing their long swords, they hacked at one another, and by the time the sun set, both were dead. Their followers brought a ship in. They put the woman inside, with a dead brother on either side, sword in hand, and buried them beneath that hill, the living and the dead together. Now when the new moon appears, or so the legend says, the flesh grows on their bones, their wounds close and their breath returns. They say that if you go up the hill on the night of the full moon, you can hear the brothers fighting in the heart of the barrow. However, once the moon begins to fade, the sounds of battle grow fainter as their armour falls to bits, their flesh drops away and the blood dries up.' The Magister grinned, patting his horse's neck. 'Easy enough to listen to on a summer's day, but on a moon-swept night, with the wind crying and moaning . . .'

'I agree,' Corbett replied, 'but let's deal with the living, they are dangerous enough.'

The Magister led them in single file along a narrow beaten track that wound around pool and marsh then up the steep incline to the derelict remains of Saltcot hamlet. The Sunne in Splendour consisted of a huddle of buildings in a cobbled courtyard bound by a high curtain wall and served by a double gate, which now hung open. Corbett rode in. To his left rose a squat two-storey tower of grey flint built alongside a rather hunchbacked manor house, its lattice windows bulging out, a mass of gables and a jumble of roofs with its lean-to buildings of wood and stone that served as stables, smithies, storerooms and sheds. The smell of cooking hung heavy in the air. Chickens pecked at the dust close to a disused dovecote, whilst the distant lowing of cattle could be heard.

Corbett and his companions slowly dismounted. The clerk could sense no danger, no threat, though he jumped as the door to the dilapidated house was thrown open and a tall, thickset giant of a man, stooping to get out, shambled into the yard, followed by a young woman. The man was dressed in a tattered jerkin and thick hose pushed into battered boots; red-faced, with popping eyes, he had a mass of unruly black hair and a tangled moustache and beard. He lurched towards Corbett and abruptly stopped, staring down at the clerk as he gestured at the young woman, no more than seventeen summers old, to join him. She had long, mousy brown hair that almost hid her pale face, with twitching lips and ever-blinking eyes. She was dressed in a shabby blue gown with sturdy clogs on her feet. Corbett immediately sensed that the pair were no threat; innocents, probably brother and sister, with the minds and ways of children.

'Good morrow.' He extended a hand, which the man grasped, staring open-mouthed at Corbett and his two companions.

'You,' he pointed at the clerk, 'you are friends of Master Rougehead?'

'We certainly are,' Corbett replied quickly. 'We are visiting here hoping to meet him, as well as to learn more about the legends and stories of the ancient grave. We are sorry to trouble you, but,' he pointed to the battered tavern sign, 'you are a hostelry and we are hungry and thirsty.' He opened the small pouch on his war belt and took out two coins, which he pressed into the man's hand, indicating that he share these with the young woman, who stood there silently, one hand pulling at her hair, the other constantly smoothing the apron around her waist. The sight of so much silver made them both smile and relax.

'I am Penda,' the man explained. 'And this is Gunhilda.' His voice was surprisingly soft, his rustic accent clear and understandable. 'We welcome you here – that's what Master Rougehead taught us to say, and what else?' He scratched his head and stared up at the sky. 'Ah yes, that's it! Now you must come in and be refreshed.'

Penda and Gunhilda led Corbett and his two companions into a large taproom: this was surprisingly clean and sweet-smelling, and, Corbett noticed, well furnished. The room also boasted a cavernous hearth with bread ovens either side, the smell from these being most fragrant. Corbett whispered to the Magister to go outside and see to their horses, and, if all was well, to light a fire so Ap Ythel would see the smoke and join them. Meanwhile, he and Ranulf sat at a table with stools set around it and were served tankards of freshly brewed ale and a platter of cured ham and manchet loaves still soft and sweet. Corbett insisted that Penda and Gunhilda join them, plying them with ale and encouraging them to talk. Then he produced two more coins and asked them to show him and Ranulf around the tavern.

He soon had the measure of Penda and Gunhilda, brother and sister, innocents before God, who had tramped the roads of Essex together, itinerant peasants looking for work on the land. When they reached Saltcot, Rougehead had hired them, providing them with bed and board and a few coins, in return for which they did exactly what he asked. They soon confirmed that the Sunne in Splendour had very few if any visitors. They knew little about Rougehead's business but did admit that ships moored in the nearby inlet, and that Master Rougehead sold them provisions, something he always insisted on doing himself. He had a cart, whilst there were horses stabled in one of the outbuildings.

Corbett questioned them about recent visitors. Penda confirmed that some of Rougehead's friends had visited the tavern and that the master had hired horses for them. They had left, Master Rougehead saying he would be back within a few days. Corbett stared at the simple faces of these two peasants and told them there was no need to worry. Penda and Gunhilda nodded wisely and said they must return to their tasks: after all, Master Rougehead would soon return, and there was bread to be baked and eggs to be collected.

Corbett plucked at Ranulf's sleeve and led him out

of the taproom. The Magister was beyond the gate, tending to the fire, placing wet sticks on the flames to create a plume of smoke.

'That might be seen out at sea,' Ranulf warned.

'Even if it was,' Corbett retorted, 'I doubt it would mean anything. This, Ranulf,' he gestured around, 'is very clever and subtle, a deserted, derelict tavern in an isolated village close to an inlet, which, by the way, we must visit very soon.' He paused, calling to the Magister Viae to alert him once he glimpsed Ap Ythel and his archers approaching.

'More lonely than a Cistercian cell,' Ranulf agreed. 'Even a hermit might baulk at this place.'

'And yet ideal for de Craon, who, I am sure, spun this web. Rougehead was ordered to go back to England to find a place like this close to the coast. The French envoy provided the money for Ausel to purchase it from the exchequer: its barons would have been only too delighted to shed this blighted place and earn some profit. Ausel stays in London; Rougehead moves out here and makes things ready. Penda and Gunhilda, two itinerant workers, are hired. Good, simple souls, they have no sense about what is happening. Gunhilda cooks, tends and cleans; Penda accompanies Rougehead to Chelmsford and the other markets. He loads the cart when the master wishes to go down to the beach to sell to passing ships. Penda wouldn't think anything wrong. In truth, however, this tavern becomes the revictualling port for *The Black Hogge*. There are plenty of brooks and rivulets to provide fresh water. Rougehead buys meat and other provisions at the markets, whilst the tavern itself provides fruit, herbs, chickens, eggs, even fresh milk from a cow. Let us say someone does come by and sees *The Black Hogge* riding at anchor: it won't display any colours, and people will think it is an English war cog taking on supplies.'

'*The Black Hogge* cannot be far off the coast.'

'Yes, Ranulf, you are correct. It disappears where it can't be seen from land, but I doubt it is far away. It will return and we must prepare.'

PART EIGHT

'If you plan to pursue a life of crime, the entire world will rise against you.'
   The Monk of Malmesbury, *Life of Edward II*

Corbett walked the tavern again, which only confirmed his suspicions that this was the supply point for the French war cog. Once satisfied, he set off, following the winding trackway across the heathland and up to the sand hills overlooking the beach. The tide was coming in, the waves rolling fast under a crest of white foam. Nevertheless, apart from the seabirds shrieking and swooping, the great expanse of sky, sea and land seemed empty and peaceful. Corbett noticed how to both north and south the beach turned to create a natural harbour or inlet. Straining his eyes, he stared at the far horizon. He was certain *The Black Hogge* was prowling not far beyond that, but until it made its presence felt, there was nothing to be done.

Recalling what Penda had told him as they'd walked the tavern, he searched the thick wall of bushes along the rim of the sand hills and came across a sturdy four-oared shore boat. He swiftly inspected this and was pleased to find it seaworthy. Corbett had a vague strategy in mind, although since he had little experience of war at sea, except for service as a mailed clerk on the old king's fighting cog, *The Glory of Castile*, he would be guided by the Magister in what was being proposed. *The Black Hogge* was a formidable fighting ship, vulnerable only to fire, even more so in enemy seas, where repairs and refitting would be almost impossible to secure.

Absorbed in such thoughts, he sat down with his back to a tree and plotted what should be done. He then reflected on the various mysteries under investigation. He had been caught up in Philip's dark design against Edward of England, yet there might be an area of this tangled, bloody situation that had nothing to do with the machinations of the Louvre: namely the murders of the Templars at St Giles and the killing of Slingsby at the Merry Mercy. Was there a killer on the prowl? Someone responsible for the deaths of the Templars, the destruction of Rougehead's coven and the murder of Slingsby? Was this assassin motivated by the cruel deaths of those two former Templars who called themselves Sumerscale and Fallowfield?

Corbett's mind went back to the devil incarnate Rougehead. According to that renegade, Ausel did not know why his comrades were being killed or who could be responsible. But surely that was not true? Again Corbett recalled Rougehead, and the clerk stiffened. Something was very, very wrong. Something he had missed. He had been so relieved at being rescued, he had not concentrated on what Rougehead had said and done at Temple Combe. He quietly promised that once he had finished the present task and returned to London, he would reflect most carefully on Rougehead's abduction of them, the journey to the Templar manor and their confrontation there.

Corbett dozed for a while. He startled awake at the arrival of two of Ap Ythel's archers, who informed him in their lilting voices that their captain and his cohort had reached the Sunne in Splendour and were setting up watches on all approaches to the tavern as well as this stretch of coastline. Corbett thanked them and returned to the hostelry, where the archers, typical soldiers, were busy cooking a meal and flirting with Gunhilda. Corbett again questioned Penda, and later in the afternoon, he summoned the Magister, Ranulf and Ap Ythel to the ground-floor chamber of the flint tower, a cavernous, spacious room, its walls freshly plastered; the floor was of scrubbed stone and the large lattice window allowed in air and light.

At Corbett's request, the Magister started the proceedings using parchment and quill pen supplied by Ranulf. He drew a crude map of the large inlet only a short walk away, as well as a rough sketch of *The Black Hogge*, with its high stern and prow castles, two masts and projecting bowsprit. Corbett had had a lanternhorn lit and placed on the table so all could see the parchments clearly, and he suppressed a shiver at the deepening tension around the table. The day had been glorious, but the juddering light of the lantern showed that it was coming to an end, and darkness was creeping towards them like some mythical beast across the moorland. The sun was setting fast, and here they were plotting another bloody life-and-death struggle, a gamble of trickery and courage to carry the day.

'Remember,' the Magister began, '*The Black Hogge* is dangerous as long as it can sail and manoeuvre, but once it is stricken, out in open water, it is truly vulnerable. Now as yet we have no sight of our enemy. I wager it will arrive on the evening tide sometime during the next few days.' He traced a line on the makeshift map. 'Gaston Foix will bring his cog in as close as he can to the shore, but he will be wary of grounding it. He will then drop the anchor stone and lower his shore boat, probably a four-oared craft like the one kept here, with extra men armed and buckled for battle.'

'What will they bring?' Corbett asked. 'What do they need?'

'Purveyance, Sir Hugh, but above all water. Remember, they have been at sea. The fresh water they took on last time has gone, turned brackish or tinged with salt, not to mention the filth from the vermin on board ship.'

'And there are casks and waterskins ready for them here.' Ranulf spoke up. 'Penda has shown them to us.'

'True,' the Magister agreed. 'Now when that devil incarnate Rougehead still crawled under the sun, this is what happened. The shore boat would pull in bringing casks and waterskins to be cleaned, scoured and made ready for next time. These would be replaced with fresh casks and waterskins already prepared, because the hours slip away and *The Black Hogge* must sail on the morning tide. Now this is what I propose . . .'

The next day, Corbett rose early. He washed as best he could using water heated in the old tavern kitchen. He ate some bread, boiled bacon and dried fruit and walked down to stand on the sand hills gazing out over the sea. Ranulf, his war belt strapped on, came up silently beside him. For a while he too stared at the far horizon.

'Will it work, Sir Hugh, the Magister's plan?'

'It has to, Ranulf. It's the only ploy we have. If we are successful – and we must be immediately – then the game is ours. Look down at that beach: many men are going to die there whether our plan works or not. There will be blood and there will be death.'

During the next few hours, the final preparations were made. The shore boat was filled with casks and skins brimming not with water but with oil, found in the tavern's storerooms. Small pots of fire were also primed ready to be lit, and placed in sacks, which were taken down to the sand hills together with other barrels, casks and skins and covered with cloths against the wind-blown sand. All the time Ap Ythel had his keen-eyed archers scanning the horizon.

Late in the afternoon the alarm was raised by one of the archers whistling long and shrill. Corbett and Ranulf, now garbed in the heavy black cloaks of the dead assassins, with their thick mantles and deep hoods, stood on the sand hills looking out over the sea. Behind them, hiding in the coarse grass, lay Ap Ythel with twenty of his archers, war bows and quivers at the ready. Corbett watched fascinated as the dark smudge became more and more distinct against the white-blue sky, like some nightmare beast crawling over the horizon to demonstrate its power, strength and speed.

'A true leviathan,' he whispered, 'a terror of the seas.'

The Black Hogge was now fully distinct, and the closer it drew, the more formidable it became. A true ship of menace with its high, powerful fore and stern castles, its deep, rounded belly, jutting bowsprit and lofty masts. As it approached, Corbett breathed a prayer of relief: the sails were being reefed, the ship turning slightly on the incoming tide. The Magister was correct. Gaston Foix was bringing his craft in as close as possible, its sails fully furled. Peering intently, Corbett could see a cluster of men in the bows preparing to cast the anchor stone on the end of its rattling chain. He did not know if those on board could clearly see him, but now and then he and Ranulf would lift a hand in greeting. He wanted the crew to study them and conclude that Rougehead's assassins had returned safely with their captives.

The afternoon drew on. Corbett and Ranulf continued their vigil from a more secure place. At last the crew of *The Black Hogge* began their preparations to go ashore. The four-oared boat was lowered. Corbett counted four mariners climbing down the rope ladder to man it and four more as an armed escort. He and Ranulf slipped back up over the sand hills to inform Ap Ythel, who prepared two lines of archers, ten in each row, a few yards from where the beach path cut through the sand hills to debouch on to the moorland. Now concealed, Corbett watched the boat push off from *The Black Hogge*: it rose and fell on the swell, the oars lifting and dipping in unison, then settled and cut through the waves towards the beach. The incoming tide helped it surge forward, until at last its keel screeched on the gravel along the shoreline. Corbett watched the men jump out, shouting at each other as they pulled the boat clear of the water and began to unload the empty barrels and flat leather skins.

'It's time,' he whispered. He emerged from hiding and strode down towards the beach. Cloaked, mantled and cowled in the assassin's black robes, he could only pray that the mariners would accept him as such. Ranulf, not so skilled in the French tongue, followed behind.

'My friends, my friends.' Corbett tried to imitate the patois he'd heard between Rougehead and Primus. 'Welcome! We have fresh food and the best Bordeaux, all is ready!'

He turned and descended the sand hill, drawing swiftly to one side. The eight mariners from *The Black Hogge* followed him over the rise, chattering so excitedly they hardly noticed Ap Ythel's archers suddenly emerge from behind a line of bush and gorse. The archers had their bows primed and curved, the twine pulled back, the deadly shafts in place. The Frenchmen stopped in alarm, too shocked to shout, turn or flee. Corbett's heart lurched at the sight of eight souls blundering into sudden and savage death.

'Aim!' Ap Ythel cried. 'Loose!'

Twenty shafts ripped through the air, followed within a few heartbeats by twenty more. The archers then moved forward, fresh arrows notched, but it was all over. The French lay twisted grotesquely, arrow shafts deep in neck, chest and groin. A few groans carried. A body twitched in the final spasms of death, but then that numbing silence that in Corbett's experience always followed a sudden, brutal assault, seemed to gather them all in its chilling embrace. Ap Ythel, his long stabbing dirk drawn, moved amongst the fallen, but there was no need for any mercy cut: all eight were dead.

Corbett shook himself free of the nightmare reverie, reminding himself how these men and their cog had waged cruel and constant war against English ships and their crews. Men such as these had slaughtered Naseby, Torpel and others.

'Quick, quick!' he ordered. 'Strip them, dress in their clothes.'

Ap Ythel and seven specially selected archers hastened to obey, doffing their own jerkins and donning the bloodied, salt-soaked garments of the dead. Once they were ready, Corbett instructed them to move the barrels and skins full of oil up over the sand hills and down to the ship's boat, a long, deep-bellied craft. The other shore boat, filled with the remaining casks and skins, was dragged from its hiding place among the rocks and down to the water's edge. All the time, Corbett kept a close eye on *The Black Hogge*, swaying at anchor.

He could see little groups gathering on board, and his nervousness deepened at the sheer size of this fighting cog and the dangers they would confront very soon.

The Magister had described his battle plan in great detail: he and Ap Ythel and four of the archers, chosen because they could swim, would take the shore boat out. They would pretend to be trying to manoeuvre around *The Black Hogge* and would become deliberately entangled with the bowsprit, which, as Corbett could now see, hung down in a mass of cordage and dangling ropes. At the same time, Corbett and Ranulf, still dressed in the black garb of Rougehead's assassins, would go across in *The Black Hogge*'s shore boat. According to the Magister, the crew would lower nets for the casks, barrels and waterskins. The most dangerous step was next. Corbett and Ranulf, leaving the four archers dressed as oarsmen, would have to climb the rope ladder and follow the net aboard. The Magister pointed out that the net would be resting somewhere close to the mast that rose midship. They must try and pull or push it closer to the mast. Ranulf, who would have slit and punctured as many of the containers as possible, would then toss the pots of fire from the sack he was carrying on to the seeping oil, and both clerks would leave as swiftly as possible.

'Are we ready?' Corbett whispered. 'Remember, do not speak as we approach. St Michael and St George guard us.'

Both boats pushed out. The Magister and his crew pulled away. Corbett watched the oarsmen of his own boat bend and pull. Closer and closer they drew to *The Black Hogge*, massive, dark and threatening. The Magister was now a distance away, his boat turning slightly in its manoeuvre to cross the bows of the war cog. The day was dying, the breeze sharper, the incoming tide powerful. Corbett pulled up his hood. The ship's hull was now very close, soaring like some monster above them. He recalled his days as a mailed clerk, scurrying to join the others at the foot of some siege ladder. This was no different.

The leading oarsman whispered an order, and the shore boat scraped against the deep-bellied hull. Corbett glanced up as a mass of cordage was hoisted down towards them. Men were shouting from the taffrail above. He drew a deep breath, gripping the tangle of net being lowered. Two of the oarsmen helped as he and Ranulf began to load the casks, barrels and skins. Ranulf drew his stiletto, winked at Corbett and began to pierce the skins and barrels as they became tangled in the hard-roped net.

'As much as possible,' Corbett whispered.

A voice rang out above them. A rope ladder was lowered and Corbett carefully stepped on to it, Ranulf behind him. The cog moved on the swell. The ladder slapped against the side as the ship twisted and turned. Above Corbett's head, the net and its bulky cargo was being slowly pulled up. The clerk closed his eyes and murmured a prayer. He could hear the shouts and cries caused by the Magister's boat, which was now tangled beneath the bowsprit. At last he reached the gap in the taffrail, and he and Ranulf were pulled on board.

Corbett became aware of a broad deck. Men milled about; they smiled and raised their hands. Corbett responded, talking swiftly in the sailors' patois. Ranulf was close beside him. The net and its cargo sprawled on the glistening deck. Corbett shouted orders, urging members of the crew to push it closer to the great squat mast. Mariners hurried to obey. Corbett stepped back. Ranulf opened the sack beneath his cloak and took out a small fire pot, charcoal gleaming through the slits. He carefully put this down, followed by another, tilting them slightly so the tops came off and the flames leapt out. At first, no one noticed. A tongue of fire ran along one of the punctured skins, a darting, dangerous blue-gold flame. Ranulf threw the third pot, its coals fully flamed, only to slip on the oil now oozing out, his hood going back to reveal his red hair. Corbett grasped his arm, pulling him back to the gap in the taffrail.

The crew were now alerted, distracted both by the flames dancing over the casks, skins and barrels and by these two strangers hastily retreating across the deck. Shouts and cries raised the alarm. Corbett glimpsed a man coming out of a cabin beneath the stern castle; he was sure it was the master, Gaston Foix, but then a sheet of flame erupted from the net now resting against the mast. More cries and shouts echoed. Corbett glanced to his left, where members of the crew were trying to untangle the mass of ropes around the bowsprit. It was time to leave. He pushed Ranulf towards the taffrail, on to the dangling, swinging rope ladder. Ranulf, nimble as any squirrel, scrambled down. Corbett followed. Above them they could feel the fierce heat from the fires raging on board.

A crossbow bolt whipped the air around them. Corbett tried not to panic, hurrying down, almost kicking Ranulf into the waiting boat. The oarsmen immediately pulled away. The light was poor, the glistening sea reflecting the fire above them. One of the oarsmen screamed, body jerking, arms flailing, as a crossbow bolt pierced his skull. He thrashed about, then toppled over the side into the sea. They could do nothing for him. Corbett recalled the details of their plan and ordered the oarsmen to turn and pull beneath the bowsprit. Ap Ythel, the Magister and three archers scrambled aboard even as their captain tossed the primed fire pots on to the open casks and slit skins. The boat they had left, saturated with oil, erupted into sheets of flame, which leapt hungrily to embrace the wood, ropes and cordage of the bowsprit.

'Pull away, pull away!' Corbett urged. 'We have been . . .' He fell silent as another oarsman screamed, kicking out in agony at the pain of the arbalest bolts that had shattered both chest and stomach. The archer lurched forward, blood spluttering out of nose and mouth. Ap Ythel leaned against him, spoke softly in Welsh, then, with one swift cut, slit the man's throat, giving him the ultimate mercy. The boat crammed with men swerved and twisted on the tide still surging in. They were now free of *The Black Hogge*, buffeted by both the breeze and the racing waves. Corbett glanced over his shoulder. The enemy ship was sheeted in flame, whilst a roaring fire had broken out around the bowsprit. Any attempt to control and quench the blaze had been given up. Members of the crew were trying frantically to escape, jumping overboard, desperate to cling to anything.

'Contrary to popular law,' the Magister declared, 'not all mariners can swim; indeed, very few can. God have pity on them.' He turned and began to count the men now crowded around him, jostling for comfort in the cramped conditions.

'We have lost three,' Ap Ythel declared. 'Two here, whilst Ap Thomas fell overboard when we were beneath the bowsprit. I tried to grab him.'

'I think the ship moved and cracked his skull,' one of the other archers proclaimed in a singsong voice.

'Poor Ap Thomas, I shall miss him.'

Corbett stretched out and touched Ranulf lightly on the arm.

'Well done, Clerk of the Green Wax.'

'I shouldn't have slipped.'

'Many things shouldn't have happened . . .' Corbett broke off as a crack echoed across the water. *The Black Hogge* was now breaking up, showering the sea around it with fiery shards and a furious blaze of sparks. A pall of black smoke was spreading around and above the ship as it continued to disintegrate in the heat.

'You see,' the Magister, crouching next to Corbett, spoke up, '*The Black Hogge* has been at sea during the height of summer, so its woodwork, sails and cordage are bone dry. Oil and fire will create an inferno fiercer than in any blacksmith's forge.' He grabbed Corbett's arm. 'You'll remember your promise, Sir Hugh?'

'I shall never forget. Rest assured . . .' Corbett broke off as the keel crunched into the pebbled beach. The rest of Ap Ythel's archers came running down to help pull the boat clear, chattering in their native tongue, shaking hands with their comrades and shouting congratulations, though one of them began to chant a lamentation for the fallen. Corbett asked Ap Ythel to impose order, pointing to what the surging tide was now driving in: pieces of wreckage and the occasional corpse, most of these displaying gruesome burn wounds. At Corbett's request, Ap Ythel deployed his archers along the beach, war bows strung, arrows notched.

The setting sun now poured across the sea, creating a glittering blood-red path that seemed to stretch towards *The Black Hogge*. The ship was no longer the majestic, formidable cog of war but a smouldering funeral pyre of darting flames and plumes of thick black smoke. Its remains were beginning to sink. Corbett could glimpse corpses, pieces of wreckage and the occasional survivor clinging on to a barrel, chest or sturdy piece of timber. Ap Ythel wanted vengeance for his three men, eager to kill anyone who came out of the sea. The Magister was equally ferocious in his judgement: the crew of *The Black Hogge* were pirates, they had been caught red-handed. According to the law, they were wolfsheads and could be slain on sight. Corbett had to exercise his authority, producing the royal seal and finally drawing sword and dagger. Ranulf followed suit.

In truth, Corbett was sick and tired of the killing. 'I do not thirst for my enemy's blood,' he declared. He wanted the survivors to remain as such. He needed these to discover how *The Black Hogge* seemed to know so much so swiftly about English ships leaving Queenhithe. Moreover, they could be exchanged for English prisoners held in France. By the time the first survivors crawled out of the sea, he had convinced his colleagues. Moreover, the sight of over a dozen bedraggled, dazed and wounded men and boys also softened attitudes. The archers lowered their bows. Ap Ythel ordered the prisoners to walk up over the sand hills whilst Corbett reassured them they were not being taken to their deaths but to be questioned. One of the prisoners appeared to doubt this and broke free, careering along the beach. Before Corbett could stop him, an archer, his bow strung, loosed two shafts in a matter of breaths; these struck the fugitive full in the back so he collapsed and lay still. Frightened by this, the rest of the prisoners complied.

Once over the sand hills, Ap Ythel made them sit down, and a water pannikin and pieces of dried biscuit were shared out. Corbett then began to question them, proclaiming that cooperation would earn them greater mercies and that if they complied, they would be held as prisoners of war and eventually sent back to France: this apparently comforted them and made them more pliable. A tall, thickset man, Sulpice, a lifelong sailor out of Harfleur, became their spokesman. He assured

Corbett that Gaston Foix and all his officers were dead. Sulpice talked swiftly, Corbett translating for the others. Apparently the oil spilt on the constantly tilting deck soon spread everywhere, dripping down into the hold, whilst the fire erupting around the bowsprit only intensified the fury of the attack. The deck became a lake of fire that spread swiftly.

Sulpice and the Magister began to exchange comments in the lingua franca. Corbett used the opportunity to walk up the sand hills and stare out over the sea. He felt an eerie sadness. The majestic and magnificent *Black Hogge* was now nothing but a mess of charred timber and dying pools of fire beneath wisps of dark smoke. He walked back to the prisoners, demanding to be told how Gaston Foix could know so much about the movements of English shipping. Sulpice just shrugged, turned away and spat. Ranulf drew his sword and dagger. Ap Ythel notched his bow.

'*Les oiseaux! Les oiseaux!*' The young man who stepped forward was no more than thirteen summers old. Sulpice shouted at him. The boy made a crude sign back and replied with an invective even Corbett couldn't follow, although he was distracted by what he'd just heard. He didn't know whether to laugh or cry: such a simple solution! Once again he, a so-called master of logic, had ignored the obvious.

He told Ranulf to resheathe his sword, then took two coins out of his belt purse, thrust one into Sulpice's hand and went to kneel by the boy, who was now beginning to shiver. Corbett wrapped his own cloak about him and pressed the second coin into the boy's thin, callused hand, smiling at the lad's narrow face and fearful eyes.

'What is your name?'

'Geranti.'

'Geranti, tell me about the birds. Courier pigeons, yes? They carry messages in little drums or miniature canisters attached to their legs. The thinnest parchment is used, the message cryptic?'

Geranti nodded, adding that he had been Gaston Foix's page, his cabin boy. Corbett translated for the rest, the news causing surprise, consternation and laughter, then demanded silence as Geranti described how the pigeons were kept in cages below the deck. Apparently they were Gaston Foix's pride and joy, his personal pets, and they regarded *The Black Hogge* as their home nest. Sulpice, now realising that refusal to answer would achieve nothing, also participated in the discussion. Stamping his feet and rubbing his arms, he described how Foix loved the birds and kept them well fed. Apparently these courier pigeons were released to some place in London, where they would be fed before bringing back messages with news about English shipping. Foix would use his sea charts to return *The Black Hogge* to the same position, or near it, so the birds could find it more easily.

'But where did they fly to?' Corbett demanded. 'To whom were they sent?' Sulpice simply pulled a face and spread his hands, whilst Geranti shook his head, and Corbett sensed that they honestly didn't know.

Deeply intrigued and wishing to reflect on what he had learnt, Corbett entrusted the prisoners to Ap Ythel and the Magister whilst he and Ranulf walked back to the Sunne in Splendour. They found Penda and Gunhilda all alarmed by the sounds they'd heard and the sight of the glow of a fierce fire against the sky. Corbett swiftly comforted them, satisfying their curiosity as well as winning their full cooperation with an offer. Master Rougehead and his minions, he assured them, would never be coming back. The Sunne in Splendour was now theirs. He solemnly promised that as soon as he returned to London, Ranulf would go to Westminster and have this offer sealed, witnessed and formally enrolled on the great exchequer remembrancer. Both innocents were delighted. Corbett gave them direct and precise instructions how, if they wished, they could collect a copy of this document from the general chancery office near the great hall of Westminster. He also made them memorise his name and those of Ranulf and Chanson before talking to them further about Master Rougehead and his journeys to London.

Once satisfied, Corbett left the Sunne in Splendour to sit by himself, even refusing Ranulf's offer of food. He reflected on his imprisonment at Temple Combe, Rougehead's drinking, his hatred, what he had spat out and how he'd acted. He also recalled the patois he'd heard on *The Black Hogge*.

'I wonder,' he whispered to himself. 'I truly do.'

Ever since leaving Temple Combe, certain suspicions had begun to flourish in Corbett's mind. He wondered whether what he had seen and heard was the truth. He suspected he had been drawn into a game of shifting shadows, of clever half-truths and subtle lies. Just because something was obvious didn't mean it shouldn't be scrutinised most carefully. Corbett, now quietly chastising himself for overlooking the possibility of the French using courier pigeons, promised himself that he would study all that he had seen, heard and learnt so that he could eventually find a path out of this tangled shadowland and confront his real opponent.

He let himself relax. He now felt tired and hungry. He returned to the tavern taproom and had a brief meeting with Ap Ythel and the Magister, who agreed to take the prisoners to the Tower and to keep them secure there. They also solemnly promised to ensure that what had happened at Temple Combe and Saltcot remained secret until ordered otherwise. Corbett thanked them, then gratefully accepted Ranulf's offer of a bowl of meat stew and a goblet of watered wine. Seated with his companion in the small buttery adjoining the taproom, he took out his horn spoon and slowly ate the spiced meat. Once finished, he wiped the horn spoon clean and sat cradling his wine cup.

'Sir Hugh?'

'Ranulf.' Corbett struck his breast. '*Mea culpa, mea culpa, mea maxima culpa*. My fault, my blame. I ignored the obvious because I didn't reflect on it!'

'Master?'

'Many years ago, Ranulf, when I was young and handsome, a mailed clerk all buckled for battle, the old king's chancellor Robert Burnel, Bishop of Bath and Wells, picked me to be his henchman, his heir, his successor. He was the hardest of taskmasters. Much harder than I ever was on you. Burnel instructed me on all matters regarding the Secret Chancery: its hidden alphabets, the scytale of the ancients, the tradecraft of the Byzantines and the exotic alphabets of the Arabs. The old king, then a young prince, returned from Outremer in love with what Burnel called the art of secret writing, of dressing messages up in parables and of communicating secrets in the safest way. Now, the use of courier or messenger birds is as old as creation itself . . .'

Corbett paused as some of the Welsh archers, never ones for ignoring an opportunity, broke into one of their battle hymns, giving praise to the setting sun, a strong, vibrant chorus of deep, heart-plucking melody. On any other occasion Corbett would have loved to sit and listen, or even better, participate.

'Noah!' Ranulf said, desperate not to let him give into temptation and join the singers.

'Noah,' Corbett agreed. 'According to scripture, he released that dove from the ark in the hope of finding dry land. Many kings and princes have used birds as couriers. I know that. Burnel made me read all the ancients, especially Pliny's *Natural History*. Pigeons have served as couriers for thousands of years. The ancient Greeks dispatched them to proclaim the victor in the Olympics. The Roman consul Hirtius also used them during the siege of Modena; the Saracens in Outremer. Saladin and his ancestors were most skilled in their management, whilst Genoa and Venice have watch towers in the Middle Sea that communicate by courier pigeon. Now according to Burnel, when the old king came back from Outremer, he was full of admiration for this system.'

'So what happened?' Ranulf asked.

'Edward Longshanks,' Corbett pithily replied, 'had, apart from his love for his wife Eleanor, one consuming passion . . .'

'Hawks and falcons?'

'Hawks and falcons,' Corbett agreed. 'He adored them, he called them his children. You have seen the great mews he had built at Queen's Cross? Once, when his favourite hawk fell ill, I had to take a waxen image of the damned bird to Becket's shrine at Canterbury and light dozens of tapers around the saint's tomb so the hawk would recover. Thank God,' he breathed, 'it did. On another occasion I had to physically restrain the king from beating to death a squire who had accidentally injured a hawk. Anyway,' Corbett glanced up at the darkening sky, 'pigeons and hawks do not mix. Hawks are ferocious hunters; their appetite for blood must be sharpened. They are trained to search out their quarry, then kill it. Pigeons are their natural prey: fat, cumbersome in the first few flusters of flight, they are easy to catch; a hawk could satisfy its appetite for days. Edward would not have pigeons close to where his court moved, be it Windsor, York or Berwick. Little wonder the old king forgot, even forbade, the use of courier pigeons – and so did we!'

Corbett paused, listening to the singing. 'Gaston Foix must have loved his birds. I strongly suspect he saw service in the Middle Sea, probably as a mariner serving on the galleys of Genoa or Venice.'

'But can pigeons find their nest at sea?'

'Ranulf, I should have known. I have read Pliny's *Natural History*. He offers a wealth of advice about pigeons, as he does about bees. These birds are swift and sure fliers. If I recall correctly, they can carry messages from anywhere back to their home. Gaston Foix made *The Black Hogge* their home; they would be raised and fed there. At first they would have to be transported to one place and released from there. However, as time passed and they became more experienced, they could pass safely to and fro, backwards and forwards, their home in one location and their food in another.'

'But *The Black Hogge* moved . . .'

'As do the galleys of Venice and Genoa, as do armies on the march. These couriers search out their home; they are remarkably accurate. In addition, Ranulf, remember what Sulpice told us. How Gaston Foix kept *The Black Hogge* at a certain location off the coast of Essex; the pigeons would return there. This system would have taken weeks to develop. I suspect the birds were first brought here from *The Black Hogge* then taken into London by Rougehead. They would then be handed to someone else, who fed them but also used them to send ciphered messages to Gaston Foix about what cogs were leaving Queenhithe.'

'Master, would it be swift enough?'

'Ranulf, I assure you, if a pigeon was released at noon somewhere in Queenhithe, it would be home on *The Black Hogge* before darkness fell. On occasion, I admit, something might go wrong. A bird could be injured, be attacked by a hawk, or killed on the ground if it rested. Oh yes, I am sure if we looked at the rota of ships, we would be mystified why certain ones weren't attacked and reached their destination safely. Of course, in the main, the courier pigeon is swift and precise, be it journeying home to its nest and its mate or back to the source of its food.'

'So *The Black Hogge* was its nest, but where in Queenhithe was its feed? Master, I have walked the Merry Mercy.' Ranulf got to his feet. 'I saw nothing suspicious.'

'No, neither did I. Let us think, Ranulf.' Corbett patted his companion on the shoulder and decided to walk around the Sunne in Splendour. He found that all was well. The French prisoners had been roped and placed in front of a roaring fire with something to eat and drink. The Welsh archers sat with them or at other fires. Corbett pronounced himself satisfied. Ranulf brought across a fresh platter of food and two goblets of what he called the best Bordeaux. Corbett sipped at the wine and agreed.

'Penda said that Rougehead loved his red wine,' declared Ranulf, 'which is why he never left here until the strangers garbed in black arrived a few days ago. Rougehead would often drink himself insensible.'

Corbett listened intently and tried to hide his surprise.

'Impossible,' he caught his breath, 'but that's impossible.'

'Sir Hugh?'

'Grandison was stabbed to death out on that lonely meadow around the midnight hour. Datchet was slaughtered in his own chamber. Boveney sitting in that enclave along the church of St Giles. Burghesh and Stapleton stuck like pigs in the sanctuary of Holy Trinity the Little. Slingsby pierced in that garderobe at the Merry Mercy. Those leper knights mercilessly executed. Nor must we forget poor old Rohesia, the collector of cat skins.'

'I do not . . .'

'We are not just hunting a murderer but a true assassin, someone who thoroughly enjoys killing as well as someone who, I suspect, is settling debts.'

'Sir Hugh, I cannot follow your logic.'

'I will come back to that, but for the moment, let's reflect on what the Magister told us about the Poultneys who once owned this tavern. Now what was it? Matilda died in 1281, whilst her son John moved to Queenhithe in London, where he died in 1293 without heir. Or did he?'

'Sir Hugh, you think not?'

'We shall see. We leave with all possible speed for Westminster at first light. The answers to these questions will be found in the city. Tell the Magister to prepare for a hard ride. We'll take the treasure with us in panniers thrown over one of the horses. Ap Ythel and his men can take care of the prisoners.'

'Sir Hugh, you talked of the murders being the work of a ruthless killer. Not Ausel, surely?'

'No, no. Ausel was a coward, a man who thought every bush was a bear.'

'Rougehead?'

'Oh yes.'

'But master, he is as dead as Ausel.' Corbett half smiled. 'He is dead!' Ranulf repeated.

Corbett just clasped his companion's hand, bade him goodnight and walked away.

PART NINE

'And so does a man offer his soul up for sale . . .'
The Monk of Malmesbury, *Life of Edward II*

Corbett knelt on the prie-dieu before the statue of the Virgin and Child close to the Secret Chancery at the very heart of the huddle and maze of buildings that housed the Crown's retainers at Westminster. A small, jewel-like oratory, the chapel of St Thomas the Apostle was carpeted completely in blue and gold. The softest turkey cloths of the thickest wool lay on the floor; boards of quilted arras proclaiming the same colours covered the walls. All sound was deadened; the silence was something that could be almost grasped and held. It was claimed that this ancient and holy place was once a chantry chapel of the Confessor: a serene abode of prayer illuminated by the light pouring through the exquisitely painted oriel window above the chapel altar to Corbett's right.

The clerk leaned back on his heels and stared at the candles he'd lit in thanksgiving for his escape as well as the safety and well-being of his family and friends. Behind him, Ranulf was whispering strict instructions

331

to Chanson. They had arrived back at the Merry Mercy before Vespers the previous evening. Corbett had assured Mistress Philippa that all was well, though he could tell that the sharp-eyed taverner sensed he was being less than truthful. After a good night's sleep, he and Ranulf had broken their fast, shaved, washed and changed their clothes. Corbett's cloak was filthy, so he handed it over to the washerwoman busy at the tavern well and Mistress Philippa lent him one of her late husband's. Corbett had wrapped this about him, revelling in its delicate and refreshing perfume as he walked the tavern.

Ranulf was correct: there was no trace of any pigeons being housed, fed or maintained at the Merry Mercy. Moreover, by judicious enquiry, Corbett discovered that Mistress Philippa and her late husband had refused to build a dovecote because of the smell and dirt such a building could cause. Afterwards he inspected the jakes where Slingsby had been stabbed, and then asked Mistress Philippa to fetch a selection of candles so he could dedicate one to Holy Trinity the Little, which he hoped to visit later in the day. Mystified, the tavern mistress had hastened to comply.

Mistress Philippa was brimming with questions about de Craon and his henchman Brother Jerome. She raised the subject in the taproom, where Corbett and Ranulf were breaking their fast. Agnes Sokelar came sidling in, eager to learn why the two Frenchmen had not returned from Westminster. Corbett blandly informed them that it was probably for de Craon's own protection; however, he promised that when he visited the palace, he would make his own diligent enquiries . . .

Corbett blinked and struck his breast in sorrow. He had not been praying but lost in distraction. He murmured a swift Ave and continued to stare at the statue of the Virgin. Feeling a slight cramp, he turned, and his gaze was caught by a vividly depicted wall fresco. The artist – Corbett suspected he was from abroad – had depicted the damned as worshipping a huge strawberry, the symbol of the earth. They had gathered around the gigantic fruit to greedily devour it, swarming so close they merged together and lost any individuality in their lust to whet their appetites. Close by the strawberry, a flock of birds stood watching. At first glance there was nothing special about these, but on further scrutiny, the sharp beaks and unblinking black eyes grew more menacing, revealing their true malignant nature: demons waiting for their chance to strike. Corbett felt the painting reflected the world he was now moving through, with its nightmare souls.

'Sir Hugh?'

He turned, rose and walked over to exchange the kiss of peace with Walter Reynolds, royal chaplain and the king's favourite cleric, a priest, according to court gossip, destined for the highest offices in both Church and state. A svelte, darkly handsome man of medium height, Reynolds was dressed in a fashionable red and gold cote-hardie over a pure linen shirt and dark-blue woollen leggings pushed into gleaming boots of blood-red Spanish leather. His night-black hair and moustache were neatly clipped, the full lips pursed, the dark, soulful eyes unblinking in their stare. Reynolds was shrewd, a court watcher, a man who liked to stay in the shadows but could make his presence felt when he wanted. Now he stood back, eyeing Corbett from head to toe.

'You are safe.' He smiled. 'Come.' He plucked Corbett by the sleeve and they walked arm in arm across the small chapel. Corbett whispered swiftly about what had happened. Reynolds broke free, his face transformed by the most brilliant smile. 'Oh Lord, Hugh!' he gasped. 'The king will be so pleased! *The Black Hogge* destroyed, its crew gone, the few who survived prisoners. Royal treasure found and seized and malefactors brutally executed for daring to invade the king's realm.'

'My friend.' Corbett seized the chaplain's velvet-gloved hand and pulled him closer, so that their faces were only inches apart. 'The king must not know, not yet. Ap Ythel's cohort will come first to the Tower. They are to be detained there, the prisoners locked away, the treasure stored in the Chapel of the Evangelist. The archers must be richly rewarded with good food and drink, but what has happened at Temple Combe and Saltcot must not be discussed or proclaimed until I say. Two things especially. On no account must de Craon and his sinister soul shadow Brother Jerome know what has happened. I want to be there when they learn the truth. Second,' he undid his belt wallet and handed Reynolds a parchment script, 'I want the clerk Fitzosbert to search out what I have written here. It should not be difficult. In a short while I am going to tell him personally, but I would like your support. Fitzosbert can scrutinise the archives. I will also ask the Wolfman and the Magister Viae to help. All three must be lavishly rewarded.' Reynolds nodded his agreement. 'In addition,' Corbett continued, 'my good colleagues can also sweep Queenhithe's taverns and ale houses for information.'

Reynolds stared at the ground, tapping his foot, then glanced up. 'Hugh, you ask for things to be kept confidential. I will do my very best, but already along Queenhithe they are talking about how easy it has become to cross the Narrow Seas now that *The Black Hogge* seems to have disappeared. Merchant ships go backwards and forwards untroubled. We are also getting information out of France that not all is well in Paris. You will be pleased to learn that the Deacon escaped to Boulogne, from where he has sent urgent messages. He believes that Pietal and Tallefert are dead, tortured and barbarously killed. I suspect you know that's the truth.'

Corbett nodded. He walked back to the statue of the Virgin, carefully lit two tapers and recited the requiem. Reynolds came up behind him and put a hand on his shoulder. 'Hugh, may they rest in peace, but the task is not yet finished. I bid you farewell.'

Corbett watched him go, then walked across to a small chantry enclave. The wooden panelling attached to the wall above the altar proclaimed the story of Adam and Eve after the fall. The artist had depicted an

Eden rapidly turning dark and malignant: a cat carried off its kill, two cockatrices fought over a dead frog, whilst nearby, a three-headed crane nested in a formidable-looking dragon tree. Once again the dark scenes seemed to be a reflection of his own experiences. Nevertheless, he admired the artist's skill and recalled a promise he had made to Lady Maeve and their two children that one day soon he would show them around Westminster. He now quietly vowed to keep such a promise. Life was short; its ending could be brutal and quick. After journeying to Temple Combe and Saltcot and receiving the tragic news about Tallefert and Pietal, Corbett wanted more than anything to immerse himself deep in the love and friendship of his wife and family, his manor, his orderly beehives and his cherished choir, where he could sing the great chants of the liturgical season. He must return to Leighton. They would soon be finished here. Deep in his soul, he felt that they were now moving to judgement.

'Sir Hugh?' Ranulf stood in the doorway. 'They are here.'

Corbett followed him out to where the Magister, the Wolfman and Fitzosbert stood in the shadow of the Lady Chapel. Once again Corbett thanked them, and insisted on the greatest secrecy and confidentiality. He then handed each of them a copy of the script he'd given Walter Reynolds. 'Please,' he whispered, 'find out as much as you can. Bring it to me at the Merry Mercy; we can meet there.'

Cowled and cloaked despite the warm sun, Corbett

and Ranulf left Westminster at King's Steps. The barge they hired made a swift run. The river swell was placid, only a calm breeze ruffling its surface. Corbett sat back under the leather awning in the stern, revelling at being back in the city. He savoured the variety of smells and odours from the summer stalls set up along the river-bank. This was a season of pageantry, when the guilds, eager to display their wealth, staged masques and mystery plays both on the Thames and along the quay-sides. Barges packed with mummers, all dressed for the part, journeyed along with a blare of trumpets, stand-ards and banners flapping. One barge rode alongside Corbett's and the clerk clambered to his feet to look more closely: there was an actor with a sow's mask under a nun's wimple next to a mummer with a moon face, whilst two monkey demons escorted a red-wigged Herod. He watched them go and sat down again.

The oarsmen were complaining about how busy the river had become. Bumboats, fruit barges, fishing smacks, herring craft as well as great war barges crammed with soldiers moved busily across the water. Corbett sensed a holiday atmosphere, a contentment. He idly wondered if news about the destruction of *The Black Hogge* was somehow seeping through London, as all such rumours did: a few words here, a conver-sation in that tavern or ale house . . . Soon the news would be confirmed, and once it was, the merchants and shipowners would greatly rejoice and flock to their guild chapels in thanksgiving.

Ranulf shook his arm and Corbett looked up. The

barge, oars raised, was now gliding to berth along Queenhithe Steps. Ranulf paid the master and they walked up on to the cobbled, fish-stinking quayside and down a runnel that led them into the maze of alleyways. A busy, crowd-thronging day. Along the riverside the stocks and pillories were being prepared for the previous night's roisterers, now a woebegone line of pathetic half-drunks who would have to endure hours of humiliation, be it curses or flung filth, whilst wailing bagpipes drowned their cries. Tinkers and traders, recognising where the crowds would gather, had set up their tawdry stalls, whilst the lard-fingered, greasy-faced wandering cooks were firing their movable grills and stoves to prepare the usual filth for eating. The dung carts were also out, piles of ordure being lifted and dumped in them, the stench so foul that Corbett bought two pomanders for himself and Ranulf. He wondered, as he always did, if the urchins who sold these nosegays were the sons or apprentices of the burly, foul-mouthed dung collectors in their leather aprons and masked hoods.

The crowds surged, pushed and shoved around them. Cripples scurried about with alms bowls at the ready, whilst the whores moved in colourful shoals backwards and forwards from one shadowy recess to another. Professional beggars moaned sonorously, surrounded by their retainers, a gaggle of orphan children, who were trying to pluck the heart strings and so open those of the purse. One mendicant had brazenly assumed the role of a wandering preacher and, perched on a barrel surrounded by a cohort of thin-faced waifs, was delivering a sombre warning to the rich, reminding them how in hell they would simmer eternally in cauldrons of burning coins and be forced to eat snakes, toads and bats.

Corbett and Ranulf pushed their way through the crowds, left the alleyways, crossed the empty concourse and pulled on the bell rope that hung to the side of the main gate of St Giles lazar hospital. A servitor opened the postern door and took them immediately to Crowthorne, the leech, now installed in the master's parlour. He greeted them very coldly, demanding why they had returned, adding how everything was now so peaceful. Corbett was equally abrupt and asked if there was a dovecote or similar building on the site. Crowthorne ignored this and replied with a spate of questions about the recent murders, the killings in Holy Trinity the Little and the whereabouts of Reginald Ausel. Ranulf drew his sword and brought the flat of its blade down on Crowthorne's shoulder: this silenced the leech.

'King's business!' Ranulf declared. 'Answer my master's question.'

Crowthorne shrugged, then led them out of the main buildings and across the great meadow to an area that Corbett and Ranulf had never visited. The dovecote he showed them stood free of the trees: a circular stone building, much decayed. Corbett stepped inside. He asked Crowthorne to take his tinder and light a sconce torch. The leech did so, exclaiming in surprise to find torches already neatly primed resting in their holders.

He also discovered two lanternhorns, each with a thick tallow candle inside, carefully cut so the wick was ready to be lit. At Corbett's insistence, he fired both the sconce torches and the lanternhorns. Corbett moved these so as to illuminate the roundel of earth-packed floor. Squatting down, poking the ground with his gloved fingers, he scrutinised the fresh bird droppings and examined the soft feathers fluttering about in the breeze. It was obvious the dovecote had been used very recently. Ranulf, searching the walls honeycombed with recesses, found fresh nesting boxes as well as small sacks of feed and bowls for both food and water.

Once they'd left St Giles, Crowthorne's sardonic farewell ringing in their ears, Corbett plucked at Ranulf's sleeve and led him to a small ale house, where barrels served as tables and crates as stools. The floor was a mess of sawdust from a nearby carpenter's shop. Ale, beer and coarse wine was sold from casks on the greasy common table. The clerks took a seat in the corner. Corbett had chosen the ale house as a good place to hide away from the public eye.

'So, Ranulf,' he began, 'we now know that the courier pigeons nested in cages on *The Black Hogge*; they were probably Gaston Foix's personal property: a pastime he pursued, one of the possible reasons he was chosen. Anyway, in the beginning, those pigeons were brought into that dovecote at St Giles, where they were nested, fed and released. This would be repeated time and again until a pattern was set. Weeks passed and eventually the pigeons flew from *The Black Hogge* across southern

Essex and into the city to feed and nest. They would then be used to send information back.'

'How?'

'Remember, St Giles lazar hospital was founded by merchant mariners. One of the clauses in the hospital's founding charter is that its inmates pray for ships and crews leaving Queenhithe. The names of such cogs are, as we know, displayed publicly in the hospital chapel. The Guild of St Martha informed us of this.'

'So Ausel didn't even have to search for the information?'

'Precisely. *The Candle-Bright*, let us say for argument's sake, sails on a Tuesday morning. Ausel knows this immediately and dispatches a courier pigeon; the message reaches *The Black Hogge* within hours. All the Frenchman has to do is plot a route as fast as possible tacking south-west. Naseby will take the shortest route to Boulogne and *The Black Hogge* simply pursues him.' Corbett sipped at his ale. 'Agnes and Philippa did no wrong. No one could have guessed at how such information could be passed so swiftly and accurately to Gaston Foix. However,' he added warningly, 'there are certain matters I must question young Agnes about. She and her mistress have played their part in these present troubles.'

'Sir Hugh?'

Corbett drained his tankard. 'My friend, no questions now; I am still searching for answers. I hope to find most of these at Holy Trinity the Little.'

In fact Holy Trinity the Little was closed, the locks on

its main door ceremoniously sealed by the archdeacon's court. A notice pinned above the locks proclaimed how the church was under interdict because of 'heinous and sacrilegious slayings in the sanctuary'. The proclamation added that the church would remain closed until purified and reconsecrated. A troupe of enterprising travelling players had caught the mood and set up stall on the steps to present their version of Cain slaying Abel with, surprisingly enough, a female member of their troupe acting the part of God. They played out their drama before a large painted canvas depicting the Chorus of Despair at mankind's first murder. Corbett, despite his own absorption with killing and chaos, studied the canvas carefully, particularly the corner paintings where fanged frog demons conducted terrified choristers who were being forced to read hellish music with notes that looked like barbs or blots of blood imprinted on a man's bare buttocks. This unfortunate lay crushed under a gigantic harp; above him, on its wire strings, other sinners hung impaled.

'This painting certainly preaches the horror of murder,' he murmured, 'though little about its resolution. Let's find Parson Layburn. He may be able to assist . . .'

They went round the church to the sacristy door, which was now being repaired by workmen. Inside at a table sat Parson Layburn and his parish clerk, who both forced hasty smiles as Corbett and Ranulf entered.

'Parson Layburn,' Corbett sat down on the bench, Ranulf beside him, 'I want to scrutinise your parish accounts from 1288 to the present. I need to look at mass offerings, chantry gifts, the purchase of funeral plots and other such necessaries. Now, whilst I do this, my good friend and learned colleague, Ranulf-atte-Newgate, would like to ask you and your clerk certain questions . . .'

Both men hastened to comply. Corbett sat at the sacristy table going through the parish rolls, ledgers, memoranda and registers. The suspicions he had entertained hardened into certainties, whilst Ranulf, skilled at questioning, managed to draw the priest and his clerk on the hidden scandals of his parish. The afternoon wore on, the ringing of nearby church bells marking the hours of prayer. At last Corbett believed that he and Ranulf had learnt what they needed. He thanked Parson Layburn and went back through the busy, hot streets to the Merry Mercy tavern.

'Are we closing on our quarry, Sir Hugh?' Ranulf asked as soon as they were in Corbett's chamber.

'Do you remember that mummers' masque outside Holy Trinity the Little? God eventually hunts down Cain the killer and brands him as a murderer for all to see. Well,' Corbett patted Ranulf on the shoulder, 'we are close to doing God's work here, and a killer will soon be trapped, a true blood-drinker.'

'But that was Rougehead, surely, Rougehead who has now gone to judgement?'

Corbett refused to be drawn further, but sat down at the chamber's chancery desk, laid out his writing implements and, using his own cipher, began to list his conclusions. The market horns had sounded and the bells rung to mark the end of the day's trading when a messenger arrived from Chaplain Reynolds saying it was proving more and more difficult to keep de Craon and his henchman at Westminster. More importantly, Reynolds declared, rumour and gossip were already hinting at the wholesale destruction of *The Black Hogge*.

Corbett sat and reflected, staring hard at a triptych celebrating the life of the great scholar Anselm. Eventually he made a decision. He sent a message back to Reynolds asking that de Craon be kept in luxurious confinement for one more day; after that, he should be released and brought back under close escort to the Merry Mercy.

The following day Corbett continued with his clerking, pausing to welcome Fitzosbert, the Wolfman and the Magister. The information they had brought was either street gossip or from the records of the chancery and the exchequer. He thanked all three, saying that what they told him only confirmed what he already knew. Later in the afternoon, he decided he was ready. He invited Agnes Sokelar by herself to his chamber. Ranulf guarded the door as Chanson had been dispatched on other business.

'Mistress Agnes,' Corbett began, 'thank you for coming to see me. I will try to be both blunt and succinct. Why do you visit de Craon in his chambers?'

'Why do you think, Sir Hugh?' She shrugged. 'I have my own reasons.'

'Which are, mistress?'

'I lie with him.' Agnes's face now lost that mousy, rather shy look; she became harder, more defiant. 'Sir Hugh, I am no maid, some lady locked in the tower.' She glanced over her shoulder at Ranulf. 'A man has his pleasures and, if single, does as he wishes. Indeed, both marriage oaths and the vows of celibacy a priest makes are easily set aside. Your learned colleague Ranulf here is proof enough, not to mention Parson Layburn and Brother Jerome.'

'Mistress, I am not here to accuse you but to ask you why. I am not your judge. There is good reason for what you do, isn't there?' he continued. 'I know you love your father deeply. I assure you that I mean you and yours every good.' Agnes put her face in her hands, her body seeming to crumple, her shoulders sagging as she quietly wept. 'Mistress,' Corbett said soothingly, 'I need you to answer me.' She took her hands away.

'I love my father, Sir Hugh. He was, he *is* a hero. When I was a child, he fought his way out of the Accursed Tower at Acre. He saved me, but despite his bravery, not my mother.' She dried her eyes and took the goblet of watered wine Corbett poured for her. She sipped at the drink, watching Corbett retake his seat. 'He has hated the Templars ever since. However, it is not only that. When the royal treasure was stolen from the abbey crypt, rumours ran rife that my father was involved. He was not. He was totally innocent. He has always believed that such rumour-mongering was the work of Templars who may themselves have participated in the robbery. Anyway, he fell under suspicion, and because of that, he received no further preferment. And then *The Black Hogge* began its reign of terror in the Narrow Seas. People wonder who is providing its master with such accurate information.' Her face became all fierce. 'Again the finger of blame is pointed at my father.' She paused to wipe her eyes on the sleeve of her gown. 'I know my father patronises that house of pleasure, the Queen of the Night, as does Brother Jerome, the French envoy's henchman. My father has his needs but he also hoped to form a friendship with the Carmelite and so discover more . . .'

'And so you decided to court Monsigneur de Craon, or,' Corbett added tactfully, 'allow him to court you?' She nodded. 'I follow the logic of that,' Corbett declared. 'And you volunteered to help Mistress Philippa at St Giles as one of the sisters of the Guild of Saint Martha. A brave decision for a healthy young woman – to enter a lazar hospital. Ostensibly you were there to help, but secretly . . .'

'My father is a harbour master. You can imagine the tittle-tattle and gossip that sweeps the taverns and ale houses where the river folk gather. We hear most of this chatter. Rumours that the Templars were involved in the robbery at the crypt, as well as being responsible for trying to implicate my father in that crime. Consequently, I wondered if they were also the source of the lies about him secretly providing *The Black Hogge* with information about cogs leaving Queenhithe. Of course then there were the murders of the Templars at St Giles, the suspicion that the French envoy was somehow involved in those, as he was in the depredations of *The Black Hogge*. So yes, Sir Hugh, both my father and I thought we should fish in such a pool. I joined Mistress Philippa in her duties to see if I could learn anything.'

'And did you?'

'No. All I saw at St Giles was a group of tired, rather weak old men; they didn't really need my help, though the lepers did.'

'And in strict accordance with the founding charter of St Giles, you provided the master, Reginald Ausel, with a detailed list of English ships leaving Queenhithe so the inmates of the lazar hospital could pray that their crews would have safe voyage?'

'Yes, yes, I did. My father gave me such a list and I handed it over to Ausel, who published it in the hospital chapel.'

'And Ausel was most insistent about receiving it?'

'Most certainly. He said on more than one occasion how such a duty, being part of the founding charter, had to be scrupulously observed. In addition, he said, he was my lord Gaveston's nominee to the mastership and so he must be seen to be fulfilling such a duty in both the spirit and the letter of the law.'

'I am sure he did,' Corbett remarked wryly.

'Sir Hugh?'

'So, learning little or nothing at St Giles, you decided to allow Monsigneur de Craon to pursue you and discovered what?'

'That Monseigneur de Craon is a gelding rather than a stallion. Quite content with the ministrations of my fingers rather than anything else.' Corbett glanced warningly at Ranulf, who slouched on his stool, one hand covering the bottom of his face.

'I wondered, Mistress Agnes, why Monseigneur de Craon never left the tavern for the pleasures of the city.'

'He said I satisfied him fully, that I must keep secret what I did. How one day he would invite me to Paris.'

'And you did all this . . .'

'To discover anything I could about *The Black Hogge*, to depict my father as the man who solved the mystery. It's well known along Queenhithe that it must be the work of the French.'

'And did you discover anything?'

'Nothing, Sir Hugh. I did closely question de Craon once, but he flatly denied any knowledge of that sea monster or its doings.' She paused, chewing her lip. 'It's strange, Sir Hugh, what I did discover.'

'Yes?'

'Monseigneur de Craon hates you.'

'I am sure he does.'

'And he truly fears his henchman Brother Jerome. So much so that I wonder who is the master . . .'

'Agnes, is there anything else you know about the murders at St Giles, or indeed anything else connected with these mysteries?' The young woman shook her head. 'In which case, I thank you. I would be grateful if you'd ask Mistress Philippa to join us.'

Agnes's smile faded. 'You won't . . .'

'No, but I do need to see your mistress urgently.'

Philippa Henman came in all a-fluster, her cheeks pink with exertion. Sweat laced her soft, sweet face whilst her veiled headdress was slightly askew and her gown stained from cooking. She kept wiping her hands on a scented napkin as she took the proffered seat, informing Corbett that the reason for her busyness was that she was preparing a splendid banquet to celebrate their return. Corbett thanked her and offered some watered wine, which she refused, then sat staring down at the manuscript before him. He wanted this woman to be soothed, to be calm before he began his journey into her past.

'Sir Hugh?'

'Mistress Philippa Henman,' he glanced up and smiled, 'I shall tell you your story.' Philippa's fluster disappeared and she straightened up, neatly folding the napkin and placing it on the table. 'Many years ago,' Corbett pulled a face, 'not a lifetime, but certainly an era when we were both fresh and hopeful, a young man appeared in Queenhithe. John Poultney had left his birth village of Saltcot in Essex and the tavern he'd inherited, the Sunne in Splendour, because both village and hostelry had become profitless, windswept and deserted. He arrived in Queenhithe with little money but high hopes and became apprenticed as a vintner, working in taverns such as the Salamander and elsewhere.

'I suspect John Poultney was a very handsome, charming and talented young man. You certainly thought so, didn't you? A mere slip of a girl, what, fifteen or sixteen summers old? You fell deeply in love with him. You planned to marry. You couldn't wait, and when you are young, the blood runs hot. You became pregnant out of wedlock. That could soon be rectified, but then disaster struck. John Poultney died from a bout of the sweating sickness that sweeps London every so often. Your family were desperate to ensure a reputable future for you, so you were hidden away like a recluse. The baby was born, a healthy male child, vigorous and strong. He was nurtured and nursed, then handed over to the Franciscan Minoresses at their house just north of the Tower.'

Corbett's heart went out to this grief-stricken woman as the mask she assumed every day slipped away. 'Mistress, I have very little proof for what I say except what I found in the records of Holy Trinity the Little: the costly funeral arrangements, requiems and chantry masses for John Poultney. Oh, they were all paid anonymously, including the stipend for a host of tapers to be burnt before the statue of St John, your beloved's patron saint. Now John Poultney had no family. Your parents have died, Philippa, but these anonymous donations continue to be made at certain times of the year: "For the repose of the soul of John Poultney." Parson Layburn believes the donor is you. When closely questioned, our good priest grudgingly conceded that there is some mystery about your past. My informants along the streets and alleyways of Queenhithe, when persuaded to answer, also talked of rumours, gossip about long-lost people and events in your life.'

Corbett paused to sip at his goblet. 'Anyway, let's go

back down the passage of the years. Your baby boy is placed with the Franciscan sisters, the Minoresses at Aldgate. Secret instructions are given that, at the appropriate time, the boy should be sent to a Templar house and trained to be a page, a squire and then a knight. If, as an adult, he does not wish to become a Templar, that would be his decision. Nevertheless, by then he would have received an education and training in both his horn book and the exercise of arms.'

Corbett glanced down, as if consulting the notes he'd written. When he looked up again, Philippa was staring at the table. He couldn't see whether she was crying or not. 'Mistress,' he continued, 'the hour rings burn away. Once again time eats itself up. I must press on. Eventually you re-entered the guild life of Queenhithe ward. You met my old comrade Raoul Henman and, due to the legacies left by your parents, you and Raoul, now husband and wife, were able to purchase this tavern.' He paused and crossed himself swiftly. 'God forgive me, at one time I did wonder if Raoul profited from the robbery in the crypt. My apologies for that.'

He rose, stretched and walked over to Philippa, gently pressing her right shoulder. 'God knows, but you may wish to tell me about Raoul learning of your love child, Henry, to whom you also gave his father's surname. One thing I am sure of, you and your son were reconciled and I believe he was more than accepted by your husband. I suggest this reconciliation took place in or around the year 1305. Your own parents had died, the

Merry Mercy was a flourishing concern. It was obvious that you and Raoul would never have children. God knows how matters would have proceeded, but Philip of France intervened. The Templar order soon collapsed; a sudden fall and a mortal one. Between 1305 and 1307 I suspect your son took the name Sumerscale and began to intimate that perhaps the accusations against his order were not all spurious lies. He wanted to deal with this vexed problem before resuming a normal life. The three of you decided to keep everything secret and confidential until the Templar crisis was over, and then you could publicise matters.'

'And this vexed problem, as you call it?' Philippa's voice was challenging.

'Something had happened in one of the Templar houses,' Corbett replied. 'Your son may have been sexually attacked. He wanted justice, vengeance, but he also needed protection. In this, he was successful. Matthew Aschroft, a Templar serjeant, became his constant companion and guardian. He too took a different name, Fallowfield. I will explain these pseudonyms later. No doubt both men feared their former order, or at least some of its members. This would explain the false names, the secrecy, the decision not to drag you into their campaign as well as their determination to lay charges against the Templars.

'They visited Blackfriars and sought the advice of Prior Cuthbert, and he passed on their concerns to other Dominicans who were acting as papal inquisitors in the investigation into the Templars. Prior Cuthbert also secured Henry and Matthew posts on board Naseby's ship *The Candle-Bright*. After all, Matthew had seen service in the Middle Sea, and captains are always desperate to hire good men. You and Raoul continued to meet Henry and Matthew secretly, putting at their disposal some chamber or other dwelling you owned in the city. I have established from the records that you do own such properties. In such a place, well away from Queenhithe, once *The Candle-Bright* berthed, they could relax. You and Raoul would ensure that they had fresh clothes, food and drink and all the necessary comforts.

'Everything seemed to be proceeding well until the wicked tragedy brought about by that limb of Satan, the renegade Templar Gabriel Rougehead. He struck at a time when the king and Lord Gaveston would brook no opposition. The trial of Sumerscale and Fallowfield, as they called themselves, was swift and summary. On reflection, what could they do? Tell the truth? Proclaim that they belonged to the disgraced Templar order and were now hiding under false names? That would only deepen their guilt. In the end, they paid with their lives for their enemy's malice!'

Philippa was now sobbing, talking quietly as if to herself. Corbett let her weep from her heart, give voice to the deep hurt, the savage wound to her soul.

'Mistress.' He returned to his chair. 'Mistress, believe me, as God lives, there is justice, there has been justice and there will be more.' She lifted her tear-streaked face. 'You have already supped from the cup of vengeance,' he continued. 'The murderous execution of Sumerscale and Fallowfield thrust you and Raoul into the deepest pit of despair. Raoul was a good man, a former mailed clerk, a soldier. It was he who approached Slingsby and arranged that murderous supper party, he who swept into that tavern like death incarnate. He joined those wicked revellers and, being a taverner, brought a sack of the finest wine – albeit laced with a powerful potion to induce sleep. Once they had sunk into a deep torpor, he took their heads. The chamber must have been drenched in the blood swilling about, but no one would ever see it. To cover what had happened, as well as to punish Slingsby for his part in the tragedy, Raoul knocked over lanterns and candles, and that chamber of death along with the entire tavern was burnt to the ground . . .'

'Justice.' Philippa lifted her head, drying her tears with the palm of her hand. 'Sir Hugh, you said there will be justice?'

'Oh yes!' He held her gaze and rejoiced at the hope in her eyes. 'You never knew the names of those Templars who abused your son?'

'Henry refused to tell me, and he bound Matthew by oath not to reveal anything until they had both confessed to the Inquisition and to some law officer. Henry believed that Temple Combe housed a devilish killer guilty of hideous murders, but he and Aschroft decided to bide their time.' She smiled wanly. 'Remember, my lord clerk, I did not want to quarrel with my son. I had a great deal to make up to him.' She sighed.

'Raoul already knew about my love child. He had heard the gossip. More importantly, he and Aschroft were good friends, both aspiring to become members of the guild as tavern masters. Of course we hoped to have our own child, but God thought different. In the spring of 1305, we decided to meet Henry at a house we owned in Cheapside. Only then did he begin to talk and hint at certain matters. I loved him, of course, I always had. Raoul was much taken with him. He considered Henry the son he always wanted. In fact it was Raoul who healed the breach between us.' She rubbed her mouth on the back of her hand. 'What made you suspect that Raoul was responsible for the judgement dealt out at the Salamander?'

'I had a cursory description of the man responsible. I recalled Raoul's size, his training as a mailed clerk as well as the wealth he had amassed. More importantly, the mysterious stranger who swept in like God's vengeance exuded the scent of Castile. Castilian soap is rare, purchased only by the very wealthy. You loaned me one of your husband's cloaks; it is still perfumed with that fragrance.'

'Master Clerk,' Philippa's voice was harsh, 'what you say is in the main true. Henry's death was so swift, so brutal, so,' she shook her head, 'so unnecessary. He was dead and all we could do was look to the cause. We were left with two corpses, one of whom was a beloved son, the other a very good comrade.'

'Again,' Corbett intervened, 'Parson Layburn talked about a mysterious visitor, wealthy, perfumed, who paid generously so Sumerscale and Fallowfield received hallowed and honourable burial. And, of course, Layburn is the parish priest of both your family church and that of Raoul's family. Did you think he suspected?'

'Sometimes,' she smiled, 'yes, perhaps he did, but what does it matter? Dead is dead; solemn and holy funerals will not bring back the departed. What we did was the best in the circumstances.'

'Did your son or Matthew ever give details about their lives at Temple Combe?'

'Very little. Henry prided himself on his manhood. He declared that he and Aschroft would settle matters then he would tell us.'

'Did you have suspicions? As a member of the Guild of St Martha, you looked after the Templars rather than the lepers. Did you do so in order to watch that group most closely?'

'Yes,' she conceded, 'but I learnt very little. The Templars, as you discovered yourself, remain tight lipped. Indeed, whatever the sins of their comrades, they close ranks, especially during these last doomed days of their order. Moreover, apart from Grandison, I did not like them very much, and perhaps that showed.'

'As it did for John Naseby, master of *The Candle-Bright*? It was you, Philippa, who delivered those warnings slipped here and there. So easy for the owner and mistress of this tavern. You could threaten Naseby whenever you wished.'

Philippa gazed back unblinking. 'Naseby hanged my son, an innocent. God damn him and God damn his ship. I have no regrets whatsoever. I did not punish him; his own sins did.'

'You also warned me. You tied that message to a spent candle, but one fashioned out of beeswax with the chandler's mark on its base. I found the same here at the Merry Mercy. It was you, but why?'

Philippa just sat, head slightly cocked, staring up at the ceiling. She half smiled, blinked and gave a loud sigh.

'Mistress?'

'Raoul always admired you, Sir Hugh, said you had an integrity that could not be bought or suborned. When Henry was murdered, Raoul thought of petitioning you. Indeed, on one occasion, he prepared to leave for Leighton. He really believed we would get justice at your hands.' She paused. 'He had truly come to love Henry. He grew ill with grief; his heart, despite the physicians, was beginning to fail. He believed you would have acted, but time was passing. As his grief deepened, his anger became more intense. He wanted justice done swiftly before he died, so he took matters into his own hands.' She shrugged. 'You know the outcome. It was easy to arrange. The killers were trapped and slaughtered as you described. Raoul had no scruples. Once it was over, he fell increasingly ill. In the end, those miscreants killed both my son and my husband.' She stroked the top of the table, watching her hand going backwards and forwards, lost in her own thoughts. 'Raoul truly admired and respected you . . .'

'So why the warning?'

'Very simple, Sir Hugh.' She glanced up. 'De Craon and Brother Jerome knew you were coming here to investigate, as did Ausel and the Templars. Grandison welcomed it but his companions certainly did not.' She laced her fingers together. 'I am no clerk, no lawyer, but I watch people. Those two Frenchmen hate you. They have a burning malice that springs from a murderous frenzy seething in their filthy souls. I am sure they are plotting your destruction. On that particular morning, Ranulf told me you were meeting the king and my lord Gaveston at the Confessor's shrine.' She leaned against the table, staring down at Corbett. 'I tell you this, clerk, both those princes, Edward and Gaveston, will also be punished for what they have done.'

'Mistress,' Corbett intervened, 'you should be careful. There are those who'd say you play with treason . . .'

'Aye, Sir Hugh, but God knows the truth and so do you. Anyway, on that particular morning, I really felt as if Raoul's spirit was very close to me. I glimpsed the hatred de Craon and Brother Jerome nursed against you. I had to give you fair warning. I went to Westminster. I watched the royal party leave. I then hired a beggar boy, one of those who plead for alms by the great door. He came with me, crept into the abbey, quiet as a mouse. He said you were still there. I gave him the message and told him what to do, and left the rest in God's hands and yours. I had done my duty.' She half smiled. 'I hired a common scrivener to disguise my hand but I forgot how distinctive a beeswax candle can be, as well as how observant Raoul said you were.' She returned to smoothing the surface of the table.

Corbett watched and quietly admired this formidable woman who hid her own sorrow, her grievous soul wounds, so cleverly behind a smiling face and kindly ways.

'You have no suspicions about others being involved in Henry's death?' he asked. She shook her head. 'Then, mistress, keep this to yourself.' She glanced up sharply. Corbett smiled and raised his right hand. 'Believe me, the court is about to reconvene and more justice will be done.'

For the rest of the day Corbett busied himself writing out lists in his own secret cipher, answering Ranulf's questions as best as he could, and preparing assiduously, as he remarked enigmatically to his clerk, for when the court reconvened. He laid out his finest cambric shirt and costliest robes. He then strolled into Queenhithe and hired a good barber to trim his hair and shave his stubbled cheeks. Later in the evening, he, Ranulf and Chanson ate the delicious supper Mistress Philippa's cooks had prepared. Corbett made his companions laugh when he conceded that all his personal preparations were for the benefit of Monseigneur de Craon and Brother Jerome when they met the following morning.

The French envoy and Brother Jerome returned to the Merry Mercy just as the church bells tolled the hour of the Lady Mass. Corbett, garbed in his best, was waiting for them in the Cana chamber, wine and doucettes on the table before him. The two Frenchmen were ushered in by a grinning Ap Ythel and an escort of archers. Corbett could almost taste both the shock and the sheer fury of both men. Nevertheless, he strode towards them as if hadn't a care in the world, bestowing the kiss of peace and proclaiming how it was truly wonderful to meet them so hale and hearty. They ignored this, slumping down on to the proffered seats, seizing the goblets Ranulf had filled with sweet white wine and gulping noisily before slamming the cups down on the table. Brother Jerome was fury incarnate, his gimlet eyes narrow and watchful like those of a hawk restless on its perch, desperate to be free and to kill. De Craon was different, his anger tempered by a fearful watchfulness.

'Sir Hugh,' de Craon's frosty smile never reached his eyes, 'why were we detained at Westminster?'

'Not detained, Amaury, rather the honoured and revered guests of His Grace the king. We sheltered you there as a hen protects its chicks beneath its wings. We cherished you as we would the apple of our eye. You must know that *The Black Hogge*, until its recent total destruction . . .' De Craon nearly dropped the wine goblet he'd picked up; Brother Jerome just gasped and gaped. 'Yes,' Corbett continued blithely, 'you must know that *The Black Hogge*'s depredations caused serious unrest along Queenhithe. The leaders of the gangs knew you lodged here. We did not want you to be swept up, hurt, even killed in some ferocious riot.' He glanced swiftly at Ranulf and winked.

'Sir Hugh,' de Craon spluttered, '*The Black Hogge* totally destroyed?'

'Oh, completely, Amaury, so rejoice with us. The monster was burnt to a cinder off the coast of Essex. Only about a dozen of its crew survived. Its master, Gaston Foix, along with his officers and his precious pigeons, which he doted on so much and were of such great use to him,' Corbett abruptly clapped his hands, 'all gone! What is left of the crew are now lodged in the Tower. They will be exchanged for English privateers, if you will excuse the term, staying as guests in some French castle or fortress.'

'But Sir Hugh, the details?'

'Oh, you will learn them soon enough! Now, what else is there?' Corbett squinted up at the ceiling as if trying to recall what he had to say. In truth he was on the verge of bursting out laughing, and the Frenchmen sensed this. 'Oh yes,' he continued, 'stolen royal treasure was seized at the manor of Temple Combe at Epping. It would appear *The Black Hogge* landed a coven of mercenaries and miscreants under two renegade Templars, Reginald Ausel and Gabriel Rougehead, to seize this treasure. They failed. All the mercenaries were executed at Temple Combe by soldiers of our king. Ausel and Rougehead were also cut down; their corpses and those of their followers lie buried at the bottom of some deep morass.' He shook his head in mock wonderment. 'We always thought Rougehead had died in that mysterious fire at the Salamander tavern, but apparently he must have escaped.'

'Details?' Brother Jerome asked, his body tense with anger, his eyes dark pits of smouldering resentment, his face ghostly white.

'You will get those eventually.' Corbett remained deliberately offhand.

'So why are you here? To welcome us back to the Merry Mercy?' de Craon snapped.

'I am not here to welcome you to anything, Amaury, but to wish you farewell. Royal letters will soon arrive from the chancery. His Grace the king and my lord Gaveston were deeply disturbed by what was found amongst the wreckage of *The Black Hogge*.'

'Which was?'

'I cannot possibly tell you,' Corbett continued to bluff, 'but His Grace is most insistent. He wants you to leave on the morning tide tomorrow. In fact, preparations are already in place. The royal cog, *The Holy Ghost* is berthed at Queenhithe. His Grace the king insists that both of you leave on it.'

'Why?'

'His Grace the king,' Corbett tried to be as pompous as possible in the hope that he would provoke both opponents, 'does not have to explain himself to you.'

'Of course, of course,' de Craon spluttered, remembering himself, 'but . . .'

'No buts, no buts, Amaury! His Grace will explain to your lord, his father-in-law, at the appropriate time and in the appropriate place.'

'Of course.'

'As for you,' Corbett pointed rudely at the Carmelite, 'His Grace has decreed that you never be allowed to re-enter this kingdom.'

'Why, how dare . . .' Brother Jerome swallowed hard as de Craon caught him by the wrist.

'His Grace will also reveal his innermost feelings on this matter,' Corbett declared sonorously, 'to your lord, his beloved father-in-law, in due course. Well, well, gentlemen. Mistress Philippa is preparing another banquet to celebrate my return. Do you wish to join us? No? Well, never mind.' He rose and sketched a bow, and only when his back was to the chamber did he give way to the laughter bubbling within him.

Once he had composed himself, Corbett began feverish but secretive preparations. Mistress Philippa, Ranulf and Chanson were summoned to his chamber and given strict instructions. He begged them not to question him but simply do what he asked and wait for the truth to emerge. Later that day, at his request, Mistress Philippa served a splendid supper in the Cana chamber, where Corbett entertained the tavern mistress, Ranulf, Ap Ythel, the Magister and the Wolfman. Chanson joined them later, reporting how de Craon and Brother Jerome were busy preparing to leave the following morning.

Corbett tried not to drink too much, but the bed he eventually climbed into was so comfortable. Before he lay down, he glanced around: Mistress Philippa's personal chamber, a place of great luxury. The turkey rugs on the shining waxed floor were of the purest wool. The oaken furniture was polished to a shimmer, whilst the walls were covered with costly arras from Bruges that presented an array of brilliant colours picked out by the light of the beeswax candles placed judiciously around the chamber. Corbett, memorising the details, extinguished the candles and lay down against the feather-filled bolsters. Despite his best efforts, he found it difficult to keep his eyes open. He neither saw nor heard the chamber door open and close: his expected assailant was towering over him, the garrotte cord brushing his neck, before the clerk fully realised what was happening and flung himself violently against the threatening shadow.

Corbett was surprised at the muscular strength of his attacker. He fought back fiercely even as the chamber door was flung open and other shadows joined the fray around the great four-poster bed. Corbett, gasping and swearing, pulled himself away as Ranulf, Chanson, Ap Ythel and two Tower archers dragged Brother Jerome back. The Carmelite struggled to free himself but at last he was thrown to the floor, arms and legs pinioned, the knife in the sheath on his belt plucked away and the smooth garrotte string freed from his fingers. The chamber was in uproar. Mistress Philippa appeared from an adjoining room. Others crowded the gallery outside. As he pulled his boots on, Corbett shouted at Ap Ythel to send everyone back to their rooms. Then he stood up, strapped on his war belt and pointed at the captured Jerome.

'Fetch his colleague. Show de Craon every respect, but if necessary, drag him to the Cana chamber.' He tapped Jerome's bare foot with the toe of his boot. 'Bind him tight and bring him too.'

Order was soon imposed. A short while later, an agitated de Craon joined Corbett in the chamber. The Keeper of the Secret Seal sat on one side of the table flanked by Ranulf and the Magister. The Wolfman guarded the door along with two archers. Mistress Philippa and Chanson sat at the far end of the table. Minehostess, although secretly advised and warned by Corbett, looked shocked and nervous. De Craon, sitting next to Brother Jerome facing Corbett, made to rise and protest.

'Shut up!' Corbett shouted at him. 'For God's sake shut up or I will have you chained. This is not some diplomatic meeting between royal representatives. I am King Edward's justiciar. You,' he pointed at the French envoy, 'may well be the accredited ambassador of Philip of France, but he,' he jabbed a finger at Brother Jerome, 'well, he can call himself what he wants. He can act the part he chooses. He can be the great Cham of Tartary but the truth is he is Gabriel Rougehead, former Templar, English-born and a subject of our king.' Corbett rapped the table. 'I wish to move swiftly. As for you, de Craon, what comes later is up to you. You can protest your heart out to your masters in Paris, but Brother Jerome will not be there. He is going to be hanged, drawn and quartered, the punishment in this kingdom for heinous treason.'

He pressed on. 'Gabriel Rougehead is a master of disguise, a man of shifting shadows. No one, and I repeat no one, has a clear description of him. I discovered that eight years ago when I was pursuing Puddlicot: a conclusion shared by my comrades here.' He gestured at the Magister and the Wolfman, who murmured their agreement. 'However, what we have learnt, Brother Jerome, thanks to the Magister, is that the ladies of the night, the *filles de joie*, at the Queen of the Night, the brothel you frequent in Queenhithe, talk of a wound on your right shoulder.' Corbett patted himself. 'Many Templars have a cross here. You've had yours removed.'

'An old wound,' de Craon retorted.

'Nonsense. Brother Jerome, you have another wound on your thigh. We know Gabriel Rougehead was smitten in such a place by a Mameluke sword during the attack on the Accursed Tower at Acre. Finally, the same ladies of the night say your body skin is that of someone who has lived in Outremer. Of course it might take time, but we could also scrutinise your credentials to be a Carmelite. They have a principal foundation here at Aylesford in Kent. I am sure such a search would find no evidence for a Brother Jerome. Finally, of course, we have caught you red-handed in Mistress Philippa's chamber armed with a knife and a garrotte, your wicked soul set on more murder. Oh no.' Corbett raised a hand. 'You are Gabriel Rougehead. The malefactor who died in the fire at the Salamander three years ago was one of your cat's paws; the same is true of the vile creature who abducted me and took me to Temple Combe.

'Now that man, the so-called keeper of the Sunne in Splendour at Saltcot, was as fit for hell as you are, but he made certain mistakes. Gabriel Rougehead's mother came from Nanterre, not Auxerre. Rougehead moved amongst the clerks of the Holy Chancery, the secret world of the Louvre Palace. He must be skilled in Norman French, as you are, Carmelite. Yes,' Corbett's voice turned sardonic, 'that's what I will call you. The creature at Temple Combe, however, could only speak the lingua franca of the gutter. When I talked swiftly to Primus, the leader of the assassins, the cat's paw demanded to know what I said. Surely a clerk skilled in Norman French would understand another clerk speaking the same tongue? Finally,' Corbett picked up the goblet he had brought into the room, 'Gabriel Rougehead eschewed wine, ale and any such heavy drink; your creature at Temple Combe could not drink enough to soothe his nerves.

'There were other mistakes. He claimed the great robbery of the royal treasury in the crypt took place on the eve of St Matthew's feast day, the twentieth of September, when of course it was on the eve of the feast of another evangelist, St Mark, which as you know, or should do, falls on the twenty-fourth of April. A leader, a participant in such an audacious robbery, would never make that mistake.'

Corbett sat back in his chair, and the Carmelite stared at him, black eyes unblinking, the bruise he'd received to his right cheekbone blossoming a bluish red, his bloodless lips moved silently as if talking to himself. Corbett guessed he was quietly cursing his confederate at Temple Combe. 'Oh, I agree.' The clerk waved a hand. 'You trained your friend and ally very well. What was he? A brother, a kinsman, a member of your acting troupe? I understand you led one of those?'

'I would like to know about the treasure,' de Craon intervened. 'If it was stolen by my colleague here, as you allege, he seems to have shared that very valuable information with a number of people: Reginald Ausel and the individual you call his cat's paw.'

Corbett pointed at his prisoner. 'A ruthless man. One, I am sure, no member of his coven would dare cross; also very powerful. He has the ear of no less a person than the king of France and that king's first minister, de Nogaret. Moreover, they were preparing to move the treasure out of England. Once in France, such items are easy to trade. In this kingdom the likes of Ausel trying to sell a sapphire ring from a royal treasure horde would be highly dangerous. You are a dark serpent, Rougehead. You writhe and turn, you hide and strike, you slough off one skin for another. Look at you now, head and face all shaven. Three years ago you were tousle-haired, bearded, ready to act as the king's approver and dispatch two innocents to a gruesome death.' He lifted a hand. 'You are like a certain reptile I have read about: you change, you assume a disguise to blend in with your surroundings, but now you have been caught out.'

He paused. Mistress Philippa was sobbing quietly; Chanson had his arm around her shoulder, trying to console her.

'True,' Corbett continued, 'I know very little about your life. After the fall of Acre, you left the Templar order. According to my comrades here, you had a troupe of actors that I understand included members of your kin. Do you play chess, Carmelite?' The pebble-black eyes never shifted. 'There's a classic move in that game where you use one piece to attack, but that's not the really dangerous piece; it is simply a front, a gambit to mask a much more devastating strategy. You became very skilled at such a game, playing it in times of danger. God knows what other mischief you became involved in. However, in 1303 you were back in England as one of Puddlicot's leading henchmen under the name of John Priknash. You helped rob the crypt and took your portion of the loot to your old comrade Ausel at Temple Combe, a good place to hide treasure. Ausel would do exactly what you said, wouldn't he?'

Corbett sipped at his wine. He was trying to provoke his victim, but so far the Carmelite seemed to be lost in his own thoughts. 'Ausel would do exactly what you said,' he repeated, 'because you knew his filthy secret. He was the abuser and killer of innocents. He slaughtered in other localities; he certainly did so in and around the forest of Epping. He also turned on a young man of his own order, a page training to be a squire, Henry Poultney, an orphan placed in the Templar order by those who received him as a baby, the Franciscan Minoresses of Aldgate.' Corbett paused at a fresh outburst of tears from Mistress Philippa. 'That lady,' he pointed at the tavern mistress, 'is the mother of

Henry Poultney. I have her permission to make that relationship public. I have also closely appraised her of your wickedness and that of Reginald Ausel, a man she tried to help.'

He smiled thinly. 'Ausel, whilst pretending to be a figure of righteousness, asked Philippa Henman if she knew of any taverns along the coast of Essex that he might purchase to start a new life once the Templar order ceased to exist. She informed him about the Sunne in Splendour, which she knew of from John Poultney, father of her love child. But,' Corbett shrugged, 'such personal details do not concern you.' He pointed at de Craon. 'Philip of France launched his attack on the Templar order, which began to disintegrate. Henry Poultney, now protected by Matthew Aschroft, fled the order. They assumed false names and tried to seek out the papal inquisitors.'

Corbett gazed into his goblet. Gabriel Rougehead, the Carmelite or whatever he called himself, was truly trapped. If he didn't confess now, Edward's personal household would ensure that he did so before meeting a violent death on the scaffold. Corbett, however, was determined that de Craon should take the full story back to Philip of France as a warning that if he and his coven wanted to enter the lists, the clerk would always be there to meet them.

'Ausel became truly terrified,' he continued, putting the goblet down. 'The former Templar had left a bloody trail wherever he had stayed. Others,' he gestured at the Wolfman, 'were becoming interested in him. Proof might be very difficult to find. However, two former Templars eager to indict him was another matter, so you returned to England. Ausel would remind you of what might happen to the treasure if he was arrested and interrogated. You decided to trap Poultney and Aschroft at the Salamander, a notorious tavern with a most unsavoury history.'

'In which case, why should they go there?' the Carmelite scoffed, determined to concede nothing.

'Sir Hugh.' Corbett turned. Mistress Philippa had now gently removed Chanson's arm and stood swaying slightly. 'I have never understood, nor have you told me why Henry and Matthew should have gone to the Salamander. They knew no one there.'

'Mistress, please,' Corbett indicated with his hand, 'please sit and I shall tell you.' Philippa, coaxed by Chanson, sat down. 'Henry and Matthew knew no one in the city apart from you, mistress, and your husband. However, that relationship was being kept most secret. I too was intrigued about their visit to the Salamander. I asked myself who else Henry Poultney knew in London. Where could he go for advice and sustenance?'

'Of course,' Philippa retorted, a wan smile on her face, 'the Minoresses who first raised him.'

'I sent the Magister to see them.' Corbett watched the accused swallow quickly time and again. 'Mother Augustine certainly remembered a visitor, a Dominican who showed her papers and seals – forged, of course – and told her he was desperate to meet Henry Poultney on a matter of life and death, an issue of great importance. Did Mother Augustine, the Dominican asked, know where Henry Poultney and Matthew Aschroft were? Of course she did. You knew that, Rougehead. The two men had visited her and told her about their assumed names and their service aboard *The Candle-Bright*. She was, I understand, greatly amused at the false names: Sumerscale and Fallowfield were two of the meadows at the Minoresses where Henry used to play as a boy. Mother Augustine's Dominican visitor,' Corbett leaned over, jabbing his finger at the prisoner, 'was you disguised yet again.'

'I did not . . .' The Carmelite's voice faltered and he seemed to slump in his chair.

'After that,' Corbett continued, 'it was easy. *The Candle-Bright* berths, you get a message delivered to your intended victims. How they must meet somebody who can help them, at a certain hour on a certain day at the Salamander. They accept the invitation and step into the trap. Henry may have wished to visit the tavern anyway, a place where his father once served – you told him that, mistress?'

'Yes, yes I did.' Mistress Philippa was huddled tearfully next to Chanson.

'What could they answer during their trial when asked what they were doing at the Salamander? How could they talk of mysterious messages, of scandals in the Templar order, of their real names and identities?' Corbett shook his head. 'It would only make a bad situation worse. Both men went to their deaths. You, Rougehead, thought that was the end of the matter and tarried a while in England. You did not know about Raoul and Philippa Henman. They were truly grief-stricken, but eventually they recovered to plot their revenge, that bloody banquet at the Salamander. Of course, being who you are, you were deeply suspicious and persuaded a member of your coven to take your place.

'On that eventful evening, you lurked in the shadows and followed Raoul Henman back here. You vowed to settle with him and Mistress Philippa. You may have been intrigued by their involvement and wished to find out more, which is one of the reasons why you and de Craon now lodge here. You were furious at the attack on the Salamander, the deaths of your henchmen; that explains your presence in Mistress Philippa's chamber tonight. She would have been found dead, but of course you were under strict instructions to leave this city and this kingdom; you might even have been gone before her corpse was found.'

Corbett paused. He'd noticed how de Craon had moved slightly away from his former colleague, though he did not seem agitated. He recalled what Agnes had told him. Did de Craon fear this miscreant? Did he resent him? Had the renegade Templar been foisted on de Craon by King Philip and de Nogaret?

'I suggest,' Corbett continued, 'you played an important part in the French attacks on the Templar order. More importantly for me, you became involved in subtle, secret stratagems to weaken this kingdom and its king.'

'Be careful,' de Craon snapped.

'Silence!' Corbett retorted. 'We all know now about the depredations of *The Black Hogge*. Its master Gaston Foix owned courier pigeons. These were brought to London and allowed to nest and feed in the abandoned dovecote at St Giles. Who would notice anything amiss? After all, the master of the lazar hospital, Reginald Ausel, was Rougehead's close confidant and ally. The names of English cogs leaving Queenhithe are published in St Giles so its inmates can pray for the safety of those ships and their crew.' Corbett forced a smile. 'How ironic! In any other circumstance a truly pious gesture, but you used that information to bloody effect. Courier pigeons would leave with their messages for *The Black Hogge*, hiding in the misty vastness off the Essex coast.'

'I was not party to any of this,' de Craon protested. 'Nor was His Grace King Philip.' He took a deep breath. 'Perhaps there are those of the French council who have taken matters into their own hands, without the knowledge or permission of my royal master. Of course, as soon as I return to Paris I shall . . .' He broke off as Corbett began to clap loudly and slowly.

'Be that as it may,' the clerk declared, 'a dark tapestry of sinister treason was unrolled. Rougehead's cat's paw manages the Sunne in Splendour, the provisioning place for *The Black Hogge*. Ausel controls the lazar house. The royal treasure hidden at Temple Combe is marked down for France. I, one of King Edward's closest advisers, will disappear along with my henchman Ranulf, never to be seen again. Your king would love to dig his hands into jewels and other precious items that once belonged to the English Crown, to play with my chancery ring knowing how its wearer lies buried God knows where.'

'I have heard enough,' de Craon snapped.

'No you have not!' Corbett lifted a hand. The archer standing behind de Craon drew his sword and brought the flat of its blade down on the Frenchman's shoulder. Corbett glanced at the Carmelite. He sat, face impassive except for the blinking of his eyes and the slight movement of his lips, as if talking to himself. Was Rougehead resigned to his fate? Corbett wondered. Or was he plotting some strategy? An offer to tell the English Crown all that he knew in return for his life? Corbett secretly vowed that he would keep the prisoner under the closest scrutiny.

'So Gaston Foix was controlling *The Black Hogge*; the cat's paw was at Saltcot, Ausel at St Giles and you, the Carmelite, at Westminster. A subtle disguise, Master Rougehead. You are lean, sinewy, head and face closely shaved, garbed in the brown and cream of the Carmelite under a religious name. A nominee to the French court, an envoy to England. No one would suspect that you were once an English Templar. You and Ausel were determined that it would remain so. The Templars at St Giles had to die for a number of reasons. King Philip did not want any of them becoming involved in a protest to the Pope at the Council of Vienne. More importantly, men like Grandison entertained deep suspicions about Ausel. Ausel was weak; if he was attacked, cornered, God knows what he might say. And of course you,' Corbett pointed a finger, 'needed little encouragement to sup another man's blood.'

'Including yours,' the accused spat back.

'Including mine,' Corbett agreed. 'You enjoyed slaying those Templars, it was easy. Frightened, tired old men, hapless chickens, whilst you were the fox allowed into the hen run. You kept your murderous work at St Giles confidential to yourself and Ausel; even that cat's paw at Temple Combe did not know the truth. It made me wonder. I mean if the Rougehead of Temple Combe spent most of his time looking after the Sunne in Splendour, then who was responsible for the slayings at St Giles? Ausel? No. And so I began to reflect, whilst the mistakes your cat's paw made helped me to my conclusion. He was a fool, wasn't he? Swept up in his own arrogance.' The Carmelite looked as if he was about to reply, but then shook his head.

'Yes, you were the fox in the hen run,' Corbett continued. 'You were brought in, concealed by Ausel, shrouded in the lazar robe he had given you. You preyed on Boveney, an old man sitting in an enclave, his eyes dazzled by the sunset. Datchet in his chamber, his back to you. And Grandison? Ausel must have told you he was a comrade of mine. He was lured to that bench in the meadow, his belly full of wine, his mind all muddled. You killed him in the blink of an eye, using the dagger plundered from the royal treasury some eight years ago. A mocking insult both to me and to the Crown of

England. A taunting reminder about the robbery and how a considerable part of the plunder had never been found.'

'And their weapons?' The Magister Viae spoke up. 'I understand they were killed with their weapons close by.'

'Oh, there is no great mystery there,' Corbett murmured. 'Is there, Ranulf?'

'The Templars were resented at St Giles,' Ranulf declared. 'Some of its inmates were leper knights; weak, blighted, but still warriors. The Templars kept their weapons close by in case of attack by these.'

'Which eventually occurred,' Corbett added, 'thanks to you.' The Carmelite's lips creased in a ghost of a smile.

'And Slingsby?' Philippa called out.

'Ah yes.' Corbett turned to her. 'I did wonder if you were responsible for his death, but,' he smiled, 'you are of good heart, Mistress Henman. You, however,' he pointed at the Carmelite, 'are a true blood-drinker. You kill like other men breathe. I don't know why you killed Slingsby. Were you concerned that he might recognise you? Did you nourish a murderous grievance against a tavern master who lured four of your companions to their deaths and nearly did the same to you? Or did you just want to silence a clacking tongue?' The Carmelite smiled, as if savouring some secret joke. 'You lured and trapped Slingsby in the entrance to the garde-robe, a lonely, deserted place at that time of day. A swift thrust to the heart as you pushed him inside to slump on to the seat, then you closed the door and slipped away.'

Corbett drank from his goblet. 'Burghesh and Stapleton were next. They too could pose a threat to Ausel and eventually to you. Admitted, aided and supported by Ausel, you sweep like some murderous fury through that lazar hospital. You cruelly and cowardly slaughter three innocent men to provoke deep unrest at St Giles. You and Ausel deliver that message about vengeance coming. Ausel ostensibly flees into hiding. Burghesh and Stapleton, encouraged by him, seek sanctuary at Holy Trinity the Little. Ausel has sworn to return and assist them. He comes in the dead of night, when Parson Layburn is elsewhere. Burghesh and Stapleton admit him. Ausel, however, has brought his cloaked, cowled friend. He assures his colleagues all is well and, I suspect, produces a wineskin of the best Bordeaux, laced with a heavy opiate. Both men, frightened and exhausted, drink and sink into a deep sleep. You deal the killing blows, then flee. Nobody sees you except for an old woman, a Sister of the Street, but who will listen to her?'

Corbett paused and pulled himself up in his chair. 'And now the final chapter in your murderous progress: your attempt to kill Mistress Philippa. This proves everything I have said. In your eyes, nobody has the right to threaten you.' He lifted his hands as he held the dead-eyed gaze of this truly murderous soul. 'Brother Jerome, John Priknash, Gabriel Rougehead, all those demons seething within you, a veritable litany of murderers: I am going to see you all hang at Tyburn. Ranulf here will tie the knot and turn the ladder. As you dance between heaven and earth, the ghosts of your victims will gather, waiting to seize your soul. You,' he pointed at the smirking prisoner, 'will pay the full cost, and you,' gesturing at de Craon, 'will watch.'

AUTHOR'S NOTE

The treason and treachery described in this novel is a fair reflection of the times. Philip of France was determined to shatter the Templar order and was equally set on bringing England very firmly within the orbit of his rule. Men such as de Craon are based on the personalities and actions of the ruthless and cruel group of lawyers who advised Philip and truly believed their master was both pope and emperor. The depredations of *The Black Hogge* also reflect the savage war waged by ships in the English Channel, where mercy, compassion and the rule of law were totally ignored.

The use of courier pigeons is thousands of years old, and the speed and accuracy of these coursers of the air is truly remarkable. Corbett's explanation of how they were ignored by the English Crown is certainly based on fact. Edward I loved his falcons and hawks more than life itself; certainly more than his eldest son, the Prince of Wales. King and heir became seriously alienated over the question of Gaveston, who proved to be a catalyst for further tragedy, totally engulfing the twenty-year reign of Edward II.